Bright as Gold

Book Four of the Georgia Gold Series

Denise Weimer

Bright as Gold

Book Four of the Georgia Gold Series

Happy birthday 9/22/14 to
Kelly Stoddard Wooten —
Job 23:10
Denise Weimer

Denise Weimer

Canterbury House Publishing

www. canterburyhousepublishing. com
Sarasota, Florida

Canterbury House Publishing

www. canterburyhousepublishing. com

Copyright © 2014 Denise Weimer

All rights reserved under International and Pan-American Copyright Conventions.

Book Design by Tracy Arendt
Cover Art by John Kollock

This is a work of fiction. Names, characters, places and incidents are either the product of the author's imagination or are used fictitiously, and any resemblance to actual persons living or dead, business establishments, events, or locales is entirely co-incidental.

Library of Congress Cataloging-in-Publication Data

Weimer, Denise.
Bright as gold / Denise Weimer. -- First edition.
     pages cm -- (The Georgia gold series ; 4)
ISBN 978-0-9881897-9-9
1. Female friendship--Fiction. 2. Families--Georgia--Fiction. 3. Reconstruction (U.S. history, 1865-1877)--Fiction. I. Title.

PS3623.E4323B86 2014
813'.6--dc23

   2014020435

First Edition: September 2014

For information about permission to reproduce selections from this book email to:
editor@canterburyhousepublishing.com
Enter Permission to Reproduce in the subject line.

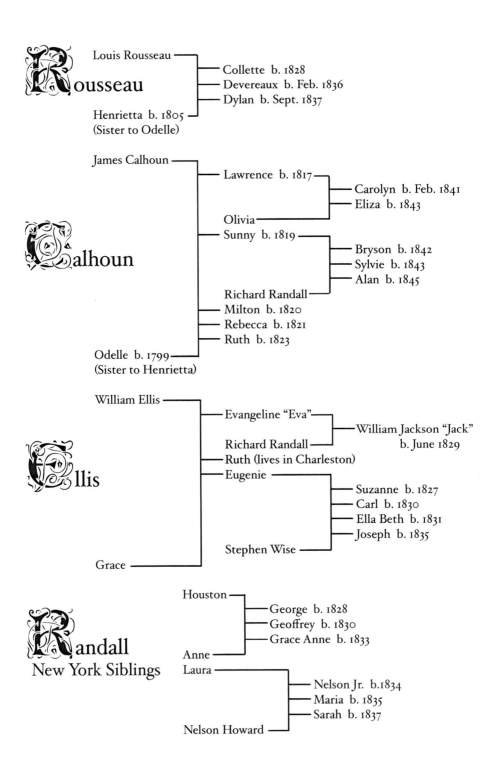

Rousseau

Louis Rousseau
Collette b. 1828
Devereaux b. Feb. 1836
Dylan b. Sept. 1837
Henrietta b. 1805
(Sister to Odelle)

Calhoun

James Calhoun
Lawrence b. 1817
Carolyn b. Feb. 1841
Eliza b. 1843
Olivia
Sunny b. 1819
Bryson b. 1842
Sylvie b. 1843
Alan b. 1845
Richard Randall
Milton b. 1820
Rebecca b. 1821
Ruth b. 1823
Odelle b. 1799
(Sister to Henrietta)

Ellis

William Ellis
Evangeline "Eva"
William Jackson "Jack"
b. June 1829
Richard Randall
Ruth (lives in Charleston)
Eugenie
Suzanne b. 1827
Carl b. 1830
Ella Beth b. 1831
Joseph b. 1835
Stephen Wise
Grace

Randall
New York Siblings

Houston
George b. 1828
Geoffrey b. 1830
Grace Anne b. 1833
Anne
Laura
Nelson Jr. b.1834
Maria b. 1835
Sarah b. 1837
Nelson Howard

FOREWORD

My personal trip back to Habersham County of the mid-1800s started with a private tour of a summer home of that period, perfectly preserved in every detail, and with the letters and diaries of that family. To the gentleman who offered this glimpse into his ancestors' lives – and who also lent me my initial stack of books and the skill of his historical editing – I owe boundless thanks. Mr. John Kollock passed away earlier this year and will be dearly missed. He was a true Southern gentleman.

Mr. Kollock's cover art for *Bright as Gold* depicts a home that once stood in Clarkesville, Pomona Hall, later known as Minis Hill. The back cover illustrates a number of summer homes surrounding Hardeman's Bottom outside town, Blythewood, LaMont, and, in the distance, Sleepy Hollow, home of Phineas Miller Kollock.

Most of the places, people and events of The Georgia Gold Series actually existed – apart from the main characters, of course. I sought to drop my characters into a very realistic time and place, and I hope you enjoy the journey with them. You met Mahala and Jack, Carolyn, Dev and Dylan in Book One, *Sautee Shadows*, set during the Georgia Gold Rush and the Cherokee Removal. You passed through the fiery days of The War Between the States with them as they found love and suffered danger and loss in *The Gray Divide* and *The Crimson Bloom*. Now, their stories conclude as the trials of Reconstruction-era Georgia refine their characters to become *As Bright as Gold*.

CHAPTER ONE

June 1865
Habersham County, Georgia

t overcame her irritation so suddenly that it burst forth – a completely foreign sound, a bubble of a laugh – right past the knuckle that she had stuffed in her mouth at her brother-in-law's struggle with the huge, cantankerous mule, the last one left on the farm. Somehow convinced by Dylan to teach him how to plow a corn field this evening, their poor neighbor kept intervening to maintain straight rows. The man had already stretched his patience yesterday by demonstrating the method for cutting the remaining wheat. In old pants and shirt sleeves, Dylan had bent and swung in a fair imitation, his russet hair gleaming in the summer sun.

Carolyn Calhoun Rousseau watched from the rutted clay lane that led to the outer fields. She had snuck out of the kitchen when her mother-in-law, Henrietta, had sought something in the butler's pantry. She had to see for herself how Dylan was faring. And she needed the break from Henrietta. In truth, the woman was well-meaning, almost to the point of aggravation, but she was a complete stranger to the duties associated with running a large farm.

Carolyn was not. And that was why her irritation surged forth to gain the upper hand again. Like his mother, if there ever was anyone less suited to farming, it was Dylan Rousseau. He might have grown up on a rice plantation, but that didn't mean he'd taken any interest in its operation. No, that had been the passion of Devereaux, the older son who had won her hand over the affectionate missives from a young Dylan at ministerial college. Dev was the one who was supposed to take over his family's 600 acres on Harveys Island outside Savannah, not to mention this upland farm in the foothills of Northeast Georgia. Dev would have known what to do. But Dev was not here. The searing pain reminded Carolyn of that. And it was she who had stepped into the void during the war with the North, coming here to Forests of Green and learning with the help of a black foreman to run this place. Now Samson was gone, too, and who did Dylan think he was?

Her face falling, Carolyn turned to walk back to the house. For once she didn't notice the peeling white paint and sagging shutters on what had once been the queenly Greek Revival residence. Her mind revisited the moment

9

two nights ago when Dylan and Henrietta had returned. She'd never been so scared in her life, except when Dev had died. Earlier that day Yankee cavalry had come and convinced the few remaining workers on the farm to depart with them, leaving Carolyn and her year-old son Dev Jr. completely alone. When horse hooves had again sounded on the drive after dark, she'd been sure the soldiers had come back to take advantage of her. She'd met her in-laws on the porch with a pistol in her hand. When she'd seen it was them, she'd collapsed sobbing into Henrietta's arms.

Her petite, dark-haired mother-in-law stood now at the door of the side porch, a crease marring her brow. "Oh, there you are! Where did you go?"

"Just a quick errand." Carolyn wiped the sweat from her brow, unable to stop herself from thinking how hot and miserable Dylan must be. She reminded herself that he had gotten used to far worse during the war.

"Well, you might have told me. I have the tomatoes ready to stew, but for the life of me I can't find anything good to put in with them. What do you suppose Esther used?" Henrietta asked, turning back to the kitchen. She missed their old cook. She'd been lucky to bring her personal maid, Lydia, back to Habersham with her.

"Whatever it was, we probably don't have it. Let's just add some onions and zucchini. It will taste nice and fresh even without spices. Would you like to cut the onion while I do the zucchini?"

Henrietta looked apologetic. She held up a hand with a finger wrapped in a cloth. "I just nicked it slicing tomatoes."

"It's all right. Why don't you set the table?"

Pleased, Henrietta hurried off. That was something she could do. Hennie Rousseau, widow of Louis Rousseau, coastal rice magnate, was born to preside over grand dinners appreciated by planters, bankers, factors and lawyers. Not to preside over a kitchen. But the slow blood-letting of Southern men and resources in sustaining a four-year war had left the countryside a wasteland, its citizens almost destitute. Carolyn reminded herself that like she had, Henrietta would learn how to make something out of nothing.

Maybe Dylan could do the same. After all, far from the shy, awkward girl she'd once been, *she* had surprised everyone. The changes the war had wrought in Dylan had already been amazing. When she had last seen him at Dev's funeral in Savannah, even then it had been hard to find the studious, gentle man who'd once courted her with letters. Now, even more so. He was tan and lean to the point of thinness, but that was just what could be seen on the surface. As he'd assessed the property the night of his return, looking for the threat that had warranted her pistol-waving welcome, the wary aloofness in his eyes had chilled her. Only when his gaze had returned to her had it softened into concern.

He'd reached for her hands, pressing them hard in his. She could still hear his low, even tone when he'd asked, "Did the soldiers harm you?" and feel the heat that had climbed across her face, knowing what he meant.

"No, Dylan."

The roughness of her hands had made him stop and turn them over. "What have you been doing with these?"

She'd named the most strenuous of her many recent tasks. "Binding wheat."

He'd said her name with regret, then pulled her into his arms. She remembered all too well how unsettling that had been. No man had held her since Dev had died. And then there had been his brother, sounding like Dev but looking so different. She had allowed Henrietta's embrace and accepted her apologies. After all, when Louis had died Henrietta's depression had been so abysmal that her older sister Odelle – in the convoluted way of many old families, actually Carolyn's grandmother – had taken her back to Brightwell Plantation on the coast with Carolyn's parents, Lawrence and Olivia. But from Dylan she'd drawn back. He'd looked surprised, and maybe she had seen a flash of hurt before he shuttered those intense brown eyes. Maybe, she thought, he was afraid she mistook his gesture for something more than it was. Carolyn knew from what had happened in Savannah that the years away from her, years in which he'd been reconciled to his brother, had finally erased romantic notions of her from his mind.

Moments later she'd furthered the tension between them by begging him to go after the workers.

"If they decide they want to be here, they'll come back," he'd said. "If not, we don't need them. We'll make a fresh beginning."

How? she had wanted to ask. But she'd been too tired to form the word.

The next day at breakfast he'd asked what needed to be done. She'd provided a litany of tasks, certain their sheer enormity would drive Henrietta and Dylan both back to the coast. But he'd given a calm nod. He'd gone to pay a visit on their neighbor, and since then he'd been too busy for her to demand an explanation of how he planned to single-handedly salvage Forests of Green.

Now, absorbed in thought, Carolyn stirred her pot. They'd gotten off on the wrong foot, but perhaps they could talk things over tonight.

But Dylan was in a rotten humor by supper time. She watched him from the kitchen door as he washed up at the pump, so stiff he could barely stand back up after he bent to splash water on his face. Then he had to sit down on the step to remove his boots, which clung stubbornly and only released with a great puff of dust. She averted her eyes as he skirted around her work station in his filthy clothes.

Carolyn was serving the plates when the only sound that could fill her heart with warmth came to her ears – that of her son's voice. She turned with a smile to behold Dev Jr., rosy-cheeked and fresh from a recent nap, jumping in the arms of Henrietta's maid. "Mama!"

She was about to hurry to him when Henrietta circumvented her, dashing around the table with her arms extended to the child. "Come to Grandma?"

To her chagrin, the dark-haired baby, the spitting image of Henrietta's prized firstborn, turned his face into Lydia's bosom.

Carolyn and Lydia said "aw" at the same moment. Henrietta's face was crestfallen. "He doesn't remember me."

"This your grandma," Lydia tried to coax her charge.

"It's all right. It's my fault," Henrietta said. "If I had come here instead of going to Brightwell, he wouldn't be afraid of me." She took a deep breath and patted Devie's plump hand. "But he'll come around."

Watching her mother's-in-law's spine straighten, Carolyn thought that maybe the time at Brightwell had done its healing work after all. Henrietta was still given to the emotional outbursts of a cosseted past, but her willingness to work and her patience with her grandson demonstrated that maybe, like most Southern women, that spine was made of steel after all.

Carolyn smiled and kissed Dev's forehead. "Please put him in his high chair, Lydia. I have to carry the plates to the table."

Once they had settled, Dylan was still not in evidence. His nephew's antics convinced the women it would not be wise to wait. As she cut Dev Jr.'s food into small bites, Carolyn decided it was a good time to broach an idea with her mother-in-law.

"I wanted to ask you about something. The wheat threshing must be done in two months, and it requires a lot of manpower. Will there be some workers at The Marshes you can spare to send up here?"

Henrietta dropped her gaze. "I'm afraid the situation on the coast is not very good. The workers have been running off ever since the Yankees took control. I did show our lawyer a copy of Lois' will stating that I, and not Dylan, owned The Marshes, but we won't know yet if that will be enough to secure it. General Sherman allowed the Negroes to take over any abandoned property. Right now The Marshes is occupied by strangers, black vagrants who will probably not leave peacefully."

"Oh." It sounded like the man who had so mercilessly razed Georgia had more on his hands now than he'd bargained for. "You know I shared Dylan's views about slavery. I'm glad the blacks are free now, but what will they do without jobs? I'd hoped some of the good men had remained and that we could pay them with a share of the crops. I guess we'll have to hire workers around here."

"No, we won't." Dylan spoke from the doorway. His auburn hair was slicked back, and he had changed into a linen vest and pants with a clean shirt. As he walked forward and seated himself at the table, his next words made Carolyn's heart leap. "A few of the previous workers came back this afternoon."

"They did?" Carolyn exclaimed. "Where are they?"

"Camped outside town. They are willing to come back to work for us, but only for cash."

"For cash? But everybody knows there's no ready cash to be had! They're accustomed to working for part of the crop. That's what they agreed to before."

"Well, not now. Their new terms are cash only." Without sparing her a glance, Dylan picked up his knife and fork.

"Why didn't you let me talk to them, Dylan? I could have gotten them to agree to their previous terms. Who was it? Was it Samson?" If their previous foreman had returned, everything would be all right. Though he'd frightened Carolyn at first by his sheer size and stoic bearing, she'd quickly surmised that he had the magnetism, knowledge and quiet confidence of a born leader. And when those pearly whites flashed in his dark face, even she had felt like laughing!

"No. Not Samson. They said he's gone. Tania would not let him return. Without his influence, I doubt you could have budged them."

Frustration mushroomed in her chest. It was the doing of her taciturn former maid, now Samson's wife, that he had left the area. Tania had always resented Carolyn, despite Carolyn's efforts to reach out to the woman and her disgust for the slave system. She couldn't stop herself from continuing. "Well, you should have let me try. If you'll take me to them tomorrow–"

"No, Carolyn," Dylan cut in, the firmness in his tone at last giving her pause. "I've dealt with it. So are you telling me you don't have any cash at all?"

His tone was even, not accusing, but she felt defensive anyway. "Nothing to speak of," she said a little sullenly.

"Jewelry?"

"Your mother can tell you we both pawned our jewels in Savannah a long time ago." Carolyn glanced at Henrietta, who nodded. "But I did bury the silver service this spring when the Yankees came through."

"Good. You can take me to it right after dinner."

Carolyn ate in silence. *Who is this man?* she wondered. He was abrupt, business-like, where he had once been sensitive and tentative. She'd realized when she'd seen him in Savannah that leadership in the army had made him more decisive, but she'd expected his interactions with her to be tempered by both sympathy and respect for all she had undergone – and accomplished

– in his absence. But it was as if a stranger, and not Dylan, had returned to them.

After dinner he got a shovel from the barn. Holding a lantern, Carolyn led him behind the house to the spot by the pond where she'd instructed Samson to bury their silver service and candlesticks.

"I'm glad you held onto the silver. This place is too big to run all by myself."

Well, that admission was a start. Carolyn just hoped one of the merchants in nearby Clarkesville would give them some money for their valuables. The storekeepers were hard up for cash, too, primarily trading for supplies now. She didn't say so aloud, but she thought that Dylan might have to go all the way to Athens or Gainesville before he found someone willing to buy the silver off him. Well, it was *his* plan. He was so determined not to let her talk with the workers. Let *him* work things out.

She pressed her lips together and pointed to the dirt at the base of the big oak the branches of which leaned over the water, on the side of the tree facing the house. "Here."

Dylan pulled on a pair of gloves. As he started to dig, Carolyn held the lantern aloft. She looked into the woods around them, presumably to make certain they were not watched, but really to keep from watching the way new muscles tugged and rippled under Dylan's white cotton shirt. She had been too long without the company of a man. And it unsettled her to be reminded of that.

"Carolyn," he said, the tone of his voice causing her to look at him. "This ground's been disturbed. It's not packed tight enough for the amount of time that's passed."

Her heart started to pound. "Are you sure?"

"How far down did you dig?"

"I told him to go down a couple of feet. Right here. Exactly here."

"*Him?*"

"Samson. I trusted him, Dylan. If it hadn't been for him, we never would have made it here during the war. I watched him start to dig, then I left. I don't believe Samson would steal from us."

"If you're right about that, maybe somebody else watched him start to dig, too," Dylan commented, tossing another shovelful of dirt aside.

A black sickness filled Carolyn's insides. She stood in silence, knowing now what the outcome would be before Dylan ever finished digging. Minutes later, the whole area excavated past two feet, Dylan stopped and leaned on the shovel, his chest heaving. Their eyes met, and his suddenly unguarded, vulnerable look of despair twisted her heart. She took a step forward, her anger at him forgotten, placing a hand on his damp shirt sleeve.

"I'm sorry," she whispered.

"It's not your fault. We'll just have to figure something else out." He turned and started shoveling and smoothing the earth in a brusque manner.

They walked back to the house in silence. That night, despite how exhausted she knew he was, Carolyn could hear Dylan pacing. Back and forth, back and forth he went. Did he even sleep? Now would he take her to speak with the former slaves? Surely he would. Finally she fell asleep, certain he'd agree to her request over breakfast.

But at breakfast he was gone.

"Twelve dollar a month," said the tall black man. "With food." His downcast eyes did little to diminish the determination evident in his tone.

Dylan shifted. The fallen log on which he perched, his seat here in the creek-side camp of several of the former workers from Forests of Green, was not the reason for his unease. He went back to his former offer. "A fourth of the crop would be an awfully good deal with room and board. Worth more than I could pay you in cash. I heard from the merchants that a lot of farmers are only giving a sixth share to their former slaves."

This was true, but so was the fact that the local merchants said they couldn't front him any money unless he was willing to try his hand at cotton, a non-domestic-use crop. Cotton? What did he know about growing cotton? Even less than wheat and corn! Even then, they didn't have as much cash to lend as he needed. He wouldn't be mentioning that. It was a miracle he'd gotten the small clutch of greenbacks he had, only thanks to that creditor who'd set up shop in town from Taylor & Davis in Athens. He'd recognized the name of the lender as an established one, but what he'd had to give as surety for the money – and only half of what he needed at that – made his stomach sour.

Markus, the apparent leader of the trio, scuffed his boot in the dirt. John sat silent, but his posture announced his support for Markus. Ham was out hunting. "Naw, Sir," Markus said. "The Yankee soldiers tell us we need to be paid in gold or Yankee dollars for whatever work we do. Then, no matter how things turn out, we be okay."

Dylan sighed. While the exodus of blacks from the county had convinced the men that opportunities in the cities would be less than abundant, they were not going to budge on this requirement.

John nodded. "Twelve dollars," he reiterated.

It was time to be tough. "You men think you're in the heart of the cotton belt? Eight, and you take care of your own clothes and any doctoring you might need." If he could get them down far enough it might help soothe the ire of Henrietta and Carolyn. Now what did he care about that? He'd do what he must and they'd live with it.

"Ten," said Markus, then added with some hesitation, "if that be all right with you, Sir."

"Nine, and that's my final offer. I can go to town right now and find ten workers who'd jump at that much money."

"Yes, Sir. We do it."

"Fine." Dylan sat up straight and brushed off his trousers. "You'll have to come with me back to the house, and we'll make up a contract. You'll stay through November, help me thresh the wheat and get in the vegetables and corn. I'll give you half up front and the other half in the fall when the job's done." God only knew where he was going to get the other seventy-five dollars!

"All right, then!" A bright smile broke out on Markus' face. He appeared inordinately pleased, as well he might be, even clapping his hands together. By contrast, Dylan experienced a sinking feeling.

At that moment they were hailed by a cry from the edge of the clearing. Ham came into view. Dylan half-rose as he saw that he wasn't alone. The colored man led an emaciated brown horse with a figure slumped over the saddle, arms dangling on one side, legs on the other.

"What in the world ..." Dylan said aloud.

"Look what I done foun'! It weren't no deer!" Ham cried, then lifted his battered hat halfway off his kinky head in recognition of Dylan. "Hello there, Mistuh Dylan."

"What you got, fool?" Markus demanded. "You gonna kill the man if he ain't dead already."

"A soldier," Dylan murmured as he came alongside the unconscious man on the stallion. The sight of the all-too-familiar gray uniform did strange things in his gut. He pulled the man's head back and felt a shallow pulse. "He's alive, but he's burning up."

"I foun' him fell off his horse mumblin' in the brush, with the horse there eatin' calm as you please. He be with the cavalry?"

"Was," Dylan said. He noticed the letter on the uniform button Ham was twisting. "He's from Tennessee."

"Musta been goin' home."

Dylan shook the man's shoulder. "Wake up!"

The man stirred. As his fevered gray eyes flashed open, he made a weak move for his pistol.

"Easy, soldier," Dev instructed in the firm voice of an officer. He placed a quick hand over the trooper's. "You're with friends."

The man's eyes slid closed, but not before deep coughing clenched his thin body. Dylan had to clutch him to keep him on the mount. After the fit passed, Dylan stood there listening to the cavalryman's wheezing breaths, his heart sinking. He had heard that awful rasping sound, and not long ago, during the long, dark days when his brother lay dying.

"What you think, Mistuh Dylan?" asked Markus.

"I think he has pneumonia. We'd best get him back to Forests of Green so the women can make him as comfortable as possible."

As the black man assisted, Dylan used the cavalryman's lariat to lash him to the saddle. "I'll go ahead and get him settled at home. You men can come on once you've packed up camp."

As Dylan set out, mounted on one of the carriage horses brought up from Brightwell that he'd ridden into town, trepidation filled him. Not only was he returning home with three former slaves he'd agreed to pay in precious greenbacks, but he was dragging along a painful reminder of the all-too-recent past – to him, to Carolyn, to his mother. He looked over at the soldier slumped hatless over the stallion's neck, his dark hair a long curling mess over the frayed gold collar. The man was mid-thirties maybe. Not a youth, and not an old man. Regardless, he was vulnerable. And given that silent tie between soldiers of the same cause, he could not let him die alone – or even in the hands of an emotionally detached doctor. He was closer to home anyway. And maybe the presence of the stranger would deter questions about his loan.

But would Carolyn forgive him for what he asked of her?

After tying the horses at the rail, Dylan climbed the steps to the side porch and stood in the kitchen doorway. Looking in, a memory assailed him, completely incongruous to the actual scene of Carolyn scrubbing sweet potatoes and Henrietta washing dishes – a memory of leading a sweetly gowned, rosy-cheeked Carolyn through the kitchen on her first tour of their mountain home, Maum Esther shooing he and Dev and the girl that divided them out of her domain. But now Esther was at Brightwell, where she'd stayed to help Carolyn's family after their cook had run off. He'd had no idea he'd find Carolyn alone up here with no help whatsoever, not even a kitchen maid. Who would have thought the once-sheltered girl would learn to run a household all by herself? He was impressed by her fortitude, there was no doubting that; but now that he was home, he was determined to take the load off her weary shoulders. He would not have her look on him as the incapable younger brother ever again.

He realized his mother was staring at him in confusion. "Dylan? What's the matter?'

"I need some help. We found a man – a soldier. He's dying."

"What?" Henrietta cried, horrified.

Carolyn tossed down her knife and ran to the door of the kitchen. "What happened?"

"I went to negotiate with the former workers. While I was there, Ham brought this cavalryman into their camp. He found him alongside the road while he was out hunting."

"The workers? Are they with you?" Henrietta asked.

"On their way." Under different circumstances, Carolyn would have demanded details of their arrangement. But as he was speaking she'd gone down to the soldier's side, her fingers searching out the thready pulse. Her blonde head cocked as she listened to his breathing. "Will you help me get him inside?"

Her brown eyes rose to his, sorrow reflected there. Dylan stepped off the porch and stood beside her. "I'm sorry, Carolyn," he said. "It's pneumonia. I just – couldn't leave him."

"If you get his upper body and I take his legs, I think I can help get him to the sofa."

Dylan nodded. He tugged the man down, bending deep to absorb the stranger's weight. A pain from his old Gettysburg wound stabbed his thigh. He bit his lip. The man he held was not so taciturn. Moaning, he came to consciousness with Dylan's arms under his torso.

"Where am I?" The stranger's voice was low, raspy.

"I'm Captain Dylan Rousseau, lately of the 8th Georgia Infantry. You're at my home in Habersham County, Forests of Green."

A bare nod acknowledged acceptance. He coughed weakly, but the phlegm that rose in his throat choked him and forced him to cough on and on. Dylan thought he might die right there.

"Mother, mix up some whiskey and cod liver oil," Carolyn called to Henrietta, who was standing on the porch. "You'll find both clearly marked in the butler's pantry."

As the older woman moved to obey, the coughing fit finally subsided. Dylan was about to ask the soldier his name when he saw that his guest had again slipped into unconsciousness.

"Let's get him in," Carolyn said, bending to slip her arms under the booted knees.

Dylan hefted the upper body and watched Carolyn's face turn red with her own effort. He backed up the steps and into the house, angling down the hall to the sofa in the parlor. Puffing, they deposited the invalid there. Carolyn began to tug off the man's boots. Dylan helped her get them off and folded the soldier's limp arm over his chest.

"I'll bring in his saddle bags and haversack. Maybe something in them will tell us who he is."

Carolyn nodded. Henrietta had arrived with a small glass of foul-smelling liquid. "Just a teaspoon," Carolyn said.

The women were working the concoction into the soldier's mouth as he left, and bathing his forehead with a cool cloth when he returned. Leaving a basin of water, his mother exited the room. She was handling this turn of events with remarkable composure. Maybe that was because of Carolyn's presence of mind. She glanced up as he deposited the bags at the foot of the sofa.

"I put the rest of his stuff in the barn. Need anything else?"

She shook her head. He saw her bite her lip. But instead of speaking, she rose up on her knees and started unbuttoning the trooper's cropped jacket. Dylan helped her raise the man up so she could remove the dusty outer garment. As he did, he saw a tear fall from her eye. He caught her hand, knowing he'd made her face death again, well before she was ready.

"I know he's a stranger," Dylan heard himself say. She paused and looked at him, and sudden awareness of Carolyn as a woman surprised him. Well, it wasn't a total surprise. The first night he'd arrived, finding his sister-in-law alone and vulnerable, the urge to take her in his arms had been overpowering. And when she'd nestled here, weeping against him, he'd experienced a tenderness of feeling he'd thought long ago stamped out by the war.

Blinking, she pulled away. "He's a human."

A motion on the front drive caught Dylan's eye. "It's the workers."

"How did you tell them you'd pay them?"

Her brown eyes pinned him, but he refused to apologize. "I got a loan from Taylor & Davis, and the men have agreed to a contract. We're fortunate they came back at all. We aren't the only ones who have been robbed recently. I heard in town the Waldburgs were on the 18th, and Blythewood was just a few days later. But with the workers to help us, we can set things right. We won't go hungry this winter."

The look she gave him was hard. "And how did you secure a loan without anything to sell? On the return of the crops?"

Here it was, no avoiding it. No use lying. She would find out the truth soon enough anyway. And he didn't lie. Did he? He never had before. Why was he considering it now? Because he knew she thought him incapable of providing for them and couldn't bear to see the lack of confidence in her eyes. "No. The only lenders or merchants giving security on a crop are those – mainly farther south – who only do so for cotton." He stood up. "I had to put up the deed to the town house as collateral."

"Oh, dear Lord," she gasped, closing her eyes. He knew what that town house meant to her. It was a connection to the outside world, and the place where she had spent most of her married time with his brother. She had been afraid when the Yankee army claimed Savannah that it wouldn't survive the occupation. Now, he was risking it again.

When she opened her deep brown eyes, they glowed like amber. He braced himself for the onslaught, be it physical or verbal. But none came. Either civility of breeding or the estrangement of the war years held her back – for Dylan was sure it wasn't respect.

He hated it, but he still wanted to deserve her respect.

"Go then," she said, which was rather worse than an attack.

And he deserved it, but he hated that her dismissal stung.

Lydia was giving Devie his bath. Carolyn liked her mother-in-law's servant, and Dev Jr. did, too, judging from the giggles that floated down the stairs, warming the solemn house with the promise of life and joy. Carolyn couldn't help but be drawn to the sound. She would see what all the ruckus was about, then give her son hugs and kisses goodnight to fortify herself for the nighttime vigil she must hold with the dying soldier. Well, not *must hold*. Dylan had offered to do that, but she'd said she'd take the first shift.

She folded the dish towel and, a slight smile lifting the corners of her mouth, crept up the back stairs to the nursery.

"Peek-a-boo!" she heard her son yell.

But the answering voice was not Lydia's. Carolyn paused at the sound of a man teasing Dev Jr.. Tingles of amazement splintered through her, but they were immediately followed by a deep, answering sense of loss. Her husband would never play with their little boy. God, how it hurt! How much Dylan sounded like his brother.

Disquieted now, Carolyn went along the hall until she had a view into the nursery that would not expose her own presence. Dylan had become a bear. He was down on all fours swinging his head to and fro, but she saw him peek over to make sure the boy was not frightened. Shrieks – not of fear but of laughter – answered. Dylan roared and lumbered forward. In his fresh night clothes, his chubby baby cheeks glowing, Dev Jr. toddled in crazy circles before throwing himself across his uncle's back, gasping with glee. Dylan obliged by leaning down to give his nephew a ride. Lydia hurried over to help place the toddler on his uncle's back.

As if sensing her, Dylan started to look up. Carolyn turned away. She hurried down the hall, unable to ignore the white-hot emotion inside her, but not sure exactly what it was. It was a terrible tangle, that was for sure. Sorrow. Anger. Resentment. It was not all because she had grown accustomed to doing things her own way. It went deeper than that, to the place where she wondered about the changes in Dylan and the changes she knew were lurking in her own future. And there was fear in that, too.

She went to check on the soldier. When she saw he was still, she replaced the cloth on his head with a cool one, lit a lamp and paced.

Why had Dylan come home, why him and not Dev? And why was he trying to act like Dev, who truly *had* known how to run a farm and oversee servants and deal with creditors? And how was she supposed to live in the house with a man who was not her husband, but who reminded her of him in unexpected and painful ways?

"Something's got to change," she muttered aloud. "Things just can't go on like this. And the house – the Savannah house! Does he want to lose *everything*?"

She told herself her anger over the town house didn't stem simply from a sentimental attachment. They would also need every asset in the future. They might need to sell it, if worse came to worst.

The man on the sofa moaned. She walked over and stood above him, hands on her hips, feeling something uncharacteristic: selfishness. "And just who are you, anyway? Besides another man creating problems?"

To her surprise, the eyelids fluttered open, and glazed, stormy eyes focused on her. "Becky," he murmured.

"No, I'm Carolyn. Mrs. Carolyn Rousseau. Mrs. *Devereaux* Rousseau." There, she felt better saying that aloud.

"Come," he rasped. He motioned weakly to her. She knelt beside him as he coughed. Suddenly, with surprising force, he grabbed her arm and drew her closer. The fever-blurred glaze clamped down on her. "I'm not empty-handed anymore! I did it for us! For us! I promised you–" A fit of coughing overtook him, during which Carolyn was able to escape his clutches. She sat back on her knees. Finally he finished, "I promised I'd take care of you."

"Yes, you did," she murmured to ease the man. "But please, calm yourself."

Who was Becky? A wife? A fiancée? A daughter? He might have any of those. Moved by compassion, Carolyn wrung out the cloth and bathed his bearded face. He was not unhandsome. She studied the high cheekbones, the strong jaw with more interest. She didn't have the heart to tell him again that she wasn't his Becky. How could she have been impatient with him, even for a minute, when he suffered as her own Dev had suffered?

Her eye fell on the haversack resting nearby. She reached for it, sliding open the buttoned tab. Tin cup and plate. Knife and fork. Hardtack. A sewing kit. Ah, a wrapped bundle – a handkerchief tied with a pink ribbon around a hard rectangle. Unfolding the cloth, Carolyn gazed at a tintype of a young woman in a Garabaldi blouse and dark skirt. She was pretty in a simple way, with a satisfied, rosebud mouth and a round face. Though there was no monogram on the handkerchief, Carolyn could only assume that she was looking at Becky.

She went through the haversack and the saddlebags in search of letters, but there were none. This troubled her. Maybe they were in the soldier's clothing. She searched the uniform coat, then bent over the man again, gently unbuttoning his vest and sliding her hand inside the pocket. Nothing.

But he stirred, muttered, "Becky."

She smoothed back his hair and said, "I'm here." She was shocked at how hot he was. Struggling, she eased the wool vest from one arm at a time.

"Chennault," he wheezed.

"Chennault? Is that your name?"

A moan was her only answer. Carolyn shook the soldier slightly. "What's your name?" she demanded. Something in her would not let this man die without a name. No, how could she let him die at all? He obviously had unfinished business. Becoming more insistent, Carolyn shook him again. "Wake up. What's your name? Where are you from?"

He spoke again, but not to answer her questions. "Don't – leave me. You said you'd wait."

"I won't leave you, but you must tell me–"

The soldier contracted in another prolonged bout of coughing. Carolyn held a cloth to his mouth. It came away yellow and red. Ah, the memories. She held up his sweaty head, slid another teaspoon of tonic between his lips.

Suddenly she had an idea. There were still several blocks of ice in the springhouse that the slaves had taken off the pond during the past winter's freeze. If she got the man in a cold bath, maybe it would break his fever. Was it too late once blood showed in the saliva? She didn't know, but she had to try.

Carolyn rose and rushed to the stairs. On the second floor, she knocked on Dylan's door, not caring how improper she was being. When he opened it, drawing suspenders over an untucked shirt, she looked away, tucking a strand of blonde hair behind her ear, but said firmly, "I need your help. That man downstairs is delirious, and we need to get him in a cold bath. We have to try to save him."

He studied her a minute, then nodded.

While he fetched the tin tub from the kitchen and carried buckets of water in to fill it, Carolyn went to the spring house. She chipped ice from a block with a chisel and placed it in a canvas sack, then took it inside. Together they stripped the soldier to his long johns and managed to get him in the icy water. He began to shiver. Not saying a word, Dylan watched her bathe the stranger's face and neck.

Carolyn felt she needed to explain her desperation. She wanted him to know she wasn't just doing this because of Dev. "I don't know who he is, but he loves a girl named Becky, and he's afraid she's going to leave him. I can't find any papers on him, Dylan, not a one. Did he lose them? Burn them? Somebody must love him. Somebody must be wondering where he is. Don't you see, we can't let him die, without – without even knowing – who to tell – who he is – what happened."

Dylan took the cloth from her to pause her frantic ministrations. "I understand," he said softly. "And you're right. You're right to try."

A tear was tracking down her cheek as she looked at the pale, trembling man in the tub. She brushed it away, angry at the hopelessness of it all. Angry that *she* was so helpless – again. Dylan had seen countless deaths, but she was tender and vulnerable now, and this rattled her. She wanted to leave, leave Dylan with this man he'd brought home, but she couldn't.

They got him out, wrapped him in wool blankets. He was cooler, and he no longer moaned or tossed about. Instead, he now lay still, like a corpse, the only indication life lingered his faint wheezing breath.

They kept their silent vigil until nearly dawn, when the breaths grew ragged. Carolyn held the man's hand and cried. He never spoke again.

hey buried the Tennessee cavalryman under the oak tree by the pond, where the ground was already soft. Carolyn brushed his hair, dressed him in his uniform, laid his haversack beside him, and folded his hands over his chest clutching the picture of the girl named Becky. The grief as she did it was intense. She knew it was because eight months ago she had prepared her own husband for burial, but there was a rightness in knowing someone grieved the unknown soldier. So she did not try to hide or suppress her emotions.

She could tell Dylan was concerned about her, but she didn't want to look at him or talk to him. He made her think too much about everything.

Dylan, too, was weighted down with troubles. There was a deep pensiveness, a distance, as if a great gulf still separated him from everyday life. Carolyn often noticed him gazing off into nothingness, his eyes full of shadows. At night, she'd hear him pacing. Sometimes she'd see a horse with a dark rider clinging to its neck shoot from the stables. The cavalryman's stallion had recovered well with decent feed and rest, and Dylan found it a much better mount than the carriage horses. Hours later the sound of its hooves would awaken her as Dylan returned home. Once she asked Henrietta where he went. Henrietta shrugged, looking troubled.

But this did not mean he was disengaged from his duties. No, indeed. In the days that followed, he did not defer to her except to ask the briefest of questions, and only when entirely necessary. A seed of resentment began to take root inside of her. *She* was the one who had worked here, had struggled and learned and made ends meet. And now here he was, taking it all over, taking all the credit, just like a man, making mistakes that could cost them everything.

The Dylan she had known would not have been that assuming.

His presence in the house began to annoy her. She didn't like the way his boots sounded as he walked through the hall. And she didn't like coming down the stairs to see his hat and coat hanging on the hall tree. No, not a bit.

Added to all this was the fact that one Sunday evening when she came back from a walk, she found Sunny Randall and her daughter Sylvie on the porch, having just spent the last hour visiting with Henrietta and Dylan. That in itself was no surprise. The Randalls and the Rousseaus had been acquainted since Richard Randall had convinced Louis Rousseau to let him export Rousseau rice in 1838. Their ties had only been strengthened when Carolyn's aunt Sunny had married Richard following the death of his first wife, Eva. Sunny was Henrietta's niece. And Henrietta had been so pleased with the way her one great niece's marriage to her older son had turned out, she had begun to think having her younger son marry another great niece wasn't a bad idea. Especially when that great niece, young, pretty, vivacious Sylvie, shared in her half-brother Jack's blockade-running, war-time fortune.

But what was surprising, at least to Carolyn, who had always thought Dylan too mature for Sylvie, was the sight of her brother-in-law's face as he bent over Sylvie's hand in goodbye. He had been pleased by her visit. And he hadn't minded the flirtatious smirk she gave him. Of that Carolyn was sure.

Sylvie was not one to beat around the bush. She knew what she wanted, and she went after it with all her feminine wiles. If she decided she wanted Dylan, where would that end? To any sensible man with eyes in his head, she would be a catch. What if Dylan came to agree with his mother that Sylvie was a good solution to all his problems? Where would that leave *her*? Did she really want to live with Sylvie Randall?

Carolyn thought about that expression she'd caught on Dylan's face all week, even when she tried to put it out of her mind. She concluded that what she felt wasn't anything akin to jealousy. That would be silly; Dylan had courted her such a long time ago, and even though for a time he'd struggled to overcome his feelings once she and Dev had wed, clearly he had been able to do so during the war. In fact, when on his deathbed Dev had joined her hand with Dylan's and asked her to let Dylan take care of her, Dylan had responded with just as much indignation as she had. No, what she felt was anxiety, for herself and for Dev Jr., and it was perfectly understandable, wasn't it?

At dinner a week or so after the trooper died, she said in a tone she hoped was conversational and casual, "After the wheat is threshed, it will be time to harvest the corn, then to sow next year's wheat. I suppose once all that is done you'll both think of spending Christmas in Savannah, and the winter season?"

If they did, she could make it until then. Then her life could return to its previous peaceful, albeit lonely, state. Dylan could provide for her from a distance by giving her a place to live, discharging his duty to his brother's widow and his nephew. She could keep a few servants at hand, and with visits to and from people in town, including occasional ones from Dylan and Henrietta up from Savannah, they'd be just fine, she and Dev Jr..

"Oh, no," Henrietta responded, looking up from her plate. "I have no desire to be in town with all those Yankee soldiers there. Remember, Savannah is occupied."

"Then – do you think you'll be able to soon reclaim The Marshes?"

A small silence fell. Carolyn wondered why no one was answering her. Dylan finished chewing his bite and laid down his fork. "I think that's something we need to talk about, Carolyn. Mother and I have discussed it, and we feel we should let The Marshes go."

"Let it ... go?" Carolyn envisioned the beautiful coastal plantation overgrown and untended, its grandeur never to be reclaimed. But then, it was already that way.

"Sell it."

She stared at him. "You can't be serious."

"We are ... very serious. Mother will probably have to take the new oath of allegiance, but once she does, the Negroes camping there can be cleared off and the place put on the market."

"How – how could you do this? And not even *tell* me? Just like gambling with the deed to the Oglethorpe Square house without consulting either of us! I realize – I suppose – I'm not officially a part of this family any more, but–"

"That's not true, Carolyn," Dylan broke in.

She continued without pause, "–but my son *is*. And that plantation was to be part of his inheritance. Or was I mistaken? I – I guess everything is yours now. But does what I think not even *count*?"

"Of course it does, but I think if you consider the facts, you'll agree…"

Carolyn could not listen to him, her anger was so quickly escalating. Her limbs trembled, and she felt cornered and alone. She glanced at Henrietta, who looked troubled, her lips compressed. "Dev *loved* The Marshes," she appealed to her mother-in-law. "And so did Louis. It was the crown jewel of your own little empire. Yet as soon as they are gone you are ready to sell it away – sell the memories, and sell the future – to some rich Yankee?" Carolyn's voice cracked, and she stood abruptly. "You can't do that! You've both gone crazy!"

So saying, she ran out of the room, out of the house, and into the garden. That was the wrong place to go, for the sweet smell of roses reminded her of Dev's proposal.

Carolyn stopped and doubled over, wrapping her arms around herself. The only person who could stabilize her world was gone forever. But that didn't stop her from longing for his arms, his whispered words of assurance.

She heard the crunch of slightly uneven footsteps, and a rush of annoyance overswept her. Could she not be allowed the luxury of falling apart in private?

She began to walk away, but Dylan's voice – Dev's voice – called after her. "Carolyn, please, wait. Please let me explain."

She halted and listened, but did not turn around.

"I can see why you are upset. First that soldier I brought home – and the loan – and now this. I don't blame you. I – handled this poorly. I should have spoken with you sooner. It's just – we can't afford The Marshes. The property taxes are killing us, and without slave labor, I don't see how we can pay enough workers enough money to break even, much less turn a profit. By now the ditches have filled up; weeds are everywhere. The blacks aren't going to want to do the hard banking and ditching labor a rice plantation demands, even if we *could* pay them. The truth is, I'm glad of it. Yes, I hate to see the land and house pass out of our family. Yes, I know we'll be closing a chapter of our lives that will never be opened again, but is that all a bad thing? We once had dreams, Carolyn, both of us, and they didn't include the old world, the dying world that was The Marshes. This place is different. I can see a future here. It will never be like it was before, but at least we won't starve. So … there it is."

"And does your mother agree with you?"

"My father was killed at The Marshes, remember?"

"I – I guess I hadn't thought of that."

"It's not exactly a place she wants to linger any more. It's too painful."

She had to admit that he made sense, but something inside her rebelled against Dylan's logic, against the inevitable. It was so hard to give up old dreams. "But you grew up there. *Dev* grew up there."

"I know. I struggled with that, but I've come to peace with it. I think you will, too, if you give it some time."

"I guess I don't have a choice, do I?" Carolyn asked, half turning to look at him in the moonlight.

"Carolyn, please don't look at it that way. We value what you've done here more than we can express, and as Dev Jr.'s mother–"

"It's all right, Dylan," she cut in softly, withdrawing emotionally, protecting herself. "I understand how things stand here now."

Carolyn turned her face away and walked back toward the kitchen. This time she ignored his pleas for her to stay. There was no point in saying anything else. The dust raised by the great conflict was settling. Dev was dead. She no longer had a defender, a representative. And Dylan was back. She no longer made the decisions. She was a young widow whose only place in the world was defined by her infant son, an attachment that would give her food and shelter, but little else. It was a situation that would continue to be awkward, at best.

Unless … unless she went back to her own family. To Brightwell.

Her heart rebelled at the thought. Forests of Green had become a true home. But did she really belong here now?

That night she cried herself to sleep … but by morning, her mind was made up.

As she fed Dev Jr. his porridge, Henrietta came into the kitchen. Her dark hair was neatly tucked under a black mourning cap that matched her well-worn gown of the same hue. She slid its skirt under her petite form as she took a seat near her daughter-in-law. She played with her fork a moment, hesitating before speaking.

"Carolyn, I felt very bad about our discussion at dinner last night. I don't want you to think we don't want you to be an integral part of our lives here. Why, if you hadn't been here all this time, hadn't held things together, where would we be now? Because of you, we have our dignity. And we love you, truly we do. And … I don't just speak for myself. Dylan cares for you, too, though showing it just now is a bit awkward, a bit hard for him."

Carolyn's hand paused in mid-air, but she did not respond. Dev Jr. kicked his legs in his high chair, so she delivered his bite.

"But … that raises a problem of another sort, something I've been conscious of since our return," Henrietta continued. "I know the rules of society have relaxed somewhat, but for people of our station, propriety will always be important. I worry … for your reputation. Of course you are chaperoned, but you and Dylan, living under the same roof … well, it just leaves something to be desired."

"And what would that be?" Carolyn asked, turning her gaze upon the older woman.

"Matrimony."

"*What?*"

"I know it's early yet, too early, but an engagement …"

Carolyn's mouth fell open. "I – I can't believe this. You are suggesting I marry Dylan? Is this his idea – or yours?"

"Well, I have not spoken to him, but I do believe, like I said, that he still cares for you."

"What about Sylvie Randall? You were so in favor of that match."

"Things have changed. I don't deny Sylvie's money would be a great boon. But the most important thing is, we need to knit this family back together again. There's little Devie to consider. Who would make him a better father? I couldn't bear it, Carolyn, for you to take him away to some other family. You can see I've been thinking about this a lot."

"Henrietta," Carolyn cut in, unable to say "mother" at the moment, "this is really too much. I can understand your feelings, but this just isn't how it works. First of all I believe in propriety, but a marriage of convenience is a bit *too* outdated. And second, and more importantly, I'm not ready to think of marrying *anyone* yet – not even Dylan. Maybe especially Dylan. I don't know if I ever will be."

Henrietta's brow furrowed in distress. "But, then how shall we go on?"

"Please do not trouble yourself. I've come to a decision. I shall return to my parents and grandparents at Brightwell." She held up a hand to ward off Henrietta's protest. "I know you will miss Dev Jr., but there will be visits – many visits – and as I see it, this is the only way for now."

Tears eased out of Henrietta's eyes. "Carolyn, I refuse to believe that. I was only just reunited with my grandson. I know I have not been involved as a grandmother, due to my grief over losing Louis, but things are different now. Dev Jr. is my inspiration, my joy. Please, at least consider what I suggest. I know if I speak with Dylan ..."

Carolyn placed a hand on her mother-in-law's black ruffled sleeve. "No, please, please ... do not do that."

She turned and lifted Dev Jr. out of his chair. Taking pity on Henrietta, who was now snuffling tragically into her handkerchief, she asked, "Would you like to hold him?"

Without reply Henrietta held out her arms. Carolyn lowered the child onto his grandmother's lap. Her heart twisted with regret as the older woman drew him close and clung as though she would never let go.

Carolyn held her ground but softened her tone. "I'll go into town today and make arrangements to leave on the Saturday stage."

Her last night at Forests of Green, Carolyn took a walk. Her eyes embraced everything: the garden, the shorn wheat fields, the rows of ripening but too-short corn, marching in neat rows to the edge of the lush woods for which the estate was named. She stopped by the pond to watch the ducks swim and listen to the solitary trilling of an early cicada. The setting sun cast orange-gold ripples across the surface of the water.

Oh, how her heart ached. She had once dreamed of a future here with Dev, here and at The Marshes, but that dream was now as intangible as vapor. Everything had changed, and her hands were empty, except for her son. Thank God for that one precious gift, the living reminder of the love she had shared with Devereaux.

At least things had worked out well for Mahala. She had visited her dearest, half-Cherokee friend at the inn Mahala and her grandmother Martha owned in Clarkesville a couple of days prior. At the news of Carolyn's impending departure, Mahala had been distressed, tearful even, but Carolyn knew nothing could completely dampen her newfound joy. And Carolyn didn't begrudge that. Mahala had been alone for many long years, when she and Jack Randall had held each other at arm's length due to class differences and Jack's stubborn refusal to let a woman into his life, and then when that heartache had pushed Mahala into an engagement with Clay Fraser, her Cherokee childhood friend. It had taken Jack sneaking into Atlanta under Sherman's very nose to ascertain the truth about Clay's death, followed by his spiriting Mahala, Carolyn and Devie to safety when Savannah fell, to convince Mahala he was a changed man ready to commit. No, she deserved the happiness she had now found with Jack. The couple was in the midst of planning an autumn wedding and a honeymoon in Europe. Mahala had made Carolyn promise to return for the ceremony.

She sighed. It was just as well she was leaving. With Mahala abroad, Carolyn would feel she belonged here even less than she did now. At Brightwell, she could think and pray. Plan her future.

She was so absorbed in her thoughts that she failed to notice someone approaching and was startled when a deep voice spoke just behind her.

"You've been avoiding me."

Carolyn whirled to see Dylan, clad in brown pants, full-sleeved muslin shirt and a striped tan vest. His collar was open, and a straw hat covered his bright hair. His pre-war clothes were in remarkably good condition. The slightest growth of stubble shadowed his square jaw.

What could she say? It was true. Several times in the past few days she had sensed him trying to create a moment to speak with her alone, and she had always managed to escape. Knowing Henrietta, her mother-in-law had poured everything out to her son despite Carolyn's wishes. Carolyn was merely trying to prevent another awkward scene.

When she didn't reply, just looked back at the pond, Dylan added, "I need to speak with you."

"Well, here I am."

"Are you still angry with me about The Marshes?"

Carolyn thought a minute. She tried to muster up some of the fire she had felt before. The protective barrier it had provided had been helpful. But she was too tired, too resigned now. "I've realized it's not my business to be angry."

"That's not true. And despite what you say, you *are* angry. Please believe that if I thought there was any other way I wouldn't have signed over the deed to the house in town. And please also believe we can keep the house. I know I haven't done things like you might have, but please, Carolyn, just give me a chance."

It was the first time since Dylan's return that he had pled for her understanding, and it softened her heart a bit. "It's all right, Dylan. I know you're just doing what you think is best. Things have changed, and we all need to be able to admit that. I just didn't want to at first."

"You are right that change is inevitable, but not everything has to change. We should hold onto all the good things from the old life that we can. For instance ... family."

"Your mother has spoken with you."

Dylan hesitated, then nodded.

"Oh, dear," Carolyn sighed, flushing and trying to turn away.

But Dylan placed a hand on her arm. "She has, but even if she hadn't, I wouldn't have been able to just let you leave like this. I need you to hear me out, Carolyn, as awkward or painful as it might be. There finally needs to be truth between us."

Carolyn wanted to look anywhere but at her brother-in-law. "Some things are better left unsaid."

"No," Dylan replied, his sharpness surprising her. "I've borne the burden of unsaid things for years, and I won't ever make that mistake again. So I'm asking you to allow me to speak my mind, whatever you may feel about what I say."

Carolyn bit her lip. She gave a curt nod. As she waited for Dylan to begin, she plucked a long grass and began to break off pieces. He stood off to one side just behind her, holding his hat, his head bowed. His first words froze her to the spot, for the tone, and the words, made her feel the Dylan of the old days was there behind her.

"I think I started to fall in love with you that day we did the polka at Madame Granet's dancing school. I guess I hoped you might look on me as a sort of prince charming coming to your rescue – silly as that might sound. And then there was Dev – as always. So much more charming and handsome and bold. I had a chance, I told myself, when we were writing to each other from school. I knew we were making a connection that went far deeper than the surface. And it might have worked, if you had not bloomed into an exquisite flower too beautiful to fail to attract my brother's notice. In the months that followed I cursed myself for allowing him to cut me out. *I* let it happen. I was convinced that I could never be as perfect as he was, at least in a woman's eyes, so I swallowed my pride. I swallowed the words I wanted to speak, because I saw the way you looked at him, and I couldn't bear to have you say he was your preference. And I let him propose to you when I had intended to myself."

"Oh, Dylan, please don't."

But he held up a hand to silence her. "Covetousness is an ugly sin, and it almost ate me alive before I confessed it to God and let go of my feelings for you. It was the hardest thing I ever did, Carolyn, but I couldn't let that envy sour my relationship with Dev – and with you. I was finally able to stop thinking of you. God restored my relationship with my brother. The years I spent in the army with Dev were the closest we ever had. He changed. I changed. And truthfully, I'm still trying to find out who I am, and what I should be doing now that he's gone and I'm here."

Carolyn felt tears near the surface – tears of sympathy, understanding and confusion. She turned and met Dylan's eyes. "Me, too," she whispered.

"I know. And I know you need time. Yet here we are in this crazy situation. We've got the rubble of our old world all around us, and we've got to figure out how to rebuild it. We need you, Carolyn, Mother and I – but especially me. You're a part of what was once beautiful that I just don't want to let go."

"W-what are you saying?"

"That I know you've been angry with me. So I tried to keep my distance, to not upset you and because I – really don't know how to … *be* … around you. Instead I just seem to keep making things worse. But I have to be honest before you leave, Carolyn. I can't picture the future without you."

She paused, catching her breath. "What about Sylvie?"

He looked confused. "What about her?"

"Don't you – care for *her*?"

"Not like that. Not like you."

"W-what are you asking?"

"I'm asking you to marry me."

A shuddering gasp tore loose inside Carolyn's chest and worked its way up her throat. She covered her face with her hands. "This is too much. You just said God gave you a brotherly love for me. And now, I'm supposed to believe you want to marry me? And that I should want to marry you? What about being f-friends?" Her voice cracked. "We were once friends. I don't feel that anymore. Shouldn't we start with that?"

She felt his gentle hands on her shoulders. "God gave me grace to love you like a sister when I had to, Carolyn, and if we have to start with friendship, so be it. But please don't ask me to remain that way. I can't do it."

A sense of panic started to rise. "Dylan, I have to go back to Brightwell. I can't stay on here with things as they are, and I'm not ready yet."

He sighed. "Fine, then, go for a visit, and while you're gone, I'll write you. We once said a lot in letters. But don't stay gone long. We all need you."

Carolyn nodded. What he suggested … letters … was it so unreasonable?

"I know right now you're still in love with Dev. Do you think you could ever feel something for *me*? Could you ever look at me and see me, and not my brother? Please, Carolyn, that much at least I have to know …"

Dylan's tone had dropped to a whisper that stirred the fine hairs at the nape of her neck. She shivered with remembered intimacies and wondered if she heard that voice in the dark, which face she would imagine. What did she feel because she was lonely, and what did she truly feel for Dylan? Right now it seemed impossible to separate the two. "I don't know. I haven't – I haven't felt like I know you anymore. And that's been – h-hard." Carolyn stumbled over the last word, choking on her rising tears. His gentleness made keeping up her guard impossible. She realized how much she had missed him!

Dylan softly squeezed her shoulders. "You once did. Maybe … maybe we can find our way back to that."

She drew in a shaky breath and bowed her head. Then she stepped closer to him, the only way she could bring herself to admit she was willing to consider his suggestion. He made a sound that was half a breath of relief and half a tearful sigh and drew her in, hiding his face against hers. He didn't hold her close with the confidence of possession, but tentatively. His nearness was both comforting and unsettling. What was she doing, what was she thinking? This solution might appear on the surface to make the most sense, but everything in her told her that it would never be easy, or painless. Dylan might have once adored her. He might sit at the head of her table. He might be uncle to her son. And he had implied that he could still love her. But he was a virtual stranger.

When at last Dylan pulled back to wipe her face, she was able to meet his gaze. "All right, then," he said quietly. "Shall I walk you back to the house?"

She nodded. He picked up his hat, and they began walking along the lane, close, but not touching.

"When will you be back?" he asked.

"For Mahala's wedding in October."

"October."

"Yes. I'll write."

"I'm counting on that." He smiled down at her.

Will it always be this awkward? Carolyn thought.

But there was also a rightness in the new understanding between them, and when Dylan's hand slipped around her own, she did not resist. In the dusk, a dove cooed, the breeze stirred the trees, and a small chorus of cicadas trilled. Carolyn heard the music of the land that was home, and her heart echoed the peaceful refrain.

In it, there was hope.

The next morning, Dylan was calm and possessed. With what she realized was disappointment, Carolyn thought one would never know he had proposed to her the night before. He did not try to touch her, or kiss her, or speak of the situation.

Wise man.

He and Henrietta drove her into town. Henrietta's tears were copious as she clung to her grandson, but Dylan merely smiled faintly at Carolyn across the carriage when she met his eyes. He was not aloof. He was just giving her the space she had requested.

Dylan handed her up into the stagecoach, and he did kiss her hand before releasing it. Then he took Dev Jr., tossed him in the air and blew on his neck before reaching him up to Carolyn. He closed the door and patted the side of the coach twice before stepping away.

"October," he said.

As the vehicle pulled away from town, Carolyn strained her neck looking back at them. When they were out of sight, she closed her eyes, and in her mind she saw Devereaux, uniting the hands of his brother and his wife underneath his own.

CHAPTER THREE

Early July, 1865
Clarkesville, Georgia

"What's the matter, Mahala?" Martha asked.

Mahala pushed a bit of stewed zucchini about with her fork, then speared a slice of squash instead. The young woman sighed, then turned her blue eyes – startling to most, contrasting as they did with her tawny skin and dark hair, evidence of half Cherokee ancestry – up to her grandmother. "Am I that transparent?"

"Well, you've been so happy lately, but ever since you got home from the store this afternoon..."

"I had to go to Fraser's. Uncle Thomas didn't have any boot laces. So instead of a single dose of disapproval and disdain, I got two."

"Oh, Mahala," Martha sighed. "I'm sorry. Next time I'll send Maddie. You'd think these people would be reasonable."

"No. I refuse to cower at home when I've done nothing wrong. The Frasers should have had ample time to get over the news of my engagement – it's not like I'm betraying Clay anyway when he's been dead a year now – and as for Uncle Thomas and Aunt Amy, their son tried to kill me! With his bare hands, blast it! What would they have me do? Would they have preferred him to kill me – in addition to my father, I might add – and escape from The Highlands with n'ary a price to pay?"

Mahala was getting incensed just thinking about it. The drama that had ensued when she had finally solved the long-ago murder of her father, Michael, Martha's son, had created waves of gossip in the small foothills town of Clarkesville. When Mahala had dug in their family hotel's compost heap in order to bury the silver service as Yankees approached Clarkesville in May, she had found the engraved lid of Michael's pocket watch. That clue had led them to realize the killer of her father had been someone very close at hand. When they had questioned Martha's nephew Leon, who managed The Franklin Hotel, he had been infuriated and had fled before they could summon the sheriff.

Now the whole town knew about how Leon Franklin had struck his own cousin with a poker from the fireplace of Michael's Sautee Valley cabin in 1838, leaving him to die, all because Michael had refused to move away from the area with his Cherokee bride, Kawani. Leon had always been jealous of Michael's position at the hotel, where he also worked, but his determination to marry a prejudiced judge's daughter had been what had caused him to murder Michael that night. Kawani had died shortly after discovering her husband's body, leaving an infant Mahala to the care of her best friend and neighbor, Nancy Emmitt. Mahala had spent her whole life, especially after coming to live with her grandmother in town, trying to unravel the clues Michael had left in his strong box – and solve the murder of his missing gold, just as Leon secretly had. Mahala had finally realized Michael had buried the gold in the spring house of The Highlands, the estate outside town which had once belonged to the family of her father's old nemesis, lawyer Rex Clarke. When she had gone there to dig, she had encountered Leon, hiding in the abandoned house. Even though Leon had always despised her for her mixed blood and her place in her grandmother's will and affections, she still could not believe he had pulled a gun on her. And that there he had admitted everything, planning to kill her and take the gold before leaving Habersham County. Their struggle had been interrupted by Jack Randall, Mahala's fiancé, just returned from taking his blockade-running steamer to the Bahamas as the Confederate States crumbled. Jack had delivered Leon straight to jail and had told Mahala that day that he had purchased The Highlands, which she had always adored, as a wedding present for her.

All this Martha knew far too well. She had always detested gossip and had tried hard to avoid it. Now she could hardly step outside without deflecting a dozen questions. And to add insult to injury, her deceased husband's brother, Leon's father, would not speak to her. And the Frasers, owners of the town's other dry goods store, were decidedly cold. They seemed to take personal offense that Mahala was engaged to the man of her dreams, all too shortly in their opinion after the death of their adopted Cherokee son, Clay. Mahala would have honored her agreement to marry Clay – a promise made to her dear friend when Jack had denied his feelings for her – had he not been killed in the battle for Atlanta. But that seemed to make no difference.

Martha didn't even censure Mahala's use of the word "blast." "I know. I know," she said. "It confounds me, too. I can only think they don't know *how* to act with the trial coming up. They are permanently shamed in town, business is ruined, and they have no one to blame. Amy has always been one for spreading poison. It's how her son turned out the way he did. I wouldn't be surprised if the two of them don't pack up and move, and that might not be a bad thing."

"Oh, Grandmother. What an awful position for you to be in. It's all so sad."

Martha nodded her agreement, spreading her beans over her corn bread. "There is much in the South that's sad now."

It was true. Things were in a fine state of affairs. Last month James Johnson, a pro-Union Georgian, had been appointed by President Andrew Johnson as governor of a shattered state. With food, supplies and cash scarce, people were starving, resorting to thievery to make ends meet. Vagabonds, former soldiers and disillusioned ex-slaves roamed North Georgia's countryside. The government was portioning out former Confederate mules and stores in an attempt to alleviate the situation. Meanwhile, Northerners flocked to the major cities of the state to grab up land deals, start businesses and offer goods to the luxury-starved but poverty-stricken citizens.

"I saw George Kollock today," Mahala offered. "He said his wife is returning from the coast. She wrote to him that there is talk of the officials making the blacks go back to their masters and work for them for small pay."

"Ha," Martha scoffed. "Most people I hear say, let the government clean up its own mess. What would the former masters pay the workers with? So many have lost even their lands."

"Yes," Mahala said, thinking of Carolyn. It was hard not to feel the sadness of the people all around her, even when her own life finally possessed the promise of joy. She had not wanted Carolyn to leave – had tried to get her to stay at the hotel instead of returning to the coast. But, perhaps her friend needed her family, and the solace of God's private healing, at this time.

"Well, folks will go on as best they know how. I hear Mr. Kollock and Mr. Waldburg were elected wardens of Grace Church. I just wish we had a pastor, Mahala. We all need spiritual guidance now more than ever, yet no one can afford to pay a preacher."

"Yes, I miss Mrs. Burns, too, very much." Selma Burns, wife of their former pastor at the First Methodist Church, had helped Mahala through her own lean time of the soul. Now that Selma's husband had died in the war, and Selma had returned to her parents, Mahala was unable to return her kindness. "It seems so many dear friends have gone, never to come again."

"But you are not one to lament, my dear," Martha said, reaching across the table to squeeze Mahala's hand. "Fortune has at last smiled on you, thanks be to God. Think of how bright your future is, full of new places and new people, all due to that man I called a rascal for so long."

Mahala felt the radiant smile break out over her face at the mention of Jack. Despite the tragic circumstances surrounding them, the joyous wonder of their love and soon-to-be life together buoyed Mahala to a height she had never before known.

At that moment a knock sounded on the door of their living quarters. Mahala raised a hopeful eyebrow at her grandmother and went to open the door. There indeed stood her intended.

36

Dressed as immaculately as ever, he swept a gambler's hat off his wavy brown hair and bowed. "Good evening. May I come in?"

"Of course!" Mahala hastened to take his hat and close the door behind him.

With a glance at Martha in the next room, he bent to place a quick kiss on her lips. But the way he looked at her – concerned, almost – as he cradled her face in his palm made her afraid. No grin, no pert comment. This was not a normal greeting.

"What's happened?" she asked, a quaver in her voice. Here it was. The thing she had been dreading. In recent days, she hadn't been able to shake the feeling that something was bound to go wrong. Some jagged piece of the world outside was sure to crash through the cocoon of their happiness as it so often had before.

"I do have news, and I'm afraid it will disturb you." He pulled her to his side. "But it concerns your grandmother as well."

"Come," Mahala urged, a lump in her throat. "Sit with us." She led him to the table where two flickering candles created a welcoming atmosphere. He apologized for interrupting their dinner, then held the chair for Mahala.

"Why, aren't you going to offer your fiancé refreshment, Mahala?" Martha prompted.

"Thank you, I don't require any."

"Jack has news, Grandmother."

"Oh?" Martha's questioning eyes turned upon her guest.

Jack nodded. "Regarding your nephew, Ma'am."

"Leon?"

"Yes. I came to tell you … there will be no trial. News is about town tonight that Mr. Franklin is dead."

"Dead?" gasped both women together.

"He attacked a guard who was bringing in his dinner. Mr. Franklin tried to wrest away the guard's weapon. In the process, he was killed. Shot in the chest."

A thick silence reigned for several moments. Mahala looked at her grandmother. What should they feel? Horror? Relief? God forbid, disappointment? Mahala shirked from the thought. Far be it from her to rejoice in any man's death. No, it wasn't that. But there was an emptiness of sorts, something she couldn't put into words until Jack said:

"I know this matter has monopolized many thoughts and emotions in your lives – your whole lives, almost. And now, to see it concluded so suddenly, but perhaps not in the way you'd wish justice done…" He allowed his voice to trail off.

Grateful, Mahala took his hand, finding comfort in the strength of it. She gave a faint smile. "Yes. Thank you for coming so quickly to tell us."

"I wanted you to be aware before you ventured out or encountered anyone in the morning."

"We can only assume this is as it's meant to be. I'm sorry for him, and for my husband's brother, but perhaps this finish will sow less blame than if Leon had been convicted at trial," Martha said.

"Perhaps," said Jack. "Yet if it's in my power to spare you any ill effects, you know I will. In fact that's the other reason I came tonight – to speak to you on a subject I've been pondering for the past few days."

"What is that, Jack?" Mahala asked.

"You remember I told you I'd had a letter from Andrew Willis, my clerk in Savannah?"

Mahala nodded. "You were thinking of buying an iron foundry the government confiscated there and now has up for sale."

"Though why you'd need another investment I can't imagine," Martha murmured. Mahala gave her a look. Her grandmother was already growing too bold with her future grandson-in-law. Jack merely grinned at her.

"Did you decide then?" Mahala asked.

"I think I'd like to take a look at it. And I think this is a perfect opportunity to bridge the gap with my family in New York." Jack's relatives owned Randall Iron, which had filled many an order for Jack's Savannah shipping firm prior to the war, and many a Union contract during it. "I've written to my cousin George telling him of the particulars and offering him passage to come down and give his opinion. Should we decide to purchase the place, his expertise in getting it up and running would be invaluable."

"And his renewed friendship would be a blessing," Mahala added with a smile. "But this means you'll be leaving!"

"Yes, and taking you with me."

"What?!"

"I can't think of a better opportunity to introduce you to my relations before the wedding and for you to shop for a wedding gown – and whatever else you need."

"B-but–"

Jack continued, raising a hand to her spluttered protestations. "I'll be in Savannah long enough that I don't want to leave you. I'm recalling my ships to port now that the blockade is lifted. *South Land II* and *Evangeline* will need repairs and refurbishment. I'd like to return both to passenger vessels. I hope the smaller ship can get what she needs done in Savannah, but *Evangeline* will have to sail to New York. I want her done up right, in grand style. Maybe, if we hurry things along, she'll be ready to steam us home from Liverpool."

"From our honeymoon?" The idea caught her notice.

"Yes. I'm just sorry she's in no shape to take us there."

38

"That's all right." Mahala returned to the subject at hand. "But I can't leave Grandmother here alone."

"I'm not suggesting that."

"But ... the hotel," Martha pointed out.

"Close her up."

"Close her up?"

"Why not? The refugees have gone back to salvage what they can of their lives, and there will be no tourists this season. If you have any guests, my staff can accommodate them at The Palace – on me." Jack winked at Mahala. They both recalled all the years they'd gone nose to nose trying to attract those guests each to their own hotels.

"Well, there are one or two," Martha said lamely, clearly tempted by his offer.

"Grandmother, you want to do this?" Mahala asked in surprise.

"I know I haven't liked to leave the hotel before, but things are changing now. Jack's reasoning seems sound enough to me, if a bit forcefully presented," Martha replied, giving Jack a censorious eye.

Jack smiled. "My apologies, Ma'am. Blame it on my eagerness to be near your granddaughter."

She harrumphed. "That's the only part that troubles me." Martha stood up, picking up her plate. "And the main reason I'll go along."

Jack stood as well, bowing his head to her judgment with only a partially suppressed smirk as answer.

Martha eyed him a minute, then added, "Go on and visit a minute in the parlor while I clean up here. Work out all your plans."

"Thank you, Grandmother," Mahala said, standing. Taking Jack's hand, she led him into the next room to the sofa. She sank down, tucking her muslin skirt against her leg so that he could sit close.

"So what's the matter? You don't want to go to Savannah?" he asked, his green eyes boring into hers. "I understand why you want to be married here – the people, the house and everything. But I thought you understood that for me to manage Randall and Ellis we'll have to spend time on the coast, too."

"I did – I do," Mahala replied sheepishly. "I guess I just didn't think – it would be so soon. Before we were even married."

"I will see that people give you the respect you deserve, Mahala".

"I – I know that. But ... will they *like* me? Your family?" Unable to meet his gaze, she twisted her fingers in her lap.

"Yes."

She looked up then. "*Honestly.*"

"Honestly. All right ... Grandfather Ellis will have no protest over you because his mind wanders–"

"Oh, thanks," Mahala said, swatting at him.

"Grandmother Ellis will embrace you and be your champion, if you need one. I don't know if she's met anyone she could not find good in."

"What exactly are you saying?"

"Aunt Eugenie – she was my mother's sister, you recall … she'll be the dark horse. But whatever she thinks, she'll tell you – no games like you get with so many Southern women. Not like my cousin Ella Beth, who always acts as though everything is fine. If she hated you, you'd never know it."

"Oh, Jack!"

"But she won't hate you. What's to hate? You wanted a true assessment, and I'm giving one so you know what to expect going in. As for the rest of Savannah, be yourself, and who cares? Besides, you'll have Sylvie for an ally, and who would tangle with her?"

"Sylvie will be going with us?"

"I'm sure she wouldn't miss the shopping."

Mahala bit her lip, somewhat mollified, though not for the reason Jack suspected. Just before Carolyn had left, Sunny and Sylvie had invited the Rousseaus to dinner at The Palace, a nice dinner prepared by the now under-worked French chef, as a farewell to Carolyn. But Mahala had gotten the impression it had been more of a hello to Dylan – from Sylvie, that was. Carolyn had acted like she had not noticed, but Mahala had.

Sylvie had seated Dylan at her own side and favored him all night with pearly-white smiles, a creamy shoulder turned toward him, a tiny hand now and then reaching towards his sleeve to accent some point. She had asked him all sorts of questions about his war-time bravery – questions Dylan clearly sought to avoid answering – and inquired into his plans for the future. She had seemed not in the least put off by the concept that Dylan was a farmer now, just a "cracker" who raised grain, no longer a rice or cotton planter. Had this not occurred to her?

"Hey," Jack murmured, touching a finger to her chin to break her reverie. She realized she had been frowning. "I have no doubts my Cherokee princess will be triumphant, even if it means you have to take a few scalps along the way."

Once upon a time such a comment would have made her mad, when it had been underlain with sarcasm. She now knew his teasing was affectionate. Without it life would not be nearly so interesting. She laughed.

It was a gay party that left Savannah aboard *South Land II* on a Sunday afternoon in mid-July. Those gathered on deck watching the city disappear behind them included Mahala and Jack, Martha, Sunny, Sylvie, Sylvie's brothers Bryson and Alan, Eugenie and Stephen, and Ella Beth with her two children, ten-year-old Sam and five-year-old Jordan. Jack's

40

grandmother had stayed behind to tend Grandfather Ellis, who was not feeling well.

"This is our first pleasure outing since the war," Eugenie commented. "I hardly know what to do!"

Mahala smiled, trying to hide her discomfort. Jack had been right about his relatives. His aunt did not like her, and she knew it. It was not what she said, however, but how *little* she said to Mahala that revealed the truth. She seemed to think that if she laughed merrily enough and looked the other way, Mahala might disappear.

The tension was enough to mar her own excitement over her first time being aboard a steam boat – Jack's boat at that. And going to Little Tybee beach! She should be delirious with anticipation. But right now she could only hope to make it through the outing with some measure of grace.

"Tide's low," Jack told them. "We should see lots of birds today."

"There's an egret," Sylvie called, pointing to the shore.

"There won't be many around for long if the hat makers keep up business," Sunny commented.

Even Mahala had seen many a hat and bonnet adorned with the bird's beautiful white feathers.

"Oh, I wish we did not have to steam past Pulaski and those disgraceful batteries on Tybee," Ella Beth said as they rounded Cockspur Island under Captain John Billingsly's skillful guidance. "It brings back such bad memories."

Mahala saw the faces of Sylvie's brothers tighten. She could imagine the sight of the bombarded fort that had once guarded Savannah so proudly and the Union gun placements along Tybee's northern face that had – with rifled cannon – proved the fort's demise would be especially bitter to the young men who had given years of their lives in coastal defense. Now, the victors were still camped on Tybee Island, which was the reason they had to forgo the more popular and nearer beach of Tybee for its southern sister.

To cover the silence that fell, Eugenie patted Ella Beth's shoulder. "Are you quite all right, dear? You're pale. I worry about you in all that black on such a hot day."

"I'm fine, Mama," the blonde woman answered.

Eugenie persisted. "Jack, do you not think she looks pale? Can we not make a place for her out of the sun?"

"Of course, Aunt Eugenie." Jack complied, carrying a deck chair from the rail to the shade of the pilot house.

As he bent over his cousin, offering a drink while Eugenie untied the strings of Ella Beth's crepe-shrouded mourning bonnet, Mahala touched Martha's arm. "It *is* hot," she murmured. "Perhaps at the prow we'll get a better breeze."

She felt relieved as soon as they reached the front of the steamer, though the wind was strong enough to necessitate them holding tight onto their wide-brimmed straw hats. She turned away from her grandmother's searching gaze, watching the shore, inhaling the salt breeze. Despite the signs of Union occupation on the island, her spirits began to rise. There was no reason to let Eugenie's ignoring her or Ella Beth's delicacy get under her skin. They were what they were, and she was what she was. Maybe one day they could find some common ground. It just probably wouldn't be today. But for now, she could at least spare the young woman some pity. She knew what it felt like to lose someone you loved, didn't she? Ella Beth's husband, Major Frank Draper of the Savannah Volunteer Guards, had fallen in the rear guard defense of Appomattox. Quite a recent loss.

Still, Mahala experienced a powerful sense of relief when Jack appeared. He was just so handsome in his fluttering white shirt, linen vest and tan trousers, straw hat in hand, with the salt wind whipping his wavy hair. Of course most women would look at him, even his recently bereaved cousin. Maybe especially his cousin.

Mahala choked that thought down and smiled.

"Here you are," Jack said. "Queasy?"

"Not in the least."

"I told you so!"

Mahala recalled their conversation that long-ago day on the way to church, when Jack had offered to take her out on one of his boats should she ever come to Savannah. She had worked so hard to convince herself she just wanted to be his friend. And now, here she was, his fiancée, on the *South Land II*, about to round the point of Tybee Island into the Atlantic Ocean! She wrapped her hand around Jack's arm, squeezing the muscle there.

"Happy?" he murmured.

"Oh, yes."

"It's not so marshy where we're headed, is it, Captain Randall?" Martha asked.

"Oh, no, Ma'am. It's a wonderful beach – long and smooth. Don't worry, I wouldn't have us picnicking in among the red cedars and wax myrtle with the snakes."

Martha laughed. "I *thought* I smelled myrtles."

"Yes, indeed, many a bayberry candle has come from these shores since Colonial times."

"Were the colonists the first to inhabit Tybee, Jack?" Mahala asked. "I heard they stopped here before settling in Savannah."

"The Euchee Indians were the first. 'Tybee' is the Euchee word for salt. Then there were the pirates." Jack's green eyes gleamed.

"Pirates?"

Pleased he'd captured their attention, he continued. "They would use the island as a hiding place. Did you know the first naval battle occurred just off Tybee? The land was once part of Spanish Florida. In the 1600s France became interested in the sassafras root that grew here. They thought that it had some sort of magical powers, made into a tea." He nodded to their looks of surprise. "The Spanish attacked a French ship that once moored off the coast."

"There's the lighthouse," Martha said. "Isn't it pretty?"

"That's the third one to be set there," Jack told them. "The first was built in the 1730s and was the tallest structure in America at that time."

"How do you remember all these things?" Mahala asked

He grinned at her look of consternation, then added, "There now. We're in the Atlantic proper. Feel the motion of the boat change?"

The little steamship angled its way south along the ocean face of the island. Jack told them with a wink that it was about two-and-a-half miles square. Mahala reminded herself that, of course, he would know all about the waterways of the Southern ports and the land that surrounded them. She turned to look ahead and had a good view of the long expanse of white beach.

"It's beautiful," she murmured. Her heart beat fast. At last she'd walk along the ocean shore. For that task she'd worn her old boots and a corded petticoat. Sylvie had lent her a leisure dress with button-up tabs and a brightly colored petticoat that was supposedly all the rage in Europe.

"You'll see," she had said. "I'm sure you'll come back from England and France soon enough telling *me* what all the latest styles are."

Mahala could hardly imagine it. Neither could she imagine the bathing machines Sylvie described as being so popular in England. Apparently women entered these rooms on wheels to change from their street clothes into their bloomer-and-long-bodice-matched bathing suits. Then the machines were pulled by horse out into the surf. With the machine blocking their view of shore, the ladies and children were then free to frolic in privacy in the water. Maybe one day there would be bathing machines on Tybee, Sylvie had said, after the war was a distant memory. For now they would have to content themselves with promenading and picnicking.

"There's no landing on Little Tybee," Jack told them. "We'll have to row into shore, and Captain Billingsly will stay aboard to watch the tide. But at least we have several strong men to man the oars."

"And we won't be bothered by blue uniforms," Martha added.

Soon there was a flurry of activity as the steamer put in to shore with care, for the water was shallow and Jack explained that it would be all too easy to get stuck on a shoal. The passengers loaded picnic baskets, blankets and a tent into the two row boats. Jack and Bryson took one boat while

43

Stephen and Allan took the other. One man descended first and the other stayed aboard *South Land* until all the women and children had climbed down the rope ladders.

Little Tybee did have plenty of marsh – the majority of the island, in fact – but its beach was just as extensive as Tybee's, its total size also being the greater despite its diminutive name. On the upland, Mahala saw pines, cedars and wax myrtles. On the sand ridges, there were cabbage palms, saw palmettos and live oaks draped with the remarkable Spanish moss. Dune plants and sea oats blew back and forth in the dunes, and sea gulls cawed overhead.

"I almost feel like a pirate," Mahala murmured to Jack, noting the deserted beach as they drew near.

Despite being soaked with sweat and out of breath from rowing, Jack managed a grin and whispered, "Argh, come ashore with me, lassie, and you'll never want to go back to that mountain home of yours."

Eugenie had heard. She compressed her lips and turned her back. When Mahala could not hide her dismay, Jack winked.

She was glad of her old boots a moment later when Jack handed her down into ankle-deep surf. In fact, as the brown, foam-flecked water swirled around her, she wished she had *no* boots, but could feel the wet sand between her toes. The other women squealed and splashed as daintily and quickly as possible for shore, holding their skirts up as high as they deemed proper. But Mahala walked slowly, staring down.

"It makes me dizzy!" she exclaimed to Jack.

As he and Bryson dragged the rowboat ashore, he offered her a hand. She clung to it, too entranced by the tide to take her eyes off it.

"Oh, look at all the shells." Mahala bent to grasp a tiny butterfly-like shape at her toe. She heard Bryson laugh and looked up.

"You'll find many more on the beach."

There was humor and indulgence in Jack's voice, but she realized he must be a little embarrassed by her behavior, too. As he secured the boat, she joined the other women on a shaded ridge. They had already begun to lay out blankets and unfold the tent.

"What can I do to help?"

Sunny smiled rather tightly at her. "Nothing. You're our guest."

"Now, Mother, don't be a pine cone," Sylvie rejoined. "Mahala's not a *guest*. She's Jack's fiancée, soon to be *family*." So saying, the young woman took Mahala's arm and led her over to a large hamper. "You can help me make up luncheon plates while the men set up the tent. I'm famished, aren't you?"

"Actually, I am rather hungry," Mahala admitted, not missing the pinched look of disapproval Eugenie sent Sylvie.

"They can be so pretentious," Sylvie whispered as she unwrapped a loaf of bread.

Mahala rued the day she had to rely on Sylvie as an ally, but she reluctantly admitted to herself that she was glad the strong-willed girl was on her side. Now, if Carolyn were here, her friend would find a way to ease her into the good graces of the women – without calling anyone a pine cone.

Helping Sylvie make sandwiches, she asked, "How far from here is Brightwell?"

"Oh, Liberty County is still a long ways south. Now, Harveys Island, where The Marshes is located, that's a bit closer. But still all the way past Wassaw and into Ossabaw Sound."

"It seems we came so far from Savannah already," Mahala murmured. She might as well put a trip to or from Carolyn from her mind.

"It's eighteen miles just to Tybee." Sylvie paused, arranging pickles on a piece of bread, then topping them with a tomato slice. "What do you think of Dylan and Carolyn? I know you love her to death, and he courted her a long time ago, but honestly, he did not seem very attentive to her the other night at dinner."

"He could hardly look at or speak to anyone else when you claimed his attention the whole evening!" Mahala blurted. She could have clamped her hand over her mouth. There was no sense in alienating her one friend.

"I did not! I was merely keeping the conversation going. Everyone else was so morose. Even you and Jack!"

Mahala hesitated, trying to be more delicate. "It's just that we can't act as though everyone else has cause to be as joyful as we do."

"But maybe they could use some cheering up – some reminding that life will go on. That's how I felt about Dylan. No man could have a more gallant record of service than he. How could I help but think well of him? And yet he is so modest, so quiet – like he's hurting. I can't help wanting to bring a smile to his face. What could be wrong with that?"

"Why nothing, if that is your only aim."

"And if it's not?"

"There is a long history between Dylan and your cousin Carolyn. I believe it ought to be settled one way or the other without interference. Regardless of what you might think, Dylan cares very deeply for Carolyn."

"How do you know?" Sylvie sat back on her heels.

"I – have every reason to believe so."

Sylvie studied her for a minute. "You think me unworthy of him."

"I never said that."

"But you thought it."

"What I wonder, Sylvie," Mahala said as gently as possible, trying to bridge the gap she felt forming, "is if you would truly care for a life of the sort of hardship and seclusion the Rousseaus must now necessarily lead."

"Hardship and seclusion? They still own two farms and a town house. That's worth something. They'll find a way to earn a decent living."

Mahala shook her head, biting her lip as she placed the knife in the butter. "With no workers, they will be forced to sell The Marshes – if, that is, they can reclaim it. And maybe the town house, too. Are you prepared to reside solely in Habersham County?"

Sylvie straightened her slender shoulders. "For the right man, perhaps. Is it too much to believe I might have the maturity to judge a man's character rather than his pocketbook? And perhaps bring a bit of joy and blessing into his life?"

"No, Sylvie," Mahala hastened to say, although she truly *was* surprised. Perhaps Jack's sister did think and feel more deeply than she had realized.

But the girl was rising from her knees and brushing off her skirt. "Of all people to be judgmental."

"Sylvie, wait!" Mahala begged, her heart sinking.

Sylvie didn't heed her. She went to sit beside Ella Beth, who had found a lounge chair under the tent Bryson and Allan had just finished erecting. Everyone began to gather under and around it. Mahala sighed. She picked up several plates and carried them over.

"Lunch, anyone?" she asked with a forced, bright smile.

Eyeing the way Mahala balanced the third plate on her arm, Stephen Wise joked, "Is there a tip required?"

Most of the party laughed. As Mahala felt her face heat, she saw Jack, who was just walking up, give his uncle a cold stare. Heaven forbid, he then glanced at her with something like pity. She'd never seen that look on his face. Making a decision, Mahala approached the dignified, still-chortling lawyer and set the first plate down on the little table in front of him.

"I don't know too many people who would turn down tips these days," she said, looking him straight in the eye.

Mr. Wise had the grace to look humbled. "Quite right, my dear. Thank you."

Mahala caught a gleam of pride in her grandmother's eye as she delivered a lunch to Allan and Bryson. That she expected. She did not expect the fleeting glance of admiration Eugenie sent her way. To her further surprise, Ella Beth bestirred herself.

"Let me help you, Miss Franklin."

"Are you sure you feel well enough, Mrs. Draper?"

Ella Beth smiled as she followed her back to the picnic hamper. She answered, "Oh, I'm fine. Mother just likes to make a fuss." She glanced over at her sons, who were playing rather rambunctiously under foot of the adults, while their black nanny fanned herself in the shade. "So much for help these days. I'm lucky if she keeps them from hurting each other.

The sooner I get food in their little hands, the sooner we'll all have a peaceful meal."

Mahala smiled back. "Your children are charming." And so was their mother, Mahala thought rather wistfully. The black of Ella Beth's sheer mourning dress set off her pale beauty to angelic perfection. Even though Ella Beth had patched the gown several times before being forced to surrender it to the dye pot, she exuded gentility and a feminine grace that made Mahala feel like a gypsy girl in her bright skirt beside her.

"Thank you. They resemble their father, in looks if not in temperament," Ella Beth commented, picking up two plates from the blanket where Sylvie had left them waiting.

"You must miss him very much."

Ella Beth shot her a glance. "Yes."

When they returned, Sunny had taken to pouring lemonade, and Eugenie had produced utensils and tatting-trimmed ecru napkins.

"I imagine business is quite slow now at your hotel," Eugenie said to Martha. "Jack says it is so at The Palace."

"That's correct," Martha agreed.

"Do you plan to reopen once you go back home?"

"Yes, I suppose I'll keep my doors open whether there's one person to tend or one hundred. I can't imagine life without it."

"We tried to convince Mrs. Franklin to accompany us to Europe," Jack added, "but she'll have none of it."

"There's no place for an old woman on a honeymoon," Martha told them.

"Unless it's *her* honeymoon," Stephen interjected, and they all laughed.

Mahala was glad to see the Ellises and Randalls were trying to make at least her grandmother feel comfortable. "Yes, Grandmother, if you go with us, perhaps you'll meet someone special yourself – a suave French gentleman?" she teased.

"Pawsh." Martha dismissed her suggestion with a wave of her hand. "I'd no sooner let a man take up the reins of my life again than I'd march over to that river and yell 'boo' to the Yankees on the landing across the way."

Hearty laughter answered her pronouncement. Again, Eugenie looked approving. Jack's aunt must admire women who were outspoken like herself. Perhaps she had been too uncertain thus far to win Eugenie's respect. What was it Martha had once told her? Every time she got dressed up she was afraid to look at herself in the mirror? Was it true that despite being confident in many ways, in the company of those the world considered her social betters, she still felt like a second class citizen?

Conversation drifted to benign topics, like the wildlife of the islands. A boat-tailed grackle that had lit on a branch nearby initiated the topic with his sharp "*cheks*" and whistles. They spoke of the least terns, whose nests might be seen along the beach as simple sand scrapes, and of the giant loggerhead turtles, likewise in nesting season. Jack's brothers and Eugenie wanted to know about the wild animals of Northeast Georgia.

"I hear the deer are bigger up there," Allan said.

"That's right," Jack replied. "Big enough to entice you to come up hunting in the future. Any of you are welcome any time at The Highlands. Isn't that right, Mahala?"

Mahala glanced up. "Yes, of course!"

"The Highlands, Jack?" Ella Beth wondered aloud. "I thought your hotel was called The Palace."

"It's not the hotel I'm speaking of, but our new home just outside town – a Federal-style mansion we're refurbishing." Jack looked over at Mahala, and her heart swelled at his expression, and the generous use of "we." Truly the whole thing was his gift to her, and she knew it well. "So you see, those of you who have grumped about extended lodging in a hotel can do so no more. Your excuse to avoid North Georgia is gone."

"Indeed, you've hardly given us any choice, Jack," Eugenie put in, "with insisting that the wedding be up there."

"Oh, you might as well let it lie," Sunny said. "They won't budge."

"Well, it just doesn't make any sense, with all of us down here, and you leaving so soon on your honeymoon anyway," Eugenie continued. She turned to Mahala. "My dear, surely as a woman who's aware of all the planning involved in such a function, *you* can see my point. It's not too late to change your plans."

Mahala swallowed. "Habersham County is to be our home, and we want to start our lives there."

"Oh, you can't tell me business won't keep you much in Savannah."

"We don't want to inconvenience anyone, but I'm afraid our plans are firm," Mahala said as gently as possible.

Eugenie huffed. "Very well," she said, but the next moment Mahala's hopes plummeted as she added, looking at Jack, "At least you've got someone who will stand up to you, Jack. I can see Sunny is right, and trying to budge either one of you would be about as fruitful as beating my head on a rock."

Mahala felt her face redden.

Sylvie suddenly stood, stretched and exclaimed, "My, all that food and the sound of the surf has made me excruciatingly sleepy! I think I'll lie down in the tent for a bit."

The rest of the party broke up, too, the nanny taking Ella Beth's boys off to play, the men rinsing the dishes in the water, and the older women cleaning up. Martha was helping them, but with her mouth pursed in the way that told Mahala she did not approve of their conduct, when Mahala touched her sleeve.

"I'm going for a little walk," she said.

"Need company?"

"No – I'm fine." Mahala lifted the corners of her mouth, but her smile wobbled. Her grandmother squeezed her arm, reading her need for aloneness.

Glancing back at Jack, who did not notice her departure, Mahala tied her hat under her chin and started along the shore. She watched the sand as she went, noting the frantic holes the tiny crabs made as they were washed in with the surf. Right now she could well imagine how they felt!

Shorebirds prowled the rills and sloughs looking for trapped fish. Way out, Mahala spied a ship with white sails spread to the wind. She wished she could swim to it, splashing through the white-capped waves. She wished she were on it, racing to some exotic port unknown. Soon enough, she reminded herself. First she just had to get through this time of proving herself to Jack's family, then the two of them could finally speak their vows and be alone, well and truly alone.

Feeling defiant, once she was out of sight of the picnickers, Mahala plopped down at the edge of the wet sand. She buttoned up her top skirt and unlaced her boots, which had never quite dried since her arrival, this having proved a source of chafing almost as irritating as Jack's aunt. Tugging them off, she rolled down her striped stockings and stuck them in the boots. Then, she waded into the ocean. How cold the wet sand was under her feet! How refreshing the lapping waves! Jack had told her the sea could look gray, brown, blue or green depending on the weather. Today, in its depths, it was a green nearly as vivid as his eyes. Mahala closed hers, savoring the roar, the breeze, the tug of power on her calves. She was here, and wasn't that a miracle unto itself?

"Thank you, God."

Mahala removed her hat so she could feel the sun on her face. She swirled her feet in the water, dancing a slow, bottom-heavy dance, opening her arms to the wind. Suddenly she became aware that Jack had rounded the bend and now stood watching her, hands in his pockets. There was that insolent grin on his face. Have mercy, but she knew what he was going to do next. If she didn't get back to shore he'd wade right out to join her!

Mahala tried to hurry inland without looking anxious. She dropped her skirt to cover her feet as he approached, still smiling.

"My, but that was a sight."

Mahala knew well enough that no lady should caper about in plain view in the ocean. Only children and mammies were allowed such freedom. "I was overcome by the beauty of the scene."

"I know how you feel," Jack replied, his eyes caressing her face in a manner more warming than the sun.

Mahala put her hat back on her head and retied the ribbon. "Please don't tell anyone."

"Wouldn't dream of it."

"You should go back to the tent now and let me make myself presentable."

"Oh, you look more than presentable to me. And I know you'd be disappointed if I acted like such a gentleman." He glanced at her boots and stockings, gave her arm a tug towards them. "Come, sit down here with me a minute and talk to me. Are you feeling better?"

She did as he ordered because the idea of a few minutes alone with him was just too tempting. Mahala sat down and wrapped her arms around her knees. "Yes, I'll be fine. It's just hard, Jack."

"You expected that, though, didn't you?" he asked gently.

She thought a moment and nodded her head.

"You're doing fine. I'm proud of you. You only met them a few days ago. Give them time. They'll come around."

Mahala bit her lip. "It's just – you won't change your mind about having the wedding in Clarkesville, will you, Jack? I do so want it to be simple and small – familiar. Getting married is overwhelming enough. I want it to be about you and me, not all Savannah society."

"Don't waste a moment of worry on that score, Mahala. I'm with you, one hundred percent."

She smiled in relief and gratification.

"As for Aunt Eugenie, she can be prickly, like Sylvie pointed out, but please believe me when I say she *is* a good woman. Over the years she's been one of my staunchest supporters."

"Which is maybe why she's acting the way she is now. She's hoping I'll come to the realization I'm not good enough for you."

"Oh, nonsense. You can handle Eugenie. You have just as much pluck and twice as much sense."

Mahala almost laughed that he would admit such a thing. "But it's not just her now, Jack. I'm afraid I've really offended your sister."

"Sylvie? How?"

"I must confess I'm quite set on Carolyn and Dylan getting together. I didn't want to allow that Sylvie might have a chance with him."

Jack frowned. "You think she *wants* a chance with him? Why? She could marry much better."

Mahala drew her mouth in, giving him a reproving look. "And you sure set the example on that."

"I'm not Sylvie. She thrives on status and material things. She'd not last a month cooped up at Forests of Green – working."

"Which is exactly what I tried to tell her, but I'm afraid we may have underestimated her, Jack. She says she really admires Dylan."

Jack shook his head, looking out to sea. "I can't see it, but I guess time will tell. I think we should leave it alone. With Sylvie, the more you interfere, the more she goes after what she wants." He glanced back at her. "And in the meantime, keep being yourself. Don't let them change you one bit. Remember I could have found a Savannah belle ten years ago – but it was *you* I was waiting for."

"Even when you didn't know it?"

"Even when I didn't know it."

Mahala slipped her hand in his.

"October seems so far away," he added. "I'm tired of waiting, Mahala."

He leaned in and sealed her lips with his. Her hat slid off again, and heat that had nothing to do with the sub-tropic sun flooded her. She turned toward him, responding, pushing her fingers into the hair at the back of his neck.

"You taste like salt," Jack whispered, tracing escaping strands of her dark hair with his hand. He kissed her jaw, her neck.

Oh, to be his, truly and fully his. It would all be worth it.

She cupped his clean-shaven jaw and met his mouth again, asking for more despite her good sense.

A cold rush of water shot under them, lapping feet and legs. Jack yelped, and they jumped apart, scrambling to their feet. Mahala snatched her skirts above the incoming tide.

"Look at those perfect toes!" Jack cried.

"Oh, you!" She dashed for shore, reaching down to grab her boots as she went, but Jack was faster. He snatched up her shoes and held them away from her, laughing tauntingly when she tried to reach behind him. He tossed the boots farther up onto the dry sand but held her socks before him. "What lovely striped stockings, Ma'am! I thought I caught a glimpse of these when you were climbing down into the rowboat earlier."

Mahala smacked him. "You scoundrel! And they worry about *me* not being proper! Give those here."

Jack wrapped the stretchy knit lengths around her shoulders, drawing her in towards him. "Another kiss first."

She tried to get hold of her stockings, but another tug landed her against him. As his warm mouth claimed hers again, she surrendered to his embrace. Breathless, she opened her eyes to see a pair of women in billowing skirts in view – Eugenie and Ella Beth, of all people – watching them.

"Oh, no," she moaned.

Jack turned to see what she was looking at. He presented his back, facing out to sea while Mahala scrambled up the sand dune and put herself back together. Meanwhile, the women about-faced and hurried the other way, their straight corseted backs telling of their disapproval.

"I'm sorry," Jack said when she called to him.

"It's all right. I'm the one who took my boots off in the first place."

Like guilty school children who knew they were facing impending punishment, their eyes met. Mahala saw an ally and a kindred spirit. Recognizing the same in her, Jack grinned. Then they both burst out laughing. Together, they would weather the silent censure they were sure to get, and whatever else relatives or society might dish out.

Post-war Abercorn Street was a scene of faded gentility, its paint-peeling and crepe-draped houses not unlike the residents within. The earliest houses had been constructed in the late 1700s nearest Factor's Walk and the riverfront. The most recent 1850s homes were likeliest to be found along the southern portion, near the more recently established squares. Sandwiched somewhere between the Owens-Thomas house and Andrew Low's imposing residence, in the vicinity of Colonial Park, was the 1840s Greek Revival abode Frank Draper had purchased for his bride in 1851.

Ella Beth pushed aside a lace curtain and gazed out onto the street. No guests yet. Everything was ready, the vanilla tea giving forth its rich aroma, the spice cakes, cream puffs and fruit neatly arranged on her silver stacking tray. On a separate silver tray were her mother's cucumber sandwiches.

"Something must be done for her," Sunny had sighed on a private aside last week. "If we don't throw some sort of party to welcome Jack's fiancée to Savannah, everyone will know we don't approve of her. And it can't be me. That would be too obvious."

"Why, you're her age," her mother had chimed in, looking at Ella Beth, not wanting to be left holding the bag herself. "It would be most appropriate. I'll help you."

What she hadn't said in front of Sunny was that Eugenie meant she would help not only physically, but financially. Buying ingredients for fancy refreshments was not in Ella Beth's budget now. And what *she* hadn't said but had wondered was why it would be a bad thing for society to know the family disapproved of Mahala. But then, she knew the answer to that. Family always rallied around each other, at least in public.

Ella Beth sighed and turned from the window. Gazing towards the cemetery made her think of Frank, and that made her think of Jack. And that made her want to do something decidedly out of control, like bang her head on the window frame. What kind of woman was she, to yearn after a man only months after losing her husband?

She had loved Frank, yes, she had, but in that warm, platonic, dutiful way she had feared from the beginning she would. She had only married him because he was the obvious choice when Jack had failed her. He had been a good man, and they'd had a good marriage, and she had kept her mind fixed on him when he had been her husband. But he had been phlegmatic if ever she had known a phlegmatic man. He had gone even to war as calmly as he went to brush his teeth. And now he was dead. She was alone, and Jack was here, alive, still single – and definitely not phlegmatic.

How her face and heart had burned when she had seen him embracing Mahala on the beach. For she longed, *longed*, to be held like that, loved like that. Before she was too old to no longer care. But here in her way was the very woman she had predicted long ago – Mahala. Beautiful, independent, mountain Cherokee girl that she was, she had transfixed Ella Beth's cousin, engaging his mind in a way no family loyalty, no tender affection, no pity could ever tie him to her.

And now she was giving a tea party for her.

"God help me," she muttered. But she knew He wouldn't. She was not the sweet and selfless girl she once had been, that she pretended to still be. A sick feeling in her gut reminded her of it in a most unpleasant manner.

"What was that?" her mother asked, sweeping in with a vase of pink powdery mimosa blossoms that filled the room with the scent of watermelon.

"Nothing."

"Are these too much? We don't want everyone choking."

"Maybe on the side table." Ella Beth gestured towards her prized veneered Empire pier table.

As Eugenie moved to comply, she glanced over her shoulder at Ella Beth with concern. "Are you certain I don't need to cover your portion of the refreshments?"

"No indeed, Mother. I must pay for *something*."

"I would say that you are." Eugenie's comment was knowing. Eugenie might be less than brilliant in other areas, but she had a mother's intuition and the accompanying sense of protectiveness. When Ella Beth only smiled in a wavering manner, she added, "Really you must tell him. I wish to heaven your father and I could satisfy your debt, my love, but you know we, too, are struggling. He'll know soon enough when your house sells–"

"If it sells."

"It will. But better to ask for his help before your desperation becomes known."

"I can't, Mother. I can't appear that vulnerable to him."

"A little vulnerability rightly presented often attracts a gentleman's notice."

"It's too late for that," Ella Beth pointed out.

"It's not too late until the bans are read."

"Oh, Mother, stop it," Ella Beth moaned in misery, putting a hand to her forehead. A headache had begun its slow, blossoming pressure there.

"I'm just saying the only person who has that sort of money now is Jack, and better he give it to you as your husband than as your cousin. If you don't talk to him, I will."

Ella Beth's stomach churned. She sat down in a wing chair the frayed top of which was cleverly concealed with a lace doily.

"And we need to talk about what you will do when the house sells. You can't keep putting off your decision. There's really no decision to make. Frank's mother, poor widow in ill health that she is, would never survive two rambunctious boys. Your father and I are prepared to take you back. If you're worried that we can't afford it, don't. We can, but only if Jack helps with the outstanding bills–"

Ella Beth waved a hand. "All right, all right," she said. "Can we not speak of something else? The guests will be here any minute."

"Of course. I did not mean to upset you. I myself forget how delicate you are. How you ever bore Frank two sons is quite beyond me. Can I get you something?"

Quiet, Ella Beth roared ungraciously inside her own tight head. "No, thank you."

How could she tell her mother she didn't know if *she* could survive moving back home? Eugenie would meddle and interfere and transpose herself into Ella Beth's and her son's lives – and her raising of them – until she'd almost rather go to the poor house.

The bell in the hall rang. Ella Beth's one remaining servant, an old woman who now served as jack-of-all-trades, went to answer the door. Ella Beth rose and went to the door of the parlor to greet the McComb sisters. As ever the first to arrive and the last to leave any function, the middle-aged twins – who had married brothers – were nosy and opinionated, but their old Savannah blood demanded their entrance into any genteel circle that would otherwise have shunned their poor manners. Ella Beth knew they would give Mahala a hard time. It would be interesting to see what the young woman did with them.

"Where is she?" Claire McComb whispered, looking about, as though Mahala might be lurking behind a potted palm or a drape. "We're dying to meet her. I've never known a Cherokee."

"You've arrived before she has," Ella Beth said as her servant took the ladies' bonnets.

Within minutes another group of women arrived, followed by the Randalls. With Union soldiers all over town, Jack or one of his brothers escorted the women to and from their engagements, but Jack left them at the door with a promise to return early.

"This is so kind of you, Ella Beth," he said to her.

She smiled, feeling like a predator baring its teeth. "It's my pleasure," she lied. She took Mahala by the arm and led her in to be introduced to those in the parlor. Mahala looked so stunning in a royal blue silk tea dress trimmed with self-rouching – not twice or thrice turned like those of the other guests – that everyone in the room paused and stared at her. Had Jack bought her the dress? No, Ella Beth had heard Mahala had some money of her own. But why hadn't Sylvie advised Mahala that wearing worn and mourning gowns was a mark of honor among Savannah women, a badge of their recent sacrifice for the cause?

Ella Beth looked from Jack's blonde half sister, who was clad in a quality but muted golden-brown dress, to his fiancée. Something had happened between them, and it wasn't quite mended yet. Sylvie could get away with dressing to the hilt. People dismissed her as young and foolish, and she had endeared many with her war-time generosity and high spirits. But without Sylvie's notable support, Mahala stood out like a bright-plumed bird in the midst of a bunch of crows. And she instantly seemed to realize it.

"What a stunning gown," Katie McComb murmured once introductions were complete.

"Thank you. I – I remade it from a party dress I wore a long time ago. There was not much occasion to wear it in Clarkesville." Her words fell like heavy stones into a pond.

"Mm, I'd imagine. Come sit next to me and tell me all about your home, my dear," Katie urged.

Mahala managed not to look relieved. She stepped gracefully across to the woman's side, Martha following her like a hen brooding over her chick, ready to snatch her under a wing if need be.

Eugenie exclaimed, "Miss Franklin, you're flushed! I believe you left your hat off too long at the shore. I tried to warn you our tropical rays are quite strong."

Mahala paused, surprised. Martha looked furious, as if she were searching for just the right words to come to her lips. Sylvie stared at her mother, incredulous. This was where she, Ella Beth, should intervene, before something even worse was said and the party dissolved in hurt feelings and insults before it had begun. But she hovered over the tea pot, biting her tongue. Then Mahala herself spoke. She actually smiled. "Oh, no, I did take your advice to heart, Mrs. Wise, and was very careful out in the sun. If I'm flushed, I'm sure it's just the excitement at the prospect of meeting so many fine ladies at one time! This is such an honor."

Touché, thought Ella Beth, vaguely disappointed, but at the same time, grudgingly admiring.

The women murmured their approval. Martha Franklin looked proud. Ella Beth began to move quietly among her guests – Mahala's guests – taking note of what they liked in their tea and whether they wished sweets or savories. All the while she was listening to Mahala field the McCombs' many questions – some of which were quite ignorant – with patience explaining her background, her heritage, and her education. Martha told the women about her hotel and how for many years they had viewed Jack as a rival. Mahala made them laugh with stories of their misunderstandings and tiffs. Ella Beth's head hurt.

At last, at last, it was over. Mahala had not won them over yet, but she had done well.

The Randalls stayed until everyone else had left. After letting the last guest out the door, Ella Beth left her mother with the Randalls, Mahala and Martha, and found a moment alone in the butler's pantry. She breathed deeply, queasy now, searching for her headache powders.

"Where are they?" she muttered to herself in exasperation. Any minute now the bright lights, precursor to disability, would start flashing before her eyes, and she'd have to spend the evening in bed.

A movement at the door startled her.

"What is it you're looking for, Ella Beth?" Jack asked.

"Oh – I'm sorry. I didn't see you there. Just a bit of medicine."

"Are you unwell?"

She offered a faltering smile. "Just a headache." But the hand she put up to smooth back her hair shook.

Concern came over Jack's handsome features. "What does your medicine look like? I'll help you find it. You should go sit down."

"No – really. I'm fine. I'm being rude. Mahala's in the parlor – go on in. I'll be there momentarily."

"Nonsense." He nudged her over and started searching through her cabinets.

"Powders in a little brown envelope."

"I was looking for you, anyway," Jack continued, sliding bottles and boxes from side to side. "I wanted to thank you again for hostessing the tea for Mahala. You have no idea how much it meant to her – to me."

A sob bubbled up, then another. She covered her face with her hands, ashamed and also unsettled by his words, his nearness.

"Ella Beth! What's the matter? Was it that taxing on you? Did things go poorly?"

Poorly, yes, things are going poorly for me, she thought, like a child crying over spilled milk. "Things went fine. I'm sorry … I just don't feel well."

Jack fished out a crisp, monogrammed handkerchief and handed it to her. She blotted her eyes. "It's not like you to take on so. You really must feel bad."

"Yes ... yes, I think a migraine is coming on."

Another moment's search produced the desired powders. Jack poured some water from a pitcher into a glass and dumped in the required teaspoon. He swirled the glass around and handed it to her. "Drink it all, and then I'll make your excuses while you go upstairs and lie down."

"No, that would be inexcusably rude."

"Not at all."

His care for her released the flow of pent-up tears again.

"Tell me what's wrong."

"I can't – I don't want to burden you." *You have enough helpless women clinging to you*, she thought. At least there was some dignity in appearing to be a self-sufficient widow. Then she remembered her mother's words. "It's just – the same as most everyone faces now. Financial pressures."

"What sort of pressures?"

"Well, the house is on the market. It's been several months, and of course it hasn't sold. I begin to worry. And – I'm not sure of the future. Mother wants us to move in with her, but, but, I just can't ..."

"I understand," Jack told her when her voice trailed off. "Is that all?"

"Isn't that enough?"

He sighed. "Of course. But something tells me there's more."

"Well, there are some unpaid bills, too. I tried very hard to make ends meet, but Frank did not get paid for so very long, and with two growing boys, certain things can't be done without."

"What type of amount are we talking about?"

She lowered her gaze, twisted his handkerchief. "Between the general store and the apothecary and a bill from the shoemaker, about nine hundred dollars. Prices were so inflated this year."

Jack nodded as though she had said nine dollars. "Have your bills sent over to my address. I'll take care of them. I'm sorry to hear you'll have to leave your home, but have you considered our grandparents? Such a big old house, and Grandmother could use your help with Grandfather. She hates to even leave him now days. I daresay she gets rather lonely, staying home so much."

"But the boys ..."

Jack shrugged. "Maybe they would be a pleasant diversion, and when Grandfather is unwell, their nurse could keep them to another part of the house. Think on it, and I'll test the waters."

Guilt, embarrassment and relief warred within her. She nodded, then began to weep again. "Jack, I didn't want to tell you – for you to think I expect–"

"Shh. Do you think I'd let a family member fall into financial trouble?"

"But it's too much–"

He put a hand on her arm. "I don't want you to think of it again."

Ella Beth leaned into him, weeping in earnest, so longing for his comfort she couldn't stop herself. Oh, for someone strong to hold her, to take away the loss and fear and uncertainty. All she did was give. No one ever gave to her.

Jack didn't embrace her, but he didn't put her away, either. He half-hugged her rather gingerly, patting her back. "That's enough now."

She realized she had embarrassed him. "I'm sorry," she said again.

He took the handkerchief out of her hand, shook it open, and wiped her face. "There now. That's better. Off to bed –" He cut off, his gaze turning to the hall, where Ella Beth saw that Mahala and Martha were now standing, aware of the two of them in the door of the pantry. As the other women filed out beside them, they tried to act as though nothing were amiss, but Ella Beth had recognized the surprise dawning on their faces before they schooled their expressions. She was glad to find that her conscience was strong enough to produce remorse rather than triumph. What a Jonah day!

Jack stepped away from her and approached his family and fiancée. "Ella Beth is unwell," he explained. "We should head on so that she can rest."

Mahala's eyes rested on her, and she felt like shrinking into the floor. What bitter reprisal might the woman rightly make now? But she actually came forward and took her hands. "I'm so sorry. I hope you feel better. I wanted to thank you for the party."

"You're welcome," Ella Beth replied, only briefly able to meet the smoky blue gaze. No wonder Jack loved her. *And if he truly knew me, what is inside, he would surely loathe me,* she thought. *I cannot wish Mahala ill.*

Mahala was upset with him. Jack could tell from the rigid way she held herself on the way back to Wright Square, only looking at him when necessary. The pulse under the black velvet ribbon supporting the cameo at her neck was slow and steady, but her fingers grasping her silk reticule were curled tight.

This was exactly how he'd feared a wife would be – making a big deal out of nothing. Creating tension where there need be none. Ella Beth was attractive, of course, but as though anyone could turn his head now! Did Mahala truly have no idea how magnificent she was? And as if Ella Beth would *want* to turn his head. If there had ever been a woman in distress, it was his cousin today. And that was all there was to it.

Jack snorted before he realized what he was doing. Four pairs of wide eyes turned on him. He coughed to cover his indignation.

At the family's Regency-styled, stucco-over-brick pink mansion, he handed them out – all his charges, he thought, plus his grandmother and Ella Beth. Really, they had to get some more men in this family. And he had to get his half brothers to re-engage with life. They were like flotsam afloat. Serious conversations with them would need to be had, and soon, to give the two young men direction for their futures.

He followed the women into the foyer, where servants came to collect the divested hats and purses. The ladies then scattered to their rooms to rest and change for dinner.

"Mahala," he called before his fiancée could escape upstairs.

Hand on the banister, she turned. Above her on the landing, Martha paused, looking down with disapproval. But she did not speak and continued slowly up the steps.

"Yes?"

"A word with you?"

Jack followed her into the parlor. She turned to look at him. "How did the party go?" he asked.

"Tiring. Your aunt observed that I was browned by the sun, and Mrs. McComb asked me if the Cherokee in the mountains still wore traditional dress, and whether I had any she might see."

Jack choked on a laugh. "Good heavens."

Mahala did not look amused.

"I'm sure you deflected their ignorance with grace."

She lifted a shoulder. "Perhaps. They are still wary of me, but at least they didn't act as if I were not even present."

"At your own party? I should hardly think so."

Mahala thinned her lips and lowered a brow. "I'm rather fatigued. Will there be guests for dinner?"

"No, but remember, my cousin George arrives tomorrow evening from New York."

"Yes, I remember. If there's nothing else, I'll just go rest a while." She started to brush past him, taffeta skirts rustling, but he caught her arm. She looked annoyed.

"I – hope you did not read anything into my encounter with Ella Beth."

"'Encounter' seems a fitting word."

Jack sighed. "Mahala, please. She's under untold pressure which I do not feel at liberty to disclose, but with which she had no other place to turn."

"Of course."

"What would you have me do? Turn a cold shoulder to my own relations?"

"It seems offering no shoulders would be more appropriate."

"I didn't think you this hard-hearted!"

"And I didn't think you this blind! *Are* you blind, Jack? Because everybody else can see what's right in front of you. Ella Beth is in love with you."

"Oh – please. That's ridiculous. Yes, years ago, she had a girlhood crush on me. But she was married – happily – and just lost her husband. The grief of that combined with her financial stress has been enough to erode her usual composure. She had a weak moment. She needed – needs – some help."

"Well, help her, Jack. But don't let her soak your lapel with her tears, because whether you believe it or not, she *does* still have feelings for you. I can see it every time she looks at you. Look more closely. Now, if you'll excuse me, I'd like some time alone."

So saying, Mahala swept out of the room, head held high. He stood there staring after her, wishing he knew what to say to call her back and into his arms. She was a proud, stubborn woman. He could see a number of such clashes ahead in their future. He thought her jealousy born of insecurity – the vulnerability of her new surroundings. But, could there be some truth in what she said?

imes like these were when he missed his father the most.

In the library of the Randall mansion, Jack sat looking at the immobile face of his half-brother, searching for a hint of interest, of eagerness, in reaction to the statement Jack had just made. Instead, his words, "I have a proposition for you," hung suspended in the air.

Refusing to be ruffled, to be pushed into appearing overeager himself, Jack reached in his desk drawer and pulled out a cigar. He held it up to offer Bryson a smoke if he cared for one and ask his permission to himself indulge. Bryson answered both questions with a wave of his hand. His face didn't change. Drat him.

Does he resent me for not fighting? Jack found himself wondering. *Has he no gratefulness for the clothes I put on his back and the gun I put in his hands? Has he no thankfulness for anything?*

He lit the cigar and took a draw. The two men stared at each other, rather like school boys in a contest.

Won't admit a bit of need, Jack thought.

He changed his tact. "What are your thoughts about your future, Bryson?"

The twenty-three-year-old shrugged. "Hear Atlanta is booming. Thought I might go there."

"And do what?" No answer. Jack continued, "Alan is thinking of Franklin College. He's young, and it's not a bad idea. It will be a new start for him. You already have GMI. But what can you do with that?"

"The railroads can use civil engineers now, what with all the repair."

"You interested in that?"

"It's a job."

Jack knew he wasn't, or he would have already made inquiries. Bryson had gone to GMI to learn how to fight, not how to build bridges. And he'd never consider service in the U.S. Army. Jack sighed.

"Well, if you want, I can ask around for you. You know I have good contacts in the industry. Or ... you can join the family industry."

"Shipping?" Bryson blew disrespectfully with his lips. "Like I know anything about that."

"You know how to do math, and you have taste. The most important prerequisites for the job I have in mind."

Bryson looked uncomfortable. "Which is?"

At least he had the young man's attention. He tapped his cigar on the porcelain tray. "As you know, all our ships have returned to port from Nassau. There're 50,000 bales of cotton sitting in Augusta from blockade running days. I was thinking of sending *South Land II* upriver to fetch a load, bring it to *Regale* in the harbor, and on to Liverpool. Should net us a nice sum. Britain and France will be offering top dollar for cotton this fall. After that's done, *Regale* needs dry docking and repairs. Her best days are gone. It's all about steam now. I want to use *South Land II* as we did before the war, local passenger transport. For *Evangeline*, I have a grander scale in mind – a Savannah-New York-Liverpool route, providing a Southern extension to the routes now run so successfully by Inman and Cunard. Our Savannah passengers could travel in comfort and high style all the way to England without even switching ships. Eventually, I'd like to expand – maybe look at ships while I'm in England and Scotland. But now, Bryson, now what needs done is *Evangeline* taken up to New York for repair and renovation. She needs repainted, her pilot house rebuilt, her engines tuned. Someone needs to research what other lines are offering on their ships, find out what's in style, shop for the best and cost-effective materials, and oversee the work. Obviously, I can't go."

Bryson started laughing. "And you think I could."

"Why not?"

"I know nothing about any of that – and know no one there."

"You're a smart young man. You'd learn, with Dean Howell's help."

"Dean Howell?"

Jack took a drag on the cigar and blew out a slow stream of smoke. In the hallway, he heard the chatter of the women as they departed for a shopping expedition. Mahala was to purchase wedding gown material today. Sylvie, unwilling to be left out of the fun and certainly not to be excluded from being a bridesmaid, had arrived at breakfast that morning all cheer and warmth. She had behaved as though she had never quarreled with Mahala. Well, Mahala would have to deal with his fickle little sister. He had enough on his mind right now. He refocused on the conversation at hand, saying, "He captained the *Fortitude* until she was beached and fired in '64. He's an excellent captain. You can trust his knowledge about all things mechanical. And as for where to stay, with my mother's family, of course."

"Abolitionist Yankees?"

Jack stiffened. His voice was hard when he said, "You will find them reasonable and gracious hosts. They will accept you with the same welcome they would offer me."

"Great land, Jack!" Bryson jumped up and started pacing like a caged tiger. "You actually want me to go up there and act like three months ago I wasn't at war with these people, that I wouldn't have shot their sons on the spot – that I don't still now want to attack at the sight of their accursed blue uniforms! Go to the very nest of vipers, live among them, do business with them, like the very basest of traitorous scalawags!"

Knowing what he would say next would be inflammatory, Jack eased back in his chair. "Well, I guess that depends on you, Bryson." Jack spoke calmly, slowly. He crossed one leg over the other, making his posture non-threatening. "If you're going to go up there with the attitude you have now, like some hotheaded Rebel bastard who hasn't yet got the fight whipped out of him, then no. No, thank you. I'll find another envoy. But if you can go as the forward-thinking son of our father, a mature representative of the Savannah Randalls – because you *are* a Savannah Randall, Bryson, whether you like it or not – then go with my blessing and my praise. After my wedding, of course."

Bryson lunged toward him, planting his hands on Jack's desk and leaning down close, his eyes ablaze. "I will *never* have the fight whipped out of me! And that's what you don't understand – have never understood!" His forefinger jabbed in accusation.

Jack ground his cigar in the dish. "Now that's where you're wrong. It's you who doesn't understand, Bryson, though I think some of your belated spit and fire come from spending most of the war on the beach. You think fighting is rushing headlong into the fray, shooting someone – cannons and shells. For some it was. But there's another type of fight, and we're in it now, the type that will only reveal who is victorious in ten, twenty years. And that's preservation. Of self, yes, but of family, of a legacy, and ultimately also of the South. Bringing business to the South will help it now more than words and widow's weeds. We have the power to do that – a power most Southerners now lack – if we're careful. So call me what you want, I'm going to drag this family into the next decade, kicking and screaming if I have to. I'd like to have my brothers beside me. I need you, Bryson. But you have to choose." He got up and walked around the desk. "You can keep your head in the sand while the world slips by, or you can make the progress and change happen. Let me know what you decide."

Jack would not give Bryson the opportunity to turn him down on the spot. He opened the door and walked out, leaving his brother staring after him, face red.

"Where are you going?" the younger man demanded.

"To the dock, to welcome my abolitionist Yankee cousin to Savannah," he returned, without looking back. He held out his hand to receive his hat and gloves from the butler who hurried forward with them.

"The carriage will be around front momentarily, Sir," the servant said.

"Thank you." Before leaving the house, Jack glanced back at his brother. Bryson still stood in the library door, glowering. He said in a level tone,

"Treat George well while he's here, out of respect for Father. Family should never be enemies."

He hoped his last words would sink in.

As he stood on the front porch, he slapped his gloves against a hand. He blew out a breath. *I should have been more patient*, he thought. *He's young.* But something told Jack being too accommodating would gain no ground with his headstrong brother. It was time the young man chose a direction for his future and stopped hanging out at God knew what clubs he frequented, swilling away his sorrows and lamenting over the good old days.

Now, another task was before him, he thought as the carriage pulled up and he climbed in.

"Riverfront," he told his driver.

He'd been so relieved when he'd received George's telegram. Jack had taken the fact that his cousin would come as a sign of good will, but what if relations were far more strained than he anticipated? George and Geoffrey had both served the Union cause, after all, just as Jack had predicted. George had been granted the rank of captain overseeing an artillery unit of guns produced at Randall Iron. He'd had men under his command die – at the hands of soldiers whose weapons could well have been provided them courtesy of Jack's steamers. Would he be ready to put all that behind him?

Jack's misgivings rose as the steamer from New York docked. The wharf area swarmed with civilians and soldiers. Black stevedores poured sweat in the hot July sun. Sea gulls cawed, and rigging clanged in the breeze off the water.

At last he saw a familiar figure. George paused at the head of the gang plank, spotting him, too. He came slowly down to the riverbank. They stood there not saying anything, sizing each other up. George's gaze lingered on the scar at Jack's temple.

"You're as natty as ever, except for that theatrical scratch. What did you do?"

"I was playing with firecrackers again," Jack quipped.

George grunted a laugh. A mischievous grin settled over his features. "I brought a peace offering," he said, making Jack's mind go back to that long-ago day in the Princeton dorm when they had quarreled over the issues dividing the nation. Jack wasn't a bit surprised when his cousin brought out a gold cigar case and opened it to reveal the finest of Cuban cigars.

"Thank you, George." His words held more than a surface significance. Jack took the case, feeling emotion rise as he put it away.

"Hey, you were only supposed to take one!"

Jack looked up, surprised. Then he saw that George was teasing, and both men broke into laughter. "I missed you," Jack admitted.

"I'm glad to see you came through the conflict unharmed," George responded. He opened his arms and they embraced, long and sincerely, throwing in a few manly thumps for good measure. When George stepped back they both tried to cover their emotions. "I brought you a wedding present. Where's your intended?"

"Shopping. She'll be eager to meet you tonight at dinner. Why didn't Anne come with you?"

"She's expecting. Too far along."

"Congratulations! This is number three?"

"Four."

Expressing his surprise, Jack motioned for his servant to collect George's luggage. Once everything was settled and they climbed inside the vehicle, Jack said, "I hope you'll stay 'til October, for the wedding. It's the first weekend."

Considering, George rubbed his jaw. "Maybe. Anna is due in mid-October. As long as there are no problems, it might be possible. So tell me about it – the foundry. Have you seen it yet?"

"Only from the outside. It's located on East Broughton near the Trustees Garden, a good source of cheap labor."

"The Garden?"

Jack laughed. "The original garden consisted of ten acres stretching down to the riverbanks, authorized by the trustees before Oglethorpe ever came over from England. Dr. William Houstoun sailed all the way to the West Indies in search of specimens to grow there. Sadly, the whole concept was abandoned within five years. The area became a hangout for slaves hired for wharf work – taverns – you get the picture. In the 1840s a bunch of Irish tenements were constructed."

"I see."

"The Federals took control of the foundry when Savannah was occupied. Now that the war is over, they are willing to sell to the right party."

"Someone willing to cooperate with authorities."

Jack nodded. "Our ties with you in New York won't hurt. We have an appointment to tour the premises tomorrow at ten."

"And what do you propose to produce, Jack?"

"Parts for our ships, of course, and railroad line. It's a rolling mill."

George nodded. "Sounds like a logical plan. I look forward to seeing it."

"I'm hoping you can advise me on what equipment I might need and help interview qualified workers."

"It would be my pleasure. What will you call the place?"

"Randall Iron, Savannah, seems appropriate." The carriage pulled to a halt in front of the pink mansion. Jack added, "I can't say how much it means to me that you are here, George. How can I thank you?"

George shook his head. "I always told you blood is thicker than water. Just don't forget it again."

"I never did. You understand – with father gone – I had responsibilities here."

A flash of something unpleasant crossed the older Randall's features. "You aided a *rebellion*."

Jack tensed. "I stood by my home state and provided for my family."

A moment went by in which the silence was strained. Finally George nodded and clapped his arm. "Fair enough. I can't say but that in the same circumstances I would have done the same. It's water under the bridge now."

If only Northern politicians shared your generous spirit, Jack thought.

In the house, George went to his room to unpack and rest. Jack found Mahala and Sylvie in the third story sewing room, bent over packages on the table. "The color choice was wise," Sylvie was saying. "I think you'll be glad you got it despite that awful woman. You can have it remade in Europe. The scooped neck and three-quarter-length sleeves will make that easy, and I don't believe anyone will fret that you show a little skin in the church. It will be so much more elegant. You'll need orange blossoms, of course –" Sylvie stopped talking and whirled around, noticing him.

Mahala folded brown paper over the material they had been looking at.

"Hello," Jack said, smiling and kissing both of their cheeks. "Good luck today?"

"Oh, yes," Sylvie breathed, glowing so much that one would think she and not Mahala was the bride. "The best! Honiton applique lace, Jack – and the most cunning little slippers!"

He raised an eyebrow.

"Well – it's not bad luck for him to see it, is it?" Mahala wondered aloud. She had been agog the past weeks at all the intricate etiquette and superstitions involved in a proper wedding. "I mean – it's not made up yet."

"I guess not."

Mahala folded back wrapping paper to reveal shimmering ivory silk-satin, the Honiton lace and machine net and bobbin lace.

"The skirt will have a deep lace ruffle," Sylvie explained, "almost half the skirt. And she will wear a veil instead of a bonnet, so you must wear all black and white, Jack. Mahala wants me and Carolyn as bridesmaids, but I said of course she'd need to write to Carolyn, as she probably won't do it. It won't even have been a year since her husband's death. She shouldn't be at a wedding, much less *in* one."

Jack thought Sylvie looked much too pleased at this idea. He glanced at Mahala, whose expression was just the opposite.

"But it's only a small country wedding," she said hopefully.

"Sylvie is right, though," Jack replied. "It is a matter Carolyn will need to carefully consider."

66

Mahala nodded.

"Who shall your groomsmen be?" Sylvie resumed.

"Bryson and George, if you have two bridesmaids," Jack answered, finding great irony in the competitive situation between both sets of attendants. "Sylvie, may I have a moment alone with Mahala?"

Sylvie pouted. "Well ... I suppose. But I'll be right down the hall, so behave yourself!"

After she had left, Jack turned to his fiancée. He smiled. "All is well between you?"

"I suppose. She told me today she understood my attachment to Carolyn but hoped one day I would care for her as a sister."

"She said that?"

Mahala nodded.

"And what did you say?"

"That I already did. I couldn't bear it when she was angry with me, Jack. I told her I sincerely hoped she will find love soon, whether it be with Dylan or someone else. I think she's just lonely. It must be hard to wonder if every suitor wants your money more than they want *you*. At least with Dylan she knows what kind of man he is. I believe that's partly why she's set on him."

Jack embraced her. "You are a good woman, and I want you to know that I'm sorry I discounted your judgment where Ella Beth was concerned. I'll be more watchful, but Mahala, know that no one – ever – will come between us. You understand?"

"Ever is a long time."

"That's what I promise."

She wiped a tear from the corner of her eye and nodded, then put a gentle hand on the dress fabric beside her. "You like it?"

"You're going to take my breath away."

"I hope so. The lady we bought this from was very rude when she found out who we were. Sylvie assures me the dressmaker is an old family friend who will be much nicer."

"She ought to be. I kept her supplied during the war with notions barely over my cost."

"But the other lady...?"

"You'll find that as many will snub you for being my wife as for being of mixed blood, Mahala. There are still many who think all blockade runners were shirkers and profiteers." He smiled at her indignant frown. "So you see, you may not be bettering your social status at all."

"I don't care about that for myself, but for you, and your family, it isn't right. I know your generous heart. There must be some way we can find to help the people who are struggling, those who might resent the money you have. Today on the streets, we saw so many poor, Jack – widows, orphans, maimed soldiers. How will they ever work again?"

"That's a good question. But they are a proud people, Mahala, who would be insulted by charity – especially mine."

"There must be some way to show them we care."

Jack tipped her nose with his finger. "I'm sure you'll think of something, my dear," he said, smiling at her troubled demeanor. "And to think I was concerned I'd have trouble getting you to spend my money!"

She play-punched him, and he kissed her. He drew her into his arms, savoring her softness, inhaling the sweet scent of her glossy hair. Why had he ever been afraid of needing her? She would be the greatest asset, the greatest ally, he could ever possess.

Sylvie was out visiting friends. Her morning call had failed to produce the desired invitation to luncheon. In fact, her hostess had seemed rather cold. How quickly people forgot that her brother had risked his neck and fortune month after month to keep the city in food during the war. They chose instead to resent the fact that the Randalls were not paupered like all the other genteel families. She sniffed. She didn't care. She'd call at Bay Street and Jack would take her to the Marshall Hotel, where they'd eat stewed oysters just to spit in their eye.

She had the driver take her to the waterfront, watching the crowds on the streets as she rode along. There were plenty of good-looking Yankee soldiers in town. Wouldn't it scandalize everybody if she let one of them start calling on her? The temptation to flout society's approval was swift and strong but did not last. She would never do that to her family. Besides, she loved the South, loved Savannah, and had supported the cause with her whole heart. It just hurt to be rebuffed.

She reminded herself that if she married Dylan, doors of the old elite would never close on her again. No matter that he had no money now. She did. And she had high spirits. He had a name, and respect, and a mysterious wounded quality which drew her irresistibly. They would be a perfect match.

Sylvie had the driver wait while she crossed the iron bridge that led to Randall and Ellis. In the space below it, cotton would soon be stacked, ready for market and shipping – but not enough cotton this year. Not nearly enough. Little had been planted on neglected farms, and what seeds remained in the South now were of poor quality. With the abolishment of the slave system, the role of the cotton factors who had once worked so diligently along this very waterfront was pretty well nonexistent. Would life ever be the same again?

She knew the answer to that.

Terrapin and oysters and maybe chilled café mocha would help.

That bumbling clerk, Andrew Willis, scrambled to his feet when she entered. Why had Jack hired him? He was dependable and must be quite smart, but he was such a mouse. He could scarcely put two words together in her presence.

"I'm going up to see my brother," she announced in answer to his greeting.

"He – he's not here, Miss Randall."

"Not here? Well, where is he? He said he would be here."

"Your mother and Miss Franklin called, and he and Mr. George Randall took them out to lunch."

"What? Without me?" Sylvie was incensed at the very idea.

"They – they did not know where you were, Miss Randall."

"Do you know when he will be back?"

"Not for a while, I believe, *if* he returns. I believe your brother planned to drive the ladies home after the meal."

Sylvie stood there a minute in indecision, huffing. She would have to go back home and eat alone. She was *not* in the mood for that.

"Are you … are you in need of an escort?"

She looked at the clerk indignantly. Surely he was not suggesting …? But he was! As he pushed his glasses back up on the bridge of his nose, Andrew Willis was turning red!

"No! *Thank you.* I am not in need of anything. I shall go home. Good day."

Sylvie whirled and opened the door, starting down the steps to the bridge without a pause. She bumped right into a solid figure coming up, a figure that said "umph!," faltered, and fell backwards while she was just able to catch herself on the rail. Merciful heavens, she had actually knocked a man down and – what was that? Sylvie looked closer. Had actually turned his foot all the way around!

"Oh! Are you all right?"

"Och, lass, I'm sprawled on my rear end for all Bay Street to see with my foot near knocked off, now how do you think I am?"

Her face flamed as she realized the dark-haired young man in front of her possessed a wooden foot that had been strapped to his leg and put into a boot. A war amputation, doubtless. He was even now working to right the limb.

"I – I'm sorry," Sylvie spluttered. "Can I help you up?"

The Irishman paused a moment for emphasis and fixed blazing green eyes on her. "No."

"Fine, then. Suit yourself." Ruffled, Sylvie started past him when she heard him mutter:

"Hopin' this isna a sign of how the interview will go."

She looked back as the young man hefted himself into a standing position. "You have an interview here?"

"It's my aim to seek out Mr. Randall."

"Jack Randall is my brother."

"Oh? Is that so?" The thundercloud lifted from the stranger's face. He stuck his hand out. "Daniel O'Keefe."

Did he expect to shake? Sylvie offered a limp hand. "Sylvie Randall."

Daniel bowed and dropped a kiss on her fingers. "Charmed," he said with an ironic twinge.

"There's no use going in – at least not now. Mr. Randall is out."

"Oh, and is that so."

The man looked so crestfallen Sylvie was prompted to inquire further. "May I ask what your business was?"

"I heard he's buying the old Broughton Street foundry. I worked there before the war, Miss. It is 'miss,' isn't it?"

Sylvie gave the barest nod. "And you need a job?"

"Sure'n I do. And not just any job. I'm the man he wants for foreman. You name it, I've done it. I started as a helper, stokin' the fires an' pushing the barrows, then was puddler, and after that, master puddler. I know how the rolling machines work and can keep them up and running."

"I see," Sylvie said, though she had no idea what he was talking about. "And … your – your leg …?"

Daniel O'Keefe's tanned face darkened again. "It's a foot, lass, and typically poses no hindrance. I can even polka on it, so long as no one plows into me."

She ought to be annoyed that he would bring up her clumsiness again. Instead she felt herself smiling. Here was a man who was not afraid of her. It was not surprising, though, considering her inglorious introduction. "I'd like to see that sometime."

Small creases appeared beside his eyes. "Well, maybe you will. Can you suggest a time for me to return to your brother's office? This afternoon or tomorrow?"

"Well …" she hesitated. She liked this man. There was a spark in his eye that matched her own fighting nature. And she *had* knocked him down. "He's due at our home within the hour. If you'd like to come and wait in his study there, you can ride with me to Wright Square."

It was Daniel's turn to hesitate. He said, "I'm afraid your brother might consider it unprofessional of me to take advantage of his sister's kindness."

"It's not kindness. It's guilt."

He laughed. "Just the same, perhaps I should call again."

She lifted a shoulder to show it mattered not to her. "Do what you like. Leave a card – but he's out a great deal. His fiancée is in town, and they are preparing for their wedding."

"I fear I'm chancin' me arm, but very well, then, lass, and thank you."

Sylvie gestured toward the waiting carriage. Daniel offered to escort her. His shirt was clean, though mended, the muscles underneath hard. He walked with a limp so slight as to be unnoticeable to one who was not looking for it. He handed her up, then paused, but when he saw her maid inside, doffed his bowler hat and took the seat opposite them. He smiled at her. Lines next to his mouth deepened.

She smiled back faintly. What was she doing, taking a strange man to her home? And an Irishman at that! Jack and her mother would be furious. Well, it's what they deserved, leaving her all alone like this. She didn't like to be alone, and Mr. O'Keefe was interesting. She eyed the cotton duck vest, the worn boots. Best to learn about him so maybe she could make it seem they were previous acquaintances. At the risk of inflaming his ire, she said, "You served in the war, Mr. O'Keefe?"

"Aye. In the Jasper Greens."

Sylvie nodded. It was an old unit, organized in 1842. The Greens had served respectably in both the Mexican War and the recent conflict, though she'd heard rumors of some of the members having raided a plantation nearby, butchering the hogs and sheep there for food. There had also been heavy desertions among the Irish when the fighting had raged near Atlanta. Was that when he had lost his foot? Some men shot themselves in the foot to get off the front lines.

Daniel saw her curious gaze and seemed to follow her line of thought. He shook the abbreviated limb. "Had to give this up outside Nashville. Did you know our brigade of 1,600 held off a Federal army of 10,000 for eight days, covering the Confederate retreat?"

He was bragging, polite society would say. But she thought he had a right to. "No," she said, humbled at the unfair assumptions she'd harbored. "I – I didn't know that. And before that, before you fought in the war and worked at the foundry?"

The skin at the corners of his eyes crinkled again. Did foundry work make men so tanned, they never lost their darker color? But then, he was still handsome, in a native, rugged way. "My family came over from Wexford County, Ireland, in '47, when I was ten. My father worked on the railroad."

She did some quick figuring. The late '40s had been the time of the potato famine. That would make him about twenty-eight now. "Have you brothers and sisters?"

"Aye. Eleven. And the care of those still at home. Da died of consumption during the conflict. I'm the eldest."

"Oh, my." No wonder he was determined to find a job. Sylvie resolved that her brother would at least speak to Mr. O'Keefe, no matter how mad at her he might be for bringing the man home. "Do you live near the foundry, then?"

The eyes sparkled. "Is this an interview, Miss Randall?"

She ruffled. "Only making conversation, Mr. O'Keefe, seeing as how I'm bringing you to my home."

"Quite right. Yes, Miss Randall, we abide in a grand house in the Old Fort District."

Sylvie let that bit of sarcasm go. Deciding that offering him luncheon was the lesser evil to leaving him alone in Jack's study – to prowl about and look at who knew what – Sylvie soon sat with Daniel at the dining room table. He regaled her with tales of his native Wexford, from its strawberries to its castles.

"Do you ever think of going back?"

Daniel O'Keefe sighed, pausing in the act of buttering his biscuit. "Only in my dreams, Miss Randall. 'Tis a sad and subjugated land."

Sylvie laughed. "Much like the South."

"Well, you're right at that!" Daniel admitted, gesturing with his knife. "May I say, by the way, that these biscuits are only delicious!" He grinned at the red-haired Irish maid who had appeared to fill their coffee cups. She colored up like a tomato.

"*Only* delicious?" Sylvie questioned, confused.

"Meanin' absolutely delicious. The Irish speech has many peculiarities." As the servant girl left, he added, "An interesting mix of help your brother keeps."

"My father had a fondness for Irish workers. He brought some down from New York with him in '38. My brother never owned slaves."

"Is that so?"

Sylvie went on to ask what she really wanted to, before biscuits and maids had distracted her. "Is that why you fought for the South, then? For freedom from oppression, like is needed in Ireland?"

"Now don't go makin' me into a hero, Miss Randall," O'Keefe replied quickly, and, she thought, rather darkly. "I did my duty, just like all those other boys. Plain and simple. I was already a Jasper Green before the war came, and I wasn't about to let them down."

Sylvie watched him as he went back to eating. There was no doubt as to his appetite. Now as to his humble motivations for fighting … she was not quite convinced. Why would an Irishman, a fairly recent immigrant at that, feel duty-bound to defend the South, if not for inbred loyalty to home, and a remembered sense of justice? She gazed at him with narrowed eyes.

At that moment she heard the front door open and voices in the hall. She jumped up, almost upsetting her chair with her voluminous skirt. Daniel looked up, surprised.

"Excuse me," she said. It was vital to intercept Jack before he came upon their cozy luncheon scene.

Her guest stood as she left the room. Out of the corner of her eye she saw him sit back down, somewhat less certainly than before. And then there was Jack's face in her view, already stony. The butler must have conveyed the information that Miss Sylvie had a strange Irishman in the dining room.

"What's this?" Jack rumbled.

Mahala, Mrs. Franklin, Sunny and George Randall gathered around him.

Refusing to be cowed, she put on her most charming smile and rose on her tiptoes to kiss Jack's cheek. "I've brought you a gift," she said brightly, "a wonderful surprise!"

"A strange Irish man in my dining room is certainly a surprise, though not a wonderful one."

Just the term she had thought he would use! She almost snorted in irritation but controlled herself. Sylvie glimpsed Mahala hide a smile behind her hand. She tossed her golden curls. "Come, Jack, don't be so testy. It's I who should be put out, going by your office as I did to find you departed – and all of you out to eat. And it was there I encountered our guest, and knew how you would wish to speak to him – to Mr. O'Keefe, Mr. Daniel O'Keefe, that is – and not let him slip through your fingers. How common is it to find a qualified foreman for an iron foundry? Why, not very, I'm willing to wager."

"Let's not add gambling to your list of charms," Jack said, but his tone was now tinged with humor. That was a good sign. "So you just brought this Mr. O'Keefe right on home with you and sat down to eat with him? What were you thinking?"

"Why, of you, Jack – only of you – and well, of him. Eleven brothers and sisters he has, and he's their provider. And he worked at the very foundry you are purchasing, Jack. He sounds very qualified."

"As though you would know," Sunny put in.

But George laughed. "I'm intrigued, Jack. We should at least talk to the man now that he's under your roof."

"Scandalous," Sunny murmured, unwilling to let it go. "I'm ashamed of you, Sylvie."

"We had a servant with us the whole time, Mama."

"A servant?" Sunny sniffed. "As if we're in the practice of–"

Jack raised a hand to deter her from speaking further in the presence of his cousin and fiancée. "Why don't you ladies go about your afternoon plans, and George and I will interview the fellow, though every notion revolts at the idea of catering to so much presumption. Sylvie, come with us to make an introduction, then I'd appreciate it if you, too, would withdraw."

"Of course, Jack," she replied with false humility.

He gave her a sharp look. "I have yet to know if I'll thank you for this. I sincerely doubt it."

As Jack placed a quick kiss on Mahala's hand in parting, Sylvie saw Mahala give him a faintly reproving stare.

Jack offered his arm to escort Sylvie into the dining room, where Daniel rose upon sight of them. In his face Sylvie saw, for an unguarded moment, how much this meeting – this job – meant to the man. After introducing Jack and George to him, she slipped out and closed the door. She leaned on the wall, a small smile crossing her face. No matter how unconventional her actions, she had done right. She just knew it.

CHAPTER FIVE

Mid-August, 1865
Habersham County, Georgia

t was still light as the Randall carriage traveled north from Clarkesville on Tallulah Falls Road, coating nodding Black-eyed Susans and pokeberry bushes in a mighty cloud of dust.

"Oh, the drought," moaned Sunny. "Will it ever end?" She held a handkerchief to her nose.

Mahala looked with concern out the carriage window, though not due to dismay over the record dry conditions. Not that the lack of rainfall didn't concern her. It was that something more pressing, and far more sinister, had presented itself in the last few days. It had her searching every shadow, gazing behind them toward town for other riders. Silly of her. Who would take a shot at a man in an enclosed carriage? No, Jack was much more in danger simply crossing the square to call on her than he was here in the country, but Mahala couldn't relax. Not anywhere. And she had tried to tell him, but he had dismissed her concerns as fanciful.

"Who knows what Maddie really heard," he'd said when Mahala had reported the conversation her servant had listened in on behind her uncle's store. The old woman had stumbled upon a gathering there of three ex-soldiers. The whispers of the men had cautioned her to eavesdrop.

"It's time we quit letting vultures and shirkers stride about as if they own our streets," one man had said. "We ought to give 'em the message loud an' clear that they're not welcome here."

"Yeah, let's send 'em back up North where they belong," another had agreed.

"What about the hotel owner? I'd like to teach 'im a lesson," the third had said. Maddie had recognized that voice as belonging to Abel Quitman, Leon's old friend. She'd strained her ears at that point as hard as she could – "lak to comin' off my head," she'd told them later – but the men had suspected someone near. With a whispered shushing, they had melted off into the shadows.

Jack touched Mahala's arm. "Worried again, my love?"

She smiled, unable to comment, because Jack had insisted she not alarm his mother and sister with the information Maddie had brought them. But – "the hotel owner"? Who else could it be? Were there really men in town angry enough at non-combatants to harm someone like Jack? She sighed. All she wanted was for the drama to end and them to enjoy life together. First there had been Savannah … all the elite gentry who had looked down on her because of her mixed blood … Ella Beth with her covert glances at Jack … the shopping, spending too much money on gowns so that she'd have a small but proper trousseau with which to begin life as Jack's wife … and snubbing by some of Jack's family. Now this. Would there never be peace?

Sylvie took Jack's comment the only way she could, being aware only that Mahala had offered resistance to the Rousseaus' invitation. "I don't know why you're still brooding, Mahala. They won't be too overworked to receive us. Everyone needs a little company and conversation. It's how we maintain society, isn't it, Mother?" Sylvie tipped her head. Tiny silk roses were pinned among her golden tresses, along with a snippet of creamy French lace that served as an evening cap.

Sunny nodded her encouragement.

"Besides, their dinner invitation was a follow-up to the one we extended to them before our trip to Savannah. It would be incredibly rude to refuse."

"I'm sure Henrietta wants all the news," Sunny agreed.

Knowing the whole truth of Mahala's reservation – the threats Maddie had overheard, plus her concern about Sylvie's fixation with Dylan – Jack took her hand and squeezed it. Their eyes met. He continued to hold her hand as the carriage trundled along, and she felt a little better. She thought of the letter in her reticule to Dylan from Carolyn, and felt better still. Good thing Mr. Blythe had gotten that in just today. She glanced at Sylvie, resplendent in her sheer cream silk organza dinner dress, and managed a smile. She had to remind herself that what was meant to be would be. Well, with a lot of prayer – and sometimes even a bit of tweaking by concerned parties!

At least she and Jack had come to terms about Ella Beth. Shortly before they left Savannah, he had told her he needed to pay a visit to his cousin updating Ella Beth regarding her financial matters – but he wanted Mahala to accompany him. He had considered the situation and determined it would be wise not to stir the widow's precarious emotions with attentions that could be misinterpreted. The significance of Mahala's presence had not been lost on the young woman. Ella Beth's manner had been grave and humble as she sat listening to Jack, her big brown eyes going from her cousin to Mahala, whom Jack kept close beside him. In imparting the knowledge that her debts had been settled, he had even used the term "we," as though Mahala was already his wife. Jack had then gone on to say that Grandmother Ellis would be delighted to have Ella Beth come and live with her once the Abercorn Street house sold. This announcement had clearly brought Ella Beth great relief – so much so that Mahala's heart had tendered. Too many women were in Ella Beth's circumstance – financially strapped and dependent on others.

But for the careful and loving intervention of the Emmitts and Martha in her life, Mahala realized, so could she be. That truth, however, had not prevented a flame of righteous indignation from flaring inside her when, as they were leaving, Mahala had glimpsed the wistful manner in which Ella Beth's eyes had followed Jack's departing back.

She had been glad their Savannah visit was over, and the next time she had dealings with Ella Beth, she would be Mrs. Jack Randall.

Resolution had also come for Jack with Bryson. The morning they'd left the young man had told Jack that after the wedding he would travel to New York to refurbish *Evangeline*. Jack had said he guessed Bryson's decision had more to do with economics than family loyalty, but maybe that, too, would come in the end. It was a step in the right direction.

Now all that remained was to see Carolyn as happily married as Mahala knew she herself would soon be.

The lamps were lit in the foyer of Forests of Green and reflected in the mirrors on the wall. Even their gentle golden light could not conceal the brackets of weariness around Dylan's mouth as he came forward to receive them, or the new roughness of Henrietta's small hands. Mahala felt her stomach tighten. What would the Rousseaus serve them for dinner? They ought to have come up with some excuse – any excuse – to have declined the invitation. There was no way whatever was put on the table could compare to the lavish spread of Jack's cook.

"I'm so glad you've come," Henrietta said, leading them into dinner on Jack's arm. How things had changed since the day she had eschewed his association. "I've been so very alone here. We hardly go into town. I'm dying for some good conversation."

Perhaps Sylvie had been right. As Sunny and Henrietta chatted – about the wedding shopping, the occupation of Savannah, old friends, and the recent death of little Susie Kollock at Woodlands – a servant Mahala had not seen before – Henrietta's maid, she supposed – brought in a thin tomato soup. It was followed by snap beans, salt-cured ham and sweet potato soufflé, which though long on the nuts and short on the brown sugar, was saved by the distinctive tang of molasses. Everything was fresh and delicious. Mahala relaxed. She ought to have known the Rousseaus would find any way in heaven to maintain appearances for company. She just hoped it hadn't cost them too dear.

"Did you receive news of the convention in Milledgeville?" Jack asked Dylan.

"Yes," Dylan said. "At least, we heard that Charles Jenkins and Herschel Johnson were elected delegates. How did it go?"

"As expected. War debt repudiated. Slavery officially abolished. And as for the ordinance of secession–" Jack gave a crooked grin – "well, it was repealed but not nullified."

"Bravo for them," Dylan cried. He commenced cutting his ham, winced almost imperceptibly, paused and resumed.

Sylvie had noticed. "Are you quite all right, Mr. Rousseau?"

"Yes, Miss Randall." It was Dylan's turn to give a wry smile. "Just started threshing wheat today. I'm afraid I'm rather new to the task."

"Threshing wheat," Sylvie repeated, as though he had said "painting a masterpiece" or "writing my memoirs." She gazed at him raptly past a showy bouquet of blue hydrangeas. "It sounds like a challenging task."

Dylan smiled again, but his tone was schooled to polite. "I find it so."

"Do tell us town folk what's entailed."

"One spreads the sheaves onto a canvas sheet on the threshing floor of the barn, with the doors open. Then one takes a flail – a short wooden stick tied with leather to a longer pole – to beat the sheaves. The flail knocks the grain loose from the stalks. The stalks are winter straw for the animals. The kernels are put on a winnowing tray and tossed in the air to remove the husks, chaff and extra pieces of straw. It's best done on a cool, windy day, but alas ... we haven't the luxury of waiting on one."

"Then – it is ready for the mill?"

"That's right." Another patient smile.

"Do you have enough help for all this?" Sylvie asked, with what appeared to be genuine concern.

"Mmm," Mahala murmured over her first taste of bread pudding.

Jack raised his eyebrows at her.

Dylan sighed, not having noticed Mahala's reaction to dessert. "I have three men. With the size of the crop – a small one, for part of what we planted was too dry to harvest – we can manage. It's difficult, though, to be quite honest. So much else needs done – clearing brush, repairing fences, and soon enough, the corn will be ready. We need rain so badly. The ears are small, the kernels small. Some stalks went straight to tassel."

"Oh, dear," Sylvie murmured. "I'm so sorry to hear that."

Mahala wondered if Sylvie knew what tassel was, apart from dress trim. She was glad this time Jack's sister was across the table from Dylan. Otherwise, she would certainly be touching his arm in deep sympathy by now.

"My goodness, it must be quite a task keeping the men fed," Sunny commented. "Your maid keeps up with things in the kitchen, and the house, too?" she asked Henrietta.

"I help her," Henrietta admitted, eyes on her plate. "It is necessary. I have to admit, I miss Carolyn. She had learned so much about this place. I must sow turnips next week, and I'm quite at a loss. But listen to us." She paused and gave a little laugh. "What complainers we're being. What type of dinner conversation is this? Forgive us. We should speak of things pleasant and uplifting."

"To be fair, Mrs. Rousseau, such topics are few and far between these days," Jack said, giving the lady a gentle smile.

"Quite right," she agreed, though an edge sharpened her face. "Though you would hardly be one to say so."

Jack chose to ignore the deeper implications of Henrietta's barb. He took Mahala's hand in his and smiled. "It's true I've found great joy in this past year," he admitted, giving her a smile.

Mahala met his eyes before turning to their hostess, mustering as much grace as she could. "And Mrs. Rousseau, as to turnips ... I recall a few things myself from my days on the farm in Sautee. Perhaps I could come out Monday and be of some assistance."

Relief and gratitude transformed the lines on Henrietta's face. "Oh, could you? I remember you were always a help to Carolyn, and taught her much when she was new here. It would be very kind of you, my dear."

Mahala smiled, remembering the day Carolyn's mother-in-law had turned up her nose at the sight of her.

"I will escort you," Jack said. He glanced at Dylan. "There's surely some task you can set me to as well."

"No – no. That's not necessary."

"I would count it a blessing. There's not enough to hold my attention at the hotel. Between wondering what I'm missing at my office in Savannah and pining for my bride-to-be, I'm about to go stir crazy!"

Everyone laughed, and Mahala flushed. She knew he kept busier than he let on overseeing renovations at The Highlands. He occasionally consulted her on decisions, but by and large he was keeping the whole operation under wraps. The finished project was to be revealed on their wedding day. Still, working alongside Dylan at Forests of Green would not only benefit Dylan; it would keep Jack safe.

"Miss Franklin, you enjoyed the bread pudding?" Henrietta asked, beaming over at Mahala's empty bowl.

"Very much. Did you make it yourself?"

"I did indeed."

"My goodness. It was even better than Maddie's, though of course I'd never tell her so."

"It will be our secret," Henrietta teased.

After the meal they all gathered in the parlor while Sylvie played the piano. She had a nice touch and a sweet soprano, Mahala thought, but not so nice as Carolyn. She watched Dylan for his reaction. He applauded with enthusiasm at the end of each number, but during the songs Mahala spied him biting back yawns. Once, he rubbed the back of his neck with a hand. As much as she'd like to believe he was unimpressed by Sylvie's skill, she knew the more likely explanation was exhaustion.

Denise Weimer

Mahala nudged Jack and nodded toward the host as he covered his mouth, then tried to sit up straight and appear attentive. After that number Jack suggested he must get the ladies back to town.

As the party filed out the door into the foyer, Mahala hung back. She caught Dylan's sleeve. As he looked at her in surprise, she felt surprise herself. Close up, with the dark circles under his eyes, Dylan appeared much older than his nearly twenty-eight years. There was already an odd combination of the plain farmer and the aristocrat in his tanned, finely chiseled features.

Mahala pulled the letter out of her reticule and pressed it into his hand. "From Carolyn," she said. "It came just today."

With satisfaction, she watched joy enliven his face. "Thank you." He tucked the envelope into his vest. "I miss her," he whispered.

Mahala placed a hand on his arm. "I know that she misses you, too. She tells me so in the letters she sends me."

He looked incredulous. "She does?"

Mahala nodded.

Sylvie returned to the parlor door and clasped onto Dylan's arm with a firmness that belied her teasing tone. "What are you two whispering about back here?"

On the way home, Sylvie did not speak to her. Mahala felt guilty, but only until she pictured Dylan's expression lighting up as he received the letter. It was Carolyn he wanted.

A few weeks later, Mahala wrote to Carolyn, still believing that it was better that Sylvie should set her sights elsewhere …

> … rather than suffer a broken heart. That's what I thought when we first returned to Habersham, for I know he loves you, but now my concern is that by your absence and her persistence he might be won over. She puts herself constantly before him. It is difficult to refuse her when she offers her services to your mother-in-law and begs to ride out with Jack and me when we go to lend a hand at the farm – which is above once a week. I know she goes to see him, but she does work hard. I fear he might begin to wonder if she could be made of sterner stuff than he at first imagined. I ought not to interfere in my future sister-in-law's business, but you, Carolyn, have been like a sister to me. If you have feelings for this man, come back to Habersham. You needn't stay at Forests of Green. Stay with me, and help me prepare for the wedding, even if you have decided you can't be in it.
> Your loving friend,
> Mahala Franklin

Carolyn folded the letter and closed her eyes. She heard the insistent tapping of a pileated woodpecker. She heard the breeze stir the leaves of the massive live oak overhead and pictured Spanish moss waving ghost-like in the wind. Then, in her mind she pictured North Georgia – like a different world. There, the cicadas would be trilling, a cool tinge would be in the air mornings and evenings, and the tree leaves would be drying, turning. It was September now. Here her father gathered a small group of loyal workers who, for the payment of part of the proceeds of the crop, agreed to harvest the delicate white sea island cotton, a long, slow process once the bolls burst. Lawrence had the advantage of a good and experienced foreman, unlike Dylan, who would be harvesting corn alongside former slaves.

She thought of his last letter. He had allowed himself to be more transparent than before. His words, his struggles, had pierced her.

"It's hard to accept the past several years were for nothing," he had written. "Except perhaps to grow character, and what can I do with that but prove the change by determination, by patience and flexibility. If I cannot take what life now offers, no matter how hard, are not those years in vain? If I cannot win this struggle to subdue this land and make it fruitful, what do we have? What am I worth?

"Carolyn, I don't mean to pressure you. You must come to your own decision. But I do need a partner in the task before me. But come – only come – if you find tenderness in your heart for the boy who adored you, and the man who needs you."

Carolyn groaned, her fingers crumpling Mahala's letter.

"Why, my dear, whatever is the matter?"

Carolyn had forgotten her grandmother was seated beside her. In the shade of Brightwell's porch, Odelle had dozed off in the coastal warmth of the Sunday afternoon, but at the sound of her granddaughter's distress, she had become alert, a thin hand reaching out to touch the black sheer of Carolyn's gown.

"Is your friend not well?"

"No, she's fine, Grandmother," Carolyn said, patting Odelle's slender, age-spotted fingers. "It is I who am unwell."

Odelle gave her a pitying look. "Thinking of my sister's son again, are you?"

Yes, and not the one in the grave, Carolyn thought, in agony. "I don't know my own heart, Grandmother. He says to come if I find tenderness for him, and I do – I care about him. And he needs me now."

"Need is not a good thing on which to base a marriage."

81

"But is this not much like a marriage of convenience, and many of those are successful."

Odelle shook her white head. "No, my love. For he loves you, and nothing is more painful than unreturned love."

"I think I could – if I don't already. It's just so different from what I felt for Dev. And I'm not sure I'm ready."

"Then stay, child, until you are."

Carolyn saw her mother approaching across the lawn with Dev Jr., who had an armful of flowers, presumably for her. Not wanting her mother to again register her input on the situation, she responded quickly and softly. "That's just it. I don't think I have the time to do that."

Olivia's ears were still very sharp, sharper than Odelle's. "To do what, dear?" she asked as Devie ran up to Carolyn and gave her the bouquet.

Carolyn made a fuss over the gift, hoping her mother would not press her.

No such luck. "I do hope you are not speaking of returning to Habersham," she continued, sweeping her skirts onto a rocker and reaching for her perspiring glass of lemonade. "There is nothing for you there. You belong here, with us. When you are ready, there are plenty of established local landowners who would call on you. It would make sense to consider one of them. Your father has proven much stronger than he feared he might be after that bout of scarlet fever, but he won't live forever."

Carolyn had been swayed by that argument before. She didn't intend to be again. "Thank you for making me welcome here, Mother, but the decision of whether I marry again and to whom is one I alone must make," she said as she drew her son onto her lap.

"What has Dylan to offer you, Carolyn? A broken-down mountain farm. And how will he even make a go of that? All you have told us yourself since you came home shows what a time he is having. In the past ten years, Carolyn, nothing has changed. The boy wasn't cut out to be a farmer."

Carolyn's guard went up at her mother's opinionated and critical attitude. "He isn't a boy. He's not the same person you knew, Mother. Not the same at all."

Olivia bit her lip and shook her head.

"Devie's wet," Carolyn said, preparing to rise. "I must go in and change him."

"Nonsense. You take too much on yourself. I'll take him to my maid."

Carolyn hesitated, then gave the boy over. She was so tired. Her mother was right that Carolyn had grown accustomed to doing things for herself while she lived in North Georgia. There was plenty of work to do here at Brightwell, though not so much as at Forests of Green, where there were so few servants to help. But it was different. At Forests of Green, she had always felt like she was working *toward* something, like the land belonged to her and she to it. Work there had left her with a satisfied peace at the end of the day. Here, work – and worry – simply left her tired.

She was glad to see her mother go around the corner. She didn't want to depend on her parents. She didn't want strangers, who knew nothing of her past, to call on her. She wanted to do things on her own. A woman of no property and no income could not do things on her own. Was there a better partner than Dylan?

She turned to find her grandmother watching her with a knowing smile.

Thinking of her grandmother's words three weeks later, Carolyn wanted to bury her head in her arms and sob. Today was her best friend's wedding, and she, Carolyn, was an emotional wreck. Here she sat at her dressing table in her suite at The Franklin Hotel, squeezed into Mahala's borrowed gray taffeta gown – because all her own dresses had been dyed black – and she could not make herself go downstairs. That was partly because Sylvie was already there, all flushed cheeks and giggles, clad in an ivory ensemble that mirrored Mahala's own right down to the veil. But it was mostly because of what was within herself. Misery and indecision. It didn't help that she was a day or two before her monthly, which made her bloated and grumpy.

She tucked a few late pink wild roses into Mahala's plain gray bonnet and put it on. It stuck up too high on her head. She took it off and added a few blossoms to the crown of her hairdo, hoping to relieve the simplicity of her appearance. The dress would serve to offset Mahala's tall, dark elegance. But it was the wrong color for Carolyn – chosen only because gray was an acceptable shade of secondary mourning – and was ill-fitting. She'd had to tack a hem in the skirt and the sleeves. She sighed. There was nothing to be done about it. It was still better than appearing like a hovering crow in her widow's weeds, which Sylvie had cried off, insisting she would bring bad luck upon the nuptial couple.

A part of her she thought dead with the war and Dev reared up and remembered with longing the type of dress she would once have worn to a wedding, that Dylan would have found her beautiful in – more beautiful than Sylvie. She chided herself. She knew Dylan wanted her, but if she could not bring herself to give him some definite encouragement, she would deserve it if he turned to her rich cousin.

He had been pleased when she came back, though she had made it clear she needed more time, and had returned to assist Mahala with wedding preparations. It had seemed strange to go to Forests of Green like a visitor, not a resident. The very sounds and smells of the place had seemed to call to her: home. Home. But she knew now it came with a price. And she would not pay that price until she knew she could do so with love.

Now she had to go down. Mahala would be expecting her. She called to Dev Jr., who was playing with a ball on the rug, and swooped him into her arms. Maddie would watch him during the ceremony and reception. Once he was delivered into the servant's care, Carolyn made her way into the Franklins' rooms. They had, of course, offered for her to stay there with them. But with the hotel almost empty, Carolyn had elected to make use of a suite instead. It was rather worn – some would say shabby – but that did not bother her. What it lacked in elegance it more than made up for in privacy.

When she saw Mahala she stopped in her tracks. She was just so beautiful. She positively radiated joy. Carolyn embraced her, careful not to crush the bride's orange blossoms, holding her a long time.

"At last, your day has come," she whispered into Mahala's hair.

Mahala nodded, wiping away a tear. "I only wish you could stand up with me."

"I do, too. Very much. But I could hardly do so with Bishop Elliott presiding."

The Episcopal minister was in town and had agreed to perform the Randall ceremony on the same weekend he was presiding over two Kollock confirmations.

"I understand. At least you'll be there."

"Yes, and you just call on me if there's anything you need."

Sylvie took that moment to step forward, handing Mahala a bouquet of white roses and baby's breath in a silver-handled tussie-mussie. "We should go now."

"Thank you, Sylvie, but do you mind if Carolyn carries my veil to the church?"

Sylvie looked surprised, then tightened her rosebud mouth. "Of course not. After all, it's all she can do today."

She was right, Carolyn thought as they set out. She was alone today, destined to sit alone in the church, to stand alone during the dancing at the reception, to go back alone to her little boy at the hotel her friend had vacated for her glorious new house and a honeymoon in Europe. She grew angry at herself. There was no room in such a happy day for self-pity.

They met the Emmitts in the parlor. On Ben's arm, Mahala proceeded out into the street.

When they arrived at the beautiful 1842 Grace Church just before noon, Carolyn saw that it was full. Buggies, horses and carriages were waiting outside. The stair rail had been festooned with white ribbon. She saw Jack standing there with his half-brother Bryson, who was to be the only male attendant, to accompany Sylvie. The expression on his face when he beheld Mahala made Carolyn want to cry. It had been decided that Jack's cousin

George would serve as Carolyn's escort for the function. He was waiting beside Jack and Bryson and offered his arm.

"I'm sorry, but the only seats still open are at the back," he told her in a hushed tone.

"That's all right."

Inside, everyone turned expectantly, then looked crestfallen when they spied only Carolyn in Mahala's gray dress. Bishop Elliott stood at the front in his ecclesiastical robes, his spectacles on his head and a book in his hand. The guests were clad in their war-worn best, the men rivaling the women in blue, claret and mulberry with lighter trousers, and top hats held on their laps. George escorted her to a rear box pew and with as little fuss as possible, they sat down.

Her gaze went straight to Dylan and Henrietta in their pew near the front. He had observed her entrance. He smiled before turning back around. She couldn't keep her eyes off his neat part ... the way the sun glinted off his hair ... the way his frock coat stretched across his shoulders. Her heart tugged in wistful agony.

From the black walnut Erben pipe organ in the gallery came the strains of the wedding march. Grace Church was not designed with a center aisle, weddings having typically been arranged for the winter social season in the city. So Mahala, on Ben Emmitt's arm, and the rest of the bridal party, had to alternate entering down the two side aisles. The space at the front of the chapel was limited, too, and quite crowded with the bishop, the bridal couple, the attendants and the parents. As Jack and Mahala said their vows, white candles glowed in the bronze altar candlesticks. It was a beautiful scene, reminding Carolyn that life would still hold grace as well as hardship.

After the ceremony, the whole congregation headed down the hill to the square. Inside the foyer of The Franklin Hotel, Jack and Mahala received congratulations. The dining room had been set for the bridal luncheon. Sunny and Sylvie had been at work. White cloths with silver candelabra adorned the tables, with place settings and cuisine from The Palace. White roses had come up from the coast. A table on one side displayed the bridal gifts, from silver service to fine linens.

When Carolyn would have passed on by after hugging Mahala, wanting only to blend into the crowd, her friend caught her arm.

"Perhaps you couldn't be in the wedding," she said, "but you can at least stand with me now. See, George is there with Jack and Bryson. Please."

Carolyn squeezed her hand. "I'd be glad to."

Putting aside her precarious emotions with the training of one of her class, Carolyn smiled graciously at those who passed by. When everyone was at last seated, she found it in her to make conversation with her dinner partner – a Yankee. She tried hard all through the meal to not picture the noses of George Randall's artillery guns aimed at the men she had known and loved.

Finally she could stand it no longer. "I'm sorry, but is it not difficult for you to be down here now?" she asked Jack's cousin.

He smiled Jack's smile. "Probably less difficult than for those I've come among," he replied with a twinkle of humor delivered gently enough to avoid offense.

"Please forgive me. Hopefully most people are more tactful than I."

"Indeed – the opposite. Most make no effort to conceal their repugnance – that is, those who don't manage to avoid me. Alas, you haven't that luxury."

Carolyn laughed. "It's all right. Were it not for you, I would be all alone this afternoon."

"I find that hard to imagine. But, as I would be alone, too, you must see that you are doing me a double honor, in joining me and in doing so graciously."

Carolyn liked him despite herself. He reminded her too much of Jack. Apparently Sylvie felt similarly, for she soon flitted over and waved her dance card under George's nose.

"You must sign up, Cousin George."

"Save me a dance, but a later one, Miss Sylvie. Remember your brother Bryson and I are to accompany the bridal couple home."

Sylvie's lip came out. "Oh, yes, but like Jack I think it's a whole lot of fuss."

"I hope you are right, for I daresay I'd make a much more desirable – and easier – target than he."

Sylvie laughed as though George had told a glorious joke. Carolyn didn't think it was funny. The men were not providing a celebratory escort, after all, but rather a guard between town and The Highlands. A business man from Washington, D.C., who had thought to prospect in Clarkesville last week had been shot at on a side road, prompting his rapid departure. George would be in no less danger.

Sylvie added to Carolyn, "Mahala is cutting the cake now. She insists all the unmarried ladies should come for their dream cake slices."

"Thank you, Sylvie."

Sylvie responded to the punctuated politeness in Carolyn's tone with a half-shrug. "No matter. I doubt it works for widows." With that, she rose and floated away.

George gave Carolyn a pitying look. She offered a vague smile.

A few minutes later, Jack and Mahala accepted the greetings of a line of couples in the Grand March that kicked off the dancing. The set flowed into the Federal Schottische. All the men loved the opportunity to pay court to the glowing bride. Standing in the foyer to watch, Carolyn thought she had never seen Mahala more animated or confident. She was glad to see Jack's relatives all on the dance floor, appearing civil with the locals and seeming to have a good time. Even the formidable Aunt Eugenie had lost her pinched look in the presence of the esteemed bishop. Of course, a bit of champagne during lunch had probably helped, too.

Finally, the floor cleared for a waltz. Jack twirled Mahala in slow, steady circles until she grew dizzy and they opened to promenade position. Still, they had eyes only for each other. Carolyn remembered feeling that way about Dev. She reminded herself that though they had always fought an attraction, Jack and Mahala had not even liked each other at first. Was there hope then for her and Dylan? Could love sometimes come more slowly, more subtly? She looked around for him and caught sight of him across the way, listening to something Henrietta was saying, though his eyes immediately found Carolyn's, as though he had just been watching her. Had he been aware of her the whole time, the way she had always been aware of where Dev had been in a room? And why didn't she respond the same way to Dylan?

Lost in her confusion, she hardly noticed the waltz had ended until Jack and Mahala appeared beside her.

"Can I leave my bride with you, Mrs. Rousseau, while I go check on our carriage?"

Startled, Carolyn smiled. "Of course." She took Mahala's hand and patted it. "You're leaving already?"

"Yes. Jack wants to show me the house while it's still light."

I'll bet he does, Carolyn thought.

"But the party will go on. Will you stay and enjoy it a while?"

Am *I enjoying it?* Carolyn wondered. "Oh – a while, perhaps," she replied cheerily. "Everything is so lovely. Most of all you. I'm so happy for you."

"Thank you." Mahala's voice lowered to a whisper, and she drew her friend aside. "Tell me honestly if I should be nervous, Carolyn."

Carolyn smiled. The feeling between Jack and Mahala was so strong, so long-lived, that she didn't have to think about her answer for a second. "No. You don't have to be nervous."

"Thank you. Now, if I can just quit worrying that someone might think his wedding day is a perfect opportunity to take a shot at my new husband!"

Carolyn protested the idea, trying to reassure her friend. "Don't think about that. I'm sure it isn't so."

Mahala hugged her as Jack came back in. "I'll come see you before we leave for Savannah. In the meantime, make the inn your home. Stay as long as you need. I'm so glad you're here to keep Grandmother company. It will ease her transition, with me being gone."

Then, as word circulated that the bridal couple was about to leave, guests thronged around them, separating Mahala and Carolyn. The couple was making their way onto the porch. People were removing their shoes in the absurd tradition of throwing them at the departing pair.

George was beside Carolyn, saying, "Will you be all right, Mrs. Rousseau? I must go now."

"Of course! Quite all right." She was like a stray animal that had to be checked on – a piece of baggage to stow away somewhere. She urged him on with a smile. He hurried to his saddled stallion at the hitching post while guests peppered Jack and Mahala with boots and slippers. Jack shielded his bride and bravely took the brunt of it. As he helped Mahala into the carriage, however, a boot caught his jaw broadside, and he no longer looked amused. Glaring, he jumped into the vehicle and slammed the door. Only once the carriage pulled away from the inn did the pair venture a wave out the window.

Carolyn spied Dylan in the cheering throng. People crossed between them, laughing and hopping while they gamely retrieved their footwear. Now he would come talk to her, she thought, seeing her standing there alone.

But as she watched, a vision in ivory with bobbing long curls came between them, capturing Dylan's attention. Sylvie grabbed his arm and led him onto the porch, announcing brightly, as if she were the newly appointed hostess of the party, "We'll continue the dancing inside, ladies and gentlemen, with a Lancers Quadrille!"

Surely Dylan would excuse himself once he realized Sylvie meant to make them the head couple!

Compelled by her curiosity, Carolyn followed the guests as far as the entrance to the reception room, where sets of four couples were forming. Dylan and Sylvie stood at the front of the room, Sylvie speaking to the musicians. They gave the introduction to *La Dorset*. Carolyn watched in amazement as Dylan bowed to Sylvie. She dimpled and her eyes locked on his. Only with reluctance did she turn to curtsy to her corner. Then she slipped her gloved hand onto Dylan's and, his limp notwithstanding, they went forward and back to greet their opposites. Carolyn felt queasy. There was no doubting the message Jack's beautiful little sister was giving Carolyn's brother-in-law … and Carolyn.

She needed a moment alone. She considered going to her room, but Maddie probably had Dev there, and if he caught sight of her, she'd never get away. And she would need to be a mother. Instead she slipped out to the garden at the back of the inn, which she was fairly certain would be deserted. She was right. She sat on the bench and breathed deeply, fighting tears and asking herself why.

Jack had watched Mahala gaze anxiously out the window into the lengthening shadows for long enough.

"I'm sure George will spot any boogey men well before you do," he said. His cousin was riding point, uneventfully, just as he had expected.

"You ought not to make light of it, Jack. He's putting his life on the line for you."

Jack almost laughed at the seriousness with which his bride delivered this statement, but he caught himself in time. He guessed he ought to be gratified that she was that concerned for him.

"It's no laughing matter," she added, having noticed his near-lapse. "That man from Washington skeedadled home with a hole the size of a quarter in his hat!"

"Well, I have no intention of skeedadling anywhere, except home with you, Mrs. Randall, but that's right here and always will be. These people know me. They know what I did for the Confederacy, the business I have and will bring to this town. They would never try to *kill* me, Mahala."

He watched her face change, from slight embarrassment at his first sentence, to reluctant resignation at the last. "I surely hope you're right, Jack. People are just not themselves these days. There's so much hurt and anger."

"I didn't see any at our wedding, did you? And I shouldn't see any worry on my bride's face today of all days." At last, a slow smile was his reward. *God, you gave me a beautiful woman!* "Come 'ere."

Shyly she slid across the space between them.

He kissed her gently and traced the rouched, scooped neckline of her wedding dress until, just beneath it, he felt the puckered scar, reminder of the time he'd almost lost her, when she'd dove in front of the deserter's bullet to save him. "Besides," he added softly, "don't you think the odds are low for *both* of us getting shot – and within a year of each other?"

Mahala laughed in the husky way he loved. "I admit chances seem rather slim."

At that moment he felt the carriage turn into their driveway. Daft man had forgotten to stop as he had requested! Jack tapped impatiently on the ceiling, and the driver pulled up.

"What are we doing?" Mahala asked.

"There's something here I want you to see." Jack opened the door and handed her down. He saw that his relatives were riding ahead to make sure all was well at the house. Mahala was looking around in confusion. He took her hand and led her to the gate, turning her to face the estate. At first she did not notice anything new. Then her eyes lit on a handsomely wrought, iron sign on the right-hand pillar.

"What's this?" she gasped.

"The Highlands was full of bad memories, don't you think? This place needed a new name, one that is reflective of its owners." Jack paused and drew her close. "The way I see it, Mahala, we're both half-breeds – misfits. We've only ever partly belonged in any place we've ever lived. But together – in these foothills – we've finally come home."

Mahala gazed at him, moved beyond words by the truth of what he said. Then she met his lips with her own in an ever-deepening kiss. She wrapped her arms around his neck and slid her fingers into the brown hair curling at his neck. As they embraced, a slow and soft rain of yellow poplar leaves fluttered to the ground around them.

"I take it you aren't angry with me for changing the name," Jack whispered when they separated.

"No," Mahala replied, slowly shaking her head. "My days of being angry with you are over. Highlands Home. The name is perfect."

"Come then, and see your new house."

Once they were inside the carriage again, Mahala began, "About that, Jack … don't get me wrong. I'm dying to see every nook and cranny, but I wonder … I wonder if everything might not look best in the light of morning. That is, if your feelings wouldn't be hurt."

"My feelings?" He cleared his throat. "No. My feelings definitely would not be hurt."

The carriage stopped. George and Bryson rode circles around them. "All is fine, according to the housekeeper!" they cried. "Tally ho!"

"Thank you," Mahala called to them as Jack helped her to alight.

They waved at the men on horseback, who then spurred their mounts in a race to the main road.

Mahala looked around her. Jack had had people working day and night to get the old place fit for habitation. Brush had been cleared, leaves raked, furniture had gone in and out, dust had flown, and polish and paint had been applied. Now, the evening light fell tenderly across the white-washed Federal façade, and a lamp glowed cozily in the foyer. A lazy plume of smoke drifted from one chimney, scenting the autumn air with the welcome of hearth and home.

Mahala swallowed back tears and clasped her hands under her chin. "Oh, Jack, it's so beautiful!" she managed to say. "I still can't believe it's ours."

"Believe it." He extended his hand in invitation for her to climb to the porch.

The simple gesture seemed too much for her, for she began to cry. "It's like a dream," she said.

"It's not a dream."

At the top of the stairs, he opened the door and allowed his wife to behold the glowing wood and fresh paint inside. A bouquet of their wedding roses graced the entrance table. She started in, transfixed, but he put a hand on her elbow, then swept her up into his arms. He shut the door with his foot and looked down at her. "Still sure about seeing the house tomorrow?"

She smiled. "Very sure."

That said, he carried her up the stairs and straight to the room where he had first told her she would be his wife. The exchange there this night was infinitely more satisfying than before.

Meanwhile, Carolyn peered under a broad green speckled leaf, unable to believe her eyes. Of all the things to add insult to injury this day!

She jumped, straightening, when she heard a step. Dylan stood there, resplendent like the days of old in his navy morning coat and tan trousers, looking perplexed.

"What are you doing?" he asked.

He had found her! Had sought her out! And all she could think to say was, "Someone stole our pumpkin."

"What? You came out here looking for a pumpkin?"

"No, I came out here – I just came out here – and while I was sitting – there –" she pointed – "I noticed our biggest pumpkin was gone. That is, Maddie's biggest pumpkin. She had great plans for it ... pumpkin pies and cookies ..." Her voice trailed off. She sounded like an absolute fool.

"It's not surprising. People are having things stolen left and right."

"I guess we should have picked it before it was too late," she blurted, then wondered if her companion caught the irony in that double meaning. That reminded her of Sylvie. "What are you doing here? Surely you didn't have time to do all five Lancers? You didn't leave Sylvie without a partner, did you?" Oops. Things were going from bad to worse. Now he knew she had been watching him, and in addition to sounding like a fool, she looked like a jealous sixteen-year-old.

With a rush of realization, the truth dawned that she *had* been jealous! It had just been so long since she'd felt the emotion that she had failed to recognize it.

Emotions slipped over Dylan's face so fast she couldn't read them. He walked closer. "No. They did three ... the other two later. I had no intention of dancing, but ..."

91

She didn't want to hear how convincing Sylvie had been. "You always liked dancing," she said, making it clear that was all the reason she needed to know.

"I was going to ask you to dance."

Carolyn laughed, unsettled. "Fine spectacle that would have made."

"How would that have been a spectacle?" Dylan looked defensive. She had forgotten about the limp.

Carolyn spread her hands over her borrowed dress. "I'm in mourning, remember? It's enough that I attended a wedding. I doubt folks would smile on me dancing at it, too."

"Well – do you want to dance here? There's no one to see."

"What? No!"

He stood there a minute, looking at her. Unfortunately a mournful Irish waltz drifted from within the hotel, punctuating the perfect timing of his invitation. Her heart fluttered in indecision. Dance? She wasn't ready to dance! She wanted to run. But she knew if she did that it might be the last time. And part of her responded, despite her confusion.

Dylan's eyes narrowed. "Carolyn, are you angry with me?"

"No. Of course not."

"Then why are you acting this way?" As she stood there mute, a slow amazement spread over his face. "Are you jealous? Of Sylvie?" He started to laugh. He was enjoying this far too much. She shifted sullenly, unable to look at him, but unable to lie as well. "You *are* jealous!"

"Don't be rude," she snapped. "I know your mother taught you not to laugh at a lady."

He was instantly serious. "You're quite right. I'm sorry. I just can't believe it. Sylvie?"

"Why not Sylvie? You must admit she has many assets, and she fancies herself in love with you. Oh, don't look like you don't know it. And you can't say you never have thought about how an infusion of Randall money could put an end to all your struggles. And – well – seeing you with her – it did occur to me that perhaps – perhaps she would make you happy." She gulped. "That's all."

Dylan moved so fast she didn't have time to resist when he took her in his arms. He held her tight. "Oh, Carolyn. Thank God for Sylvie – if she's what it took. Yes, she has money, and beauty, and charm. But I don't care – because all my life I've loved one woman, and that's you. Why do you think that's changed? That it *could* change? You're the only one who knows me, who belongs at Forests of Green."

Carolyn felt the repressed tears loosen, and she couldn't stop them. She wept into Dylan's chest. He held her like he had on the farm, stroking her back, murmuring words of comfort. She was so ashamed. Would she ever stop falling apart in front of him, soaking up his support, and then putting him off? It had to stop. She couldn't imagine life without him. So … it was time to make her decision. As he wiped her tears away, she closed her eyes, angled her face, expecting him to kiss her – now *wanting* him to kiss her.

Instead he said, "But I think you're not ready."

"What?" Her eyes opened in shock.

"As much as I want you, I won't hurry you. It's clear you're still not ready. I competed with my brother all my life. I won't do it now, now that he's dead."

Her mouth fell open at his firm forthrightness.

He continued, "If you need more time, I'll wait. You don't have to worry about Sylvie Randall. Perhaps I should have a talk with her, set things straight."

Jealousy followed by being put away from him aroused a surprising determination within Carolyn. She wiped away the remainder of her tears and adjusted the ill-fitting dress. "You're wrong, Dylan. I don't need more time. I told you I would have an answer for you by October. It's October, and … well, I'll marry you. It's what I want. It's what you want. It's the best thing for everyone."

He stood silent before her, studying her a painfully long time. Where was the blazing joy she'd expected? "It's what you want?" he finally repeated.

"It's what I want."

"Why?"

Why? She looked askance at him. He *knew* all the reasons! Why was he being difficult, making her repeat them? It was awkward and embarrassing. She shifted to one foot. Then she knew the reason he wanted to hear. He didn't want a litany of his good qualities or their common ties. He didn't want to be told about her bond with Forests of Green or his bond with her son. He wanted to know that she loved him.

Oh, God forgive me … this is how Mahala felt with Clay, and I was so, so hard on her!

Carolyn swallowed. Her mind went back to the time when she had chosen between the two brothers. It had become clear after her marriage to Dev that he'd merely wanted to capture the prize. Winning his love had been the hardest thing she had ever done, and one of the most painful. Once she had it, though, it had been glorious. And the short taste of it had made his death all the more bitter. But – he had not necessarily been her first choice. The feelings for Dylan had been there long before Dev had given her a second glance. What would have happened if Devereaux had never interfered? Now was her chance to find out.

She stepped closer, traced the outline of Dylan's jaw with her fingers. Tears filled her eyes again at the thought of how she had hurt this man. Could she make it up now, years later?

"I want to marry you," Carolyn said, "because I love you."

Dylan closed his eyes, leaned his forehead against hers. He could kiss her now. She wanted him to, to show her he could wipe away the memory of other kisses. They were engaged. She had said the words he wanted to hear. But he again drew back, looking at her.

Carolyn took a breath, closed her eyes, and pressed her lips to his. He stiffened in surprise and clasped her elbows to hold her in place, but he did not deepen the kiss. It was a very chaste kiss as kisses went. She could tell little from it – except that he did not yet trust her. She drew back, jaded.

He tipped up her chin and searched her eyes. What was he looking for? Did he find it?

"A few months' engagement," he said. "Christmas. Will that do?"

Carolyn nodded. "Christmas will be fine."

That night she placed her neatly wrapped slice of bride's cake – cut thin enough to slide through a wedding ring – under her pillow. Silly, to expect that she might dream of her potential groom three nights in a row over a bunch of squished crumbs.

She dreamed of Devereaux.

CHAPTER SIX

At the close of the first week of October 1865, a chill breeze nipped through Clarkesville, scattering drought-dry leaves loose on the streets. As a carriage and two saddled horses waited, a party gathered in front of The Franklin Hotel. Martha Franklin came out, wiping her hands on her apron, and Carolyn Rousseau, holding her son. Jack and Dylan were busy stowing luggage as the women – Henrietta, Mahala, Sunny and Sylvie – said their farewells.

For Henrietta, little needed to be said. She and Dylan were traveling to Athens and back, though from the pinched look on her face one would think she had a long journey to dread. She had received a letter from her Savannah solicitor stating that in order to lay claim to The Marshes and oust the vagrants living there, she must sign the new loyalty oath. As for Dylan, it didn't matter. As a former Confederate officer, he was disenfranchised, his political rights suspended for who knew how long.

Dylan had elected to take his mother to Athens in the company of friends. The countryside was still full of drifters. They would return to Habersham by stage while the Randalls proceeded to Savannah.

Mahala clung to Martha and couldn't stop her tears. "I still wish you were going with us," she said. "I don't know what I'm going to do without you."

Martha was trying to be stoic, but Mahala saw the glint of tears in her eyes just the same. "Make that new husband of yours much happier than you would *with* me, that's what. He's your concern now, not me."

"You'll *always* be my concern!"

"I'll be all right. I have Carolyn here with me." Martha glanced at the blonde young woman standing nearby, saying her goodbyes to her new fiancé.

"I'm glad. But as soon as we return from Europe, I'll come home."

Martha kissed her and held her a long time. Finally she said in a throaty voice, "Go on with you, now."

Mahala blinked and turned to Carolyn. She saw Dylan kiss her cheek, then kiss Dev. Jr.. In the carriage, Sylvie looked the other way. As Dylan took his leave, Mahala moved to her friend and clasped her hands. She noted the misgiving in Carolyn's eyes as Dylan mounted his stallion.

"Don't worry – I'll keep the spider from spinning any more webs between here and Athens," Mahala whispered.

Carolyn laughed.

Dev Jr. clapped his hands. "Spider!" he yelled.

"Shh," Mahala told him, tweaking his button nose. The last thing she needed was for Sylvie to hear and punish her with silence all the way to Savannah.

"Oh, Mahala, you have the whole world before you." Carolyn's face was both wistful and happy.

Mahala smiled. Strange how after so many years the tables had turned. "Yes, but I don't leave you empty-handed."

"My world is here now."

"It's not a bad place to be."

"No, indeed not. Write and tell me of all your wonderful adventures, though, and you will brighten a long, cold winter."

Mahala squeezed her hands. "You know I will."

Despite the sorrow of goodbyes, Mahala's heart lightened as they left town. Jack rode out in front. She leaned out occasionally to see him – oh, so handsome in his brown morning coat, fawn breeches and polished boots. Beside him Dylan handled his mount with the ease of an experienced horseman. The men talked and gestured, easy in their companionship.

"Mr. Kollock took the Yankee oath last month," Henrietta said, as if to console herself. "I know I have no choice. None of us do. But it seems such a betrayal of our boys – of Dev, and Dylan, kept even from the right to vote, the right to hold his own land! What would we do if something happened to me now? Where would he be? And these very people – who would steal everything from us – to demand we bow the knee when they guarantee us no rights …"

Mahala reached out to pat Henrietta's hand, as she knew Carolyn would have done had she been there. "Mrs. Rousseau, you musn't work yourself up. You're doing what you must. So will Dylan."

Henrietta withdrew from her coolly enough that Mahala realized the older woman's initial outburst had been intended for the ears of the Randall women, not hers. Henrietta didn't say it out loud, but her look stated: *Easy for you to say.* Not to be put off, Mahala sat back, pretending ease as she signaled a change in subject. "How are your turnips doing, Mrs. Rousseau?"

Henrietta looked startled.

Sylvie's cough into her handkerchief sounded suspiciously like a snort of laughter.

They rode quietly for a ways after that. Mahala wished she was on horseback next to Jack, enjoying the cool fall day and better company. They had just passed the area known as Tom Paine's Post Office – a clearing where early settlers had stopped to trade for leather at the tanyard there, but best appreciated for the nearby whiskey still – and began the descent towards Hollingsworth when a shot rang out on the crisp air. Hunters, Mahala thought, not alarmed, because the sound was reasonably distant. She smiled when she thought of the buck Bryson had bagged two days before the wedding. He'd been so proud. Jack had hoped the experience would help lure him back again.

Then another shot sounded, and Mahala's hand flew to her breast, for this one was right next to the road! She heard Dylan and Jack yelling to each other and to the driver, who had stopped the vehicle. She pushed Sylvie aside and looked out the window.

Pop!

Both men had drawn their pistols, and Jack fired into the heavy woods beside them.

Bang!

Jack cried out, grabbed his arm. Mahala screamed his name and wrested open the carriage door.

"Go! Go!" Dylan was yelling to the driver, riding circles around Jack and firing off rounds. He had not noticed Mahala framed in the open door.

Bright red had appeared on the upper arm of Jack's coat. "Get in the carriage!" he bellowed, forcefully enough that she obeyed, gulping back a sob. As she did, she saw it: a movement behind a wide pin oak tree – a floppy gray hat as its owner scurried farther into the underbrush.

"Jack, it's Abel Quitman!" she tried to call, but the driver had gotten his horses to stop backing and rearing and start pulling together. She fell back against the seat, hard.

Henrietta was weeping.

"Who is Abel Quitman?" Sunny gasped. "A Yankee?"

"No," Mahala said, heart pounding. "He was a Confederate." And the only white Southerner with loyalties misguided and undying enough to lay an ambush for Jack. She didn't need to wait for the men to tell her that all the bullets fired from the woods had sought but one target.

Sylvie stood up on the lurching floor. She pounded her fists on the ceiling and yelled, "Stop this carriage! Stop this carriage this instant! Or you'll never work another day in Savannah."

The carriage stopped.

Sylvie swung open the door. The voice came from above: "Miss Sylvie, Mist' Jack says 'go.' What you doin'? You stay in that carriage! What if them bad men come this way?"

Unheeding, Mahala and Sylvie both climbed out, leaving Sunny to calm the hysterical Henrietta.

"Oh, my son! My only son!" she was wailing. "Lord, I can't stand it if he's taken from me, too!"

"Hush, Mama, I can't hear a thing!" Sylvie ordered.

Henrietta desisted on a gulping sob.

Denise Weimer

Mahala was about ready to go running down the road the way they'd come when she saw a rider come into view. Dylan! And – God be praised – Jack was right behind him! She and Sylvie hurried toward them.

"Jack!"

He was holding the reins in one hand. He drew up right beside her and slid down. Sylvie was there to take the reins from him as Mahala threw her arms around his middle, then tugged at his jacket. There was a lot of blood. "How bad are you hit?"

"It's o.k.. I'm just nicked. But we've got to get out of here quickly in case they circle back."

Dylan rode closer and took the reins from Sylvie, peering at Jack's wound. "That's more than a knick."

Unexpectedly, Jack started laughing, looking at Mahala. *"Déjà vu.* I think this road is cursed for us."

"Don't say that! Get in the carriage. We'll go back to town to the doctor."

"What, so they can finish me off? We'll go to Homer. Give me that horse."

"Don't be an idiot. Get in the carriage."

"Get in the carriage, man." Dylan looked at Jack firmly.

"Jack, please," Sylvie said.

"Homer," Jack told them.

"Raise your arm up and keep a tourniquet on it," Dylan instructed as Jack went with the women to the waiting vehicle. Dylan trotted his mount in the same direction and prepared to get down. Mahala realized he was going to tie Jack's horse to the rear of the carriage. "I'm going back," he announced. "See what I can find."

"Dylan, no!" Sylvie cried.

"And leave us unprotected?" Henrietta wailed from the carriage window.

"One against how many?" Jack questioned, turning to face Dylan with a glare. "Now who's being the fool?"

Mahala watched as Dylan considered, the hardened set of his square jaw testifying to his anger, his inner struggle. "Cowards!" he spat at last. "Scum! Have they no honor? To attack their fellow citizens – with women along! We can't just let them skulk away and do this again!"

"We won't," Mahala said. "I know who it was -- at least, one of them. A man angry at me and Jack for turning in my cousin Leon. We can talk with the sheriff in Homer. He can see that word goes out."

Dylan wanted to fight. That much was clear. Yet Mahala saw the anger in his eyes wax, then bank. It did not fit with the picture of the calm, easy-going minister Carolyn had once described. But at last he growled and nodded, saying, "Let's get going, then. You're bleeding like a stuck pig."

Henrietta had stopped sobbing when she had ascertained that her son was unharmed. But when Jack removed his coat and got into the vehicle, she began to carry on again about the amount of blood.

"If you would please give us your scarf, Aunt Henrietta, maybe it wouldn't be so bad," Sylvie stated sharply.

Mahala gave her a quick look of gratitude for her presence of mind. She took the cloth and wrapped it tightly around Jack's left arm above the wound, which she had ascertained through the torn shirt to be a sizeable gash – certainly not life-threatening if tended soon, but loss of too much blood was always a cause for concern. She took a lap blanket from under the seat and draped it over her own shoulders.

"Put your arm around me," she ordered.

"Please, my dear!" Jack said in tones of feigned shock.

She sighed and reached for his hand, gently raising his arm until he winced but complied. He slouched beside her then, any jesting spirit gone, his mood growing darker as they lurched their way out of Habersham. If she thought about the ambush, she would soon be in a similar frame of mind. But all she could concentrate on was getting her husband to a doctor.

By the time they reached Homer, Jack's attention was beginning to drift. They pulled up outside Dr. Parker's practice as Mahala directed. She was almost tempted to seek help elsewhere due to the embarrassing questions their reappearance in such a state would raise, but she had liked Mrs. Parker, who had tended her own gunshot wound from a deserter's bullet the year before.

Jack was wobbly on his feet. Mahala and Dylan rushed to support him.

The door was opened to their knock by a dignified-looking man of about fifty. Mrs. Parker appeared behind him, her eyes widening as she took them in.

"Dr. Parker?" Mahala questioned. "Hello, Mrs. Parker. It seems we again require your assistance."

To his credit, the doctor did not voice the question his face reflected. Instead he ushered them into his surgery. But as he set about cleaning Jack's wound and preparing to sew stitches, Mrs. Parker could not restrain her own curiosity.

"Who did this? The same man who troubled you before?"

Mahala bit her lip, uncertain how Jack would have her respond.

"Different men," Jack answered through stiff lips. "Drifters."

"Plenty of those about," Dr. Parker mumbled, pulling the thread through Jack's flesh.

Mahala looked away.

"Still, what luck you've had," Mrs. Parker said, then proceeded to tell her husband about their previous meeting, when Jack, Mahala and Carolyn had fled Sherman's descent upon Savannah. "It's a shame when one can no longer travel the Old Federal Highway in peace. Where were you set upon?"

"Near Hollingsworth," Mahala replied. "We're on our way to Savannah."

"We'd like to make it to Athens tonight," Jack announced. "Just as soon as you finish and I again visit your sheriff."

"No chance of that, young man. You're the color of a sheet of paper. You'll spend the night here, where you can get a good night's sleep after Mrs. Parker gets you full of broth to thicken up your blood."

"It would be best if my husband sees you again in the morning," Mrs. Parker told Jack. "*Then* you can see the sheriff. The rest of your party will have no trouble finding accommodations at the hotel."

"I'd like my wife to stay here, if you have room," Jack replied.

Mrs. Parker raised her eyebrows. A smile crossed her face. "Of course. We can make up the guest room you used before." She winked at Mahala. "I see the accommodations were so good the week you became engaged you just had to return for your honeymoon!"

Mahala helped Mrs. Franklin set a fire in the bedroom to chase away the evening's chill, then offered to assist with dinner preparations.

"Indeed, no," the woman said. "I was thinking of putting on a beef stew anyway. Please just rest. If your husband feels up to it, you can join us at table like proper company. It will be nice."

Mahala knew such treatment went well beyond what was professionally expected. She spoke her gratitude and only hoped that their payment in greenbacks would do the rest.

That night, after a meal at which Mahala had to hold up their end of the conversation due to Jack's unnatural moroseness, Mahala climbed into bed next to her husband. He lay facing the other way, his weight on his good shoulder. She put an arm around his waist and snuggled against his warmth, delight filling her – as it had every night since their wedding – at sharing a bed with him, despite his injury.

"Does it hurt much?" she asked.

"Only smarts a little. We should have ridden on."

"Nonsense. You didn't need to be on horseback all afternoon. In fact, I think you ought to ride in the carriage tomorrow."

When there was no reply, Mahala knew he was going to be stubborn. After a long silence, Jack asked, "Do you think they were really trying to kill me – or just tell me to stay away?"

Mahala thought a long moment. "I don't know."

"*Why* would they do it? How long have I lived and worked among them? And yet they still see me as an outsider – a Yankee."

Mahala's chest tightened at the rare sound of hurt in Jack's voice. She knew this incident touched on pain from his past. Incident? Too light a word. Someone had shot him. Trying not to give into the dismay and alarm that fact aroused, she said softly, "It was Abel Quitman."

He pointed out what she had left unsaid. "There were others with him."

Mahala stroked his hair and leaned up to kiss his cheek.

"You know what this means," Jack added, "unless all those men are apprehended."

"Yes," she whispered, feeling tears rise to the surface. "It may be a long time before we can go back home."

There was a man in a Confederate great coat sitting on the steps of the church across the street. That was not surprising, as many impoverished ex-soldiers had chosen to remove their military buttons and wear the garments, though other military articles had been denied them. But Sylvie pressed her face closer to the wavy glass of her upstairs hotel room. The man was Dylan.

She glanced back over her shoulder. Her mother and Henrietta were already asleep in the bed. Sylvie swung a cloak about her shoulders, put up the hood, and exited the room, stepping around the trundle bed meant for her.

The street was deserted, but if Dylan saw her coming, her hem stirring up dry leaves, he gave no sign. He said nothing even when she stood in front of him.

"Are you all right?"

When he raised his head, she realized his eyes had been closed. What if she had interrupted his prayers?

But he didn't chide her, merely looked at her.

She decided on another question. "The church wasn't open?"

"No."

"It's pretty." Presbyterian, his denomination.

"Yes." Another pause, then he asked, "Are the others asleep?"

"Yes."

"Why aren't you?"

It sounded like a rebuke. She sat down beside him to show she wasn't going anywhere. "My mind was too busy, so I sat by the fire a while. Then, I decided to come out here." Hoping he'd assume she'd merely sought some fresh air, she chose not to mention she had only come out to see him. "That was quite a bit of excitement today."

"Mm."

"You were very brave."

He turned his face to her and searched hers incredulously, almost with disgust. "That was nothing," he finally said.

"I realize that after the war it must seem so. I'm sure you faced much more galling circumstances in battle – but to me, what happened this morning was quite enough."

"Yes," Dylan said. "It *was* quite enough. But please, Miss Randall, don't make me out to be some sort of hero. I'm not a hero."

"If you aren't, who is?"

"You wouldn't say that if you really knew me now. War changes people – for the worse. Changes them until they don't even know themselves anymore."

"I know what you are. Loyal. Dependable. And brave – yes – as brave now about the future as you were about battle."

"Is that what you think?" Dylan sat up, removing his arms from his legs and resting his feet on the ground. "'Cause you got it all wrong. I had no idea what I was doing going into battle, and I have no idea what I'm doing now, and frankly I'm scared spitless. Do you admire that?" He stood up. "I'm going in."

Sylvie stood reluctantly, not yet willing to let the conversation go, not when he was being so open with her. That counted for something, didn't it? "At least you're honest. I think a lot of people are scared now."

"What do you know? The war didn't even touch you, except for maybe an occasional twinge of worry for Jack as he dashed about on the high seas. Thanks to him, you didn't even have to sacrifice your pretty dresses. And your other brothers were right there in Savannah for most of the war."

Tears filled Sylvie's eyes at the sudden attack, and when she spoke, her voice wobbled. "Why are you saying that?"

"To try to rid you of your romantic notions of me, and anybody else like me. Take my word for it. You have no idea what suffering is. So please, don't try to understand me."

"I'm just trying to reach out to you. I can tell you're hurting. You may think that Carolyn has suffered, and that makes her like you. But even Carolyn doesn't have any idea what you're going through. It's easy to see that. But you don't have to go on like you are now. It doesn't have to be bleak and hopeless and hard."

He didn't pretend not to know what she was talking about. "I'm not looking for any handouts or even any sympathy, Miss Randall. Fall or rise, I'll do it on my own. Thank you for caring, though. It does you credit. Now, you really ought not to be out here alone. Let me walk you in."

"Caring? Is that what you think this is? You idiot! You can't even call me Sylvie! Why can't you call me Sylvie?" she cried, her anger at last coming to the fore. She was making a fool of herself, but she didn't care. She wouldn't lose her last chance to let him know how she felt. She wanted to grab him, to shake him, to force him to hold her, and then he'd see – then he'd feel. But his next words extinguished any remaining hope.

"I'll call you Sylvie if you wish, but only because you're the cousin of the one soon to be my wife." Looking down at her, Dylan must have seen the shock and pain she couldn't hide, for his face and tone gentled, and he extended his arm. "Please – let me take you inside."

"I'll take myself."

The fool! How could he not want her, want all she offered? He deserved to fail, and she hoped he did.

Sylvie half turned, ready to march back to the hotel, but Dylan's voice stopped her.

"Miss Randall – Sylvie – I'm sorry if I've hurt your feelings. It just goes to show that what I'm saying is true. I can no longer always say the perfect thing – say things I don't mean. Life just isn't like that anymore. It's not some game where we dress up and use our manners and everything is perfect. That world is gone – at least for me. But you – you're young. Untouched. You're fortunate. You still have your idealism. Hold onto it. Hold onto it, and find some young man equally untouched who can make life what you want it to be."

She stood frozen for a minute, feeling the dagger of his words pierce her heart. Then she hurried away.

She tiptoed up the darkened stairs and entered the bedroom where both of their mothers slept. She had to be quiet, to hold in the pain. She hadn't even the comfort of tears. She undressed and lay in the darkness, staring into nothing with burning eyes.

She didn't really want him to fail. She wanted him to want her, and together, for them to make a good life together. She knew what kind of man Dylan was – knew better than Carolyn, blind with her continuing devotion to her dead husband – knew better than Dylan thought, than all the people thought who assumed her to be silly and simple. But he would marry Carolyn, and she would have no one – because she wouldn't settle for less – and there was nothing she, wealthy, spoiled Sylvie Randall, could do about it.

The mellow glow of evening had faded to dark when Max Reed entered the kitchen, kicking the big orange cat out of the way. It was a gentle kick, not enough to hurt the animal, for Max was rather fond of the old mouser, but enough to remind him to keep the path clear. Max had been at Highlands Home for three months. Before that he'd worked at The Palace. Since Jack Randall was closing up the hotel, and he'd been impressed with Max's work, he had hired him to help clean up Highlands Home's grounds and keep them looking nice, and hired his wife Callie to do the same for the house. The master had put in plenty of hours himself. Between the three of them, Max would say they'd done a right good job. The new Mrs. Randall must have thanked them a dozen times. It was clear she loved the place so much she was somewhat loathe to leave it, even for Europe. And as for Max, he was pleased he and Callie would have a snug home over the winter while the newlyweds were on their honeymoon. When lots of Negro couples were struggling to find jobs in the city or still working like slaves on plantations, they couldn't do much better. He knew he had a good thing with Mr. Randall. So good that Jack's warning for him to keep an eye out for Abel Quitman's vagabonds did not scare him one whit. He'd do what he needed to to keep the place safe.

Callie was bending over the fireplace, stirring their supper. Soup and cornbread sure smelled good.

"Got the hogs fed?" she asked.

"Yep."

"You washed up?"

"Yep."

She put dinner on the table, and they ate right there next to the warm fire. They had married during the war, and Callie was expecting. Living here in this big house, just the two of them, was rather like a honeymoon of their own, too.

Their quiet conversation was interrupted when Callie froze, her gaze going over Max's shoulder to the yard and the trees beyond. "Max, I thought I saw somethin' move out there."

The hairs on the back of Max's neck tickled. "You sure?"

"Pretty sure."

He got up and reached for the gun above the mantle. He kept it loaded.

"Torches, Max! They's men with torches out there!" Callie cried.

"Stay inside, woman. And git down."

Late October 1865
Savannah, Georgia

Mahala frowned at the explosion of hats, shawls, dresses and shoes on the bed. She still felt guilty when she looked at them. In addition to the few dresses she had purchased with her own money when previously in Savannah, Jack had licensed Sylvie to take Mahala out this month to buy much more. Several dressmakers had just completed their frantic ministrations, and their creations had arrived today. Mahala had been forced to swallow her pride and visit only the city's native elite *modistes* – even the one who had snubbed her before – for Jack insisted that they should not patronize the new Yankee shops. Everything they did, every penny they spent, Jack assured her would be noted by Savannah society.

Sylvie turned a dinner dress inside-out and huffed. "This is not properly finished. I know it was a rushed job, but *my word*. The way she's left it, it will surely fray."

"It looks beautiful to me."

"That just shows how badly you need my expertise."

Despite Sylvie's frequent hints about accompanying them to Europe, unlike Martha, she had not been invited. Since their return to Savannah, Mahala had grown concerned over a sensitivity that her new sister-in-law's bravado couldn't quite mask. She felt sure it wasn't all about Europe. No, something had happened on the trip from Clarkesville, something she didn't know about, despite her promise to Carolyn to be watchful.

"Will you be all right while we're gone, Sylvie?" Mahala asked gently.

Sylvie glanced at her. "You don't think you can talk Jack into letting me go?"

Mahala bit her lip. "I'm sorry," was all she knew to say. An awkward moment came as silence fell. Mahala realized that Sylvie was not used to anyone having more influence over her half brother than she. "I don't want you to think I'm coming between you, Sylvie. You've talked to Jack yourself, and, well, you know he makes his own decisions."

"Yes, I know. It's not your fault."

Mahala smiled and put a hand on Sylvie's sleeve. "Jack loves you very much. There will be other trips."

"Of course."

Feeling the strain, Mahala took a breath and tried to change the subject. She looked back at the clothes on the bed. "It just seems like an awful waste of money at a time like this."

"No, indeed. A woman of station must not be seen in the same dress twice in one social circle. You'll have to do more shopping in Paris. And what you will get there – ha! – will put all these garments to shame."

Horse hooves sounded in front of the house, and Mahala ran to the window to look out. "Jack's home!"

Sylvie rolled her eyes. "I'll make myself scarce. Nothing like invading the nest of two love birds."

"Thank you for your help, Sylvie."

"My pleasure," Sylvie said wryly as Mahala hurried out of the room.

She hastened down the steps and met Jack on the landing, flying into his arms for a hug and kiss.

"Miss me?" Jack chuckled.

"Outrageously. How are things at the foundry?"

Denise Weimer

"All arranged for our tour tomorrow. Are you ready for our departure the day after?"

"Almost. I don't know how I'm ever going to get everything into the luggage."

Jack wrapped an arm around her and led her upstairs. "Leave that to the maid. I have something for you. Letters from home." He reached into his jacket and produced a thick envelope.

"Oh! News from Clarkesville! At last!"

At the door of their room, Jack stopped and said, "Good heavens."

"I told you! I'll clear a spot and you can rest while I read what they've written." Mahala hastened to do so. When Jack sat on the bed, preparing to swing his legs up, she stopped him. "What are you thinking? Take those boots off."

"Yes, Ma'am." Jack looked at her with a twinkle in his eye.

Finally he stretched out with a sigh while she slit the envelope, perching beside him. Mahala unfolded the note in her friend's fine, neat script first. After a minute of silent reading, she said, "All is well with Carolyn. She especially thanks us for arranging a room at the Commercial Hotel in Athens Christmas week. Oh, Jack, I'm so glad you thought of that. I felt so bad I won't be there for her wedding – but this is a perfect present. I know they could not afford it otherwise, and she felt she didn't know my friend Patience well enough to impose." Jack grunted. Mahala paused while her eyes ran down over the page. She resumed, "Dylan is sowing the wheat. She doesn't see him as often as she would like. He's come into town on the weekends to take her out driving, and once she went to dinner at Forests of Green. Things are fine at the hotel, but she says Grandmother has important news in her letter. I wonder what that could be."

"Maybe it's about Quitman."

Mahala hurried to open Martha's letter. "They must have written about the same time," she said, looking at the dates. "Yes, this does seem to be about Quitman! She says, 'the sheriff from Homer wrote to the law in Clarkesville regarding what happened. Our sheriff paid us a call and said there just wasn't enough evidence to arrest Quitman. According to him, there are too many floppy gray hats out there. It could have been anyone.' Oh, Jack! I can't believe it! They're really going to do *nothing*, after that man shot you?"

"Perhaps they're afraid of getting on the wrong side of that particular group of ex-Confederates." Jack's expression was controlled. "Go on. Anything else?"

"Yes. 'We were mighty disturbed after that, feeling that no citizen and no property was safe with the likes of those vigilantes riding around acting out on personal vendettas. And it seems we were right. You won't be-

106

lieve what happened next. But first let me tell you, Mahala, *everything is all right now*. However, a couple days ago Jack's groundsman Max came into town for the sheriff. Seems he had two men out on the property he'd shot and killed. Quitman's ruffians had come upon the house after nightfall with torches, apparently set on burning down your home.'"

Mahala dropped the letter and clutched her heart. Jack sat up, grabbing up the paper. She waited for him to read more while she struggled to breathe. She gasped, "Did they burn it, Jack – any of it?"

"No," he said. "It's all right, Mahala. Max shot the men before they could succeed in igniting the porches. Thank God. Remind me to send him a hefty Christmas bonus."

"And the other men?"

"Scattered. He rode to the neighbors for help after they left, leaving Callie to stand guard."

"Poor woman! How terrified she must have been."

"Yes. The sheriff got up a posse and tracked Quitman and the man who fled with him to the Unicoi Road. It would appear they're long gone."

"Yes, but for *how* long?"

Jack looked at her regretfully. "That I don't know. We can only hope – for good."

Mahala started to cry. "Hoping isn't good enough. What if he comes back? He could come back at any time and finish what he started. When will it ever be safe? Even if Max saw Abel Quitman's face, Abel could return without any fear. A black man cannot testify against a white."

Jack gathered her into his arms. "Don't cry. Don't assume the worst. I really don't think he hates us that much that he would come back just to do us in. I think he's just angry and looking for a target, and we happened to make a convenient one. He'll probably move on and find trouble somewhere else."

"You weren't right before," Mahala muttered petulantly.

"Look on the bright side," he said. His famous words made her roll her eyes. "Max and Callie are all right. The house is all right. Two of the gang are dead, and the other two are gone. We have to trust this is the end of it."

Mahala wiped her face. Suddenly she realized Jack had to believe that, or he would find the continued attack on his character more than he could stand. She nodded. They did have to believe it was over, that by the time they returned from Europe, they could safely go home.

"Your nose is red, and your eyes are puffy," Jack told her, cupping her head in his hands and kissing the offending areas. "What a sight you'll make at dinner." He kissed her mouth, and she sensed his need. "I'm ready to leave it all," he whispered, a trace of anger threading the desire in his voice. "All of it. For it to be just you and me for a long, long time."

She flushed with expectant warmth as his fingers tugged open the top hook on her bodice. Ever since their wedding night she'd never once regretted that Jack was the only man she'd ever taken to bed.

"How long 'til dinner, anyway?"

Mahala pushed forward until he fell back on the pillow. "Long enough."

Ella Beth had thought that Sylvie would help her endure this night. They had both lost the men they wanted. Just knowing someone else was suffering like she was would have strengthened her when she had to make pleasant conversation – had to look at the happy couple at this, their farewell dinner. She had expected Jack's sister to be quiet and withdrawn. But no! Sylvie was animated and vivacious, though Ella Beth thought she detected a barb to her wit, an almost frantic need to seem gay. The girl appeared determined to engage the conversation of the man on her left – Daniel O'Keefe – as if in exclusion of the man on her right – Andrew Willis. Both guests were rather irregular. The Randalls had taken a tour of the foundry that day. It was set to open on Monday. Jack had been so pleased with the manner in which O'Keefe had readied the facility and hired workers in his absence that he had decided to honor the man with an invitation to the going-away dinner. He said he deemed it the perfect opportunity to introduce his foreman to his family. Likewise, his right-hand man at Randall and Ellis Shipping had been included.

Sylvie was annoying her, like the buzzing of a bee or the whirring of a hummingbird in a tranquil garden setting. She sat in the middle of the two men, looking like the center of the pendulum – Willis appearing anxious, fidgeting with his tie and silverware; O'Keefe at ease, slightly reclined and waxing eloquent on the topic most familiar to him.

"Oh, you should have come along, Ella Beth," Sylvie insisted. "It was so educational. Really we all ought to know what the men in our family are up to – so Mahala and I said. Mr. O'Keefe was so obliging, to meet us at Broughton Street and give us a tour. He explained everything in such a way that even I could not fail to understand. You would not be adverse to telling Mrs. Draper a little bit about the operation of the foundry, would you, Mr. O'Keefe?"

The dark-haired young man glanced at Ella Beth. She covered her dismay in time. "I would be short a shillin' if I believed you fine ladies truly wished to hear the details of such a trade."

"No indeed, Mr. O'Keefe," Ella Beth interjected. "I would be fascinated to learn more about the operation of a rolling mill."

"As would I," Andrew Willis added, leaning forward to see past Sylvie.

She made no effort to adjust her posture for him.

"Very well, then," Daniel said. "In the foundry, basically, we have several single puddling furnaces. We do what we call 'pig boiling' – or, to say it proper, wet puddling."

Ella Beth raised her brows. It all sounded like another language to her. Against her will, she glanced at Jack, seeking clarification.

"It's the process by which pig iron is changed to wrought iron," he explained. Why did he have to be so handsome? "Pig iron contains impurities – silicon, sulphur, phosphorus – which make it brittle – breakable. Boiling the iron at the right temperature to remove these impurities requires both strength and skill."

"Oh," she said, studying her leg of mutton. She delicately picked off a bite. Ella Beth looked back at Daniel O'Keefe. He had been waiting patiently to continue. "So you just heat the iron in the furnaces?"

"Six hundred pounds of pig iron goes into a single hearth, the fires of which are stoked to a perfect pitch by the puddler's boy. We have to be rid of the phosphorus and sulfur ahead of the carbon. The iron turns to slag and flames break through. When the carbon bubbles out, the slag pours out over the hearth and is taken away in a cart. Then the puddler starts to stir, and stirs almost half an hour straight with a big paddle. It's like the biggest, hottest pot of soup you ever saw. The iron will eventually sponge up and has to be balled into three loaves – the orneriest loaves you ever saw. Each one weighs two hundred pounds."

"How do you know when you've got them to the proper size?" Grace Ellis asked.

O'Keefe shrugged. "Like a cook knows how much salt to put in a recipe – or a lady knows just where to pin a flower to her dress." He winked at Sylvie.

She giggled. "Then you take the loaves out with the huge tongs you showed us – and off they are wheeled to the squeezer. Right, Mr. O'Keefe?"

Daniel bestowed one of his dimpled, charming smiles upon her. "You were an attentive pupil, Miss Randall."

"Why, thank you!"

In placing a hand at her breast in a gesture of dramatic gratitude, Sylvie's napkin fell to the floor. Andrew Willis retrieved it for her, and she took it without thanks.

Daniel continued, "From the squeezer a river of lava pours onto the floor. The sponge left is white hot and goes to the rolling machine. At last, iron bars emerge from the different sizes of rollers – and the process is done."

"But it's all done with a terrific roar and lots of clanking and whirring and terrible heat," Sylvie put in. "Jack said that was why we ladies would not enjoy a tour when the foundry was operating – besides the fact that it would not be safe with our long dresses."

"I can imagine," Ella Beth murmured. She looked at Daniel O'Keefe. "It sounds like very hard work. What made you undertake it?"

He paused with fork in midair, thinking. Then he swallowed and said, "Many a thatch and daub cottage I saw tumbled like matchsticks when its owner was in o'rear of rent back in Ireland, Mrs. Draper. Perhaps it was somethin' in that memory that made me want to make a lastin' material. Think on it. What we build – the ships, the railroads, the fancy tall buildings – they will outlive us, eh, Mr. Randall?" O'Keefe gestured at Jack, who nodded. "It's man conquering nature. We do it, ladies, because we can."

Ella Beth was surprised that a common worker could be so eloquent, in his own way.

"To man conquering nature," Jack called out, raising his glass.

"Hear, hear!" Daniel agreed.

Everyone raised their glasses and clinked them together.

"Wait – I have one," Sunny chimed in. Her face took on the shine of sweet memory, then she smiled at Mahala, who blushed with her next words. "To woman conquering man!"

A warm eruption of knowing laughter followed her toast. More clinking. Ella Beth could not bear to watch Jack and Mahala, who were smiling, their eyes locked on each other adoringly.

"So tomorrow you depart for New York, Jack?" Grandmother Ellis asked. "And then on to Europe! Share with us the cities you will visit."

Ella Beth had to look away from them, or she wouldn't be able to hide her dismay. She glanced somewhere, anywhere else. In the process, her gaze stumbled onto the Irishman sitting across from her. Daniel O'Keefe was looking at her, and his face reflected a surprise which he then veiled in a faint, almost sad smile.

CHAPTER SEVEN

December 1865
Habersham County, Georgia

Two weeks 'til her wedding, and Carolyn was happy. Happy because today she was at Forests of Green, and it felt like home. Her nose was cold and her fingers stiff as she squeezed the handle of the cutters until the bough of evergreen snapped off. She bent and picked it up, adding it to her big basket.

Her cloak dragged a denuded branch, and she detached it with an impatient swish as she headed toward a wild holly tree. She smelled wood smoke on the cool, still air, spied a cardinal flitting ahead of her, and hummed a Christmas carol. Stopping when crunching leaves signaled footsteps behind her, she turned to behold her intended, bringing along the basket she had left. He wore old clothes, the coat straining on his shoulders.

"Ah, good," Carolyn said. "You can help me. See that branch, up there? The one with all the berries? Can you pull it down for me?" Dylan obliged, and she reached high with her cutters. Not quite high enough. He took them from her and lopped off the branch. "Thank you. All done with your chores for the day?"

Dylan nodded.

"Shall I make us some cider? You can relax while your mother and I decorate the house."

"That sounds good. I'd like to spend some time with Devie before you go. The house seems so empty without him."

Carolyn glanced up at him, smiling. "Not for long."

He did not respond with the expected anticipation. A cloud seemed to pass over his features. "I need to talk to you, Carolyn."

"Now's a good time," she replied, trying not to show her misgivings as she set out toward the house.

He followed. "I met with the workers yesterday. Told them I went into town and took the proceeds of the crop to the mill. I was able to sell just enough to pay back the lender from Athens – to cover the up-front cost for the workers, and some supplies I got when I first came home. There was nothing left over. We have barely enough for us to live on through the winter."

"Enough to feed the workers, too?"

"Enough to feed them, maybe. Not enough to sell to pay them the cash they wanted."

"But you promised them!" Carolyn didn't mean for the statement to sound accusing, but in her dismay, it came out that way. And the tightening expression on Dylan's face was instant.

"There was nothing to be done about it, Carolyn. It was a poor crop – nobody's fault."

"I know, Dylan. Were they angry?"

"They seemed to think I had cash squirreled away somewhere. They just can't believe the Rousseaus aren't made of money, I guess. They questioned me about half an hour – the same questions over and over. I just kept telling them I had no cash – not for us, not for them – that I could only pay them with a portion of the crop. And that was shameful little."

"Oh, Dylan." Carolyn paused and reached for his free hand. Her glove slid over its bare roughness. "Did they agree?"

"I broke the contract, dishonored my word as a gentleman. But I couldn't help it. I think finally they realized that, though I fear I've lost their respect."

"But they haven't left, have they?"

"Not yet. I think they'll stay for the winter. I tried to convince them jobs were bound to be scarce in the cities, and at least here they had a guarantee of shelter and food."

"It's true," she said. "You told them the truth. They are better off here."

"I suppose. By spring, though, I expect they'll still leave."

There was such humility in his once-proud face she couldn't stand to look on it longer. They were near the hog pen. The half-pink, half-dirt-streaked animal within – which she had hidden from the Yankees when necessary – rooted among the scraps Dylan had thrown to him earlier that afternoon. "At least the hog is fat."

"I've been feeding him with the unmarketable squash and pumpkins and potatoes, like the *Cultivator* recommended. We'll need to slaughter him when we return from Athens."

"The meat will help us make ends meet next year," Carolyn agreed. "A local farmer's wife showed me how to process it last year. I can do it again. The salted meat from last March is very low."

Dylan squeezed her hand. "Carolyn – what I meant to tell you was – it's going to be lean, hog or no hog. To be fair, you and Dev Jr. would be better off in town, if Mrs. Franklin views your help and companionship as an even exchange for room and board."

Carolyn withdrew from his grasp. Her heart had started a heavy thudding. "What are you saying?"

"I'm offering to postpone the wedding."

112

"What? No! Why would I agree to that? Don't you remember how I worked and helped? You think I'm a stranger to hardship – that I'm afraid of it?"

"I think maybe you should be afraid of hunger. As much as it shames me to admit it, that's a real possibility. I'm just trying to do what's best for you and Dev Jr.."

"Well, you're not! We'd pull our own weight, if that's what you're worried about–"

"It's not."

But she was too upset to hear him. "I'm just so tired of not belonging anywhere. Don't you see I'd rather have my belly empty here than be full and lonely there? What about for better or worse, richer or poorer? You're just like everybody else – ready to throw us over when we're an inconvenience. " Carolyn shoved the cutters at him, whirled and stomped toward the house. She heard him coming after her and threw over her shoulder, "I'll take my son and go back to my parents!"

"You will not! Stop, Carolyn."

She ran up the steps of the front porch with full intentions of finding her son and packing. "Devie!" she called him.

Dylan grabbed her arm and swung her around. "Wait."

"What kind of man goes back on his proposal?" Carolyn asked on a sob. She was shocked by the strength of her own reaction. She felt tears of betrayal ease out of her eyes.

"One who loves you very much." Dylan pulled her to him and smothered her in a tight embrace, so tight she could hardly breathe, holding her middle, her head, putting his mouth on hers in a way he never had before. But then, they'd hardly been alone since his proposal. The closeness and taste of him began to break through her wall.

When she had a chance to speak she whispered, "If you love me so much – why are you so willing to let me go?"

"I'm not! I was truly trying to do what was best for you, but I didn't know – I didn't know you felt that way."

He kissed her again, hard, his mouth crushing hers, parting her lips. She shuddered and went limp in his arms. And she had wondered if there could be passion between them! It was true, she didn't know him, not anymore, and the thought both excited and terrified her. But she did know this ... the idea of him pulling away from her had terrified her more.

"Unc'lyn!"

The cry came from the landing along with a muffled "Good heavens!" from Henrietta, who held a struggling Dev Jr. in her arms.

Carolyn broke away and turned ten shades of red.

Henrietta started to turn and go back up, but Dylan, unruffled, said, "It's all right, Mother. Just kissing my bride-to-be. Let him come on down."

"Kissing," Henrietta huffed. "That looked awfully close to ravishing to me." But she released the wiggling toddler, who repeated his greeting of "Unc'lyn" and started down the steps on his bottom. Ignoring his mother, Dylan grinned and swung the baby up into the air.

"Me hug!" Dev cried.

"Hey, little one! Of course you can have a hug. Want to build with your blocks while Mama and Grandma decorate for Christmas?"

Carolyn trailed them awkwardly up to the front door.

"Unc'lyn help."

As Dylan took the child off to the nursery, Henrietta put her hands on her hips. "Well? Where are the trimmings?"

Carolyn couldn't look at her. "The trimmings? Oh! I guess we left them outside." She blushed again and hurried back out the door. If she didn't know better, she could have sworn she heard Henrietta laughing as she went down the porch steps.

When the time came for the wedding, the Rousseau party spent the night at the hotel in Homer to allow a more restful journey and an earlier afternoon arrival at their destination. When they finally arrived in Athens, Carolyn was taken aback by the number of Union troops present there, and she could tell from his stiff posture Dylan was, too. He kept a sharp eye out as they drove into town in the buggy and pulled up in front of the three-story Commercial Hotel at College Avenue and Broad Street, built in the 1840s by E.L. Newton. A balcony extended from part of the edifice on the second story. Since commercial shops and a saloon were housed on the bottom floor, Carolyn and Henrietta waited while Dylan made arrangements with the hostler. Henrietta's maid, Lydia, held Dev Jr., who was pop-eyed at being surrounded by so much activity. Across the way they noted the arch and three columns – representing wisdom, justice and moderation – constructed at the entrance to Franklin College. The arch had been put in place to keep stray animals off campus, but it was quite attractive as well.

Suddenly a sharp cry barked out: "Clear the sidewalk!"

Carolyn looked in the direction from which the order had issued to see a contingent of infantrymen marching swiftly their way. She noticed that a burly sergeant had been the one to speak. The next moment a hand seized her elbow, and the sergeant set her down from the boardwalk with the hissed words, "Pardon, Ma'am, but you are about to be trampled."

Dylan was at her side like lightning, taking her other arm with a glare at the sergeant that could have melted steel. "Get your hand off the lady."

"Easy, son," the man said before turning and marching alongside the tail of his column. He tossed over his shoulder, "Watch out for your women better next time."

For a moment Carolyn thought her fiancé would jump on the soldier's back. She put a hand on his arm. "Please. It's all right."

"It's *not* all right. Noncommissioned upstart scum – coming down here and strutting about, saying what they want, doing what they want, and getting away with it." He cursed under his breath.

Carolyn stared at him. She was so astonished at Dylan using profanity – the first time she had ever heard him do so – that she was rendered speechless. The Dylan she remembered had been humble, never throwing around his wealth or position, considering all men equal under God. Now that wealth and position were gone, and circumstances made those who were once powerful less than equal, was humility gone, too? Replaced by anger and resentment? It was one of the many changes in Dylan she was only now discovering. *He needs me now more than ever*, she realized.

Dylan was instantly penitent at the sight of their shocked faces. "Sorry," he whispered. But Carolyn noticed his jaw was still stiff as his narrowed gaze followed the occupying soldiers.

"Come, Son, take us in," Henrietta prompted.

He escorted them onto the hotel porch, where he held the door for them and two crepe-clad widows. "I'll make your dinner arrangements, then I'll need to go on over to the church and speak with the pastor," he told them as they climbed the stairs.

"But when will *you* eat?" Henrietta wondered.

"Later."

They sat in the lobby as Dylan approached the desk. The widows were standing nearby. *Why, we're all widows*, Carolyn realized, and offered the women a slight smile. It was all the encouragement needed. The tall, skinny one leaned over and said in a conspiratorial tone, "I saw what happened on the street. Shameless, isn't it?"

"I guess we didn't realize there would be so many of – them – in Athens," Carolyn admitted.

"Oh, yes, my dear. We are traveling to Nashville, but our aunt took ill and had to rest here a bit. We've been here several days. It's a wonder if a woman can walk down the street without being jostled by Negroes and ogled by bluecoats."

"We heard the command center for Northeast Georgia was in Augusta," Henrietta said.

"True, under General King – but I think they have an outpost of that new Freedman's Bureau here." The lady gave Carolyn a knowing smile. "Your husband seems quite the fighter."

Carolyn laughed. She would never have applied such a term to Dylan. Then she sobered. "He's not my husband – yet. But yes, I guess he is."

"Protective. That's good. I'm Sally Jones. This is my sister, Roberta Nicewood." Sally tilted her hawk-like face to her companion. Roberta was shorter, rounder and fair next to her sister's spare figure, and she appeared to be the younger of the two.

There was nothing to it but to introduce themselves, too.

"We're about to go into dinner. Will you join us?"

There was nothing to it but to accept. At least Henrietta seemed to think so – as ever eager for conversation and news. The sisters proved a fount of that, Carolyn discovered, once they were seated and Lydia had taken Devie upstairs with their own plates of food. She would have preferred to eat her delicious dinner of baked chicken with them, away from the curious eyes of strangers, mulling over thoughts of her imminent wedding. Was imminent a negative term? But her mother-in-law seemed very content to hear all their companions could tell her.

"Surely you've heard the results of the election in Milledgeville," Roberta said. When Henrietta shook her head, adding that they had been quite isolated in Clarkesville, the lady went on: "It was expected Joshua Hill and Alexander Stephens would be chosen, but as it turns out it was Stephens and Herschel Johnson. Of course they had no choice but to ratify the Thirteenth Amendment. Our only hope is to go along with them and trust that they may let our men stay in office. Johnson was a moderate on secession, but at least he's from Georgia, you know."

"You seem quite well versed on politics," Henrietta commented, sounding like she was realizing just how uninformed she was.

"Well, knowledge is power, they say. I say, why are black men voting and white women are not?"

Carolyn raised her eyebrows. She had never met such an outspoken lady.

"You don't agree?" asked Sally Jones. "Surely you agree. You must."

"Well, yes, but – it seems a pipe dream."

"That's what the slaves said," Roberta chimed in. "And look what happened."

"If another bloody war is required for women's suffrage, Mrs. Nicewood, I would gladly forgo the vote," Henrietta said with cool dignity. "I have already lost far too much."

Mrs. Nicewood sighed. "Well said, Mrs. Rousseau. Haven't we all? One day, though. Mark my words. One day."

"Oh, they've been so sheltered, Roberta, I bet they haven't heard of the scandal in Washington, either," Sally said, lighting up as the idea came to her. "That terrible business that went on at Chennault. Just one more example of the types of ills women are subjected to."

Carolyn felt her stomach sink to her toes. She almost dropped her fork. "Chennault?" she echoed.

Sally turned to her with sharp eyes. "Oh, you've heard of it?"

"Well – not really. I just heard a soldier mention it once. Is Chennault in the capital, then?"

"No, indeed. Washington, Georgia!"

"W-what happened there?" She had a sick feeling now, along with as much drive for information as Henrietta had ever possessed. Hadn't the dying soldier buried under the oak tree at Forests of Green said "I did it for us"? What had he done?

"Why, that's where the Confederate gold was stolen!"

"There was Confederate gold?" Henrietta asked in amazement.

"Well, what was left after it traveled by train and then wagon all the way from Richmond, with army pay-outs along the way," Sally said. Her thin nose fairly quivered with excitement.

"How much *was* there?" Carolyn asked.

"Oh, hundreds of thousands, they say, to begin with – in gold and silver bullion, jewelry – even floor sweepings from the mint right here in Dahlonega – worth maybe up to as much as seven hundred thousand." She paused as her listeners gasped, then wiggled a hand to show concession. "Maybe way less. Estimates vary widely on the exact amount. But by the time the wagon train made it from Danville to middle Georgia – only a small fraction was left."

"A small fraction is still a lot of money!" Henrietta exclaimed.

"Indeed. So thought the robbers when they learned the wagon train was camped at the Chennault Plantation on the night of May 24."

"Robbers?" Henrietta squeaked.

"May 24 ..." Carolyn said, thoughtfully. "Who were the robbers? Were they caught?"

"*I* hear they were cavalrymen from Vaughn's Tennessee Brigade," Roberta Nicewood confided, as though someone important had personally whispered confidential information in her ear. "They thought the money belonged to the Confederate government and thus, as unpaid soldiers, to them. They're saying now the money was to be returned to banks in Richmond to pay Confederate widows and orphans. But I don't know. Some say the thieves waded knee deep in it when they filled their haversacks and pockets and whatever they could find. They left easy trails for bank officials to follow. Some local blacks watched where some of the robbers hid their gold and ratted them out. One robber who got only four thousand dollars in silver got mad when his companions refused to share their ten and twenty dollar gold pieces, and he turned them in, too. Eventually, about a hundred and ten thousand was recovered."

"But not all," Carolyn stated.

"No. Not all. Some got away ... probably clean to Texas by now," Sally told them.

Carolyn's thoughts rushed like a mountain freshet after a rainstorm.

Oblivious, Roberta went on. "But that's not all. It gets even more like a novel. The Yankees sent in this awful man named Edward Wild. I thought Sherman was bad, until I heard about *him*. War sure breeds some maniacal characters. This Wild, he worked for the Freedman's Bureau out of Macon, establishing agencies in Columbus and Atlanta. He was in Augusta when all this happened. He already had a reputation for recruiting black soldiers, violence upon Rebels, and even rashness and insubordination to his own officials –but they sent the one-armed devil right to Chennault, where he was convinced the family was hiding more gold. He arrested the two brothers and their wives, and the two daughters of the older brother. Two of the men he trysted up–"

"What's that?" Henrietta asked in a strangled voice.

"A sailor's punishment – hanging by the thumbs."

"Oh!" Henrietta cried. She hid her face in her napkin, sliding back from her plate.

Roberta seemed not the least nonplussed by her listener's reaction. She was into her story, and with a morbid fascination, Carolyn wanted – needed – her to go on. "The Rev. Dionysus Chennault weighed over three hundred pounds. You can imagine the results. John Chennault was ill with consumption and was cut down upon fainting. During this, which I believe happened in the woods, another group of soldiers entered the house, and you'll never believe what happened to the women."

"Please, tell us no more," Henrietta said. "We don't need to know."

But Carolyn said, "Yes, we do. Please go on." She ignored her mother-in-law's shocked look.

"Well, thankfully the younger children had been able to escape, but the one seventeen-year-old daughter of John Chennault was forced to remove all her clothing – and I do mean *all* – and be searched in the presence of a lieutenant – as were the other women – all the while subject to the taunts of their former maid."

Henrietta moaned.

"But they found nothing?" Carolyn asked.

"Nothing but the barest trivials. Charges filed against the women were unrelated and had to do with cruelty to their servants – an embarrassing enlightenment, to be sure, but surely no justification for their own treatment at the hands of strange men. They were held for some time in an upper room on the town square but finally found innocent. It just goes to show you a woman can't be too careful with such hooligans about – *in charge*, no less. And so you see it's a good thing for your men to be protective."

118

Before Carolyn could speak, Sally Jones said, "But Wild didn't get away with it – not totally. He was arrested in late July in Washington – at Robert Toombs' house, of all places, which he'd confiscated after throwing Mrs. Toombs out onto the very street!"

"No!" Henrietta cried.

"Oh, yes."

"Where is he now?" Carolyn asked.

"Back in New York, I guess, and safer than he deserves to be. Someone down here tried to assassinate him before General Grant relieved him of duty. Would have been a fitting end, I say. I can't believe you heard nothing of all this. There's been such a public outcry about it all!"

Not exactly nothing, Carolyn thought. Like a ripple in a pond, a dying man had reached their far shore and had said the word "Chennault," a word only she had heard. She was sure now he had been among the robbers. But had he lost his prize – been forced to give it up, escaping only with his life, his bitterness, and his love for a girl named Becky – or was he one of the few who had hidden a secret? Her brain whirled. She had gone through his clothes, haversack and saddlebag herself. There had been no sign of Confederate treasure, great or small. That must mean his last daring exploit had gone unrewarded. What a way to die – a failure at all things. No wonder he'd been tortured with misery.

Pondering all that, Carolyn scarcely noticed Dylan had walked up until he stood right over their table. Their faces must have registered a blank sort of shock, for he asked with some alarm, "What's wrong, ladies?"

"Oh – nothing," Henrietta said. "Mrs. Jones and Mrs. Nicewood were just telling us the most remarkable ... story." She proceeded to make introductions, making a visible effort to shake off the pall the recent conversation had created.

Carolyn did likewise.

Dylan bowed and sat down, but Carolyn noted his manner was restless. "Did you speak to the minister?" she asked.

He nodded. "I did, and he will do the ceremony, but it must be tonight. He leaves town in the morning."

"Tonight!" Carolyn grasped her tea cup with both hands to keep it from slipping to the table.

"Can you be ready?"

That was a loaded question. "I suppose I must be," she replied faintly. Realizing how unenthusiastic that sounded, she shook herself. "I mean – of course. It's just – a surprise. I must go change right now, and someone must alert Mrs. Sprite, who is going to serve as a witness."

"I can do that," Dylan said, watching her carefully.

"Oh, a wedding, today?" Roberta exclaimed. "How lovely! Might we come along? Passing the hours here grows so tedious."

"Of course," Carolyn said. Her first instinct had been to find some reason to refuse, but what could she say? And besides, she would be in such a daze she would hardly notice *who* was there. She had counted on the ceremony being tomorrow, giving her an evening to rest, pray and prepare her mind and heart. Now, she felt like everything was spinning out of control.

Dylan touched her hand. "Are you sure?" He looked into her eyes, and she knew he wasn't talking about the guest list.

She remembered the kiss at Forests of Green, the words he had spoken that day – words she hadn't been able to get out of her head since – and nodded. "Yes," she said with a smile.

But as she dressed the feeling of ambiguity returned. She was reminded of Dylan's stubbornness as she donned Mahala's gray taffeta dress. He had firmly rejected the notion of Carolyn wearing her old wedding dress. She could understand that, really, but when everything else she had was black, might he not have considered her request to remake the gown so that she could feel beautiful on this day?

Also there were to be no rings. Carolyn had put away the wedding band Dev had given her when she had accepted Dylan's proposal. All other family jewels were gone. Dylan promised to one day rectify the situation.

But now, it all felt thrown-together and sham-like. Not like a real wedding at all. Not like her first wedding. Not even when they went inside the Presbyterian Church on Hancock Street. Even the Italian marble pulpit, pine pews trimmed in hand-hewn walnut from a local plantation, and the presence of the Rev. Nathan Hoyt added credence to the occasion.

Stop it, she told herself.

It was real enough that night, though, when they returned to the hotel. Devie was taken – with tearful protestations – into Henrietta's room, while Dylan led Carolyn into the other bedroom of the suite and closed the door behind them. A fire crackled on the hearth. They warmed their hands there, removing their outer garments. Dylan drew her close and kissed her, a long, tender, possessive kiss. When he started unbuttoning her bodice, his hands shook.

Slow down. Slow down. Carolyn took his hands in her own, took a breath, closed her eyes and whispered, "Hold me."

He did so. He held her a long time, until the world slowed down and their hearts beat as one. Carolyn felt time coalesce into a single moment, as though this night was the most important of her life. The notion alarmed her.

But as Dylan made love to her for the first time, her body responded of its own accord. She couldn't have stopped it if she'd wanted to. But when, unexpectedly, she felt herself sliding away, she did want to hold onto a corner of herself. She hadn't expected so much more than the words he had used to say he loved her. Now, he told her without words that not only did he love her, he adored her, had longed for her, needed her beyond what he could express.

Finally, he lay beside her in the dark and whispered, "That was my first time."

Her lips parted in amazement – though she should have known – not only that it was true but that he had chosen to tell her. She put his head on her shoulder and stroked his hair so he wouldn't see the tears that eased out of her eyes. She didn't want him to recognize her guilt. Though she had given her body and even a measure of love, the stripping down of his tender passion had revealed to her that there was something she *couldn't* yet give – a whole heart.

Christmas 1865
Savannah, Georgia

Sylvie had pulled another surprise out of her hat. Ella Beth was sure not even Sunny had seen this one coming.

Ella Beth stood in a corner of the Randalls' parlor, like a great black moth drawn to the myriad candles and lamps that illuminated the holiday party scene with a golden glow. She should not be here. She was still in mourning and should not have allowed her grandmother to persuade her to stop in even for a brief time. *A family gathering, my foot*, she thought. *This is a full-fledged party.* They would talk about her tomorrow for attending.

A fire sizzled on the hearth. The mantle was decorated with oranges, apples, cinnamon sticks, evergreen and red candles. A Christmas tree – maybe the only one in Savannah this year, Ella Beth thought sourly – was dressed out with cranberry and popcorn garlands but not lit. The rug had been rolled back, and on the polished hardwood floor slippers slid and leapt, sacheted and turned. A polka was in progress. Sylvie was in the arms of a young man known to have his way with women. She initiated a pursuit, hands on her hips, throwing a tantalizing smile over her shoulder at the grinning fool who followed her.

"Shocking," murmured a white-curled old lady on the sofa.

Ella Beth agreed. Her own face was red to prove it. Even more outlandish than her cousin's flirtations with the rake was the fact that, between dances, she directed all her charms at Daniel O'Keefe. Sylvie had invited him on the sly. She had told Ella Beth as much. Now that he was here it was too late for Sunny to ask him to leave, and apparently he did not have the social sense to know no one but Sylvie welcomed him.

As for Sylvie, someone should really take her in hand. With Jack gone, and Dylan now married to another, she was absolutely incorrigible. For the past month, she had flirted shamelessly, going from party to party, riding out with anyone and everyone – and now sneaking an invitation to the foundry foreman and cavorting about with him for all Savannah to see.

Ella Beth could bear no more. She started to edge her way out of the packed room into the foyer. She passed a servant with a tray and set her empty eggnog glass on it. Once in the library, she sank back onto the sofa before the fire and sighed, putting her head back and covering her eyes with a hand.

Chances were good Sylvie was just trying to dull the pain of Dylan Rousseau's rejection. That Ella Beth could understand. But her manner was far too wild. She would ruin her reputation soon, and no one would have her.

"Aha! There you are!"

She jerked up to behold Daniel O'Keefe with unbelieving eyes. "Did you follow me?"

"I came looking for a bit of peace, don't you know, and here you were."

"If it's peace you're seeking, perhaps you should call for your coat and hat and go home."

The man walked around the sofa and stood there staring at her through incisive, narrowed eyes. "Back to Old Fort where I belong, y'mean?"

Ella Beth was too grumpy to mince words. "Something like that."

"That's not very civil of y'now, is it?"

She frowned. "Obviously you need someone to tell you the truth. Have you no idea that everyone is wondering why you are even here and talking about the way you and Sylvie are carrying on? Do you not care if her reputation is ruined? Or maybe that's it – you hope in ruining it that she'll fall into your unlikely arms?"

Daniel tilted back his head and laughed. "Hardly so! The lass and I would nit-pick each other to death in the space of one week. I think perhaps you're making a mountain out of a mole hill. She only wants to have a bit of fun. The lass is hurting … do you not recognize it?"

His knowing gaze, and the memory of him catching her staring at Jack that time, burned like a lance. Ella Beth snapped, "There are other ways to deal with one's hurt."

"Such as keeping everyone at arm's length with a sour face and biting word?"

She jumped to her feet, shocked and incensed. "How dare you speak to me so? You've overstepped your bounds, Sir!"

"I'm sorry, lass." Daniel made a calming gesture. "Perhaps I did go too far. I just thought you'd be able to take what you dish out: plain speaking." When her mouth fell open in astonishment, he touched her arm. "Truly I'm sorry. Y're right. Y're a lady, and I'm a common man. And I should not have been so harsh."

She hesitated, her upbringing battling with her ire. "Neither should I. I'm sorry, too."

"There now. Can we sit down and try again?"

Ella Beth nodded. "All right."

They sank onto the sofa. Ella Beth folded her hands and watched him. An alarming thought came to her. She was really glad he was in here with her, instead of out there with Sylvie. How could she possibly feel that way? The man was coarse, argumentative and completely inappropriate. What about him could possibly arouse jealousy?

"We're much alike, you know," he said, as if reading her thoughts, "apart from our origins. My da always told me anyone could read me like a book. I don't much believe in pretending, Mrs. Draper. What you see is what you get. I think you're like that, too."

"No, I'm not. At least, I wasn't always. I used to be very good at pretending. I don't know what's happened to me."

"Folks react to heartache in different ways," O'Keefe observed with a slight, sympathetic smile. "Or maybe it's just that like knows like."

She was unsettled that he persisted in making that point. "You're referring to your background and your experiences in the war. With the weight you carry for your family, don't *you* feel discouraged at times?"

"At times," he agreed, shrugging. "But I guess I reckon there's no use looking back when I've got the rest of my life in front of me."

Ella Beth sighed. "I wish I could feel that way, but a woman has so few options."

"We have what options we make, Mrs. Draper, if we don't let others dictate to us what they are."

She looked at him with disbelief. "That's not true for women of my class. Perhaps you can rise, but we can only fall."

Ella Beth could not believe she was having this conversation with the man. The other part of her couldn't seem to stop herself. Was this openness of nature what drew Sylvie to him? The refusal to be bogged down by what ensnared others?

O'Keefe was hesitating, perched there beside her. He had a rumpled black tie that she noticed needed fixing. "There's something I'm wantin' to tell you – an old Irish saying – but I'm not wanting you to fly at me again."

She found herself biting back a sudden giggle. "And what's that?"

"There is no stocking that doesn't find an old boot. So … if you can believe that … maybe you won't be sad forever." He rose and smiled down at her. When he walked out of the room, he didn't bow, but she found she didn't mind.

CHAPTER EIGHT

January 1866
Paris, France

hen they pulled up at 7 *rue de la Paix*, the street was so jammed with carriages there was no place to pull over. They had to circle a couple of times before there was a spot their driver could wedge in the vehicle.

"It must really be good to be worth such a fuss," Mahala, who was the recipient of yet another of Jack's surprises, commented.

His eyes twinkled. "Oh, it's *Worth* it all right."

"Worth? Is that where we're at?"

"Worth and Bobergh, to be exact."

"Oh, good heavens, Jack." Mahala stepped down from the hired vehicle and stopped short. "Who *is* that magnificent woman?"

A lady was exiting the popular shop with a retinue of servants behind her. Her glistening brown hair was swept up under a jaunty hat, and she was clad in a fur cloak. A coachman opened a carriage door sporting an elaborate coat of arms and helped her inside.

"That is the Empress Eugenie," said their driver from above.

Mahala glanced up at him, and her mouth fell open. "As in the emperor's wife?"

"Of course, Madam."

"That would be Napoleon III," Jack whispered in her ear, grinning.

"Empress Eugenie is both capable and stylish," the driver added. "She acted as regent last year while her husband was away. There must now be something she could not wait for Monsieur Worth to attend her. He is couturier of the French court, you know. And the Empress sets all the fashions in Paris."

"Oh, no," Mahala said, making a move as if to get back into the carriage. Jack caught her arm. "Where are you going?"

"Certainly not in *there* on the heels of the empress!"

"Come on. The shop is crowded morning to night. If you don't present yourself, you'll never get an audience."

"I have no intention of presenting myself!"

A man on a wagon loaded with bricks yelled out behind them, "Hey! *Voulez-vous!*"

The end of their carriage was sticking out into the street.

"Best to get out of the way," their driver told them. "I must drive on."

"Come back in an hour," Jack instructed. He grabbed Mahala's arm and pulled her along. Mahala did her best to match his stride. After all, it would not do to have everyone think he manhandled his wife.

"Come now, you're not to be undone by a bunch of French royals." He smiled, opening the door for her.

Oh, yes, I am, she thought. *Absolutely rusticated, intimidated and undone.* Couldn't Jack see that by forcing her into situations where she was so out of her element he was not helping her, and could be setting up the both of them for humiliation?

But alas, the clerk had now approached and was bowing and waving her into Worth and Bobergh. He waved in a rolling motion low from the waist, as if she were some visiting dignitary. Jack handed his calling card to the clerk.

"There is no fashion show today," said the little Frenchman in a pinched, nasal voice.

Jack said, "I would be most obliged for my wife to consult personally with Monsieur Worth."

"Please – have a seat." The man gestured toward a pair of gilded chairs. He cast a skeptical eye at Jack's card before disappearing down a short hallway.

A pair of women sat waiting as well. They eyed the newcomers down their thin noses before turning away. Mahala guessed they must have been waiting long before the appearance of the empress. They would surely take precedence over Mahala. She and Jack were wasting their time, and there were so many things waiting to be seen.

This trip was opening Mahala's eyes to the wonders of the world. The transatlantic crossing on the maiden voyage of *Aleppo* had been amazing in itself. Jack had told her how, after being interrupted by the war, the transatlantic telegraph cable was again being laid. Mahala had stared into the foamy fathoms they steamed over, unable to believe the whole world would soon be connected under its depths.

She had sat in with Jack during his private conversation in Captain Howard White's luxuriously appointed cabin. The men had discussed the growing rivalry between Inman and Cunard passenger lines, for which White was employed. As Jack had praised the *Aleppo*, White had encouraged him to visit Finnieston Street, Glasgow, to see the *Russia* under construction. A veritable floating hotel at 358 feet long by 42 feet on the beam, *Russia* would accommodate 235 first class passengers.

"There's your challenge," White had laughed. "Build one bigger and better than that."

Jack had laughed, too. "Indeed I might."

They were only beginning their time in France. That morning they had gone to the art museum, where some of the paintings and sculptures had caused her to blush. But she had been fascinated by the paintings done in a new method which used short, thick brush strokes and mixing of colors to create a realistic sense of shadow and light. She would like to have spent more time looking at those, and the architecture of some of the buildings they had toured. She could hardly see how they could get it all in before moving on to Italy. Mahala barely kept herself from squirming in her seat just thinking about it. She had been like a child waking with such eagerness each morning.

Indeed it did seem they would be making a quick departure when an imperious voice drifted from the back room. "*Non, non, aprés Empress Eugenie, je suis fatigué – trés, trés, fatigué. Je ne suis pas les temps pour un americain.*"

Even if Mahala had not understood French she would have understood that. She saw the clerk lean into the room and say, "*Oui, monsieur, mais Madam Randall est trés unique. Elle …*"

Mahala could hear no more, for the man had dropped his voice beyond perception, in fact, even to a whisper. Then, to her startled eyes, a head appeared at the door of the back room – a black velvet skull cap, dark eyebrows, a full mustache over a chin which receded loosely into an enormous bowtie. The eyebrows raised. Mahala quickly averted her gaze, trying to appear impervious to study.

Beside her, Jack chuckled. "It seems your beauty would open more doors than my name," he whispered.

A moment later, the master himself swept into the room in a velvet jacket and bowed from the waist. He was about forty, Mahala guessed.

Jack rose and shook the proffered hand.

"Monsieur and Madam Randall," Worth said. He reached for Mahala's hand and leaned over it, looking deeply in her eyes. "Ah – *azure*! Enchanting. You come to me all the way from Savannah. It is a long time since I have had customers from the southern part of your country. *Trés desolée*. What can I do for you?"

With his typical charm, Jack explained that making the acquaintance of Monsieur Worth – not to mention the purchase of one of his creations for his new bride – would be the highlight of their European honeymoon. Mahala glanced at the older women sitting along the wall. The clerk was explaining something to them in hushed, obsequious tones. Whatever he was saying was not soothing their indignant expressions. Finally, they rose and followed him into a side room. Monsieur Worth never glanced their way.

Mahala started when Worth took her hands and urged her to rise. She did so with reluctance, uncomfortable under the piercing gaze.

"What did you have in mind?" Worth asked them.

Mahala glanced at Jack, who said nothing. Why wouldn't he help her out? Coming here was *his* idea, after all. "A – a visiting dress seems practical," she stammered. "And, I do have my wedding dress with me, if you would prefer to look at it, possibly remake it …"

"Please remove your cloak, Madam."

She obeyed. His eyes took in every detail of her appearance. He took her hands and turned her.

"This color – *non, non, non*," he said. He tweaked a ruffle at her neck. "This is all wrong for you, too – how do you say? – fusty. What you need, Madam, is clean, elegant lines – vivid color. None of the gowns my models wear in the shows will do. How long are you in Paris?"

Jack did speak then. "As long as necessary."

"*Bon*! We shall do both dresses. I cannot go wrong with such a model to represent me – but then, I never go wrong." Worth clapped his hands, just two sharp claps.

Mahala blinked. A woman and a man appeared from the back. The woman had a measuring tape draped around her neck.

"Coffee, Monsieur Randall? A newspaper? We shall be a while. Come, Madam Randall, and let me show you the exquisite new silks just in from Lyons …"

In Savannah, while trying not to think of the fun Jack and Mahala were having in France, Sylvie received a single red rosebud with a message attached. She opened the envelope, her mind running back over the young men who had been present at the dinner party last night. It had been dull as tombs, the whole conversation a refighting of the battles for Atlanta. "If, if, if." "If" did not change anything.

My love is like a red, red rose,
That's newly sprung in June.
O my love's like the melody
That's sweetly played in tune.

"Bah," said Sylvie, casting aside the card.

She now knew the rose could not be from Daniel O'Keefe. He would not borrow another's tired verses, even if those verses be from a Scotsman. He no longer accepted her invitations, anyway. Even a lowly factory foreman didn't want to lead her on. And him the only man around who wasn't lost in "ifs."

She looked out the window and tried not to think of Carolyn and Dylan, snug on the farm in Habersham.

Carolyn was in the small hothouse constructed at Forests of Green before the war, kneeling beside a raised bed. With a trowel in her gloved hand, she mixed manure into dark topsoil. It was cool in the potting shed but – due to the numerous high windows – not nearly so cold as it was outside, where a brisk winter wind chased wispy clouds across a high blue sky. She could hear it blowing over Devie's chatter. She had given him a pot to put dirt in, and he was busy "helping," scattering more soil on the floor and smearing it on his face and clothes than he got in the planter. She took a look at him and laughed despite herself. He was such a beautiful child, more like his father every day – handsome, opinionated and unafraid of anything. Dev would be so proud of him. She found herself imagining how he would react to his son, if he got to see him for the first time.

She shook her head. Daydreams were no good. But she had to wonder how often Devie made Henrietta and Dylan think of Dev. Carolyn was sure her mother-in-law did, for she'd sometimes catch Henrietta gazing at her grandson with a soft, distant look that told Carolyn she was in the past. Dylan gave no sign that Devie's resemblance to his brother disturbed him. But then, he was only around him for limited time in the evenings. Maybe soon, she would be able to give Dylan a child of his own.

Her stomach rumbled, reminding Carolyn that that might best happen when summer's garden produced its plenty, helping supplement their meager diet.

She was planting lettuce now. The soil ready, she opened the brown envelope resting nearby.

"Carolyn?"

She jumped, almost spilling the tiny, precious seeds. "Yes?"

Henrietta appeared in the doorway. "I brought you some coffee. I have enough for Dylan, too, but I thought you might want to take it out to him."

"Oh, yes. Of course. Thank you." Carolyn closed the envelope, set it aside, and rose to gratefully accept the steaming mug her mother-in-law offered her. She took a tentative sip, pondering how Henrietta had showed amazing sensitivity to the newlyweds the past month. It was almost as if she were aware of the awkward, uncertain stage their relationship was in, filled with the embarrassed tenderness of intimacy one moment and strained by strangeness the next. While Carolyn was thankful for her mother-in-law's attempts to give them extra time alone, the idea also made her nervous. She and Dylan didn't always agree on how to go about things. It was a constant balancing act of trying to share her views without making him angry – for when angry he became aloof. That was not easy, for these days it seemed there were a good many subjects that he did not want her to raise. One in particular had been nagging her for quite some time now.

128

"My, you're a mess!" Henrietta said to her grandson, who pulled himself up off the floor, bottom in the air first.

"Mess!" he exulted aloud. Then he smeared his hands down his pants.

"Come with Grandma. You've done enough damage for one day."

Carolyn drank her coffee, savoring the warmth of it in her stomach, as she followed Henrietta back to the house. In the kitchen a tin cup with a lid waited on the table. Removing her dirty apron, she took the coffee pot and poured its remaining liquid into the cup. Then she pulled her old coat from the peg and shrugged into it, drawing on the mittens which waited in the pocket.

"Back soon," she said, cradling the hot cup and heading out the side door.

The cows were in the barn, where one of the workers was singing, mixing up the feed. Dylan was repairing the fence nearby. Carolyn could hear his hammer thumping. Soon she saw him, bent over in his gray wool coat, his breath coming out in frosty puffs.

"Time for a break!" she called.

He straightened and, spotting her, smiled.

"Coffee!" she added.

He tossed down his hammer and approached, opening one arm. As she looked at him, she still couldn't believe she was married to him. Carolyn pressed herself to his side and raised her face for his kiss. His lips were warm in the cold air. She handed him the tin cup.

"Thank you," he said, taking a sip.

"You're welcome. Almost done here?" She always looked forward to the early winter evenings which allowed them to gather in the parlor before the fire, the women knitting and mending, Devie playing on the rug, Dylan behind an old newspaper or an issue of *Southern Cultivator*. Last night Dylan told her he had read from a newspaper he'd picked up in Athens that General Tilson of the Freedman's Bureau had met with planters in Savannah last month. Just before Christmas, Tilson had issued a circular dictating acceptable pay rates for black workers in the different areas of the state. According to its pay grade, they would have to offer their men several dollars a month more each, plus board and lodging.

She wondered if Dylan was thinking about that as his gaze wandered out across the hard, bare fields. "Soon time to break the land," he stated, as if in answer.

"Can we pay them?"

"You know we can't."

"What will we do?"

"God only knows, Carolyn. We can take some poultry to Athens next month. That will give us a bit of cash – but not enough. They'll have to settle for a portion of the crop again. When I tell them – I expect they'll leave. We need a miracle if we're to hope otherwise. I've been thinking, we need a crop we can sell at market. It's the only way to get ahead. Jarvis Van Buren swears by grapes – muscadines."

"To make wine?"

Dylan nodded.

"You – a Presbyterian minister – are thinking of entering the wine industry?" She couldn't keep the disdain from her voice.

"I'm not a Presbyterian minister anymore. I'm a farmer, one just trying to find a way to survive."

The sharpness in his tone told her his wall was going up. But here was the perfect opportunity to broach the subject that had been on her mind. She forged ahead, resting a tentative hand on his arm. "I've been thinking, too, Dylan. I really miss going to church. I know others do as well. We need each other more now than ever. It can be discouraging to be isolated, to work and work, with no fellowship. Have you considered preaching in town, just once a month perhaps?"

"I'm sorry you're feeling cut off from the social world, Carolyn, but I'm not willing to preach for free. I don't have time for sermons."

This was a far cry, she thought, from the man who had started a mission in Savannah's Yamacraw slums before the war. "I bet there are a few like Mr. Van Buren who could scare up a few coins for the offering plate, if you were willing to come. And even if they couldn't at first … maybe later … and think what a blessing it would be to everyone."

"Think what a burden it would be to *me*." Dylan handed Carolyn the empty coffee cup and picked up his hammer.

"A burden? What was once the love of your life?"

"Things change."

"But Dylan–"

He pinned her with his gaze. "*People* change. I was a different man then, in case you haven't noticed. I'll never preach again."

Carolyn stood in place while he started hammering, feeling as if he had punched her in the chest. "Don't say that."

"It's true. Put it out of your mind."

"But Dylan, I don't understand."

"I said *leave* it, Carolyn," he snapped, partially raising up and fixing her with a cold eye. Then, as if regretting having raised his voice – perhaps the effect of her startled expression – he went on more gently, while holding a board in place. "Mr. Van Buren would give me cuttings, I'm sure. Next time I'm in town I can talk to him."

"That would be a mistake." She couldn't stop herself. He was so stubborn, she burned with indignation. "There are people in the congregation who will never tolerate a full-blown wine industry. Not from him, or from you. I just don't understand why you'd consider something so foolish but refuse what you're meant to do."

Carolyn bit her lip. He paused, clenched his jaw, and started hammering. She whirled and stalked off toward the house.

Why was Dylan shutting her out? Why?

He hardly spoke at dinner. Afterwards he pushed aside Devie's clamoring – too brusquely for Carolyn's taste – and went to the study.

"What's eating *him*?" Henrietta asked Carolyn as they rose to clean up supper.

You're asking me? Carolyn wanted to retort. But she answered in a quiet voice. "I think he's angry that I suggested he consider preaching again." Well, that wasn't the whole truth. She had also dismissed his idea for a vineyard – rather forcefully.

Henrietta looked pained. "I *have* noticed he neglects to read his Bible, and he used to be so faithful. He always had a Scripture for every situation ... before the war. I had hoped that once you married ..."

That I would be a gentling influence? Carolyn asked in her head as she turned away. *Well, apparently I'm not. The truth is, I really don't know how to be married, to be a wife. Dev and I were never close until he was gone away to war.*

That night she fought her own war inside her head when Dylan entered their room and undressed in the dark. Should she present him her back or reach out to him? She decided on the latter, rolling part way over as he raised the quilts and climbed in next to her.

"Dylan?"

"Good night," he murmured and kissed her forehead.

So that was to be it. They were not very good at this. She lay there a long time, feeling the weight of her inadequacy. *God, help me to be a wife to this man*, she prayed.

Hours later, after an interlude of fitful sleep, she was awakened suddenly. She sat up in bed. Next to her Dylan was thrashing. The covers were entwined about his lower body.

"They must lie down. Tell them they must lie down, sergeant!"

Carolyn grabbed his arm. "Dylan!"

"The shrapnel is too heavy!"

"Dylan!" She shook him.

He came awake, lunging forward with an intensity that startled her.

"It's me," she said. "You were dreaming."

With eyes that glistened white in the moonlight, he stared at her. He rubbed a hand over his face, then ran it through his hair. Carolyn saw his chest rise and fall rapidly.

"Are you o.k.?" she asked, reaching out toward him.

He brushed her hand away. "Fine," he rasped. "Just a dream – like you said."

It was the first one she was aware of, but far from the last.

Two weeks later they cleared brush at the edge of the corn field. Carolyn joined the men in her old coat and one of Mahala's remade cotton dresses, which Martha had generously donated when she heard Carolyn mention that Dylan complained about his bride wearing black. Thick gloves protected her hands as she used a small scythe. She bent and swung, bent and swung.

Of course Dylan had told her she need not labor in the field – had in fact discouraged it – but she had insisted that she was sick of being cooped up in the house, and one more set of hands would ready the field for plowing all the sooner. They wanted to try to plant a few more rows of corn again this spring. She figured they better get it done while they could. Over the weekend, Dylan had spoken with the workers about the continuing absence of cash with which to pay them. They had almost walked out on the spot. "No diff'rent than bein' a slave," Markus had muttered. Now, from their sullen demeanors, Carolyn could tell they might leave at any time. Might well be today, with the advent of heavier work following the more restful winter.

Suddenly the ground tilted. She stood up and blood rushed from her head. Then the sky tilted. She staggered and dropped the scythe. Dylan came running and caught her before she fell.

"What's the matter? Are you all right?" he demanded, holding her with one arm while stripping off his gloves. "Water! She needs some water!" He put the back of his hand to her face, checking for fever.

"I – I'm all right," she said as he eased her into a sitting position. "Just too long bending over."

Ham jogged up. He carried a sloshing water dipper. She thought about all the men having drunk from it, but Dylan was looking at her with such pleading that she took it and sipped. The metallic taste of tin filled her mouth and slid disagreeably to her belly. She pushed the dipper away.

"Come on, I'll take you inside," Dylan said. He gently pulled her to her feet. "Can you walk?"

She nodded. "I'm fine now – really."

He looked unconvinced but conceded by giving her his arm. "Have you been unwell, Carolyn?"

She shrugged. It was too early to tell him of her suspicions. She was almost hoping she was wrong, the timing was so poor.

He instantly picked up on her ambiguity. "What is it? If there's anything wrong, you should have told me."

Carolyn stopped walking. "I missed my monthly."

"You ... what?"

She waited while her meaning dawned on him. She hadn't been able to tell Dev the same news in person, so the transformation that took place was amazing to see. Confusion, understanding, disbelief, and – oh, thank God – joy.

"You're not upset? It's so soon, with things so tight ..."

Only then did Carolyn see that awareness pass over his face. She was adding to his already heavy load. But he groaned and clasped her to him, laughing in amazement. "Our own child! Carolyn, I can't believe it."

"It's early days yet ..."

It was the wrong thing to have said. It made them both remember her first baby, Dev's baby, born early, dead. "Why were you out in the field?" Dylan demanded. "What were you thinking? You're going in to lie down." He took hold of her elbow and steered her toward the house.

"Oh, no, don't you become overly protective of me."

"Who just nearly passed out in the corn field? A nap for you, and I'm going for the doctor."

"No! A doctor comes too dear. I'm all right now, I promise."

Dylan paused to consider. "All right," he said, "if you promise to nap."

Carolyn nodded. Having him concerned and solicitous might be a nice change. He had been distant lately, preoccupied, and the lack of sleep often made him touchy during the day. Perhaps the anticipation of becoming a father would provide hope for the future – maybe even enough to outweigh the burden.

Warmth. The winter sunlight touched her face. The wind whisked against the window, but it sounded far off. She was in a cocoon, but someone was tugging her from it. A hand caressed her back, pulling her from sleep. A voice murmured, "You've made me so happy," and she remembered *she* was the cocoon.

With a faint smile, Carolyn stretched and turned toward the face she knew was near, knew so well she didn't have to even look. She murmured, "I love you, Dev."

The immediate silence and stillness in the room penetrated her fogged state. Too late, she opened her eyes. Too late she realized. Dylan's expression was the most shocked and frozen she had ever seen. He withdrew, physically, emotionally.

She sat up on the bed, grasping for his arm as he pulled away. "Wait – I didn't mean – you *know* what I meant!" she cried. "I was just half asleep."

"Right." He was walking away.

Carolyn scrambled up. "I'm sorry!" The words sounded pitiful even to her own ears. Oh, God, what had she done?

Dylan waved a hand to show she should say no more and should not follow him, but nothing would have kept her from it, even her stockinged, shoeless feet. She hurried after him down the stairs and out onto the porch.

"Wait!" Carolyn called. "Stop walking away from me! Where are you going?" He kept walking. "Dylan, I didn't mean anything by it."

"It's fine."

"It's not fine. We have to talk about this."

He turned in the dried leaves that covered the lawn. The pain on his face sent an arrow to her hammering heart. "Don't you think you've said enough for today? Maybe for a lifetime."

Starting to weep, Carolyn ran after him, all the way to the barn, where Dylan was saddling his stallion. He proceeded as if she wasn't even there, his face like an awful, set mask. She was trembling.

"Please listen to me. I know you're angry, and you have every right to be. I don't know why I said that. I swear I don't. It's you I love, you I'm married to. I love you, Dylan. Please believe that. I was just half asleep, and I thought – I thought ..."

He stopped what he was doing and fixed her with a cold stare. "'Out of the overflow of the heart the mouth speaketh.'"

Carolyn gasped. *Now* he wanted to quote Scriptures at her? "You're being unreasonable. Stop this right now!"

Dylan swung the saddle up and leaned under the horse, pushing his shoulder against the stallion's belly to release the excess air before he buckled the strap.

"Where are you going? It's almost dark!"

Ignoring her, he buckled the saddle and swung himself up onto it. He looked down at the hand she put on his boot. "Please get out of the way."

"No, I won't!"

Dylan pried her fingers loose and used his other leg to urge his mount forward. "Ha! Ha!" he called as soon as he was clear of the stable door – and her.

As he thundered out of the barn, Carolyn yelled, "'Don't let the sun go down on your anger!'" Then she burst into tears, hard sobs that shook her whole body and forced her to crumple in the hay.

Oh, God! Oh, God! she sobbed. *With one word – one name – did I just ruin my marriage?*

Of all the hurtful things she could have said – belittling comments, fierce accusations – a declaration that she still loved her husband's brother was, Carolyn knew, by far the most damaging. Hadn't Dylan told her he had lived his whole life in Dev's shadow, he wouldn't now compete with his memory? She

134

longed to take it back, to erase that moment in time when she had opened her mouth without thought and the wrong name had come out. But that was impossible, and she feared the repercussions would run deep.

Why had she said it? Carolyn searched her mind and heart as she wept. A part of her would always love Dev. To ask her to have no lasting emotion for her first husband was unfair and unrealistic, she thought indignantly. Couldn't he see that what was important was that she was doing all she could to make their marriage work? Didn't that show her love for Dylan? He was overly sensitive, demanding, jealous. It was he who needed to be looking into his heart now, not her.

Carolyn jerked her sleeve across her face. Her eye fell on something at the back of the barn. The light was dim now, but she could still make out an unfamiliar saddle draped over a sawhorse against the far wall. A voice in her head echoed:

"*I* hear they were cavalrymen from Vaughn's Tennessee Brigade."

"Some got away ..."

Why had she forgotten about something so important? Because she'd been absorbed trying to please her exasperating husband, that was why!

Glad for the distraction, ready to turn away from her pain and a glimmer of guilt she didn't want to examine, Carolyn half-crawled to the saddle. She ran her hand over it, looking for identifying features or irregularities. It seemed to be a typical English-style cavalry saddle, well-worn but well-made. At the foot of the sawhorse were a blanket roll and a canteen. She picked up the canteen. Empty and unremarkable. Shuddering, Carolyn reached for the blanket, thinking of bed bugs and lice but deciding that any such vermin would be long gone. She unrolled the heavy square of wool. With a solid thump, a hand sewn muslin pouch fell to the ground.

Her heart raced, a queer exhilaration that almost obliterated the memory of her suffering only moments earlier. She knelt, reached for the bag, and had to pick it up with both hands because of its size and weight. Carolyn pulled open the drawstring and dumped out the contents into her lap. Various denominations of gold pieces, some five and ten dollars, winked bewitchingly in the evening light!

Confederate gold.

Confederate gold in her hands. Gold that would solve all her problems. Well, almost.

Gold Federal authorities wanted back.

She sat there a long time, thinking, counting, fingering the coins. She had heard that after the Confederacy took over the Dahlonega mint in April of 1861, a small quantity of half eagles and gold dollars had been struck by amateur Rebel minters. It would appear some of the coins in the pouch could be among those. Even though the wording and symbols were the same, the

135

imprints were weak, so much so that on a couple of the dollars the "U" in "United States of America" was missing.

Wasn't it fitting that these coins should come home to North Georgia? And did it really matter if the money had been Confederate payroll or intended for widows and orphans? She had been a widow. Her son had lost his father. And now she was again married to a former Confederate officer. Any way she looked at it, she would have been due some of this money.

But this much? How could she even consider such a thing?

It was so much easier to be highbrow and moral on a full stomach, knowing one would have a place to live and someone to take care of you, than when each day was a battle to meet one's most basic needs.

Wasn't the recovered Confederate gold in a vault somewhere now, to be tied up in litigation for who knew how long? This money, it could make a real difference to their family.

Carolyn suddenly knew that if she kept the money, she could not tell Dylan. At least not now, with his pride and anger at the fore. He would rather let them starve than take money dropped providentially on their doorstep by a dying soldier, especially if *she* suggested it. Even if he did keep it, he would insist on paying the workers with it, rather than standing his ground and demanding that they split the crop like everyone else was doing. Best to let him arrange things with the workers first. It would be wise to have something set by in case this year went no better than last. She would hold onto the gold for a while. What a relief it would be just to know it was there.

But first she had to get it out of the barn where anyone could find it. She started slipping coins down her bodice, where they lodged cold and hard in her corset. A small portion she left in the bag and looped the drawn string around the tab of her petticoat. She left the barn, wondering why she felt like a furtive thief when she was only moving something that had been right there for six months.

Dylan had said it would take a miracle to get the workers to stay, and that was exactly what happened the day after Carolyn almost fainted in the field because she was carrying his child, the day after she spoke his brother's name as she woke from sleep. It didn't feel like a miracle was coming, and he sure didn't deserve it. Dylan sat in his office as it was coming down the road as yet unbeknownst to him, holding his head in his hands and staring sightlessly at the account books. He was nursing a headache brought on by his foolishness the night before.

Carolyn didn't even know there was a tavern out near Unicoi Road, away from town where it was less likely its more upstanding customers would be seen coming and going. He hadn't set out for it – had just ridden until he and his mount were both tired and thirsty – and the thirst and the anonymity and the need for a blurring of the cutting hurt had led him to order something he normally never drank. Just a couple of glasses, but it had been enough to soothe the rough edges of inadequacy.

Carolyn wasn't *going* to know, either. He'd fallen into the guest bed long after the house was asleep. But he'd been unable to find unconsciousness again after one of the more and more frequent nightmares had roused him early this morning shaking and sweating.

Now, though, the numbing had fully worn off and the hurting was back. It sharpened the bottomless feeling of uncertainty he experienced at the start of each day. When he had first become a soldier, like now, like he'd told the foolish and adoring Sylvie Randall, he'd had no idea what to do. But then there had been people to give directions, to watch and learn from. His insides twisted. *People like Dev.* Now, there was no one. He was on his own. No one to advise him or bail him out if he failed. No one to watch his back. And plenty of people counting on him for their livelihood – with one more just added. A child of his own. He had to make a success of this place. The transition from fighting a war to a bitter peace would have been hard enough without the new responsibilities. Now, regardless of his words of bravado about doing things on his own, the raw burden of survival clung savagely to his shoulders like a beast about to drag him down.

Added to that, his own wife, whom he had thought to make a partner, secretly longed for his brother.

Part of Dylan told him he was making far too much of a whispered name. He should let it go and give Carolyn the chance to prove her devotion. But another part still smarted at unfair comparisons … remembered the pain of never quite measuring up … and wondered if every time he touched her she wished for another. Most of the time she seemed to care for him. But there had been those haunting moments when he had known she was holding part of herself back.

Dylan rubbed his hands over his eyes. The numbers on the page jumped and blurred.

"Dylan! Dylan!"

Carolyn's voice sounded alarmed, but not anxiously so. She had some-thing important to tell him, probably nothing to do with yesterday's drama. He felt incensed. How could she let it go so casually, just come bounding in as if nothing had happened? They had not spoken since he had ridden out of the barn the evening before. She hadn't sought him out this morning to demand where he'd gone. That had surprised him. Maybe she was afraid to know. She appeared now in the doorway, her brown eyes wide, her hands clasped to-gether. He scowled. "Yes?"

"You'll never believe who's coming up the drive!"

She could be excited about company? "Well?" he growled.

"Samson and Tania!"

That did give him pause. Samson and Tania? It was indeed hard to believe.

"They've come back, Dylan! It's the miracle we need! Shall I show them in here?"

Dylan stood up, resisting the urge to clasp his head in his hands again. "Just calm down. We don't know what they want yet."

"Of course they must have come back to work, Dylan, and if you can convince them to labor for part of the crop, *they* can convince the others!"

"Perhaps. But they can't think we're desperate for that. And there's still the question of whether *they* might have been the ones who dug up our silver."

Carolyn bit her lip. He could tell she didn't trust him to be delicate enough in his questioning. Not for one minute did she believe Samson and Tania were the culprits. He waited for her to warn him to be careful not to accuse, to send them away offended, but instead, her face smoothed out. "Very well. I'll let you handle it. I'll go prepare some food. They're bound to be hungry."

He watched her walk away, a frown again creasing his brow. Why had she not insisted upon advising him, staying to put in her two cents, or at least greeting the returning workers? Her response now on top of the fact that she had not accosted him earlier about his whereabouts left him totally confused. To give up so easily was not like her.

Dylan didn't have time to examine that now. He shoved it aside and went into the hallway as Samson's heavy boots thudded on the front porch.

Dylan and the two former slaves had been in the study for half an hour or more before the door finally opened. Carolyn, who had scarcely refrained from eavesdropping, was ready with a tray of hot cider and ginger cakes. Upon sight of her, Samson stood with a huge smile.

"It sure be good to see you again, Miz Carolyn," he said as she set the tray on the desk.

Carolyn made the gesture he could not, reaching for his hand and squeezing it. "I'm so glad you came home, Samson. So glad." She broadened her gaze to include Tania, who nodded stiffly. Carolyn smiled at her and nodded back. She must have peace with this woman. "Please, have some cake, Tania."

Tania took a piece and ate hungrily. Carolyn handed Samson a steaming cup.

"It bothered me a long time, Miz Carolyn, the way we done leave you," Samson told her. "I couldn' clear my mind on it. I so glad to see Mist' Dylan come home an' took care of you an' the little one."

Dylan cleared his throat.

"Yes, he did, Samson, but we still need you," Carolyn said, not taking her eyes from the big black man's face. "I hope you'll stay."

"I'm aimin' to. There's a lot of shiftless folks out there, Miz Carolyn, but I ain't one of them. Tania an' me, we want to make our own way, but we find no place that feels like home … 'cept here."

"That's wonderful." Carolyn glanced at the coffee-colored woman sitting proudly in the leather chair. Tania's face gave nothing away. Carolyn could hardly believe that her former maid shared Samson's sentiments.

"Carolyn," Dylan said. "We need to have some discussion with the other workers. Would you go call them in here, please?"

She looked back at her husband. "Of course."

Once she had rounded up Markus, John and Ham – which took some effort, since two were in the field and one was fishing at the pond – Dylan thanked her in a way that told her she was again dismissed. She stood outside the study fuming. If yesterday had not happened, would she be in there with them now? Was this how it was to be? All his talk of needing a partner, needing her expertise, was as nothing beside one whispered name?

She went back to the kitchen and helped Lydia with lunch preparations. At last she heard the study door open. She hurried into the hall as the workers filed out. Markus and John would not look at her. Confused, she glanced at Dylan, who walked past her on his way to the kitchen. At the door he began putting on work boots and outer wrappings.

Carolyn hovered over him. "Well? What happened?"

"Ham and Samson and Tania will stay. You were right; Samson honestly feels bad about leaving. I don't believe he stole the silver. So, we came to an agreement."

"And will you tell me what that was?"

He paused and looked at her, one foot poised at the top of a boot. "All the men want their own piece of land to work. It's what Samson saw being done when he was down near Athens. So you can rest easy – I didn't even have to argue about cash payment. But they don't want to work in a gang anymore. That's too much like the old days for them. They want to be responsible for their own section of the crop. Tania wants her own place. It was her condition for returning. She and Samson will build a cabin in the wooded area near the edge of the property. Until that's done they'll share their former cabin with Ham."

"But – the others?"

Dylan shoved his second boot on. "Not enough land for everybody."

"But you'll still be in charge, right?"

He buttoned up his coat. "We'll share equipment and work together at harvest, and other times when necessary. I'll make sure the land is being well-tended. But as you already know, I won't need to worry about that where Samson is concerned. I can learn from *him*. He's a more than even trade for the other two."

"But the land is still ours."

"No – I gave it away." His sarcasm took her by surprise. He drew in his lips and added, "I certainly know by now what having a bit of earth means to you, Carolyn. They'll be like renters. Until there's a profit, they'll keep their third of the crop."

"Will we have enough to live on?"

"The same as if we paid them cash, don't you think?"

He was making fun of her. She straightened and bit her lip, saying more imperiously than she would have otherwise, "It isn't what I'd pictured, but I guess it could work."

Dylan stood up. "I'm glad you approve. Did you actually think my clumsy handling would scare them away?" he asked. His face twisted then, and she glimpsed something that clutched at her heart. "Is that what I did to you?"

"No, Dylan – no!" She started to reach out to him, knowing she only had seconds before his wall went back up. Already he was turning away. "Wait – we've got to make peace between us."

"There *will* be peace between us."

"Not inside, not where it counts, until we talk about this."

"There's nothing to say."

"Won't you at least accept my apology?"

He turned on the step. "How can you apologize for something like that? It just happened. It just is."

"It's not the way you think." Carolyn clasped her arms around herself. The chill in the air and on his face sliced through to her bones.

Dylan studied her. "Isn't it?"

Carolyn didn't know what else to say. She had affirmed her love for him, cried, begged and now apologized. If he didn't accept any of those things, what else did she have to give?

She knew the answer. But how could she give her heart to a man who chose suspicion over belief, who pushed her so far away she despaired of ever being able to reach him?

Another rose came for Sylvie in February. There was a Valentine attached. She had no idea who it was from. She hadn't seen Daniel O'Keefe since Christmas. All the men who had once vied for her attention had now turned on each other, and on her. At a party last week she'd heard a former friend whisper that Sylvie Randall was fast. She wasn't fast. She just didn't trust any of them. None of them wanted her for *her*. Not even an Irish foundry foreman.

140

She hadn't gone out of the house since the party.
When she read the verse on the card she cried.

As fair art though, my bonny lass,
So deep in luve am I;
And I will love thee still, my dear,
Till a'the seas gang dry.

CHAPTER NINE

Early March 1866
Savannah, Georgia

lla Beth always enjoyed her walk to market. It was not far from St. James Square, where she now resided at the Ellis mansion, to Ellis Square, and it was a pleasant walk. Some of the homes were run down now, but they were still beautiful. On the corner of Barnard and Broughton, she looked appreciatively at the 1812 house that had belonged to General John Charles Fremont – even though he'd been a traitor and fought for the North.

The orange trees had blossomed, and the cherry laurels. Around a stand of them near a fence bees buzzed among the dark green leaves and small white flowers. Birds twittered overhead. The sun was warm on her mourning bonnet and could not fail to lift her spirits.

Accompanied by her maid, both of them carrying large straw baskets, Ella Beth entered the open Colonial-era brick building designed by Augustus Schwaab. The market was always such a stimulant to the senses, with its cacophony of voices and brightly colored and sweetly scented fruits and vegetables. It was almost like pre-war days now, with the port back up to speed, except there were always bluecoats present and the civilian shoppers looked less affluent than before. That was not the case for Ella Beth, whose grandparents now provided for her needs in exchange for her care of them. Well, really, they all knew the money that flowed into Randall and Ellis coffers was all generated one way or another by Jack and his investments – railroad stocks, the foundry and the renovated *South Land II* which again shuttled customers to Pensacola, Hilton Head and Charleston. She had money in her purse to spend, but she wished like crazy it had been of her own making.

I should count myself lucky, she thought, noticing a filthy little boy sidling up to a baker's stand. Before the child's thin hand could snake out to steal a bun, Ella Beth grabbed it and pressed a coin into the palm. When he looked at her in surprise, she tilted her head toward the baker's ample back. She watched until the boy edged around the stall to pay for his goods.

Satisfied, she turned to meet her maid's firm look and shaking head. Ella Beth did not let it bother her. Had it not been for Jack's intervention, her boys might have met a similar end.

She thought of him less now, but it still smarted at times.

While the servant fetched beef for dinner – Ella Beth hoped a strong broth might strengthen her grandfather – she purchased onions and carrots. She had wandered to another stand to consider bananas when a solid form suddenly appeared before her.

"I thought I saw a lass I knew," Daniel O'Keefe's voice said, "though it's hard to tell one from another with so many wearing black."

"But I have my veil back."

"Aye, but that only helped me a little, as the face under it was smilin' instead of frownin'." His contagious grin softened his words.

"Are you always so incorrigible?" Ella Beth asked.

"My mother tells me so."

"Well, you won't get the best of me this time. I'm determined to show you just how pleasant I normally am, even in the face of bad manners." Ella Beth put on a smile and dropped a little curtsy for good measure.

Daniel bowed. "It's well you are doing, then?"

"Well enough."

"You sold your house on Abercorn."

"How did you know that?"

A half shrug. "I hear – things. I hear also your grandfather's bad ailing."

"Yes," Ella Beth admitted. "We fear he hasn't long to live. The dementia takes his mind most days. It's powerfully hard on my grandmother. But she handles it with such patience and sweetness."

Daniel looked thoughtful. "I like to think time and experience are like the ovens in the foundry. If we submit to them they'll burn away our flaws. Those who have endured the fire are able to face life with more grace."

Ella Beth frowned. It always unsettled her to hear statements like that coming from the lips of one the world deemed second class. Class conscious sorts in Savannah even called the Irish "Negroes turned inside out." To cover her emotions, she asked, "Do you always talk about iron?"

That grin again. "It's what I spend most of my time with, Mrs. Draper. It's either find lessons for life in it or go mad with the repetition of my duties."

He would not be a foreman for long. He would own his own foundry in five years or she was a fool.

"But I'm rudely interruptin' your shopping," O'Keefe continued.

"Yes, you are."

"May I carry your basket for you?"

She raised her eyebrows. "Haven't you somewhere to be?"

"Aye. Here."

"What about the foundry?"

He smiled. "'Tis Saturday."

"Oh, yes. So it is. Well, if you're determined …" She let her voice trail off, handing him her basket even as she pretended to examine grapefruit.

Why was she so flustered? Everything she'd ever been taught said that he was far beneath her, but in his presence she tingled all the way down to her toes. Had it been that long since a man had paid attention to her?

He followed her along like a dutiful puppy as she made her purchases, talking about the wares, pointing out bargains, making droll observations about the unique people they passed. She was painfully aware of his presence, so much so that she hardly knew what she bought.

"Walking back home?" he asked when she announced she had everything she'd come for.

And then some, she thought wryly. "Yes," Ella Beth said. She saw her servant across the way and motioned to her.

"This basket's too heavy for ye now. Why don't I just go along for the walk?"

"Well, I …" Ella Beth didn't dare glance at the black woman who joined them. She could feel the servant's disapproval emanating from her ample body like steam. She decided that for once she would do what she wanted to. "I'd be pleased to have an escort."

"Fine, then." With a bright smile, Daniel held out his free arm.

Shyly Ella Beth took it.

On the way home, she matched her pace to his slightly limping one. They talked of the foundry and of Daniel's family. He spoke with great fondness of his mother and siblings.

"But did you never want a family of your own, Mr. O'Keefe?" Ella Beth heard herself ask. Her servant's eyes bugged out. Where had such boldness come from?

But Daniel was nonplussed. "Aye," he answered readily enough, though his tone lowered and softened. "A bonny lass I had before the war. I was pledged to marry her. But while I was gone she died of the fever."

"Oh! I'm sorry," Ella Beth gasped, regretting she had pried.

He shook his head and looked over at her. "It's all right, Mrs. Draper. Maybe 'tis why I recognized the same sort of sadness that you bear."

"But I wore mine on my shoulder while you … you face life with such joy," she murmured, embarrassed to recall her jealousy and self-pity. "What you must think of me," she added quietly.

The knowing look he gave her confirmed her worst fears, but again his voice was gentle. "There's no shame in mourning, nor in looking for love again once the sorrow fades a bit. The important thing is not to rush it. When it's right, your heart will know."

What was he trying to tell her?

"Ma'am, we almost home," the servant said. She was trying to warn Ella Beth that it would be best to part ways with Daniel here on the street, rather than to raise questions among the staff and family by bringing him to the door.

"Yes, well, here we are ..." Reluctantly Ella Beth let go of Daniel's arm.

"You go to market every Saturday?"

"Usually."

Their companion gave a disgusted harrumph.

Daniel lifted his hat off his dark head and bowed. "Then perhaps I'll run into you there again."

"Perhaps."

Sylvie Randall snuffled tragically into a handkerchief, not because she was at a wake, but because every woman there had either turned up their nose at her or pretended to look straight through her. It was unfair, ridiculous and hurtful. If only her mother would finish paying her respects to Jack's grandmother and take her home.

"I miss Jack," she mumbled to herself, dabbing her swollen eyes.

At least this would bring him back to Savannah a week or so early. She had already posted a letter telling him of his grandfather's passing. He would be so upset that he would have to miss the funeral. There was, however, nothing to be done about that.

Sylvie was seated in a small anteroom across the hall from the parlor where William Ellis was laid out, the clock stopped and the mirrors draped in black. People were so silly about superstitions, like believing that the next person to look in the mirror in a house where someone had died would be the next one to pass.

Thinking she had successfully secreted herself, Sylvie was startled when the door cracked open and Ella Beth, with Andrew Willis, peeked in.

"I thought I heard someone talking in here," Ella Beth said. "But whatever are you doing, Sylvie – and so upset?" She said the last as if no one but she and Grace had a right to be upset – whether it be about William or not.

Sylvie turned sulky eyes on her. Ella Beth had not helped her situation, strolling about the market and the park nearly every Saturday with Daniel O'Keefe. Everyone in town knew and was talking. Sylvie had written Jack about that, too. The most annoying thing was, no one seemed to be snubbing Ella Beth. Why was that, because she was so serious and boring people thought her incapable of creating a scandal?

"I merely am trying to have a *private* moment."

"By all means, then." Ella Beth put her nose in the air and went to close the door, but Andrew's hand actually shot out and stopped it.

"If you would, Mrs. Draper – if Miss Randall would – I would have a word with her," he said.

Ella Beth looked as surprised as Sylvie felt but withdrew with a decorous bow of her golden head. Willis edged in to the chamber and settled on the chair beside her. She watched him with wide eyes. *Well?* What could he possibly have to say to her?

"Mr. Willis ..." she prompted, a little impatiently.

"Ah – Miss Randall, it distresses me to see you so grieved. I thought you looked in need of company, despite your protestations."

"I assure you I am fine."

"There is nothing I can bring you, nothing I can do, in the absence of your brother?"

As if he could fill a toe of Jack's one shoe. "Thank you, no."

"Then ... allow me to express my condolences on your loss."

"Mr. Ellis was not my grandfather," Sylvie reminded him.

"Ah – yes. That's right. I had forgotten. But – you were so ..." Andrew's look of confusion filled in the void his voice left. Sylvie squirmed when understanding dawned. So even he had heard the ugly talk. The last thing she needed was sympathy from this self-effacing clerk.

To her surprise, though, he changed the subject. "Do you have a date for your brother's return?"

"I hope he will be in Savannah by the end of April."

"Oh, yes, I think ... I think he might have mentioned something like that to me as well. This will be hard on him. I know how much Mr. Randall admired his grandfather, how integral he was in the early years of our firm."

Willis sat there, annoyingly stiff and proper. And yet ... he had not condemned her. His manner was kind and gentle. A spark of gratitude toward him ignited inside her, followed by a moment of curiosity. Who were his people? Where did he even live? He seemed like he must have had a genteel raising, despite his rather humble occupation.

The spark died out when she considered the way in which he had said "our firm." Presumptuous.

As if sensing her irritation, Andrew Willis rose, pushed his glasses up on his nose and said, "Well then, Miss Randall, I will leave you to your private moment. It was a pleasure speaking with you."

He bowed his way out. He must be daft as well as stiff. She had in no way tried to make it pleasant.

Jack's six-month period of bereavement for his grandfather precluded his participation in any of the balls and dinners customarily bestowed upon newlyweds returning from honeymoon, but, Sunny had pointed out, Mahala at least could be properly welcomed home. A brunch, she decided, would be just the opportunity for the ladies of Savannah to feast on tales from the couple's European hiatus. It would be elegant but subdued, only the best of society invited.

The dining room table was extended and set with the best crystal and china. Fresh flowers were arranged. A pianist and a violinist were engaged to provide music. And the French chef, sent down from Habersham since business there was so slow, stirred and fussed all evening and all morning in the kitchen.

At the appointed hour, Sunny, Sylvie and Mahala gathered in the parlor, ready to receive their guests. All were gowned in their finest morning dresses.

"The McComb sisters will be first," Sylvie declared.

But the minutes ticked by. No McComb sisters. No one.

"Were the time and date correct on the invitation?" Sunny fretted, going to get one out to check. "Yes, yes, they are. And I had a good response. Most everyone said they were coming. Perhaps we set the hour too early."

Mahala got a sick feeling in her stomach. She listened to the clock tick and waited. The feeling grew and came into focus. While on her honeymoon, she had been fêted by the open-minded French as unique and beautiful. Worth's attention had done much to bolster her self-esteem, as Jack had known it would. In Italy, the only second glances her darker skin attracted were admiring ones. Upon their return to England, they had spent a week at the grand estate of friends they had made on the *Aleppo* voyage. But here, where she longed to be embraced the most, nothing had changed.

At last she spoke aloud. "I don't know why I expected it would be different. I shouldn't be surprised. But I dread to tell Jack." He would be upset, upset for her. And hurt again himself.

"I – I don't think it's you, Mahala," Sylvie said in an unsteady voice.

"What do you mean?"

The young woman burst into tears. "I think it's my fault! My reputation is ruined!"

"*What?*" Moving to comfort her, putting her arms around Jack's sister's thin, shaking shoulders, Mahala looked askance at Sunny.

Sunny looked troubled, shaking her head. "Impossible," she said. "A few flirtations should never bring about total censure. And that is what this is. No coincidence, but an organized boycott. It makes me so angry. Sylvie may have been rash, but she doesn't deserve this. No, I think it must be due to Jack's cousin's going about with that Irishman. You should have him speak to her, Mahala, and at once."

It was Mahala's turn to shake her head. She knew Jack would no more want to get into Ella Beth's business than Mahala wanted him to. "No. I don't think this is any one person's fault. I think – if I may be so bold as to say it ..."

"Go on," Sunny urged.

"I think it's the way the whole family is perceived. You're – *we're* – too unconventional. Jack was already riding a fine line with his Northern ties and his blockade running. Now, perhaps the people think the Randalls take their wealth as a license to wink at society's rules."

"It could be," Sunny said thoughtfully. "We have always been watched with a fine-tuned telescope."

Sylvie snuffled and blew into her handkerchief. "This is terrible," she moaned. "We've been excommunicated. It's not like you can help where you fall in love, or who your parents are." In the face of her anguish, she was willing to give even Ella Beth a break. "Why are people so cruel?"

"People never like what's different," Mahala said.

"And they're jealous," Sunny added. "But this can't go on. I won't have Sylvie's future threatened because of a few mean old biddies."

"I have an idea," Mahala said.

Both sets of eyes turned on her.

She'd had it while picnicking on the grounds of the Pantheon in Stourhead, watching graceful swans glide over the surface of the pond in front of the temple's majestic white columns. It had come to her so suddenly she'd sat up straight and declared the same thing to Jack. A perfect solution, she had said, to both Savannah's need and the ostracism of the Randalls. It was a way they could give back, to show they cared. It would also give her days meaning while Jack was absorbed with business. Jack had agreed with her idea, had even offered to fund the whole thing should she so desire. Because she wanted this to be *her* project, they had decided it would be partly funded by her father's money. But it was important the whole family be on board.

"Ella Beth's situation made me start thinking. How many women there are now without means! How many children with no father! Most of them don't have family who can afford to care for them, and they long to be independent – like you said Ella Beth does. Then there are the men maimed in the war who can never work again, or if they do, will receive only the paltriest of wages. What if we provided a place for these people to stay, a boarding house where the rent is fixed on ability to pay?"

Sunny's eyes widened. After a moment she said, "Charity work. I like the idea."

"And there's more," Mahala ventured, not certain how the women would react. "What if eventually we drew in other landlords, society people with big places they can no longer afford to keep up? Opening portions of their homes could allow them to stay in residence."

"And bring us a debt of gratitude. I follow your thinking, but there's a major flaw in it. These people would never allow themselves to become indebted to the 'scalawag Randalls.' They are far too proud."

"Perhaps. But maybe not, if there was first a model – a successful foundation. Those receiving help would talk. Word would get around. We could put notices in the paper when we were ready to start a second home. Money could be made available – only a set amount, mind you – grants with a strict application process for some upstanding family willing to reach out to those in need by opening their property on the principles of our first boarding house."

"You make it exclusive ..." Sunny began.

"And they will want it!" Sylvie finished for her.

"But where would this first home for the widows and fatherless be? Would we purchase a place?"

"There are certainly plenty such places on the market, but I was wondering ... about the Ellis mansion."

Mahala paused while both women looked at her. She hadn't yet told Jack about this portion of her plan. But if she could get him to approve the public use of his family's estate, if Grace and Ella Beth could experience a new purpose in life by overseeing a boarding house, the old Southern Ellis name would lend a dignity and credibility that little else would.

"Jack's grandmother is in good health," she went on, trying to sound convincing, afraid she had just lost her audience, "and she and Ella Beth have so much time on their hands now. My grandmother's servants might come down to help them since our hotel is closed–"

"It's brilliant!" Sunny exclaimed.

Mahala stopped, surprised.

"I don't know if the Ellises will consent to their house being occupied by strangers, especially when you consider that it would necessarily have to be altered to make that possible, but ..."

"That's true."

"But I do think they will like the idea of helping."

"I hope so."

"I admit I didn't know at first what my stepson saw in you, Mahala, but I think I'm catching on." Sunny stood up and took a deep breath while Mahala watched in silent amazement. "Well, we have all this food, and it needs to be eaten. Now that there's no party, what do you say we send over our carriage for the two widows? We can talk everything over with them."

Mahala and Sylvie rose, too. Sylvie laughed, and the sound was wonderful to hear. "I think that's a great idea," she said.

As the younger woman reached out and clasped both Mahala and Sunny in a trio of an embrace, Mahala felt tears fill her eyes. She had been wrong to think nothing had changed.

Late April, 1866
Habersham County, Georgia

Mahala was coming to Clarkesville. As soon as Martha had received a letter indicating the expected date of her granddaughter's arrival, she had sent word to Carolyn that her old friend would be calling on her. Carolyn had mixed emotions about such a visit. Many a day she had missed Mahala's easy company of the past, the way she would lighten the load of chores with her talk and laughter. But now there were things Carolyn had to hide – things she was not sure she *could* hide – from Mahala's perceptive gaze.

It would only be one afternoon, she told herself, for Martha had already relayed Mahala's intention to return quickly to Savannah. How hard could it be to act as if everything was normal for that long? And how hard could it be to let the one person who had always understood her in the past leave again?

In preparation for the visit, Carolyn baked up a pound cake – an extravagant luxury to be sure, but what delicacies must Mahala have grown accustomed to in Europe?

At last a message came from town that Mrs. Jack Randall requested to call the following afternoon. Carolyn sent a note back with the errand boy that she would be pleased to accept a call. When had Mahala grown so formal? Used to be, she would not have been able to restrain herself and would have ridden straight out on Unagina, knowing she needed no introduction. But then, Carolyn wasn't being fair. Mahala would need time with her grandmother first. And just maybe she had been a little disappointed that Carolyn had only answered Mahala's correspondences from Europe with one short note. What had there been to say?

The morning of Mahala's visit Carolyn was queasy, but it had mostly passed by mid-afternoon. She sat in the parlor with Henrietta, mending a shirt. Even with that task she felt lazy. There was so much to do this time of year. Dylan, Ham and Samson were planting corn, nestling the seeds an inch deep and six inches apart in rows they had painstakingly watered by hand, since there had been precious little rain. In the evenings, Samson worked on his cabin. They could hear the hammering up at the big house. Tania was putting in her own garden at the site, while Henrietta and Lydia worked the big house garden. After a day in the field, Dylan always had chores to do with the livestock and the buildings which were in disrepair, or some errand in town. She scarcely saw him, but he had strictly forbidden her to ride or to work outside the house. Carolyn had expressed her guilt to Henrietta that she wasn't able to be more helpful, but Henrietta backed Dylan up, saying that nothing was more important than the health of the coming baby.

Now, Henrietta looked relieved to be able to sit quietly with her knitting. In fact, she was about to doze off. Carolyn said nothing to wake her, noting the dark circles around her mother-in-law's eyes. She could not even bring herself to resent Henrietta's presence in what she might have wished to be a private interview with her friend. She knew the older woman was starved for a reminder of life outside Forests of Green.

When the knock came on the door and Carolyn heard her friend's familiar voice in the hall, all Carolyn's apprehensions fled. She hurried out, ready to embrace Mahala. But the sight of the woman in the flame-colored dress brought her up short. Could this be Mahala, the girl who'd once been frightened to set foot inside the Rousseau home?

Now, she was as vivid as life, with her hair in an elaborate and sophisticated coil beneath a white hat trimmed in black braid and burnt orange rouching. Garnets winked at her ears, and taupe kid gloves were on her hands. More than that, more than the outward embellishments, was the way she held herself, as though she had finally found her place in the world. Well, she had.

"Carolyn!" Mahala opened her arms.

Carolyn embraced her, holding her friend a long minute, almost afraid to pull back and see again the changes.

But Henrietta reminded her, having come to the parlor door and said, "Mrs. Randall! How good to see you again. And how elegant you look."

"It's Mahala – please."

"But whatever are you wearing?"

Mahala smiled. "It's the new princess dress style. The panels are fitted together and gored from shoulder to hem. Quite different, isn't it?"

"Well, turn around. I've never seen anything like it!"

Carolyn suddenly realized she was wearing one of Mahala's old dresses. "Why don't y'all go and sit down and I'll bring some refreshments," she said.

Mahala looked startled at Carolyn's abrupt directions but recovered her poise quickly. "Of course," she agreed.

"I can't wait to hear all about Europe," Henrietta said.

"I can't wait to tell you about it. I haven't had much chance to share about all we saw and did, except with Jack's family of course. The Ellises being in mourning has limited our socializing."

"Oh, yes, I was so sorry to hear about William Ellis."

When Carolyn returned and put down the tray, she felt Mahala's eyes go sharply over her, not with judgment, but with something worse ... concern. Carolyn tried to imagine what she saw and pitied. The old dress, the plain hairdo, the lack of jewelry, a too-thin body despite the rounding abdomen that strained under her waistband. Yes, Mahala's gaze was there. She stood up and reached for Carolyn, embracing her again.

"Why did you not tell me? Congratulations!" she exclaimed.

"I – thank you."

"When are you due?"

"Early October, it would seem."

"Dylan must be very happy."

"Oh, he is," Henrietta said.

Mahala glanced at her, then back at Carolyn, who smiled. There was no telling anyone her most painful secret, that her husband now used her delicate condition to avoid intimacy with her. There had been just enough hint of trouble in the pregnancy to validate his excuse. The more time went by, the higher Dylan's walls grew. Nothing Carolyn did seemed to be able to breech them. But this was the last thing Carolyn wanted to share with Mahala, who so obviously was flourishing in her own marriage.

"Well, I envy you," Mahala said then, ironically. "For I have no such news to share, and it would have been so wonderful to have children close to the same age."

Carolyn glimpsed a fleeting sadness on Mahala's face. "You know when I was married before, it took quite a long time," she said. "It will happen for you soon enough. Until then, you have so many opportunities. Your grandmother tells us you are renovating a house for widows and orphans."

Mahala's expression brightened. As she told Carolyn all about the project, her enthusiasm was unmistakable. The Ellises had decided to keep their own house intact, so Jack had located a large property for sale quite nearby on Broughton Street. However, Grace Ellis and Ella Beth Draper would be involved in operating the home. Mahala was bursting to meet with the architect next week.

"It's a project for the women of our family," Mahala said, "a way to get involved in giving back to the community. We've decided to call the fund The Phoenix Foundation. Jack is setting up all the paperwork now."

"That's wonderful," Carolyn said. "So ... I guess you won't be returning to Habersham for some time." She couldn't keep the disappointment from her voice.

"No," Mahala agreed quietly. There was a pause, then she added, "Grandmother told me Abel Quitman has returned."

"That's true," Carolyn had to admit, "but I hear that he's behaving himself. The sheriff can't arrest him for what happened in October, but he's let Quitman know he's keeping very close tabs on him."

Mahala sighed and shook her head. The feather on her hat draped elegantly against her dark hair as she sipped her tea. "That may be the case, but Jack and I feel it's too early to test his limits."

Jack and I. It would be so nice to say "Dylan and I," thought Carolyn.

Mahala continued. "So I've decided to keep myself busy in Savannah. I'm not even going out to Highlands Home this trip. It would hurt too much. I'm just staying at the hotel and then taking Grandmother back to the city with me as soon as possible. Maddie and Zed have even agreed to come along, to work at the boarding house. But I do promise …" Mahala leaned forward and reached for Carolyn's hand. "I *will* return. One day, this will be home again."

Carolyn nodded and managed a fleeting smile, pulling her hand away. She was not used to being at the needing end of things. She felt hollow inside.

"But tell us of Europe," Henrietta urged. "It's been so long since I was there!"

And you will never go again, thought Carolyn, her bitter emotions stirred. She sat and nibbled pound cake as Mahala talked. She related visiting the French court in Versailles, dancing in the ivory wedding dress remade for her with tulle, swansdown, crystal beads and glass pearls by Worth himself, admiring Greek sculpture in Florence, and visiting the Coliseum and Spanish Steps in Rome. She spoke of European politics, intrigues and innovations, then of her visit to her new friend in England and to Jack's family in New York.

The world is going on without me, and I am stuck forever in the war that is not over, Carolyn realized.

"Oh, dear," Mahala declared at last. "I'm afraid I've run on far too long. Please forgive me. I was so looking forward to talking to someone about the trip, someone I knew had been there and would appreciate it."

"Of course," Henrietta murmured. Carolyn could see Mahala's money and new polish had made great strides with her mother-in-law. Though she might never fully approve of Jack, a cultured woman was always attractive to her.

"I'm afraid the reception in Savannah has been rather cool," Mahala admitted.

Carolyn tried to stir her sympathy, but social snubbing seemed a small thing now next to the threat of starvation. "Folks will come around," she said. "There are just a lot of people struggling due to the war."

"Yes, which is why we want to help. Speaking of which, how are you managing here? Grandmother says things are tight for everyone."

"Oh, we're doing all right," Henrietta replied, her wall going up again with her back.

"Samson returned, and Tania," Carolyn added as she reached for a second slice of pound cake. Right now, she could eat the whole thing if she let herself. "So with Ham that makes three strong men to work the place." She went on to describe the arrangements they had made with the former slaves.

"It sounds wise," Mahala said.

"It may take us some time to find the right crop to get ahead with, but we will," Carolyn stated, far more optimistically than she felt. It seemed everyone she knew was trying whatever they could to make a dollar, things they would have considered hair-brained and outlandish before the war. It was almost embarrassing. But one did what one must.

"I know you will. And if there's anything we can do to help, let us know."

"Thank you, but we're fine," Henrietta said.

"I just meant … oh, never mind. Well, I'd better get back to town."

"Will you stay to supper?" Carolyn asked. *Please don't. If you do I'll break down and cry because I can't keep up this charade any longer and I don't know what in the world I'd serve you.*

"Thank you, but Grandmother is expecting me."

The ladies rose. Mahala glanced at Henrietta and said, Carolyn thought with a clear but well-placed hint, "Mrs. Rousseau, it has been good to see you again. Thank you for having me."

Henrietta bowed her head. "It was our pleasure."

Filling in the expected gap, Carolyn murmured, "I'll walk out with you."

As they did, Mahala took her arm and drew her close to her side. "How I've missed you. How I needed you to set the Savannah biddies in their places."

Carolyn laughed faintly, feeling like she looked back on another girl, the Carolyn of the past. "I'm afraid I might not be much help. I've been out of polite society for so long."

"Oh, you would. Your name and your manner alone would whip them into shape in no time."

Her name? What did it mean now, to be a Rousseau? They still held the town house, but it was being leased out this year. They had finally reclaimed The Marshes and authorities had evicted the vagrants, but Dylan was putting it on the market. He had just taken out a line of credit again for the supplies they needed for spring planting. With any luck, they would grow enough to live on, but little more. The state legislature had passed a stay law allowing an extension of payments on farmers' contracts made prior to June

1 of the year previous, but Dylan had made his arrangements just after that date. After they'd honored their financial commitments, only a few coins had been left. Was one's name only related to how much money one had in the bank, or what patch of ground one owned?

"A good name is rather to be chosen than great riches, and loving favour rather than silver and gold…" Unbidden, the Scripture popped into Carolyn's mind.

And her manner. It was not what it used to be. Shame filled her at her husband's rejection, guilt at the secrets she kept.

Mahala no longer knew her.

But she still cared. That much was evident as she paused on the porch, her gaze going over the peeling paint on the columns – at odds with the fresh spring life shooting forth around them – then returned to Carolyn, searching. "Is everything really o.k.?"

"Pride goeth before destruction, and an haughty spirit before a fall…"

A smile and a nod. "Of course."

"And with Dylan? I thought to find you blooming with contentment, but …"

"Do I not seem content?"

"You seem altered."

A surge of resentment rose in Carolyn, that Mahala could have seen all the ills in Savannah but would expect no change here. While she had basked in blessings, others suffered. Why would she think Carolyn would not be among those? "So I am, and so is Dylan. The war has changed many things for us."

"And yet you can find comfort in each other, can you not?"

If only it were that simple. *I can't tell her. What could she do, but pity me?* Carolyn put a hand on her swollen abdomen and smiled. "And in our coming child."

"Of course." Mahala smiled in a wistful manner and patted her hand. "Well, if you ever need to get away, come stay with us on Wright Square."

"Thank you. I'll remember that."

Mahala looked unsatisfied, but she said only, "I'll miss you!"

The women embraced, and Mahala climbed into Jack's handsome carriage. Carolyn waved as she departed.

When she went back into the house, Henrietta was cleaning up the tea things. "Well, that was a lovely visit, was it not – apart from her presuming we needed rescuing."

"Indeed. I'm feeling a bit queasy again. Do you mind if I go lie down?"

"Not at all. Do you need anything?"

Carolyn shook her head. Too much cake, too much richness on an unaccustomed stomach. It was her own fault.

Upstairs, she fell across the bed and managed to still her churning middle by lying there unmoving. At last, she curled into a ball. She put a hand on her stomach and thought about the child within. Dylan hardly spoke of the baby. Did he even want it, or had he pushed thoughts of it away as he had of her? Would a son or daughter, once born, bring them closer? She could only hold out for that hope.

The uncertainties of the future crowded in on her, and tears found their release. She wept for what had been, what should have been, and what was gone forever. Finally Carolyn rose and went to the bureau for a handkerchief. As she moved the linens in the top drawer, she felt a small, hard rectangle. She picked it up and gazed at Devereaux's likeness. It had been a long time since she'd seen it. In an attempt not to fuel Dylan's jealousy, she had put it away. Now, looking at the familiar, handsome face and dark hair curling over the collar of his uniform reminded her that she had overcome adversity and obstacles once before. She could do so again.

The room spun, and she clutched the dresser to keep from falling. She shoved the daguerreotype toward the drawer before staggering to the bed, closing her eyes against the dizziness. No one called her to supper, and at last, she slept.

Ghosts filled the halls of Forests of Green. Carolyn could feel their crowding, oppressive presence before she ever came to wakefulness. She heard their moaning and felt their suffering.

Suddenly she sat up in bed. Awareness and surprise came simultaneously. Dylan was beside her, thrashing, groaning in his sleep. She was astonished to find him there. He must have thought her exhausted enough that she would not wake when he joined her during the night. As she watched him, pity washed over her. What horrors did he see in his sleep? How many dead men haunted him from their graves? And why would they not let him go?

Carolyn reached out and touched his shoulder. "Dylan. Dylan, wake up."

He opened his eyes, but it was a minute before lucidity settled over his features. His breath was fast, and perspiration beaded his upper lip. With a deep sigh he drug an arm across his face, as if dispelling cobwebs. "I'm sorry," he said, sitting up.

"For what?"

"For waking you. I worked so hard today I thought ..."

Carolyn waited for him to finish, but he didn't. Tentatively she laid a hand over his. "Why don't you tell me about your dreams?"

"There are some things best left unsaid." He swung the covers back and got out of bed.

Carolyn scooted to the edge. "Didn't I tell you that very thing one time, and you said you had lived too long with things left unspoken – and would never do so again?"

"That was different."

"What are you doing?" The answer to that was obvious. In the pale moonlight he was pulling pants over his long johns. She felt a rising sense of panic at being abandoned again. "Where are you going? It's the middle of the night!"

"Nothing clears my head like a ride."

"Please, Dylan, come back to bed. Talk to me. Help me to understand."

He whirled around to glare at her. "Good land, Carolyn – I'm going crazy here, can't you tell? Pressure from every direction every day, no sleep at night, and you want to pick my brain? You won't like what you find! Do you think by sharing my demons I'll be cured of them?"

"It might be a start! Just tell me – tell me what's making you so restless, so angry!"

Dylan paused, his shoulders slumped, back turned. She swung her legs over the side of the bed. But then she saw him reach for a small object on the dresser. When Carolyn caught the glint of glass in the moonlight, her heart seemed to stop before it started thundering. She remembered the room spinning, tossing the picture in the drawer. Only it hadn't landed there. Her husband turned to look at her, the daguerreotype in his hand. A muscle worked in his jaw.

"Just tell me," he said quietly, "why I should open my heart to a woman still so clearly yearning for one of the very ghosts that haunts my dreams."

"Dylan–"

"He's dead, Carolyn. Dead! Rotting away in a grave! Imagine *that*! But it doesn't matter, does it? His noble demise made him all the more an idol. You'll always remember him just like this." He gestured with the photograph. Before she could reply he whirled and threw it with all his strength into the darkened hole of the fireplace. The glass struck the bricks and shattered.

Carolyn jumped and caught her breath, edging back on the mattress.

He saw and laughed at her. "You think I'm coming for you? Don't worry."

She cowered while he yanked a shirt over his head. Then, once Dylan stormed out of the room, she got to her feet and with trembling fingers lit a lamp. Going to kneel by the hearth, with care she swept up the glass with the broom. She picked the broken bits from the frame and briefly held the likeness to her breast before putting it away in the drawer and firmly closing the dresser.

Carolyn lay sleepless the rest of the night. She did not rise to help with breakfast. She heard Henrietta go in and get Dev Jr.. Her limbs felt like they had turned to jelly. When she smelled bacon frying, her stomach tied in a knot. She rose and dressed sloppily, not bothering to wind up her braid.

At the kitchen table Henrietta's servant Lydia was spearing slices of meat onto the plates of those gathered: Henrietta, quiet and pale in black; Dev Jr., who greeted her with a smile and a cry of "Mama!"; and Dylan, who rose as she entered but did not look at her. He wore the same clothes he had left in last night, and his eyes were red-rimmed. As he held her chair he detected the unmistakable smell of whiskey. Her stomach tightened even further, and she thought she might burst into tears.

Oh, God, what's become of us?

Oblivious to the drama, the black woman plopped meat onto the plate she brought for Carolyn and said in a sing-song voice, "The last of the bacon. Best eat up!"

Carolyn cut and chewed the salted meat, but tears blurred her vision. She couldn't muffle the snuffling breath she drew in.

Dylan stood up. "Please excuse me. I'm not hungry." He pushed back his chair and started to walk away, then paused. With his knife he stabbed his ham and transferred it to Carolyn's plate. Then, without saying a word, he left.

Tears overcame her.

"What wrong with that man?" Lydia exclaimed.

Carolyn broke into uncontrolled sobbing.

"Mama!" Dev Jr. pleaded, distressed. Lydia went to distract him.

Henrietta came and stood behind her daughter-in-law, wrapping her arms around Carolyn's shoulders. She waited until Carolyn could speak.

"It's all my fault!" Carolyn cried, turning her face into Henrietta's embrace. "He thinks I don't love him. He doesn't love me. What am I to do?"

"He does love you," Henrietta insisted with surprising firmness. "I know he's confused right now, but with Dylan, you must read between the lines. As for what you are to do, well, eat that bacon."

Startled, Carolyn gazed at her mother-in-law. What she saw in the older woman's expression caused her to suck in her breath and mop her face with her napkin. She had never felt more miserable in her life. But she focused on the piece of meat on her plate. If this was the only token of affection Dylan could spare in his anger, she would have to accept it. Steadying her shaking hand, she took up her fork and ate.

Three days later, Dylan had just gone back out to the fields from lunch when Carolyn heard the rattle of an approaching wagon. She hurried onto the front porch and watched as the vehicle with two black men on the seat stopped in front of the steps.

"I'm sorry, we don't have any work for hire," she called out, well accustomed to drifters wanting an odd job for a bit of pay. Problem was, as soon as she told them they couldn't pay laborers, those inquiring always asked for a meal. Carolyn braced herself.

But the driver's answer surprised her. "Yes'm, you do. This house need paintin'. We unload the paint here, if you kindly tell us where to put the wagon once we done."

Carolyn put her hands on her hips. This was the most presumption she'd ever seen displayed. "Now you just go along. I said we don't have any work, and I mean it. We can't pay you. Don't make me call my husband."

"We done been paid, Miz Rousseau."

"Mrs. ...? How did you know that?"

"I'm sorry, Ma'am. I reckon I done forget my manners again. We only got a week afore we hafta get back to Athens, an' by the look of things it gonna take all that time an' more." The driver lifted his holey hat off his head and scratched in his curly hair. "I'm Abe, an' this here's Clancy. We got a regular business down in Clarke County, an' we do your house up nice. So we promised Miz Randall."

Carolyn's mouth fell open. Mahala had done this! Shame, followed by tender gratitude, bubbled up in her heart. "Very well," she spluttered. She gestured to her left. "You can unload right here. The barn's around back. I – hope you don't mind sleeping there, too. We're all full up."

"No problem, Ma'am."

As she watched the workers swing paint cans, tools and boards that would make scaffolding down at the corner of the house, Carolyn decided she'd let them get a good start before she announced their presence to Dylan. A freshly painted house would lift everyone's spirits – especially Henrietta's. Even if it was only like whitewashing a sepulcher. She wouldn't let his pride ruin that little bit.

CHAPTER TEN

Early May 1866
Savannah, Georgia

ahala and Ella Beth were working in their late herb garden at Pheonix House. They had made use of the original raised beds, but the plots had been neglected and had required the germination of new seeds and the generous application of fertilizer.

Mahala glanced up, tilting back her netted straw hat to wipe her forehead. "I'm sorry we didn't get the place early enough to re-seed the parsley."

"It's all right," Ella Beth replied. "We'll plant it next year. Until then we have plenty at Grandmother's house."

Mahala nodded. She tossed another spadeful of dirt at the foot of the plot containing dill, basil, anise and cumin. "Did you see my ad in the paper?"

"Yes." Ella Beth didn't want to say so, but the wording had been ingenious. It had called upon any genteel displaced widows to apply for lodgings in Savannah's newest and finest boarding house – on a first-come, first-served basis. Application was to be made to Mrs. Grace Ellis. There had been no mention of the Randall name, only a statement that the Phoenix Foundation was a Southern company committed to serving Southerners. Word would get around soon enough who was behind the whole venture. By then, Ella Beth guessed that there would be a wait list. She said, "I like the idea of charging rent based on income."

"Yes. We decided to fix their monthly rate on a percentage of their income, or what they have in the bank. Jack thought people would feel good about paying what they can."

"Of course." Ella Beth glanced up. "Ah, here's your mother-in-law."

"Hello!" Sunny called as she hurried across the lawn. A black man with a wheel barrow trundled after her. "I brought your spearmint and peppermint plants!"

"Oh, thank you!" Ella Beth cried. She rose to her feet and brushed off her skirt. While Sunny paused to survey the crew whitewashing the rear brick side of the Federal-style house, Ella Beth stepped over and sniffed the herbs appreciatively. Rubbing their soft leaves, she imagined the soothing teas they would create.

Sunny frowned. "That Irish man is installing the gate," she pronounced. "He asked after you, Ella Beth, but I told him you were busy."

160

"You did?" Ella Beth did not quite manage to hide the dismay in her voice.

Sunny didn't miss it. "I did, and you would be wise to stay that way. Your walks home from market with him have not gone unnoticed. I swear I don't know what you young women see in the man. He's a ruffian, Ella Beth, a worker. Not our equal."

Ella Beth glanced down. She could feel her cheeks burning under Sunny's rebuke. She knew the truth was that she was doing the very thing that she had scorned Sylvie for. In fact, she now realized her early irritation towards them had been jealousy. But she couldn't seem to help herself. Each time she saw Daniel O'Keefe coming, with that peculiar, jaunty, limping walk and that grin on his face, her heart leapt. The short visits were never enough. She could talk on and on with him, his stories making her laugh, his accent so filling her head she heard him speaking when he was not there. But did she have the courage to defy society? And would he ask her to?

Mahala stood up. "The design on the gate was specially ordered from Randall Iron, New York, where they do beautiful decorative wrought iron. It's supposed to be a phoenix. I for one would really like to see it. Wouldn't you, Ella Beth?"

"Why, yes!"

Sunny's dark brows winged down. "Your status as a widow will only grant you so much license, Ella Beth," she said as the younger women turned away.

Mahala linked her arm through Ella Beth's. "It's a gate, Sunny. While we're gone would you have your servant put the plants atop that bed near the chamomile, please?"

Ella Beth hated to feel grateful to Mahala. She told herself there was no need to hold onto old jealousies. That would be grievously inappropriate now. But the transition from enemy to friend was awkward, and could not be accomplished too swiftly, though Daniel O'Keefe was helping her with that. How much of her interest in him was the balm his attentions smoothed on her wounded vanity?

She saw him there by the gate and knew it was not all. Oh, that it were. That would be simple. But she had had simple and had struggled to make it enough.

"Hello, Mr. O'Keefe!" Mahala called out.

He turned to them with a bright smile. "Ladies!" He raised his hat and bowed, swinging the new gate open. "Come and see the newest improvement to Phoenix House."

"Oh, it's splendid!" Mahala cried, putting a hand to her chest as she gazed at the spread-winged bird depicted in the ironwork.

"I think so, too. It's a fine thing you're doing, Mrs. Randall. In fact, I have to tell you as I was screwing this in a moment ago, two ladies happened by. You could tell they was ladies, of course. They stood right over there and talked as though I was deaf."

"What did they say?" Mahala questioned with wide eyes.

"One said the old place was looking right nice. The other answered and said 'it's high time the Randall fortune is used for something worthwhile.'"

"Oh, really?" Mahala murmured, drawing out the words thoughtfully. She tapped a speculative finger to her chin and quirked an eyebrow at Ella Beth, who merely raised hers in silent response. Maybe, just maybe, Mahala was right and this idea of hers might work. Wouldn't it be ironic if a half-breed mountain woman became the savior of the family reputation and the blessing of Savannah?

Daniel was smiling at Ella Beth, looking over her stained dress like she was gowned for a ball. Come to think of it, this was probably the most mussed he had ever seen her. Of course he seemed to like it.

Mahala interpreted their glances and said, "You know, I've just remembered something I need to tell the carpenters working inside. Will you excuse me a minute?"

Ella Beth didn't know whether to be pleased or dismayed. As Mahala scurried away, with Daniel lifting his hat again, she turned to him with a small smile.

"I'd – better get back to the herb garden. We left Mrs. Randall there."

"Ah, and doubtless she wasn't happy."

"…no."

"Won't you stay and talk to me just a minute, Ella Beth?"

It was Ella Beth now and not Mrs. Draper. She still called him "Mr. O'Keefe" but made no effort to correct his use of her Christian name. She glanced at a woman pushing a shaded baby carriage by on the sidewalk. "I – I don't know."

"You like talking to me, don't you?" His tone was soft, almost wheedling.

"Yes."

"And I think you enjoy my company. If you don't, please tell me now."

"Why?"

"Before I say what I'm going to say next."

"What are you going to say?" she asked breathlessly.

"Come in." He opened the gate again and gestured to a bench on the lawn in the shade of a magnificent magnolia tree. "Over here."

Against her better judgment she followed him, like a horse scenting a sugar cube. They sat down.

"I want to ask your cousin's permission to officially court you, if you'll allow it, but before that, I want to take you to meet my mother and sisters and brothers. I want you to know exactly how low society will deem ye're stooping should you allow yer name to be linked with mine. You ought to be able to make a fair judgment of if you think it will be worth it."

Ella Beth sat in stunned silence. She had grown accustomed to his directness, but this was amazing.

"I've shocked you."

"Yes."

"Am I presuming too much?"

"Yes."

"I'll go then, an' trouble ye no more." He stood.

She put a hand on his arm. "I never said I didn't want to meet your mother."

His expression was like the gray clouds parting to reveal a ray of liquid sunshine. "Aye, I guess you didna."

Early June 1866
Savannah, Georgia

Sylvie held to Bryson's arm, fingers flittering over the red rose pinned into her golden locks. She couldn't remember the last time she had been nervous at a party.

She hadn't found what she had sought during the winter social season. She now knew she had gone about things wrongly in her desperation, in the hurt of Dylan's rejection, but it was too late. The vicious gossip and disapproving frowns had taken their toll, penetrating her armor and forcing her into a tactical spring retreat. She had spent long hours alone, something she had never done before. And she felt she had grown up, shedding the outer skin that had been the young and assured Sylvie, emerging as someone entirely different, more thoughtful, more serious.

Only this month had she ventured out, and that was mostly when she joined a society of virtuous matrons who took food to Savannah's slums. Sylvie was finding that focusing on others, trying to relieve their burdens, helped her own wounds. Now she wondered if anyone could see the change in her. She feared they'd assume she would behave as she had before. So she left her dance card virtually empty and stayed close to her brothers, all three of whom were in attendance. That fact made Jack very happy, she could tell. And Bryson stood straighter tonight than he had since surrendering his Confederate uniform. Tonight was really as much about him as it was about Jack, for the refurbished *Evangeline*'s unveiling – her sleekly polished wood, gas lamps, plush upholstery and inviting staterooms – were his doing. Sylvie could tell the compliments he was fielding gave him a sense of accomplishment, and she was proud of him.

The Federal naval commodore Bryson was currently talking to seemed particularly impressed. Bryson had tensed when he had approached, but Sylvie had steadied him with a squeeze to his forearm, silently reminding him of the necessity of a good professional relationship with local authorities, especially those in charge of the waterways. It was a strange gathering tonight, though, she had to admit. At least she wasn't the only uneasy person, she realized as she glanced around. There was an undercurrent of tension in the ship's ballroom between the native Savannahians and the Yankees present. Everyone was far too preoccupied to worry about *her.*

Like Bryson, she gradually relaxed under the warm accolades of the tall, florid officer. Commodore Duncan's wife was equally pleasant, despite the fact that her clipped accent stood out like an iceberg amid the soft drawls.

"We will be returning to New Jersey for a Christmas visit," she said. "I hope your sailing schedule will accommodate our family."

Bryson bowed slightly. "Captain Howell plans a trip north for the holidays. I'm gratified that you're impressed enough with what you've seen tonight to want to sail with us."

"Oh, yes, young man. Your taste is impeccable. And your brother tells us that you are quite new to the family firm."

"Yes, Ma'am. While I was in New York, Jack's connections there enabled me to study the innovations Inman and Cunard have made in passenger transport. I looked at *Malta, Tarifa* and *City of London* while they were in harbor. Captain Howell was also a great help. I've certainly learned a lot about screws and engines and all that goes along with marine engineering."

"I'm sure you have," Commodore Duncan agreed. "What will you do now that your project is so successfully completed?"

"I'm off to Scotland next month. While on his honeymoon my brother visited George Thomson at his shipyard in Bankton and convinced him to build a steamer for Randall and Ellis."

"*Really?*" Colonel Duncan's heavy eyebrows shot up.

Over his shoulder Sylvie watched the dancing. Despite herself, her feet itched to move to the music. When the commodore noticed her distraction, she quickly focused on him and smiled. She did not want him to translate her desire and ask her to dance. A fine howdy-do that would make, fast Sylvie Randall hopping around the floor with a New Jersey naval officer!

"Another large steamer?" Duncan asked Bryson.

"Yes, larger than *Evangeline*, and faster, too, with more staterooms."

"Will there really be that much traffic between here and New York?" Mrs. Duncan inquired.

"Eventually, we believe so. Jack is a visionary, Mrs. Duncan. To be honest I've often resisted his ideas only to find five or ten years later that he was ahead of the curve all along," Bryson said.

Sylvie squeezed his arm in silent approval.

"Quite a *young* visionary," the older woman added, looking across the room to where Jack was talking with a knot of Savannah railroad men. She might as well have said "handsome" instead, for her tone clearly implied it. Of course Mahala was at Jack's side, a deterrent to female admirers, married or otherwise. She was absolutely resplendent in Worth's ivory ballgown, the tiny beaded trim dancing and sparkling in the gas light. Sylvie was pea green with envy. She had taken her cue from Mahala's style and herself chosen a white, double-skirted grenadine. The material had been brought back from France and fashioned in the latest mode, with a broad, fringed rose silk sash that fastened at her belt, draping around to one side in the rear, where it was clasped with roses and leaves, giving the appearance of a third skirt. The scalloped rose silk was also echoed in the underskirt and the pleated bertha. The flowers on her skirt were silk, but the one in her hair was real, another token of her mystery admirer. This last flower had been accompanied by verses apparently composed by the sender.

A sniff of an orange's orb
At the gem within only hints.
Its skin though bright must be peeled aside
To reveal the hidden true gift.

The burst of a grape may taste sweet
When taken straight off the vine,
But once pressed and many years confined
Will yield the rarest and finest wine.

Some may judge what the surface shows –
Of a look, a word, take great note.
But others wait for the rose to bloom
While to its tender care their attentions devote.

This time she had not said "bah" when she read those lines, but rather scanned them over and over, strangely touched, intrigued, looking for some clue about the writer. His attentions, understated but consistent in the face of her public disgrace, had been a buoy to her spirits. And now ... it seemed he saw the true Sylvie. All night she had wondered if he might be present, and if he would take her rare public appearance to make himself known at last. She scanned the crowd again, curious and hopeful.

"It was a wise move of Mr. Randall – your older brother – to offer the Savannah natives half price fare in the first year," Mrs. Duncan said. "Oth-

165

erwise I can't see that many of them could have afforded it – if they can even now."

As if she isn't talking *to two "natives,"* Sylvie thought irritably, noticing that Bryson, too, stiffened.

"Well, those of us with Northern ties have to do what we can to foster good will," the commodore added magnanimously. "My poor wife has had to endure so many hurtful social cuts that she hesitates to venture out in public."

"Well, we hope you feel comfortable here," Sylvie offered sweetly. Too sweetly?

"Oh, we do, thank you. It's been a very nice evening for us."

"We're so glad. But I wonder if you might excuse us? I'd like to steal my brother away for a dance. Remember you promised me the next schottische, Mr. Randall?"

"Oh – yes." Bryson looked like he might be going from the frying pan into the fire, but he bowed to their guests, taking a proper leave, and led Sylvie toward the dance floor. "I hate the schottische," he muttered. "All that gliding and hopping. But I'd stand on my head to be free of those Yankees."

"Now, now, they weren't so bad."

Byrson held her hand, facing the cleared floor. The band shuffled through their music. He sighed. "I hate to admit it, but you're right. I didn't see any horns under all that hair. Did you?"

Sylvie giggled. "No forked tongues, either. Though the accent was frightful."

"It's just hard, Sylvie. Three years of firing at blue on sight. A man can't change instinct overnight."

"I know, Bry. I'm proud of you for trying ... though it *has* been a year now."

He glanced over at her wryly.

"Excuse me," someone stammered behind him.

They turned to behold the slight form of Andrew Willis, surprisingly dapper in evening dress. His hair was slicked back with a great deal of pomade, and for once his glasses were perfectly in place.

"Yes?" Bryson asked.

"I – I was wondering if you would mind – that is, if Miss Randall would honor me – with this dance." Andrew never once glanced at Sylvie.

"I guess you'll have to ask her," Bryson prompted. He pushed Sylvie forward slightly, as if offering a choice morsel from a plate.

She didn't really want to be shoved off on the clerk. She clung to Bryson's arm stubbornly, protesting, "But Bryson, you so adore the schottische."

He sent her a dark look.

166

Willis was fumbling in his pocket. "I beg to remind you, Miss – Miss Randall, if you will but consult your – your dance card ... you will recall I marked off this dance at the beginning of the evening."

"You did?" Sylvie stared at the small square of paper Andrew presented her, pencil attached. Sure enough, his forefinger underlined her name on #11, couples' schottische. She had a vague, sudden memory of dashing it off up on deck. Willis had been there when she'd intentionally penciled her brothers in for all the couples' dances. She'd just been too distracted – too concerned as to whether everyone around her was looking at her censoriously – to notice much when Andrew had asked for a dance.

Her face turned red. As unimpressive as Willis was, she hated for anyone to think she was purposely toying with them. Especially now. "I'm so sorry, Mr. Willis. It quite crept up on me."

Bryson chuckled quietly as Sylvie transferred her hand to Andrew's arm. The music was beginning. He led her out and took her hand. Almost immediately, with the next phrase in fact, Sylvie found herself drawn into the step-together-step-hop pattern. They glided along like that for the length of the floor until they encountered a couple with the gentleman down on one knee, his lady circling around him with one hand joined to her partner's. Sylvie couldn't imagine Willis performing such a jaunty move. But he did automatically split from her during the step-hop sequence, so that they could pass the other couple. Looking very serious, he rejoined her. She smiled.

"Something is amusing, Miss Randall?" he said, so quickly that it was clear he needed to spend as little time as possible speaking so as not to disrupt his counting.

"I'm sorry. I just never imagined you doing the schottische," she replied truthfully.

"You should see polka," he retorted.

Sylvie giggled. "You should see *me* polka, you mean."

"No. Me."

She stifled the first rich laughter in months. "Never mind," she said. "You have far more gumption than I'd imagined. We'll just dance. No talking. We can talk over punch."

Andrew flashed her a bright, grateful smile. "Thanks."

He actually wasn't so bad, as long as he was silent. On the next phrase he tugged her into waltz position. Sylvie tried to look at him, but his gaze was fastened intently on her ringlets. He must be too shy, or too preoccupied with getting his feet in the right places, to look her in the eye. His feet *did* go in the right place, though he held her as far away as possible in closed position. She had to concentrate herself to interpret the pressure on her hand and on her corset.

When the dance ended, Andrew bowed formally. Sylvie smiled, curtsied, and nodded as he thanked her.

"You said you'd take punch?" he asked.

"I will, thanks."

Appearing rather dazed, the clerk offered his slender arm. They went to the table spread in Jack's generous style with lavish goodies and drinks. As Andrew requested two punch glasses and took them from the server, Sylvie's eyes widened. His hands were trembling so, she immediately imagined the red liquid all down the front of her ballgown. She stood well away while carefully accepting her drink.

"Sorry," muttered the young man. "Dancing makes me nervous."

"Then why do you do it?"

"Oh – I love it. I just don't get to dance much, and well, I – I guess I'm just so afraid I'll mess it up. If I don't dot an 'i' or cross a 't' at work your brother – he'll usually forgive me. But if I forget a step, well, you know how it all goes downhill from there. Didn't want to embarrass us both."

"Well, you did quite well, Mr. Willis. You were bold to try the schottische. If you get off count on that, it's pretty obvious. You end up looking like popcorn."

Sylvie expected him to laugh, but Andrew answered seriously, "It was the only couples' dance left on your card."

"And the group dances?" she prodded, eyebrows raised.

"Heard you say you didn't want to dance those."

Had she?

They stood there a minute in silence, sipping, looking around. Why had she agreed to prolong her interaction with him? Six months ago she would have brushed him off like a fly. She must be desperate. And now, desperate for something to say. "Good punch."

"Mmm. Yes. Oh! Would you like to sit down, Miss Randall?"

At last. Her toe was cramping in her slipper. "Yes, I would, thank you."

They perched on two nearby chairs. Sylvie wore one of the new narrower, elliptical hoops with a slight train to the skirt of the gown, but the dress was still wide enough to force Andrew to leave an empty seat between them.

"So glad your brother has come on board," he said, looking out into the dance set forming. Bryson and his partner, a blushing young lady in blue, had joined a quadrille with Jack and Mahala.

Sylvie watched the two half-brothers exchange pleasantries and share a joke. The sight gave her a warm feeling inside. She glanced at Andrew. How much did he know about the past tension between Jack and Bryson?

"Yes," she said. "Me, too." *It really begins to feel like one family now.* "What about your family, Mr. Willis? Do they live here in Savannah?"

"Oh – my family – no. Augusta." He nodded.

"Augusta!"

"Yes, Augusta. My father – he is a lawyer."

Sylvie raised her brows. Surprisingly respectable. "And you didn't want to follow in his footsteps – join his practice?"

"I'm the fourth son, Miss Randall, so you see, I had to make my own way. There was only so much money for college."

"Oh, yes. And you've done quite nicely."

"I like my job – though perhaps some would find it – unimpressive."

Was he fishing for her opinion on the matter? Had she not thought of him as exactly that word – *unimpressive* – only minutes before? Trying to make up for it, as though he might read her mind, she said, "I know Jack feels you are quite indispensable. I don't know what he'd do without you ... he has to be away so often."

"Thank you." Andrew's face colored up.

Another long pause ensued. Sylvie watched the dancing and sipped her punch. Oddly enough she was not irritated at Andrew for his faltering manner. She felt safe beside him. No one would say anything ugly about her, and Andrew would certainly not say anything ugly *to* her. It was clear he held her – and her whole family – in high regard. That was refreshing. She might just dance with him again, if he asked.

"May I ask ..."

"Yes?"

"Do you like roses, Miss Randall?"

Sylvie hesitated. This was not the question she had been expecting. "Roses? Why?"

"Well, you have so many about your person tonight. They are lovely, I must say. Quite lovely."

She sat there with her mouth slightly agape. Unconsciously she touched that special flower in her hair, a nervous and uncertain gesture. Andrew's eyes followed the motion. It couldn't be ... No. He was just making conversation. Wasn't he?

"Thank you. Yes. I like them very much."

She glanced up as Jack approached, Mahala on his arm.

"I believe I signed up for your redowa waltz," her brother said.

"Oh. Yes!" She rose and let Mahala have her seat. "Thank you, Mr. Willis, for the punch."

"It was my pleasure," he replied, rising as well and bowing awkwardly while at the same time trying to greet and seat Mahala. He looked like a bobber jerking to and fro with the rise and fall of incoming waves. Sylvie turned away and sighed. He would never have the confidence to send her roses and poetry, she thought. But then, she would have never thought he

Denise Weimer

would dance the schottische, either. She glanced back over her shoulder once as Jack led her away.

For a moment Ella Beth wanted to withdraw back into her grandmother's carriage and return to St. James Square. Even the overcast nature of the late May Saturday could not soften the faults of the one-story frame house wedged between two tenement buildings. Oh, it was in good enough repair. But it was so small, so humble and squat in its little dirt yard. The wash was hung on the side, for the residence backed right up to another building. And the neighboring tenements! Rambling, hulking structures, they gave the impression they might swallow up any who entered and never spit them out again!

Ella Beth shuddered. *This* was where Daniel O'Keefe lived?

It was true. He was coming out the front door. His usual bright smile was missing at first, lost in a look of sheepishness, but when he saw her peering out the carriage window and their eyes met, it winked out as if he could not help himself. Now appearing more eager than embarrassed, he strode toward her, avoiding the droppings of stray animals in the street.

"Ye're at the right place," he assured her, swinging open the door and helping her down. "Ye have that look of a scared rabbit, but ye musn't run. My mother's been baking all day."

Ella Beth directed her driver to return in an hour. Turning to Daniel, she said, "I wasn't going to run."

"Oh, yes, ye were."

Refusing to argue further, she pursed her lips. He kissed her hand, and she said, "I *do* want to meet her."

"Well, ye look just right." He approvingly scanned her simple muslin frock and older silk bonnet before leading her towards the front door. It opened to reveal a boy who looked like a junior version of Daniel. "This is me brother, Connor. He's the next oldest son. He works as puddler's boy at the foundry."

"Oh – I didn't know that." Ella Beth curtsied. The adolescent bowed to her as she said, "Pleased to meet you."

She noticed Connor's nails were dark around the edges, but he was clad in a neat shirt and breeches with a linen slouch cap. Behind him appeared a dark-haired woman with a toddler on her hip and a girl, barely older, clinging to her skirts. Ella Beth curtsied again as Daniel introduced his mother.

"I'm so pleased you accepted me invitation to tea. These are me children," Moreen O'Keefe told her, gesturing to the brood that congregated around her, pressing forward to stare at Ella Beth with curious eyes. "I see

170

you've already met Connor, then there's Rose, Davina, Deirdre, Brian, Brock, Anya, Myrna and baby Fergus. Don't worry ... we don't expect you to remember all of that."

Ella Beth laughed, flustered and relieved. She was sure she never could have succeeded, except for maybe Rose, who was clearly the oldest girl, and the smallest two, Myrna and Fergus.

"And that doesn't count my oldest two sisters, who are married and gone," Daniel told her.

Ella Beth nodded. He had spoken of them before.

"Won't ye come in?" Moreen offered. As she turned to lead the way, she spied one of the girls clutching a scruffy-haired black cat. One of its ears appeared to be fixed in a permanent droop, and its sole redeeming feature was a white blaze on its chest. "Deirdre, why do you have that cat in the house? Ye know what I've told you about it."

"But, Mother–"

"No 'buts.' Put him out, *now.*"

"But that other tom–"

A warning glare silenced the red-haired child, who promptly did as she was told, plopping her unwieldy bundle on the stoop. Moreen shut the door practically on the cat's back and smiled at Ella Beth.

"Such a pleasure, to have the cousin of Daniel's employer over for a visit. You do us quite the honor, Mrs. Randall."

"Oh – it's Mrs. Draper." Ella Beth shot Daniel a confused look, but he focused on his mother.

"You know I told you Mrs. Draper is a widow," he put in.

"Oh, yes, so ye did. I just had Randall on my mind. The family's been so good to us. I've baked up my lemon and vanilla curd cake, and currant squares, and fruited scones to go with our tea, Mrs. Draper. Rose here made the scones. Brown scones I thought too plain for the occasion."

Ella Beth opened her mouth but didn't know what to say. She got the impression Moreen O'Keefe thought she was making an employer-employee duty call, not a social visit to one who might just become her mother-in-law. Had Daniel not told his mother the nature of their relationship?

The girl named Rose seemed to sense Ella Beth's sudden uncertainty and offered her a shy smile. She was willowy and brown-haired, just beginning to display a woman's shape. Ella Beth warmed to her instantly.

"I like your dress," Rose murmured.

"Thank you. I'm sure I'll like your scones."

"Well, on that note, I'll leave you ladies to your visit," Daniel announced.

"*What?*" Ella Beth gasped.

"It would hardly be fitting for me to join a ladies' tea party, now would it? Connor and I have some business down the way. We'll be back in half an hour or so. Give you a chance to get acquainted."

Ella Beth could clobber him. It was true men generally didn't participate in tea parties, but wasn't this an exception? Did he have to abandon her so soon, with so little said? As if she didn't matter at all? Her face turned red with all she was holding in, and she whisked away, following Mrs. O'Keefe into the sitting room.

"Do take the wing chair, Mrs. Draper."

It was the best seat in the room. Some of the others looked worn and shaky. But the place was neat and clean, rather like the children in their simple frocks and old boots. The boys were shooed out while Rose organized a small tea party on the rug next to the hearth for the younger girls. As Moreen poured tea for herself and Ella Beth, Ella Beth watched them. She was impressed by the prim way they spread their skirts and quietly waited their turn for refreshments under Rose's watchful eye.

All except for Deirdre, who blurted out, "I want a piece of cake!"

"Hush," Rose said.

Moreen whispered as she handed Ella Beth a tea cup, "Her name means 'chatterer.'"

Ella Beth bit back a smile. "It must be challenging, seeing to so many young ones with your husband gone and your oldest daughters now married."

"Aye, it is. But it keeps life interesting. And you, Mrs. Draper? Daniel said you have wee ones of yer own."

"Two boys."

"Oh, is that all?" Moreen sounded disappointed.

"My husband went away to war, Mrs. O'Keefe."

"Ah, of course. And never came back, what a sad shame. I thank the good Lord every day He returned Daniel to me, for what would I have done otherwise? Starved is what. But forgive me. You might not think Him so good for not returnin' yer husband."

"I had my moments."

"I hope ye came to the conclusion He's always good, an' always knows what He's doin', even when we don't."

Ella Beth nodded. "Yes. He's always taken care of us, though sometimes through others."

"That'd be yer good cousin Mr. Jack Randall."

"Yes."

"Will ye take a bun and a scone?"

"I must try Rose's scones."

Moreen smiled and placed a fat triangular pastry beside an equally large slice of cheesecake, which evidently wasn't optional. "The curd cake recipe has been in our family for well over a hundred years," she said as she handed Ella Beth the plate.

Both desserts were delicious, and Ella Beth said as much. Rose blushed with pleasure.

A rumble of thunder made Moreen glance up, as though she could see the sky through the spotted ceiling. "Oh, my," she said darkly.

"A bit of rain would be wonderful," Ella Beth commented. "I only wish we could share the little showers we get here on the coast with the rest of the state. The farmers are having such a hard time of it."

"Yes indeed," Moreen agreed, though Ella Beth intercepted a peculiar worried glance the woman sent Rose.

"Are the children in school?" Ella Beth asked, watching the girls on the carpet sipping their juice, which had been given in lieu of the strong, dark tea.

"Rose teaches them," Moreen replied, a bit defensively, Ella Beth thought. "And Daniel taught her." Then the older woman pursed her lips and admitted, "It's a concern of mine, Mrs. Draper. I don't agree with the notion that girls don't need no learning. How can they expect to take a good position – to marry up – when they're ignorant? Maybe if you need a maid, or know of someone who does, you might think of my Rose?"

Ella Beth almost choked on her scone. If Moreen was asking her to take Rose into service, Daniel certainly had not told his mother he hoped to court Ella Beth.

Moreen misinterpreted her reaction. "I know it's a lot to ask, when your family has already been so kind," she hastened to add.

"No – no. Not at all. But I – I don't know of any positions."

"Oh."

Ella Beth felt like her heart was sitting at the bottom of her stomach along with the heavy curd cake. Why hadn't Daniel been eager to tell Moreen about her? Because, unlike her, he *had* already thought of the incongruity of having a wife who was in a position to employ a sister?

Another rumble of thunder sounded much closer, followed by a crack of lightning and yet more rumbling.

"Danny and Connor are gonna get wet," Deirdre piped up.

The next minute a heavy deluge of rain fell upon the roof. To Ella Beth's surprise, Rose jumped up without a word and ran out of the room, with no reproof from her mother, who was again staring at the ceiling. Her expression looked dismayed. Ella Beth followed her gaze and saw the reason. A darkening circle near the light fixture spread ominously and finally dripped, once, then methodically.

Rose was in the foyer, plopping down a bucket. She hurried back in and sat another one in the middle of the parlor floor.

Ella Beth looked back at her cake. Moreen must be so embarrassed. As Ella Beth cut a small bite, a strange yowling sound rose above the storm. She sat up straight and looked around.

"Rrr-owlll!" it came again.

"What in tarnation?" Moreen cried.

The sound seemed to be coming from behind the house. Rose hurried out again and came back with a red face. "It's just that cat," she said. "There are two of them that tried to take cover under the back porch, and now they're getting ready to fight."

"I tried to tell you, Mama, that the other tom was outside," Deirdre exclaimed.

"Oh, for heaven's sake!" As another yowl rent the air, Moreen threw up her hands.

Ella Beth stifled a laugh. Moreen looked at her, clearly disgusted with the disintegration of her perfectly planned visit. Then she cracked a small smile. Ella Beth giggled. The tension in the room dispelled as, one by one, everyone else followed suit. Laughter rose in a chorus that almost drowned out the sound of the cat fight outside. When they began to taper off, catching their breath and wiping their eyes, another feline howl could be heard, and they went into gales of laughter again.

"What you must think of us!" Moreen said at last.

"Oh, not at all," Ella Beth retorted, unceremoniously gulping the last swallow of her tea. "I can't remember when I had such a good laugh."

"You should come see us again," Deirdre said. "We laugh a lot here. Mama just told us to be on our best behavior today."

"Oh, she did, did she?"

"Yes, come see us again!" Anya, who was a year or so younger than Deirdre, intoned. Ella Beth was enchanted by her gap-toothed smile.

"Well, perhaps I will at that," Ella Beth said. She wanted to, but the remembrance of Daniel's strange behavior subdued her. "Has your roof been long leaking like this?" she asked Moreen. She looked at the stained ceiling. The rhythm of the droplets was slowing.

"Yes. We've almost enough put by to repair it. We need the whole roof redone." Another cry from the back stoop interrupted her. "Rose, I can't believe I'm saying this, but why don't you let that droop-eared cat in so that meowling stops."

"Yes, Mama."

As Rose cleaned up the dishes, then went to do her mother's bidding, Anya came over and surprised Ella Beth by climbing up into her lap. The little girl with brown hair a shade darker than Rose's – streaked with molasses – screwed up her round face in severe concentration on Ella Beth's brooch.

174

"It's a rose like Rose, right?" she questioned, tapping it with a forefinger.

"That's right. Do you like it?"

Anya nodded and played with it. Ella Beth reached up to unclasp the pin and attached it to the shoulder of the girl's cotton smock. She whispered in the child's ear, "Perhaps you should keep it, then, and loan it to your sister when she has an occasion to wear it, for such a fair young lady surely will soon."

Anya's face lit up in wonder, but her mother heard and said, "Oh, no, Mrs. Draper. It's far too precious."

Rose came in holding a housewife and a folded garment, deciphered what was going on, and blushed again. Ella Beth liked her immensely. "I would be pleased if you would keep the brooch," she insisted. "I have another very like it. What's that you've got there, Rose?"

Moreen shook her head but relented at the change of subject. Rose perched on the corner of the sofa beside Ella Beth. "It's a shawl I'm mending for Mama."

How refreshing. A girl who did not know she was supposed to put away necessary work and pretend to embroider when a guest came.

"Can I see it?"

"Yes. See, it tore here, so to cover the repair I'm stitching on this fringe."

Ella Beth took the paisley shawl and examined the work. "This is very good. Your stitches are quite fine."

"Thank you." Rose ducked her head as she took the material back onto her lap.

"In fact, have you considered sewing for ladies who hire out?"

Rose shook her head. "We don't know any such ladies, Ma'am – excepting yourself, of course."

Ella Beth smiled. "Well, I do. I can pass your name on if you'd like. And it could enable you to stay home."

"Oh, and that would be a boon!" Moreen exclaimed. "Lord bless you, Mrs. Draper."

Ella Beth smiled again as Anya nestled against her. "It's nothing."

"Thank you, Mrs. Draper, for the pin and the reference," Rose stated in a calm tone, but her pink cheeks gave away her excitement.

The front door burst open, and Daniel and Connor trooped into the hall, wiping their boots and throwing off hats and coats.

"As sure as the blessed virgin we got a *soaking*!" Daniel called into them.

"Gracious, you surely did," Moreen cried.

"Are ye done with your tea and talk?" he asked from the parlor doorway. "Mrs. Draper's coach is outside." He paused in surprise when he saw the cozy scene, Anya on Ella Beth's lap, wearing her brooch, Rose sitting close by sewing.

In that moment Ella Beth knew exactly what he had been up to.

With all the graciousness she could muster for the benefit of the ladies, she smiled and said, "It has been a lovely visit. You've made me feel so at home, Mrs. O'Keefe. I thank you for all the hospitality."

"Oh, and we thank *you* for coming. We do wish you wouldn't hurry off." Moreen rose, reaching to take Anya from Ella Beth's lap.

"It's best to not keep the coach in the street for too long. And I'm sure you have evening plans." She gently embraced Moreen and Rose, then let Daniel help her with her accessories in the hall. As he opened the door she saw that it had stopped raining, and the sun was already trying to break out, illuminating the soggy streetscape.

"How did it go?" Daniel asked as soon as they stepped off the small porch.

"Wonderful, no thanks to you."

"What?"

She rounded on him. "Oh, have the brass to admit it. You thought I'd come here and be horrified by the poverty and simplicity, that I'd brush my skirts aside and hightail it home! That's why you didn't bother to tell your mother about me."

"I did tell her about you. I said that Mr. Randall's cousin was a most particular friend of mine."

"And yet you never mentioned you were hoping to court me – because you never thought I'd want you to after I met your family." She paused, waiting for him to speak, praying he'd deny her accusation. But he dropped his head. She groaned and put her hands to her cheeks. "Heaven preserve me, Daniel. Is your opinion of me so low? Are you such a coward? Such behavior is not worthy of you. And now there's all the more pain, for I liked them and I think they liked me. But there's an end to it."

Ella Beth turned and started picking her way through the mud puddles. Daniel reached for her arm. When she turned, his eyes were pained. "You're right," he said. "A hundred times right. It's to me living shame that I thought you would turn your nose up and put an easy end to me misery. For misery is what it has been, Ella Beth, pinin' for a woman so high above me, knowin' yer a fool's dream but unable to stay away from you."

"How can you care for me and yet think so little of me?" she whispered.

"I do ... I don't." Daniel's face looked tortured. "I'll go to yer cousin. I'll make it up to you, Ella Beth."

She stepped around a slimy pool and climbed up the steps the footman had put down, into the carriage. The man stood waiting to close the door until Ella Beth waved him off. He left Daniel there by the open carriage.

"No," Ella Beth told him. "You won't. Because there's no use courting a woman when you can't afford a wife. Any wife. Not that I'm determined to be kept in any certain way, or unwilling to come down in the world. But I won't add to your burden. If I did, you couldn't carry it. Meeting your family showed me that, too. Fix the roof. In fact, find them a better place to live. Jack can help you do that. But there's no way you can take care of them and me and my sons, too. Goodbye, Daniel."

She reached out and took the door from his frozen grip and shut it.

"Ella Beth ..."

She knocked on the ceiling of the coach. The driver called to the team and the vehicle lurched forward, spraying muddy water onto Daniel's feet and legs. He still stood there staring after her. She leaned back in the seat and shut her eyes to close out the sight of him. She hurt, but the blessed numbness of sure actions stole over her. *Better now than later*, she told herself, *when I love him even more*.

CHAPTER ELEVEN

July 1866
Habersham County, Georgia

The shocks of wheat – what bound grain that did not shatter from drought when cut – had been brought into the barn. Dylan knew it would not make enough flour to get them all through another whole year. The knowledge sat in his gut like a boulder. If it did not rain, the corn crop would fare no better.

Everyone was glum, even Samson, whose pearly white smile was seldom seen. They were all weary in spirit from the routine of work with no reward. Something had to be done. Dylan declared a Saturday off. The blacks could rest, hunt or fish, or go visit friends. Dylan had no spending money, and the stimulating presence of baubles and novelties for sale was sure to create unneeded temptation, but he decided he would take the women and his nephew into town.

That morning when he sought out Carolyn to see if she was ready, he found her lingering over her top dresser drawer. It was not that fact only, but the guilty manner in which she quickly closed the drawer that brought to mind the daguerreotype and hardened his face and voice when he said, "Buggy's ready."

He'd seen her cover up a small cloth sack. She must have put that darn picture in there to better hide it. What else could it be?

He turned from the sight of her blossoming figure. How could he treat her like a man ought to treat his pregnant wife – how could he treat his nephew like his son – when the woman persisted in mental infidelity? Would the knife of her betrayal never cease to cut him? You'd think he had enough scar tissue now that he wouldn't even feel the pain.

But Dev Jr. ... there Dylan *had* to make an effort. The child did not understand why "Uncl'yn" was always so busy, and he could not be faulted for his mother's failings.

Dylan smiled as Henrietta brought the boy down the porch steps. She held him by the hand, just in case, but at two, he was steady and sure. Two! Shoot. Devie's birthday was this month. It could not be overlooked entirely. Something would be gotten and put on the ever-mounting tab at the dry goods store. He hid his consternation, squatted and clapped his hands, holding his arms out.

"Look at you! Walking like a little man!"

Devie grinned and ran to him. Dylan swooped him up into his arms. He tickled the boy's side. The feel of the solid little body trembling with a belly chuckle softened his heart. He reminded himself that for a father figure he was all the boy had.

"Someone dressed himself today, too," his mother put in.

"Did you, now?"

Devie nodded with pride. "*I* do it."

"Good for you. You're growing up. Sit right here by Uncl'yn, and you can help me drive." Dylan deposited the toddler in the front seat. Devie scooted across and promptly reached for the looped reins. "Whoa!" Dylan cried, lunging to disengage the chubby hands from the leather straps. "Not yet, young man. You need at least a decade before you get to take over those. Sit there on the seat and behave yourself."

He heard a soft laugh and looked up to see Carolyn on the porch. He wished he could say pregnancy made her unattractive. But even in Mahala's remade blue muslin dress, expanded in the middle with material from the hem, she would turn any man's head. Her skin was flawless, her hair lustrous, her lips pink and full. The sight of her smiling made a wistful longing rise inside.

He turned to help his mother into the buggy. "I'll sit in the back," she said ever-so-helpfully.

On the driveway, Dylan gave in to Devie's begging and sat the child on his lap. He even let him help him hold the reins. But the child persisted in shaking the leads up and down, up and down.

"Guess I was right about the ten year thing," Dylan said, sliding him over to his mother.

"Devie want to drive," came the protest.

"Not now, dear," Carolyn told him. "See, Uncl'yn has to go fast on the main road."

"Devie drive fast!"

Carolyn laughed, but Dylan frowned. Whenever the boy displayed too much determination, it brought up less-than-pleasant memories of his brother from his own childhood. "What do you need in town today?" he asked Carolyn.

She bit her lip as if calculating whether to give him the whole list or an abbreviated version.

"You know it will have to go on credit," he put in before she could answer, hating himself for saying it.

"Buttons for the coat I'm sewing for Devie. Some paper. And Lydia is low on cinnamon and sugar."

"Carolyn needs shoes," his mother said from behind, leaning forward. "The soles are separating. And also, when her feet swell, the boots are too tight."

179

"Is that true?" Dylan looked at his wife.

She shrugged and slid her toes well under her skirt.

"And of course it's Devie's birthday soon," Henrietta added, with a gleeful poke at her grandson.

Drat his mother. Did she live in such a make believe world as to suppose they could afford the things she named? Did she have no idea how her words caused the ever-burning knot of tension to rise in his throat, practically choking him with frustration?

"Birthday! Birthday!" Devie shouted and clapped.

As usual, Carolyn seemed to sense his mood and reached out to touch his arm. He tried not to flex away. He hated it when she was understanding. "It will be o.k.," she murmured. "Devie's birthday is more important than my shoes. My feet don't swell that often, and I know Samson can stitch up the soles. They've got plenty of wear left in them, anyway. It would be wasteful to buy a new pair now."

What was he supposed to say? He was hardly in a position to argue with her, but not doing so made him feel like a Scrooge.

"Really, it will be all right," she said again. "We'll make it, Dylan."

He couldn't stop himself. He turned to her and bit out, "And just where does your optimism come from?"

How could she look so surprised?

Henrietta said reprovingly, "Dylan, please."

"Well, what is it?" he persisted, ignoring her, looking at Carolyn. "Can't be God. You don't hold by that any more than I do these days. So what do you know that I don't? Why pretend, Carolyn? If it doesn't rain, starvation is no farther from our heels than it was last year."

He had effectively silenced her, snuffing out whatever bit of joy the trip into town had mustered. She drew Dev Jr. against her and bit her lip, looking straight ahead. The blackness of his mood hovered around the wagon like a dense fog. It was too late to dispel it. He didn't want to dispel it. He wanted a drink. He needed to forget that he couldn't buy his nephew a birthday present or his pregnant wife shoes. He needed to forget the hopeful way they had all looked at him, as though he could draw water from a rock.

When they got to town, he handed them all down in front of Fraser's store. "Get him one toy, but choose a nice one," he told Carolyn, much more quietly now.

She nodded and looked like she would cry.

"I'll go to the post office while you shop." He couldn't bear to face Fraser just now, adding more to a tab he had no intention of paying any time soon.

There was a letter from the solicitor. He slit it open and sat down on a bench to read it. A rush of relief made him pause in wonder. He caught himself forming a silent prayer of thanks. Long-standing habit. It was the first good thing to happen in a long time.

Dylan rose and hurried to Fraser's, where he found the women in a deliberation between a toy train and a set of soldiers in a box. Normally the soldiers would have given him pause, but in the swell of emotion produced by the lawyer's letter he blurted out, "Get them both."

Carolyn turned questioning eyes on him. "But you said–"

"I know what I said. You were right. Things will be o.k.." When she remained standing there staring at him, trying to figure out his abrupt change of demeanor, he urged, "Trust me. If there are boots that will fit you, get them, too."

He waited while his family gathered up their purchases. As Carolyn reluctantly set a pair of glossy black boots on the counter next to the toys and spices, Dylan selected peppermint sticks for everyone for the ride home. Dev Jr. was ecstatic. As Dylan lifted him into the buggy, he thought about the little boy, how proud Dev would have been of him. And yet he – himself – had not been near patient enough when the child had attempted to toddle after him, as Devie often did. The child was getting old enough that he needed a man's example now. He didn't know why it was so difficult to open his heart to the boy.

Yes, he did. The scars from past wounds – and recent ones – closed around that organ like rawhide, effectively squeezing everyone out.

They had just left town when his mother's musing voice came from behind him. "What happened while we were in town, Dylan?"

"I got a letter from our Savannah solicitor. He's found a buyer for The Marshes. Soon there will be money in the bank account."

Henrietta gave a soft gasp. "It's a sure thing?"

"The family has left no doubt that they intend to purchase the plantation, and that they are able to do so."

"They're Yankees, aren't they?"

He had not planned on divulging that fact. "Yes."

Carolyn studied his face. A moment later he heard the sound of quiet weeping from the back seat. He glanced around to see his mother with a lacy handkerchief pressed to her face. Carolyn met his look of astonishment.

"What in the blazes ...?" he questioned.

"I'm sorry, Dylan. I can't help it."

"But this is a good thing, Mother," Carolyn pointed out. "You know how desperately we need that money."

"I know, but ... you should understand, of all people, Carolyn. You were so angry when Dylan first told you we had to put the plantation up for sale. You hated the thought of some conquering carpetbagger living there. Just because I agreed to the sale doesn't mean I don't feel the same way!"

Carolyn pressed her lips together. "I do understand, but – that was a long time ago. Before things got so bad." She glanced at Dylan guiltily.

He shouldn't be angry at her for admitting that. Whether or not some of it was his fault, things *were* bad. But hadn't he warned her they would be? Hadn't he offered to let her out of the engagement – and she had chosen – *chosen* – to stay by him for richer or poorer?

The familiar ugly feelings reared their head, warring with his initial appreciation that she was trying to encourage his mother.

"I know it has to be," Henrietta whispered, "but I'm still sad to see it go. Allow me my moment of grief."

The moment stretched out over the first two miles. Every time Dylan thought his mother would be quiet, a new spasm of tears would seize her. He had not expected this reaction. It wore on his nerves. He ground his teeth to keep from snapping at her.

Dev Jr. was concerned about his grandmother. He kept turning around in Carolyn's arms to look at her. He even offered her the toy soldier Dylan had allowed him to hold on the ride home.

"Oh Devie, what a sweet boy," Carolyn said. "But you just keep it. Grandma is a little bit sad. But no, don't put it in your mouth."

"Mouth," the child repeated.

"That's right! You are so smart. Mouth. And what is this?" Carolyn asked, putting a finger on her son's nose.

Dylan looked over at them. The next instant, there was a terrific crack. As the buggy lurched and gave a violent jolt to one side, still skidding down the road, the women screamed, and Carolyn grabbed her son and the dash. Despite that, she was still thrown against Dylan. It was all he could do to brace her and not slide out onto the ground.

"Whoa!" he called to the skittish horse as the vehicle half-dragged, half-rolled to a stop. "Are you all right?" he asked Carolyn, and as she nodded, turned around to view Henrietta. "Mother?"

"Yes. What happened?"

Well, obviously the wheel on his side had broken. He didn't feel the need to point that out. Devie was crying loudly in Dylan's ear, and Carolyn was trying to quiet him.

"See, we're all right now," she reassured the boy.

"Climb over me while I hold him," he told her.

She did so, laboriously, struggling for a firm foothold in the leaning vehicle. He handed her down while keeping Dev Jr. under his other arm.

"Hush now," he told the sobbing toddler as he gave him to Carolyn. He looped the reins, climbed out and helped Henrietta. Then they all stood looking at the left front wheel. It was broken virtually in half. A large, pointy stone in the road was the obvious culprit. And they were still only halfway home. Groaning, Dylan went to check the horse, making sure he had not pulled a muscle when the wheel cracked. He seemed sound. Dylan slowly, gently urged the stallion to the side of the road, dragging the vehicle behind.

"There's no fixing this," he told the women. That went without saying. Carolyn still looked so dazed he asked her again, "Are you *sure* you're all right?"

He was taken aback when she threw her arms around him. Hesitantly he returned her embrace.

"Yes," she said. "It was just so sudden."

It had been a long time since he had really held her. She smelled sweet and felt good, but he was surprised by the round hardness of her abdomen. She sensed his awareness and drew back.

"I think the baby was startled," she added. "He's kicking."

"*He?*"

"I've felt all along it's a 'he.'" Carolyn took his hand and placed it on her stomach. Before he could withdraw, sure enough, he felt it, a fluttering and a thumping beneath the cloth, beneath the skin. A life that was both his and hers, and its own. Or 'his' own, as Carolyn insisted. He could not hide the wonder. She saw and smiled.

Snuffling, Devie pushed his way between them, clinging to his mother's skirts. Dylan felt an unreasonable irritation toward him. Stupid, to be jealous of a child. He turned away and reached for his mother's elbow.

"I'm fine," she said rather angrily.

"We'll have to walk," he told them. "You can take turns on the stallion if you want."

"There is no way in heaven I'm getting up on that thing!" Henrietta announced.

Dylan had forgotten that she had not ridden in years, and the carriage horse was a good three hands taller than her last docile mare. He looked at Carolyn and realized that in her condition there was no way she could or should straddle the animal, and she would have too much trouble staying on sideways without the saddle.

"Maybe someone will happen along. Gather what you need from the buggy while I unhitch the horse."

When they were ready, Dylan scooped his nephew up. The toddler's short legs necessitated that he be carried, and Dylan was the only choice to do so. Devie was happy at first, tall on Dylan's shoulders, as Dylan led the stallion. He viewed the trek as a glorious adventure, chattering, bouncing and helping his mother look for small animals. When Devie grew restless they fished out a peppermint stick and handed it up to him.

While the child started licking and sucking his candy, content again, Carolyn paused to tighten her shoe string. As she bent over, Dylan winced to see the effort the motion cost her, and the poor condition of her shoes.

"Do you want to put on your new boots?"

She shook her head. "I think I'd regret trying to break them in now."

"Probably right."

Carolyn was bearing up admirably despite the old boots *and* the late afternoon heat. Henrietta was not doing so well. She sighed and paused often as if overcome with woe or exhaustion. Carolyn went back and gave her an arm. Dylan wanted to scold her for taking more on herself, but the steadier pace was too valuable a thing to squander. Even when Henrietta's handkerchief reappeared, Carolyn tugged her along.

Dylan felt a slumping body rest on his head. He realized Devie had fallen asleep. Better that than more fussing. In the process of lowering Devie to his arm, Dylan stopped. "Ugh – his peppermint's stuck in my hair!"

Carolyn started to laugh. Even Henrietta smiled. He had to stoop down so that Carolyn could get the candy off of his head and out of the child's hand.

"Thank you," he said.

"Thank *you*," she replied, catching his eye.

It was dark by the time they reached Forests of Green. Henrietta was limping. Dylan's arms felt like they could fall off. Lydia came running out to greet them, waking Devie with her stream of worried exclamations. But thank goodness she took the hot little bundle into her grasp. She headed towards the house, crying, "What you got into, son? You a mass of drool and stickiness, you are. You needs a bath."

With a hand beneath her elbow, Dylan helped Henrietta up to the porch. Carolyn mounted the steps behind them, faltered, then sank down. When Dylan turned back to her, she waved them on.

"Go on and help her to her room. I'll make it into the parlor presently."

After delivering his mother to her chamber, Dylan got a glass of water from the kitchen and brought it to Carolyn in the parlor. She had bent down to unlace her dusty boots. "Here," he said, handing her the glass. As she drank thirstily he knew what he needed to do – but he hesitated, caught in awkward indecision. Then he took a knee and pulled at the lacings of her shoe.

"What are you doing?" she asked in amazement.

Since the answer was obvious, he didn't respond to the question. Instead he said, "Your feet are swollen." One boot thumped to the floor, and he set about removing the other. Then he tugged down the filthy stockings, pulled over a stool, and propped both her feet up. Taking one of them between his hands, he kneaded gently while he said, "You didn't complain the whole

184

day. Not about the plantation, not about the long walk, or the heat. You even helped Mother. Thank you. I'll have Lydia bring you something to eat once she gets Devie settled."

Carolyn's lips were parted in silent amazement. He didn't meet her eyes. He started to rise, but Carolyn dove towards him. He only realized what she was doing when her mouth met his. Her arms wrapped around his shoulders, and she kissed him passionately. All weariness washed away in a warm flood of sensation.

Instinctively, Dylan pushed back against her, meeting her ardor with his own, drinking in her taste, her scent, the sweetness of welcome. It had been a long time since he had made love to her, and his natural response *was* to love her. He had done so most of his life. On the surface, it was the easy thing to do. Giving in to her would end physical and maybe even emotional need – end the ever-present tension and conflict. Temporarily. But then, he realized, it would only be a matter of time until it seethed forth again, all the more painful as it broke through any veneer they tried to coat it with.

Dylan pulled back, removing her entangling arms.

"I can't do it," he said, standing up.

"What do you mean – you can't do it?" Her hurt and accusation seared him like a hot iron.

He bit his bottom lip. The flavor of her was still there. He almost folded. Struggling to form an answer, he turned slightly so he wouldn't have to look at her. He wanted to say, "I won't settle for part of you ever again." But she would say, "It's different now. I'm ready now." And he would want to believe her but wouldn't be able to, because he would fear too much that down that road would be another rejection, or if not rejection, another failure – of his – that would wound, disappoint and bring back the memories and comparisons. And even if not that, if fortune could so shine upon him, closeness would breed demands. She would need him to be who he couldn't be yet. She would pick, pick at the fragile scabs that covered the wounds. Those scabs were all that held him together now. Eventually they would open and she couldn't deal with – he couldn't deal with – what was inside ... the emptiness ... the things he had done ... things his nightmares resurrected ... the ways he had failed himself, failed God, failed his convictions. Ah, she was too close, even now, because he was skirting the abyss he had to avoid. He could feel the blackness inside threatening to devour him.

"Not now."

"Not now? When, Dylan, when? Or do you intend to live this sham of a marriage forever? When will you forgive me?"

"I have forgiven you," he said softly.

She stood up, put her hands out to him. "Then what is it? What do I have to do to prove myself? When will it be enough?"

He clenched his fists at his sides. He had been foolish to show her tenderness, foolish and cruel, because it led down a path he couldn't yet travel. When? "It's not you. It's me. And I don't know when. I'm sorry. But it's not now."

As he turned to go, he saw a hardening of her face that he'd never seen before. It was as if she had come to a decision. He realized then he would regret this moment, but he couldn't find the power in his soul to do anything differently.

August 1866
Savannah, Georgia

The tent erected by Sylvie's ladies' aid society offered little relief from the tropical humidity and scorching sun. Sylvie could feel rivulets of sweat running down her chest and back beneath her corset, despite her thin voile dress and straw hat. It was only mid-morning, but the temperature was already almost past bearing. She could add to that a strong bout of unexplained nausea. She decided it must be a result of overheating and continued to hand out food to the line of blacks and Irish who came from the slums where Daniel O'Keefe's family lived, according to Ella Beth.

When the first cramp struck like a snake she nearly doubled over. She caught herself, breathing in small gasps.

The directress, a tall, angular woman named Mrs. Perdue, noticed. "Are you all right, Miss Randall?"

"Yes, just a pain. It's passing." Her corset was too tight for the heat was all. She straightened and smiled at the little Negro girl who came up to her table, watching her with wide dark eyes. Sylvie handed her a loaf of bread. "Don't forget we have salt pork, too, at the other table."

"Thank you, Ma'am."

Another pain started and tightened – tighter and tighter – until Sylvie gasped to Mrs. Perdue, "I think I need my carriage."

"Of course." Mrs. Perdue looked worried. She only stared a moment at Sylvie's face, which Sylvie could feel had drained of color and broken out in a clammy sweat. Then, as the woman hurried away to send word to the Randall driver, Sylvie hunkered on a nearby stool. It was impossible to act normal. It felt like her heart would thunder right out of her chest, and her legs would not support her.

When the driver came, he practically carried her into the vehicle. Sylvie was dismayed to be attracting so much attention. But moments later, when she realized with horror that she had soiled herself, she was abjectly thankful her humiliation had not been even more public.

At home, Sunny and Sylvie's maid half-dragged Sylvie upstairs. Her legs kept faltering.

"I'm sending for a doctor," Sunny declared before Sylvie closed the door on her.

The maid helped her get into a clean shift and bed, then left with her dirty underclothes. But Sylvie was up and on the chamber pot within minutes of lying down. She heard her mother return and start knocking on her door.

"Not now, Mother."

"Do you need help? Let me in."

She stood up. "I'm –" Sylvie took a step toward the bed, put a hand out and promptly collapsed. She was surprised how loud her slight body thumped on the wooden floor.

Sunny beat on the wood separating them. "Sylvie? *Sylvie!*"

Sylvie just lay there staring at the locked door, unable to move, unable to answer.

"Look at the size of these staterooms," Jack said to Andrew Willis, pointing to the deck plan he had just unfurled with an enthusiastic flourish across the clerk's desk. "And the ballroom! She's going to be a floating palace. Have you seen this new photograph Bryson sent, Willis?"

On the desk, atop the deck plans and exterior sketch, Jack laid a likeness of the partially finished ship George Thomson was constructing for Randall and Ellis. "Huge," was all Andrew could say.

"I haven't decided whether to call her *Mahala* or *Cherokee Princess*," Jack confided. "Which do you think?"

Willis stifled a snort. Or was it a laugh? "I think – you'd better ask her, Sir."

"What? And spoil the surprise?"

Willis was too careful to say that the surprise might be Jack's instead of his wife's should he not broach this particular subject with Mahala beforehand. But Jack knew his clerk well enough to read what he was thinking on his face. Maybe the man had something there. Mahala could be a bit unpredictable.

Jack was about to comment when the front door burst open and a footman from his own household ran in. He straightened, instantly on guard at the expression on the boy's face.

"What is it?" he demanded. Mahala. His grandmother. Who?

"Your sister, Sir. She collapsed in her room. Mrs. Randall – your stepmother that is – sent for the doctor, and he says – he says–"

"*What?*"

Jack looked in shock at Andrew, for it was Andrew who had spoken. Bellowed, more like. Just as Jack had been about to. The clerk had risen to his feet, his hands balled into fists at his side.

The footmen's eyes flitted to Andrew's face, then back to Jack's. "Ch-cholera."

Oh, God, no. Not cholera. Not the dread disease that was even now sweeping parts of England and Russia. The epidemic was leaving thousands dead in its wake even as London's scientists scrambled to determine whether it was water- or air-borne. This past month the sickness had been discovered among the Yankee troops stationed on Tybee. Many were deserting, running from entrapment and mortality. So far it hadn't gotten a foothold on the mainland. How had it reached Sylvie? Sylvie, of all people?

"Is he sure?" Jack's voice came out in a whisper.

The footman nodded.

Jack swallowed. "I'll come home at once."

"Your stepmother is tending her. Won't let anyone else near her – except Miss Randall's maid, as she's already been exposed. But your wife sent me to you. Knew you'd want to know at once – and be there."

"Yes. Let's go now."

Andrew Willis shot out a hand and grabbed his arm. Jack looked impatiently back at him. The clerk had risen, sat and risen again, and in the interim had apparently tousled his fine blonde hair with anguished fingers. "Please," he said now, "keep me updated."

Why? Jack wanted to ask. What right or reason had he to look so tortured? But there was no time for explanations. And something in the pale face compelled Jack to nod.

In the carriage, Jack mentally thumbed through all that he knew about cholera. It was believed to be dangerously contagious. Most of its victims were quickly dehumanized by continuous diarrhea, usually leading to hypotensive blood pressure and collapse within half a day. Death often followed in one to three days. *Death.* There was no killer – short of a knife, bullet or lethal dose of straight poison – as sudden and fierce as cholera.

How had Sylvie, his sheltered, pampered little sister, gotten this terrible disease? Jack thought of her new charity work. A spasm of panic tightened his chest. Someone she had helped. Some water she had drank in the slums, perhaps. Had she been so careless? He had warned her. But it was like Sylvie to do without thinking twice. Like his mother had done. Oh, Lord, like his mother.

God, Jack bargained with the Almighty, *please don't take her, too. Not Sylvie. So young and bright. Just now coming into her own, finding her place. God, not her. Please not her.*

He kept up the silent litany all the way to the front door of the pink mansion, where the doctor was emerging, repeating to Mahala as he hurriedly exited, "Liquids. Continuous liquids. A dire necessity. A matter of life and death."

Jack brushed by him and took his wife in his arms. Mahala sobbed tears of fear and anxiety on his shoulder. He held her there in the foyer. Looking up, he caught sight of his face in the mirror. Only love afraid of losing looked like that. He had looked that way when his mother took the yellow fever in 1838. Andrew Willis had looked that way today, too.

It was midnight, and still he couldn't sleep. Jack was too attuned to the sounds in the house – the cook stirring about in the kitchen creating various mixtures of water, salt, sugar, soda and fruit juices – and Sylvie's maid running between kitchen and bedroom. He had kept abreast of his sister's condition hourly until eleven, when Mahala had looked so exhausted he had urged her to go to bed. But the only way he could convince her to go had been to join her. It had felt good to hold her, he had to admit, though she sniffled on his shoulder. It was the second time that day she had cried. Now because of Sylvie. This morning because her monthly had come. Every time it did she grew more disappointed, more difficult to console.

He'd tried to lighten the mood that morning when she'd cried. As he'd dressed for the office he'd quipped, "Did you ever consider it might not be your monthly clock that needs repair?"

The stunned, silent look she had given him had made him realize she had not. He'd turned quickly to her, taken her hands and said, "Don't ever blame yourself, Mahala. No matter what happens, you must know that if I never have anyone but you, it will be enough." She had to know what a gift she was. He'd watched the tears coalesce in her eyes, and he'd had to ask, "Am *I* still enough?"

"Oh, Jack, you *are* enough," she'd replied. "I just want your child so badly. And I – I can't make that go away."

Now he stood there with the window cracked open and watched her sleep. He worried about her being exposed to the disease, but he knew she would fight him tooth and nail if he tried to get her to leave. She was so worn out with the work at Phoenix House. They had it almost ready for occupancy, and the occupants were eager to move in. Thanks to Mahala's excellent publicity, and his grandmother's connections in the right circles, more families down on their luck had applied than they could house. Mahala had already been talking with a war-impoverished matron about using a wing of her home for a second location.

In addition, Ella Beth had related to Mahala, Sylvie, Sunny, Martha and Grace the conditions under which the O'Keefes and other Irish were living. Sylvie had confirmed her concerns. Something had to be done, the women had decided among themselves. They couldn't bring Irish boarders into the homes of proud Savannah natives. So they would create a home for the Irish near their own turf, by renovating a rambling old house on the fringes of the slum area.

Jack had been so proud of all of them, the women of his family – the way they had come together around The Phoenix Foundation. Every one of them had a finger in the pie in one way or another. Their work was clearly so fulfilling – and peace-making – that he had restrained from voicing his concerns that they might be over-doing it. And now this.

Jack blew out a smoke ring, thinking of his sister so weak and helpless in the next room. And his stepmother, tirelessly, constantly spooning liquid down her parched throat – even when Sylvie's stomach threatened to rebel – hoping her efforts and prayers would prove enough to combat the relentless specter of death. It made everything pale next to it, even Ella Beth's continuing sadness and Daniel O'Keefe's continuing surliness, both of which had been a thorn in his side the past weeks.

He leaned forward to tap his cigar on the dish and, doing so, caught a movement outside the window. He leaned farther. Someone was standing across the street on the square, staring at the house. Jack stepped right up to the pane and muttered, "What in the world …?"

He banked his cigar and quietly left the room, jogging down the steps and outside. Andrew Willis was still standing across the way. Jack crossed the street and stopped in front of him. Willis looked like a ghost. His arms hung limp at his sides, and his face was even more tortured than before, if that was possible.

"Good heavens, man," Jack said.

"I – I'm sorry. I – I had to know. I thought if I saw the house, I might get a clue as to what – as to what might be happening."

"It's cholera. Nothing new to tell."

"She's – holding on?"

"Just. Sylvie's a fighter, as you know. If anyone can make it, she will."

"It's an unfair thing," Willis said. "This should not have happened to her. She deserves things good – beautiful. Like her."

"How long have you loved my sister?"

At the direct question, Andrew hung his head. "I think since the first day I saw her. She was like a butterfly. I knew I could never catch her. But I couldn't help it."

Romantic balderdash. Jack would have snorted if the situation were not so grave. "The roses?" he asked.

Andrew nodded. Jack shook his head. "Please don't tell her."

"Why not?" Supposing she lived.

"If she knew it was me it would ruin it for her."

"But why do it, then?"

"Because she was sad. I couldn't bear to see her sad. I – wanted her to know someone still admired her. Very much."

Jack sized up the smaller man thoughtfully. "Go home," he finally said. "I'll send a message 'round tomorrow."

Sylvie would make it. Her system began to stabilize on the third day, marking a change for the better. When Jack told Andrew the news he looked like he might cry.

"Would you send her my regards – my wishes for a speedy recovery?" the clerk asked.

"No," Jack said. "You can bring them yourself in person."

Willis looked thunderstruck. He shoved his glasses up on his nose, turned red and spluttered, "But – but – are you saying …? I would never have presumed …"

"I know you wouldn't have. That's why I'm telling you. If you have anything to say to my sister in the future, present yourself properly at our front door." Jack could have laughed at the combination of awe, gratitude and terror that passed over the younger man's countenance.

Terror won out. Willis pressed his lips together, then said, "Sir, please do not believe I deceive myself as to Miss Randall's opinion of me. Her low regard is exactly what I expected. I know I am her inferior in breeding, station, appearance and deportment."

Jack did have to grin at that. It would have been fun to rake Willis over the coals and see him squirm, but where Sylvie was concerned Jack had a soft spot. Willis was one of the last people he would have chosen as a potential brother-in-law, but he had to respect the clerk's honest self-assessment. Still, the other part of the truth deserved to be spoken. "Yet not – I dare say – in intellect. Or heart, either."

Willis brightened. "Thank you, Sir. And that's just it. Despite all of the impediments to relationship I named, my attachment to Miss Randall has only grown. I have examined myself, and I do not believe that attachment to be unhealthy." Jack smothered another smile as Willis continued. "But neither do I expect your sister to welcome me."

"You will find her altered," Jack said. "And that is as much warning as encouragement."

Long enough after Sylvie's illness that she had regained some flesh and strength and that it was clear no one else in the household would take sick, Jack said to his sister, "There is someone who would like very much to call upon you and wish you well."

"Oh?" she asked, reclining on her bed. "Who?"

"My clerk, Mr. Willis."

Sylvie felt her face redden at the name. She muttered, "I can't imagine. That mousy man."

"He has asked about you most kindly during your illness. I suggested, since he has such a pleasant reading voice, he might make a brief call and divert you with some lighthearted entertainment."

Sylvie could have choked. "You *suggested* –?" She took a deep breath. She didn't have the strength to get up her ire, and Jack knew it. She kept trying to get back to her normal self, to pretend to be feisty and pert, but the memory of humiliating illness was all too recently imprinted on her mind and body. What was Jack doing, forcing her into Willis' fawning company? And if he no longer fawned – well, that would be far, far worse, wouldn't it? Proof that *no one* would fawn now.

Jack pierced her with his green eyes. "He's been very kind to you," he reminded her. *Kinder than you deserved*, his tone implied.

Sylvie sighed. "Very well," she said. "Fifteen minutes should allow him to be disposed of his duties, I suppose. But if he's to come today I'll need my maid right now, and my hand mirror."

She saw her brother's face tense. A feeling of dread blossomed in her chest. Was it that bad? She waited. No one moved. If she had been standing she would have stomped her foot. "My mirror. Someone. *Now.*"

Her maid bit her lower lip and obliged. When Sylvie raised the looking glass she let out a little cry. Her hair hung limp and frizzy around her dry-skinned, thin face. Her flesh was slack and pale, and she knew her body to be no better. She dropped the mirror onto the covers and put her hands on her face.

"There now, Miss, it's not so bad. A shampoo and some cold cream, and you'll be right as rain," her anxious maid exclaimed, flittering around her. "Please don't cry." While Sylvie's head was bowed she fished the mirror from her lap as though Sylvie might slap her.

Jack drew close to the bed and touched her arm. "You look beautiful to me, sweetheart. We're just glad that you're alive. I know Mr. Willis will feel the same."

"It's no use. I look too terrible to receive any callers."

"Even him, mousy man that he is?"

She turned her face away. "Even him."

Without a word of argument Jack walked away. It was the fact that he did not accuse, not even with the posture of his body, that sent the arrow of self-recrimination straight to her heart. She liked to believe she had changed. Would she still be this vain and selfish, or would she hear the gentle words of a kind man who – heaven knew why – had always looked at her as though dazzled by her very presence?

Sylvie let out a gusty breath. "Fine." Let Willis look at her now and still think she was a goddess. The visit could prove a fit test. Of her – she was doing her part, nobly sacrificing all her pride – and of him. This would put an end to his mooning for sure. She waved her hand at her maid. "See what you can do to make me presentable."

Jack paused holding her door and closed it with his face framed there, with his insolent grin and a wink thrown in for good measure. She would do anything for his approval. Why did he want her to see Andrew Willis?

Three hours later, after Sylvie had napped, bathed and been trussed up, Jack returned to carry her down to the parlor. He frowned as he lifted her. "You little sprite, you're a sack of bones."

Sylvie stuck out her tongue at him.

Mahala waited in the receiving room. She was there to pour tea. Sylvie was glad for her company.

"Don't let her be shy with the pastries," Jack said to his wife as he deposited Sylvie on the couch.

Sylvie poked her lip out. Then she pulled it back in. Doubtless pouting did not have the same effect when one looked as she now did. The fresh hairstyle had brought some luster to her locks, and lightly applied rouge brightened her lips and cheeks, but nothing could hide her skeletal frame. Her muslin dress hung on her, even without her corset. The undergarment had been so large it had been pointless to put it on.

Mahala covered her modestly with a light lap throw. She smiled. "I'm so happy to see you out of bed, Sylvie." Mahala reached for her hand and gave it a gentle squeeze. "We were so scared for you."

"Thank you."

Within five minutes the clerk arrived. She waited to see what his reaction would be when he saw her. To her amazement, he paused in the door of the parlor, blushed and adjusted his glasses as though everything were quite normal. Something deep and warm, utterly foreign, swept over Sylvie. She could love him just for that blush, that telling reaction that could not be faked. If he had been handsome and confident, would she have cared for him before now?

Illness had turned her head. What *was* she thinking?

Sylvie raised her chin a fraction and held out her hand. "So kind of you to call, Mr. Willis."

Mahala bit her lip.

Andrew came and gave her hand a reverent kiss. "Dear Miss Randall." He held her hand and gazed at it in a troubled manner. Somehow the look made her feel not ugly, but treasured. "Are you really going to be all right?"

"Yes, I will, if you read me whatever you've got there." She peeked at the small red volume she saw in his coat pocket.

He cleared his throat. "It's *The Lady of the Lake*. Sir Walter Scott. Would that be acceptable?"

"It would, for I've never heard it."

"Really?" Andrew looked intensely interested. "Then you're in for quite a treat. Of course I'm partial, poetry being my favorite form of verse."

It was Sylvie's turn to say "*really?*"

Mahala cleared her throat. "Would you both like tea first?"

Andrew spun around. "Oh, Mrs. Randall. My deepest apologies. I – I did not see you there ... sitting – as you are – well, rather in the corner."

Mahala giggled softly. "That's quite all right, Mr. Willis. What may I serve you?"

Over small talk Mahala prepared cups and saucers and small plates of treats.

"But are you not going to have something, Mrs. Randall?" Andrew inquired when he had handed Sylvie her scone and Mahala tidied up the tea tray.

With a kind smile, Mahala said, "Thank you, but I must ask that you excuse me. The painter is coming by in fifteen minutes or so to settle his account on the boarding house, and I must make myself available."

"Of course."

"I'll just leave the refreshments here in case you want more." Mahala looked pointedly at Sylvie.

Andrew bowed her out, then came back to sit across from Sylvie. He adjusted his frock coat, took up his plate and smiled at her. She studied him intently. He reached for his tea. The cup made a clattering noise in the saucer.

"Why did you come, Mr. Willis?" She had to ask.

"W-what?" He set the tea down again, almost on the edge of the table. He took a minute to push it back. "Why – your brother mentioned he thought some verses read aloud might hearten you. He said – being in your room all the time bores you."

"Of course it does. But he said that – just like that? Quite out of the blue?"

"Why – I suppose so – yes."

"It's unlike Jack to arrange poetry readings. And why should ... oh ... say, *his wife* not be suitable for such a task?"

"He ..." Andrew sighed. "He knew of my regard for you."

"Thank you, but you hardly know me."

He leveled a surprisingly direct stare. "I have known you for a long time."

"Know *of* me perhaps, but not *known* me."

"I would like ... to – to rectify that, then."

Sylvie resisted squirming. She waved a hand airily. "Well, here you are then," she said, an attempt at lightness. "Talking is so tiring. How about you read now?"

"Of course." Not in the least unsettled by her demand, the clerk reached into his pocket and opened the little volume. Sylvie saw it had a golden harp on the front, and that her companion seemed instantly more comfortable behind it. He adjusted his spectacles and read, "'Argument. The scene of the following Poem is laid chiefly in the vicinity of Loch-Katrine, in the Western Highlands of Perthshire. The time of action includes six days, and the transactions of each day occupy a Canto.'"

Willis peeked up at her. She gave a little nod, and he proceeded. "'The Lady of the Lake. Canto First. The Chase. Harp of the North! That mouldering long has hung On the witch-elm that shades St. Fillan's spring, And down the fitful breeze thy numbers flung/ Till envious ivy did around thee cling ...'"

He went on. Interesting change, that which came over him. The meek manner fell away. He did have a golden voice, and not soft, either. There was none of that stuttering or those half-sentences. Willis actually became animated.

Frowning, Sylvie finished her scone and sat back.

A few pages later, her companion glanced up again, seeming concerned. "'And on the hunter hied his way, To join some comrades of the day; Yet often paused, so strange the road, So wondrous were the scenes it showed." He looked up again. "Do you wish me to continue, Miss Randall?"

"Why wouldn't I?"

"Well, you looked a little fatigued. I thought maybe Sir Walter Scott failed to interest you."

"I *am* fatigued, but not of Scott. If you wouldn't mind so terribly, perhaps I might just stretch out my legs and lie back a bit."

"No! Of course! Let me help you!" Willis jumped up, reached toward her, then reddened as he realized he was about to get a good glimpse of ankles. Clearing his throat, he cast about for something to occupy him – carrying the plate with his half-eaten scone back to the tea tray – while Sylvie raised her legs and tugged the hem of her gown down to her slippers. As he turned he noted her lap robe had fallen to the floor. He quickly spread the blanket over her, saying, "I'm glad you don't despise the poem, Miss Randall. I admit Scott is a writer to whose style I aspire."

"You write poetry, Mr. Willis?"

He paused and turned redder than before. "Sometimes. Though poorly."

Sylvie knew then, and she knew Jack knew. And that was why Willis was here. She caught his eye as he sat back down and said, "Perhaps next time you could read me one of your own poems."

He cleared his throat. "Perhaps. But – I fear – it might fail to keep your attention."

"A brush with death gives one an entirely different perspective on things, even things one may have scorned before … like poetry." Feeling the weight of the silence between them as Andrew absorbed her words, she plucked at the fringe on her throw. Then she added airily, "Jack was right. You do have a pleasant voice. You may come again to read to me." She caught herself and added with more humility, "That is … if you will."

"I will."

"Go on."

He picked up the book, and his hand shook. Sylvie hid a smile. She leaned her head back.

"'The Western waves of ebbing day …'"

She was warm and comfortable, happier than she had been in some time. Sylvie closed her eyes. The cadence of the poem made her sleepy.

"' … the whole might seem The scenery of a fairy dream …'"

She opened her eyes. Had she missed something? Andrew was still reading.

"'A chieftain's daughter seemed the maid; Her satin snood, her silken plaid …'"

If she let him keep calling, people would say she could do no better. Well, it just might be true, might'n it?

Some time later she awoke and knew she had slept deeply. Andrew was gone, but a rosebud was lying next to her hand. Sylvie snorted a little laugh, then gave in to a secret smile.

Andrew Willis became a regular visitor at Wright Square. After *Lady of the Lake* it was *Ivanhoe*, then there were morning walks in the park and dinners with the family. Sylvie slowly regained her health. She was altered, though. Her girlishness was replaced by womanhood, her spirit tempered by grace.

"This cannot be," Jack said to Mahala one day.

"What?" Mahala asked. "Sylvie is better. She's happy. What's the matter?"

"The constant presence of my subordinate in my home is simply intolerable!"

"But you are the one who told him to start coming," Mahala pointed out.

"I know, but I had not considered all the ramifications."

"What do you mean?"

"It seems clear to me that I now must promote not one but two of my employees."

Mahala stared at him blankly.

"Well, I cannot have both my sister and my cousin marrying beneath them, can I? I'll simply have to take on a new partner at Randall and Ellis Shipping *and* Randall Iron. Then there will be salary increases and new men to hire and train to fill the old positions – and necessary stock shares, too. It puts me in a bad humor just to imagine how much all this romance is costing me."

"Oh, Jack." Mahala flung her arms around him. "I love you even more than words can say. Does that put you in a bad humor?"

"*That* is what started it all." He drew her face down and kissed her soundly.

CHAPTER TWELVE

Late August 1866
Habersham County, Georgia

A pounding headache crescendoed in the blazing mid-morning sun as Dylan snapped and twisted, snapped and twisted the ears of corn from the stalks. The stalks were short, not lush green and head-high like they should be, testimony to the hard, cracked earth under his boots. Every day they had watered a different row. And every day the parched ground had sucked up the moisture to no avail while the sky remained ironically cheerfully blue.

Anger rose like bile in Dylan's throat. *Why, God? Was it not enough for us to lose the war, lose family, lose homes, lose money and position? Are we not humble enough yet for You? When will the punishment end? With death by starvation? What do you* want *from us?*

Emotions rose so fast and heavy the corn field spun around him. Dylan stopped, doubling over, and drew in a shuddering breath.

"You o.k., Mist' Dylan?"

Samson's voice came from the wagon into which Dylan had been tossing the paltry ears. They had been spelling each other, trading out picking and driving. He was fair, wasn't he? Dylan looked back at the concerned black man, who was leaning forward slightly on the seat, waiting for his response.

Okay, God, I'm sorry I owned slaves. Although I didn't actually – my family did – but apparently that counted. So sorry, so dad-blamed sorry I didn't rock the boat.

He couldn't quite curse when talking to God. Why was he talking to God? Whatever favor he had once enjoyed had long since dissipated, with boyhood, with decisions, with the war. Now, for all the good talking to God did him, he might as well shake his fist at the sky, curse the Almighty and die. Only if there was a hell he would go to it – and that was supposed to be worse than even drought-baked Georgia in August – and if God was no longer listening it would do him no good. And if God was no longer there, well, that changed everything. That notion was so big Dylan couldn't get his mind around it and so bleak he didn't want to. If that was the case he ought to give everything up, throw all his morals to the wind. But what kind of man abandoned his family, his defenseless women and children? Not the kind he was raised to be. Not a Southern gentleman.

He cursed softly under his breath – a string of curses. "We're done," he told Samson aloud. "I'm done, anyway."

He walked out of the field. Samson followed with the wagon as Dylan had known he would, faithful and unquestioning.

In the barn, the men worked silently, placing the ears in crates.

"Check the field in a couple days, get in the rest?" Samson said.

It was phrased like a question, but only for the sake of politeness.

"Sure," Dylan said. He ought to be grateful. Without the blank man's expertise and muscle, he would have gone belly up months ago. But just now he wasn't grateful for anything.

Ham, who came in to help with the unloading, muttered, "This be pretty poor-lookin' corn crop. I ain' never seen nothin' so sad. Shoulda gone with Markus and John."

Dylan rounded on him. "You think so? Go on down to Atlanta, then, and try your luck there. Maybe you'll get a belly full of lead like those poor Negroes on Decatur Street who were having dinner and a sing-a-long for the Fourth of July. Didn't hear about that? Well, that's what drunk Yankee soldiers think of black rights."

Ham stared at him bug-eyed. As Dylan wheeled around he saw Samson shake his head at the other black man, a look of warning in his eyes. Dylan didn't care.

He headed to the house for lunch. As soon as he opened the kitchen door he knew something was wrong. Someone must have come by with mail from town. Carolyn and his mother were poised over the work table, a letter in Henrietta's hands. She had been crying.

"What is it?" he demanded.

Henrietta put the paper away. She and Carolyn exchanged a glance that said: *we have to tell him. It might as well be now.*

"There will be no sale of The Marshes." Carolyn spoke quietly. At the same time, Henrietta resumed her weeping. "In fact, there is no Marshes – no house, anyway. It's burned to the ground. The fire was most likely started by vagrants. Or Yankees. Who knows. In any case, the result is the same. The buyer has backed out."

The day they learned The Marshes had burned was the first time Dylan didn't return by the next morning. He came home late in the afternoon of the following day, closed himself in his room, and slept until dawn. By the day in late September that Carolyn had her first pains, this behavior was becoming a pattern.

She was angry at first that when her labor started Dylan wasn't home, and once again, no one knew where he was. All day long as the contractions grew more intense she focused on that anger, breathing and counting through it. There was no Mahala to help her this time. Henrietta came in and out but never stayed long, so overcome was she by anxiety. Lydia had attended births before, so the servant put her mistress to work running errands and herself stayed by Carolyn's side. When it came time to push near dawn, Carolyn bore down with all the churning emotions in her body.

"That's good," Lydia said.

But a few minutes later, Carolyn curled around a furious twisting and burning inside, crying out. "Something's wrong," she gasped as it abated somewhat. It frightened her that Lydia looked blank and uncertain.

The contractions still wracked her body with the same furious intensity, but there was no visible progress.

"Stop pushin', honey," Lydia directed. Her strong black hands pressed firmly on Carolyn's distended belly. "Oh, Lord. This baby done turn half-way around."

As Carolyn's stomach tightened again, she sobbed with pain. "What are we going to do?"

"Send for the doctor! We must!" Henrietta cried from where she had appeared like an untimely cuckoo in the doorway.

"They no time. This baby gots to turn *now*," Lydia said. "Hold on while I try to mash it into place." She placed her palms on Carolyn and pressed, harder and harder until Carolyn cried out.

"Do you know what you're doing?" Henrietta voiced Carolyn's own concern.

"We bes' hope I do." So saying, Lydia angled her body and tried again from another direction.

Carolyn felt something give.

"There we go!" The black woman looked triumphant as she brought a drink of water to Carolyn's lips. "Now next time you feel a pain, push again."

Carolyn was growing weary. "Is Dylan home yet?" she asked her mother-in-law.

Henrietta shook her head.

"Maybe you ought to send someone for him."

"Of course." Henrietta hesitated then, wringing her hands. "If only we knew where he is! But – I'll send someone out – somewhere." She turned and left the room.

Carolyn's labor soon became exhausting, and again unfruitful. Her limbs trembled, and the blanket that Lydia pulled out from under her legs was streaked with blood. There had not been blood with Dev Jr. until after he was born. Her anger turned quickly to fear.

200

Lydia was hovering over her with a handkerchief. Carolyn's eyes rolled up to the wadded fabric with a silent question. "Miz Carolyn," Lydia said apologetically, "jus' you take this in your mouth. I believe that baby turned again an' I'm gonna hafta force him back – the hard way."

"No – no," Carolyn protested, but the servant stuffed the handkerchief in her mouth anyway.

It did little to muffle her scream, though it did keep her from biting her tongue. The next moment Carolyn blacked out. The dark insensibility was a welcome relief, but the respite it provided was all too brief. Another contraction, coming like a dark wave in to shore, broke upon her, forcing her back to consciousness. It felt like her body was being torn in two. She tried to scramble back on the bed to get away from the merciless vise that clamped down on her.

Lydia was there to calm her. "It be all right now, Miz Carolyn. The head be down. You be a brave gal. Now work with me."

"I can't," Carolyn gasped. She saw Henrietta's small figure hovering in the doorway. "Dylan," she whispered.

"I sent out Samson and Ham, but I don't know–"

"Dylan!"

Carolyn sobbed as the contraction demanded her attention. Hot liquid gushed out between her legs. Blood? Was she going to bleed to death? She was too weak to push. Tears ran down her face, and she tried to curl into a ball. She just wanted it to be over.

"No, Ma'am! Push. Push!"

Lydia's hands straightened her out. Her voice demanded obedience.

Some time in the next half hour, Carolyn decided that even if she was going to die she would do her best to bring her child into the world. But perversely she longed for the man who had caused her so much pain, longed for what might have been. Asked God for a few minutes with him before her final breath so that they might remember the tender love of youth that had first united them, and make peace.

Lydia yelled when she saw the baby's head, but her exultation turned to panic the next instant. "Help me, Miz Henrietta," she gasped.

"What – what's wrong?" Henrietta whispered, finally compelled to come to Carolyn's side.

"The cord – it's the cord."

Carolyn felt Lydia pull the child from her body. There was a strange caving sensation and another hot gush of liquid. She imagined blood everywhere and Henrietta ready to pass out at the sight. Lydia's hands were working fast. The servant held the child upside down and slapped it. Nothing.

"Oh, God, oh, God, please no!" Carolyn whimpered.

Lydia laid out the tiny blue body, ran her finger inside the mouth, pressed the chest – once, twice, three times. Then she hung the baby by the feet again and slapped its rear end twice.

A tiny cry rent the room. Carolyn and Henrietta wept.

"Thank the Lord," Lydia said. "The cord was aroun' his neck."

"His?"

"Yes'm. It's a baby boy."

Carolyn fell back on the pillows. She knew no more until Lydia nestled a bundle into her arms. She opened her eyes and looked down at a tiny face with a fuzz of blonde hair.

"He a scrawny thing." Lydia said. "What his name be?"

"I don't know." Tears fell from her eyes. She had hoped Dylan would help choose the name. He never had. "I can't – I can't hold onto him." Her arm was so weak she was afraid she'd kill the newborn after all, by dropping him on the floor.

Henrietta slid another pillow under her arm.

"You goin' to be okay, Miz Carolyn," Lydia told her. "Just gonna take time to build back up your strength." She paused and cocked her head, listening to a commotion coming from downstairs. "Mist' Dylan be home."

Her heart twisted. How could he come now? How could he show his face? Now that she knew she would live she didn't want to see him. The anger returned. Though her limbs were too weak to even tense, it burned like a hot coal in her chest. Worse than that – there was hurt, too. She longed to be past being hurt by him.

He was clattering up the stairs. Raised voices and an extra set of heavy footfalls testified that Samson was just behind him. Henrietta hurried into the hall, from where Carolyn could hear her accusations.

"Fine timing you have. We've had a terrible ordeal. The baby turned twice, and the cord was around his neck. He and Carolyn both could have died. And where were you?"

"Is she o.k.? Is the baby o.k.? Let me in."

"You think you can just go barging in there? That she wants to see you now? Didn't you hear me? They both could have *died*," Henrietta hissed. "When she thought she wouldn't make it she asked for you, though heaven knows why. And you weren't here!"

Carolyn heard a gasping sob.

"Are you drunk? Shame, shame on you!"

Carolyn turned her face away. She pulled the soft blanket around the infant's head. Dylan burst into the room despite his mother trying to bar him, the stench of whiskey coming with him. He stood there by the bed so long she had to look back at him. Tousled, shirt tails half out, eyes bloodshot, he was gazing at his son with a mixture of awe and regret.

"Carolyn, I'm so sorry." Dylan fell to his knees beside the bed and burst into tears. "So sorry. So sorry ..." His voice held an agony of sorrow. She had never seen him cry. Shoulders heaving and head down, he reached across the covers toward her hand that cradled his son. It was too late. She couldn't bring herself to reach back.

The next evening Carolyn and Henrietta were examining the baby as Henrietta proudly held him when a soft knock sounded on the half-open door. Dylan stood there, gazing downward as if ashamed to meet their eyes. He had slept, bathed and dressed in fresh boots, breeches, shirt and vest. His hair had been carefully combed.

He cleared his throat. "May I come in?"

Carolyn said nothing. Henrietta stood, the babe in her arms. Her face was set and angry. "Well?" she asked.

Dylan came closer. He stopped near Carolyn but still did not look directly at her. "I'd like to apologize again for not being here last night. I'm sorry – that you had such a hard time – and that I was not with you."

Carolyn waited until he glanced at her. Then she nodded once – briefly, unwillingly – and looked away. Dylan looked at his mother. She knew what he wanted and drew near, folding back a corner of the blanket. Dylan smiled for a moment.

"Would you like to hold him?" Henrietta asked. "I guess you are sober enough to do so now without dropping him."

Dylan took the tiny bundle and held the child up to the evening light coming in the window. Carolyn's heart wrenched, and she could not bear to watch.

"What shall his name be?" Henrietta inquired of her son. "Carolyn wanted your opinion."

Dylan glanced at Carolyn, surprised. When she would not meet his eyes his face twisted in a slight sneer. "Let's call him Jacob."

"Dylan, that's not funny," Henrietta warned.

"Was I being funny?"

Supplanter. The one who grabbed the heel of his older brother. That was, of course, what Henrietta was thinking. But Carolyn saw a fitting irony in the name – a promise, despite the way Dylan meant the suggestion. "It's not a bad name," she pointed out. "Jacob was a father of Israel. Maybe this Jacob will be a leader and a father of many as well."

Dylan held her gaze a long moment, then nodded.

Later that night, Carolyn awoke around eleven to feed little Jacob Louis. He seemed uncommonly demanding, even for a newborn, only content when he was in her arms. He was going to drain the last bit of energy from her wasted body, she thought. As if he hadn't given her a hard enough time being born!

Then she considered the possibility that even so new a person might only be responding to the tension in the atmosphere – and in her. She softened, caressing one tiny cheek. Despite her impatience, she loved the baby deeply.

When she was sure the infant was sleeping soundly, she stepped carefully, slowly, to put him in his crib. As she tucked the blanket around Jacob's middle, she heard voices in Dylan's room.

Instantly alert, Carolyn shuffled across the floor and leaned against the adjoining doorjamb. A woman. Henrietta. Thank God for that. She would have killed him if it had been anyone else – if she'd had the strength. Despite her concerns about where Dylan went and what he did the nights he left, she had no proof that he visited another woman – or women.

"Dylan, we need to hire a maid for Carolyn, someone to help her with the boys," Henrietta said. "It will take her a while to recuperate from such a difficult labor, and Lydia can't be spared. She has too many duties already."

An exasperated sigh. "I agree with you, but you just don't understand. Next month the credit line is due at the store, and that's only the beginning. January first property taxes must be paid on The Marshes, this place *and* the town house."

"Can't you use what we make from the lease?"

"What we make from the lease will cover the taxes on that house and the debts you incurred during the war. We also have Lydia's salary to consider. There's nothing extra for the plantations."

Henrietta sounded like she was growing panicked. "Well, you aren't charging the Moores enough for rent. Maybe you should raise the payment."

"It's all they can pay, Mother. They're good people. Hiram Moore fought with me from the Wilderness to the surrender. I won't make them homeless on our account."

"But you'd see us thrown out for back taxes instead? What are you going to *do*?"

"I don't know!"

"Perhaps … I could speak to my sister about a loan."

"No. Absolutely not. We owe them enough already."

"But they're family–"

"I said no. They don't have that kind of money to spare, anyway. I'll figure something out."

"How? How will you do that?"

Carolyn backed away from the door. Sore and aching inside and out, she climbed into bed. Henrietta's desperation and Dylan's pride still echoed

204

in her head. She thought of the gold coins lying in the drawer nearby and knew what she had to do. She just had to figure out how, and wait 'til she had the strength to do it.

Soon after, the strength came. Not from the good place of trust and faith of her innocent youth, but from a hard, closed-up core that felt like iron. Still, it gave her something to anchor to. Nothing would breech her heart again. Carolyn drew on that cold certainty as she told what would be her first lie. She announced in a manner that brooked no argument that she intended to travel to Savannah to visit Mahala, then repair to Brightwell. She disarmed Henrietta's tearful protests by insisting that her parents should be able to see their grandsons for Christmas, and that Mahala had sent ahead ample travel fare – enough to hire the needed maid to accompany her. A recommendation from Lydia procured an experienced black nurse named Delia from town. Carolyn invited Henrietta to join her at Brightwell, which, as she'd anticipated, Henrietta declined. They both knew she would not leave Dylan now, and he could not leave the farm. What Henrietta didn't know was that Carolyn had no intention of staying with Mahala, and that she planned two stops before she ever even considered calling on her old friend.

He had been blissfully, numbly drunk the night before, and he intended to get drunk again. In the study, Dylan was nursing his third glass of whiskey, after bolting down the first two. Blessedly, the lights from the candles and the fireplace began to take on a bright blur. Soon the memories should start to blur, too.

She had taken his son and left. His baby son he had only held that one time, because she had looked at him with such loathing it was too high a price to pay to be near his child. But Carolyn hadn't known he had crept into the nursery every chance he'd gotten to gaze at the sleeping infant. And now, they were both gone, and the searing truth of it rocked him even harder than the nightmare memories of that boy at Thoroughfare Gap.

The door knob rattled. Thankfully he'd had the foresight to lock it. His mother's voice said, "Dylan, let me in."

He didn't answer. As if he would willingly make himself audience to her tears and complaints.

She banged on the door. "Let me in right now. I mean it!"

She did sound like business, but he didn't budge. He took another swallow of whiskey, waited, and sighed in relief when he heard her footsteps retreat.

She would be much happier in Savannah, close to her friends and family. But she would never leave him here. However, if he were gone, she could sell this miserable patch of cracked earth, have no compunction about giving the Moores the boot, and exist without shame in Savannah off the proceeds of the sale and any necessary aid from her sister. Or, of course, she could move in with Collette in Charleston. Dylan hadn't seen his sister in years. They had never been close. But Henrietta exchanged letters with her regularly, and while Fred Lambert didn't have the excess funds to bail them out now, Collette would gladly take Henrietta in.

Dylan began to picture the widow's walk on top of the house. It would be an easy thing to climb the low railing and step off the edge. People would say he had gone up there when tipsy and simply slipped. What gentleman didn't indulge in an evening cocktail once in a while? That would not be frowned on. No shame for the family. Only relief, long overdue ...

A fitting place to end it, after all ... where Dev had stolen Carolyn from him and never given her back.

The temptation was shocking at first, then sickly sweet. It all just seemed to fit, to be inevitable. It was the only clear way to solve everything.

Crack!

Dylan jumped nearly out of his seat. The study door shuddered.

Crack! Crack!

What in the name of all that was holy?

He stared at the door and saw the tip of an iron ax head pierce the heavy wood! He blinked to make sure he wasn't imagining it, then fumbled hastily for his revolver.

He heard his mother's voice, breathless with exertion: "I said I meant it, and I meant it! If you won't open this door, I'll hack it down!"

Dylan cursed. "Are you insane? Stop! I'll open the blessed door." He ran across the room, nearly falling in his haste and alcoholic delirium. "Don't swing that thing again! I'm opening it now."

As the door swung wide, the sight of his petite mother standing there in her widow's weeds clutching an ax was so startling he fell speechless. Behind her in the hall, Lydia danced about with a hand clutched to her heart, fluttering like a moth.

"Oh, Lawd, Miz Henrietta done gone crazy!" she moaned. "Sweet Jesus, save us!"

"Lydia, go upstairs," Henrietta ordered her. As the maid disappeared, Dylan's mother marched into the study like a general going to battle. But when she saw his revolver lying on his desk, she dropped the ax with a thud and ran over to the weapon. "Oh, Dylan, no! I knew I had to get in here, and now I know why. What were you *thinking*?"

Some strange magic was at work this night. He shook his head in an attempt to clear it. She'd guessed his dark temptation, but not his method. He was not about to let her know how close she'd come to the truth. "That you were an intruder," he said, "and I'd better defend myself."

She wheeled on him with more ferocity than he had ever seen. "You let her go!" she practically shouted, pointing her shaking index finger. "You let her go and take my grandsons! Now do you think I'm going to let you leave me alone in this house while you drink yourself to death – or whatever else you have planned? No. I say no. Enough is enough." Henrietta actually stomped her foot.

Dylan stared, stupefied. His mother came forward, jabbing her finger in his chest. "What do you think gives you the right to give up? Do you think you're special, that nothing hard should ever come your way?"

"*Nothing* hard!' he spluttered. "There's nothing in my life that *isn't* hard!"

"You think you're the only one? How could you be so selfish? These past months I've watched you turn your back on Carolyn, on Devie, on me – on the world. You've turned your back on all you believed in. All that you fought for. Honor. Integrity. Faith. Are those things suddenly worthless? Is nothing worth fighting for? Your father didn't raise a son who would roll over and die when things didn't go his way. Even Job said in his afflictions 'Til I die I will not remove mine integrity from me. My righteousness I hold fast, and will not let it go.'"

Henrietta's words cut too deep. "Enough!" Dylan cried. For a moment he saw her waiver before his superior size and force, and he felt a pang of guilt. When had he ever shouted at his mother? He turned his face and said bitterly, "Sorry I'm such a disappointment. If Dev had come home instead of me none of this would be."

Henrietta took one step toward him, her hand raised. It made swift contact with the cheek he had turned. The slap made his eyes water. He looked at her in astonishment. "Don't you ever say that again. Never. Do you hear me?" she cried. Then she let out her breath painfully. "He was my first born, and I loved him. Too much. He could do no wrong. For that I take blame." Henrietta's voice broke. He stared at her, knowing she was struggling to continue. "I'm sorry, Dylan. So sorry. I was young and foolish. But lately I've come to see ... you always had the better character."

Dylan could only stand mute. He'd never thought he'd hear such an admission from his mother – never even realized how much he'd *needed* to hear it until now. Then she did something even more unexpected. She placed her hand again on the stinging mark she'd made on his cheek, but softly, gently. Something within him began to crack just a little bit.

"I've made so many mistakes with you. I've not been the mother I should have, and I fear part of the blame for your actions now rests on me. Can you ever forgive me?" When he still didn't respond, she continued.

"I've failed as a mother and a grandmother at points in my life, but I don't want to fail now. This is not a time for weakness, but strength, and we need each other."

Henrietta caressed his bright hair, and Dylan felt no more strength to even hold his head up. He was so much taller than she was, yet when she pulled him close, he drooped to let his head rest on her shoulder. To his shame, he realized tears were running down his cheeks.

"Forgive me?"

"Yes."

She pushed him away to look into his eyes as he wiped away the tears. "It pains me so much to see you destroying yourself this way – throwing away all you held dear. Just answer me this: do you love her?"

"What?"

"Do you still love Carolyn?" She captured his roughened hands in hers.

He didn't want to answer that question. "Doesn't matter. It's too late."

"It's never too late."

"She hates me now."

"Hate is just love twisted around. You do love her, don't you?"

He cursed softly, and his mother stepped back, frowning. "Yes." God help him, he loved her so much it hurt.

"I'm going to go back to washing your mouth out with soap. And I'm going to follow you around while you show me where all your devil's brew is hid. We're going to pour out every ounce. And then you're going to go after her."

"What? No! Are you crazy?" he shouted at her petite back.

"If I am, it's you I have to thank." Henrietta was nosing around his desk now. She seized the whiskey decanter by its neck and headed for the window. When he realized what she intended he instinctively put himself between her and the frame. Her brows came down threateningly. "Get out of my way, or I'll crack this over your head."

The way she was behaving, he believed her. He stepped aside. While she tugged the window open, a broken admission escaped him. "I can't do this."

The whiskey was splashing on the ground outside. Rising panic surged inside Dylan's chest. If she was anyone but his mother, he would have leapt across the floor and throttled her to get that decanter back. "You have to." She faced him, putting the cap on. "I still believe you can turn things around."

"I can't single-handedly beat the drought, pay the tax collector, and win back a woman who doesn't want me."

"Maybe not single-handedly, but with my help, and with God, you can take one step at a time. First off, prove yourself worthy of being wanted.

208

She'll come back to you. Then, together, we can do this. I promise. Please just stop closing everyone out."

He hung his head, took a shuddering breath. "O.k.," he whispered, though inside he thought, *if this fails, I won't have the strength to go on.*

"All right, then." Henrietta put her arms around him. "Now show me where the next bottle is hidden."

Mahala was doubly busy these days. It had been necessary to move ahead with renovating Mrs. Harper's mansion and purchasing and renovating the Irish boarding house simultaneously. That their work was moving ahead with such success – and was beginning to make a difference – brought an exhausted satisfaction at the end of each day. She didn't even mind that due to Sylvie's and Ella Beth's very recent engagements, she was putting in most of the work. It kept her mind occupied.

She was sitting at the dining room table with plans for the Trustees Garden home spread out before her, her morning tea cooling off to one side, when the butler entered. He paused behind her and held out a silver tray with a single calling card. The fact that it read "Mrs. Devereaux Rousseau" pierced her with pity and joy. She jumped up and rushed right past the servant into the hall, where Carolyn was standing. She had a bundle in one arm. Behind her a black woman Mahala did not recognize had charge of a Dev Jr., who had grown much taller.

"Carolyn!" Mahala hurried to embrace her friend, not hiding her happiness or astonishment.

Carolyn hugged her back. "I'm sorry to surprise you. I just came to town yesterday, and of course I wanted to call."

"Yesterday! But where are you staying?"

"At my family's old home. It's empty presently."

"Oh, of course. And who is this?" Mahala bent to see the baby.

Carolyn angled the child in her arms for a better view. "Jacob Louis Rousseau."

"Oh, he's so tiny! But look at me. Keeping you here in the foyer. Come – come into the parlor. Can I ring for some refreshments?"

"No. We've already eaten. I know it's an odd time of day," Carolyn said by way of apology, but Mahala waved her off. As she did so, though, she caught a flash of undisguised yearning on Dev Jr.'s face.

She bent down to the dark-haired toddler. "Hello, Devie. Would you like some milk and a scone?"

He nodded, shy but enthusiastic.

"Well, then, your maid can take you right back to the kitchen. Just straight down this hall."

"Thank you," Carolyn said when Mahala had ushered the boy and nanny in the proper direction. She followed Mahala into the parlor. As the butler hovered, waiting for her coat, Carolyn glanced at Mahala. "Would you like to hold him?"

"*Would* I?" Mahala held out her arms. Cradling the infant, she sat down and stared at him, examining his tiny features with wonder – and an envy she could not deny. She tried very hard to hide it from her guest, though. "He's *beautiful*."

"Thank you," Carolyn said again.

Mahala forced herself to look up. "Well, if you haven't come just to see me, what brings you to town? Is everyone here?"

"No. Dylan could not leave the farm. I'm taking the boys to visit their grandparents at Brightwell for Christmas. I expect we'll be there for some time, maybe through spring."

It sounded logical, but Mahala frowned, considering how young the baby was. "So long?" she couldn't keep herself from asking. "Didn't Dylan protest?"

Carolyn shifted on the seat before her. When she frowned, for the first time Mahala noticed her sunken eyes, her pallor. Something was wrong. Before Carolyn could hedge or prevaricate, she insisted, "Tell me what's happened."

Carolyn's lips quivered. "I need a steamer," she said, "to take me to Liberty County. As soon as possible."

"Carolyn, what is it?"

"Can Jack's boat take me there?"

Mahala reached out and grabbed Carolyn's arm. "Not until you tell me why. You owe me the truth." Her strident tone made the baby start to cry.

Carolyn took him and held him up to her shoulder, jostling him gently. Who was this thin, desperate woman with the darting gaze? Mahala waited until Carolyn met her eyes. Tears shone in Carolyn's. "All right. I'll tell you, to my everlasting shame. I should have known I couldn't hide anything from *you*. My marriage is a failure. The crops have failed from drought two years in a row. The house on the plantation – which we thought we had finally sold – burned. We don't have enough set aside for winter. And that's just the beginning."

"Oh, Carolyn. What else?"

"Don't – don't pity me! I won't say another word if you do. I'll get up and walk out of here, and you won't ever see me again."

Carolyn's threat felt like a dart thrown at Mahala's heart. She could take no more. "Stop it! You don't talk to your friends that way. What have I done to deserve it? You're here, aren't you? And I'm just trying to help."

210

Carolyn's voice caught on a small sob. "I'm sorry. You're right. I know it's not your fault. I'm just so ... ashamed."

"What do you have to be ashamed of?" Mahala moved closer and placed a tentative hand on Carolyn's shoulder.

"Didn't you hear me? I said my marriage is a failure." Despite her defensive tone, and a harsh swipe of her sleeve across her eyes, Carolyn did not shrug Mahala's hand away. "Dylan is changed. Since the war, he has nightmares, he's angry all the time, and the only solace he finds is in a bottle. Sometimes he stays gone for days."

"Oh, no!" Mahala's chest wrenched with this revelation. It was so unlike the gentle man she had first met she could hardly believe it, except when she remembered how angry Dylan had become when Jack had been shot on the Old Federal Highway.

"It's true. He won't come near me. You asked if he protested when I left. No indeed. I even overheard Henrietta telling him he should insist that I stay ... but he said it was best this way. I think he knows this isn't just a holiday visit. I don't know when I'll go back – if ever."

"Oh, Carolyn. Oh, dear Lord," Mahala breathed in anguish. She tried to draw her friend into an embrace, but Carolyn remained stiff. Watching her sadly, Mahala sat back. "I'm glad you've come to me. I'm sure if things turn around financially – if Dylan has some help – things can start to change for the better. You must let me help you."

"No." Carolyn moved away, her back erect, shaking her head. "No. That's not why I've come. I merely wanted to pay a call and inquire about the use of *South Land II*."

"Of course Captain Billingsly can take you. He's up the coast just now, so it will be a few days, but–"

"I can pay my way."

"No, you won't. And you must tell me what we can help with."

"Nothing, I said! And I meant it. I've taken care of things." Carolyn froze then, as if she had said too much.

"What things?"

"Nothing. I just meant that all will be fine once I'm at Brightwell." Carolyn attempted to smile, but the gesture was stiff and fake.

Mahala wasn't half Cherokee for nothing. When she got her jaws around something important, she could be as tenacious as those snapping turtles she used to fish out of Sautee Creek. This was important. "*How* did you take care of things? And *how* will you be fine? You're running from something, Carolyn. What is it?"

Carolyn stood up. "You spent too many years trying to solve your father's murder, Mahala. You think there's a mystery under every bush. I had a bit set aside Dylan didn't know about, is all. Now, can you tell me when I should be ready to go?"

Mahala rose, too. Her instincts told her not to give up, but the wall Carolyn had thrown up was about as daunting as Fort Sumter. Their visit was at an end. Perhaps their friendship was, too. "About three days," she said finally. "I'll send word around."

"Thank you." Carolyn hesitated. Then she leaned in quickly and kissed Mahala on the cheek. "Thank you very much."

"Don't do this."

Carolyn just shook her head. Then she called her son and left.

After the front door closed, Mahala stood in the parlor for a long time, her mind confused and her heart heavy.

CHAPTER THIRTEEN

ylan surveyed the Italianate stucco-over-brick mansion and adjusted his cravat. Around him, the scene was tranquil. November's nip had not touched the coastal area as it had the mountains, and people were out driving and strolling in the square – children and their mammies, women with baby carriages, old gentlemen discussing politics. But inside, Dylan was as anxious as he'd been when facing battle.

It was mid-morning. He'd stayed the night before with the Moores. It had been too late in the day when he'd arrived in Savannah to seek Carolyn out. Such a feat was best accomplished after a bath and a good night of sleep. Well, he'd had one of those. And time to think, though that might not have been a good thing. But did it really matter how prepared he felt, if Carolyn refused to even hear the fine lines he'd rehearsed?

Dylan raised his hand and knocked. Within minutes a butler had shown him into the parlor, and Mahala Randall had appeared. He stood up. He was prepared for her surprised response. No telling what Carolyn had said about him. He was even prepared for recriminations.

"Mrs. Randall, I know how inopportune my visit is, but I've come to see my wife."

"Mr. Rousseau, I – I simply can't help you with that." Mahala spread her hands and looked befuddled.

He frowned. "I understand you were not expecting me, and she may not wish to see me – and has probably told you so – but ... but there are some things I simply must say to her. If you'll call her, please."

Mahala stepped toward him. "You take me wrongly. I'm very happy to welcome you, but Carolyn is not here."

"Is not here?"

"No. She came to visit, but she is staying at the Calhoun residence in town."

"But – she told me she would be here ..."

"I assure you she is not."

Dylan's face turned from blank to red. What an idiot he must look, not even aware of his wife's whereabouts.

Mahala continued, "If you wish to contact her, you must hurry. You would probably be safer in trying to catch her at the wharf than at the house. She is to leave this morning on *South Land II* for Brightwell."

"Today?" Dylan was aghast. "I knew she was headed there, but she'd given us to believe she would pass a great deal more time here in town ... with v~ She – must have changed her mind."

Mahala looked sad. "She did not visit long at all. In fact, she seemed in a particular hurry to leave Savannah."

To leave me, Dylan thought. Before he could think of what to say aloud, they both noted that the butler had come to stand in the hall. The man quietly cleared his throat.

Mahala held up a finger in Dylan's direction. "I'm sorry. One moment."

She and the servant conferred in low voices. When she returned she wore a frown. "Mr. Rousseau – Dylan – that message pertains to you. I think we should both go with all haste to the Calhoun house. Captain Billingsly sent up an inquiry of whether I knew if Carolyn had changed her plans to sail, for she hasn't showed up at the wharf, and the time he gave her is well past."

Dylan fought down panic. What in the world was going on? Nothing was making any sense.

The butler had brought Mahala's wraps. Dylan helped her on with them. "I have only my horse out front," he said.

"You can leave him here. I've had a buggy made ready."

"What did Carolyn say when she saw you, Mrs. Randall?" Dylan asked as they hurried to the front door.

On the porch she met his eyes. The concern evidenced there only increased his worry. "She was not at all herself. To be quite truthful, she was anxious and impatient. She wanted to leave for Brightwell right away. She did say ... she had plans to stay there indefinitely. That there had been some ... troubles." Mahala's gaze flickered uncomfortably away from his.

The buggy arrived, and he helped her up into it. Once they were settled inside and Mahala had given the driver the address, Dylan said, "I won't pretend with you, Mrs. Randall."

"Mahala – please."

"Mahala. You have been a good friend to Carolyn for many years. A far better friend than I. We've had some serious struggles, but I came after her to try to fix them, to ask for another chance."

"I'm glad you did."

"I just hope it's not too late. And I don't know why she would not show up for the boat after she'd gone to so much trouble to arrange for it."

"I know. I have a feeling something else is afoot – something she didn't want to talk about with me. I think ... it might have to do with money. If it 'es, if there's a need, please, Dylan, let us help. I *want* to help."

Dylan shook his head. Except for that one loan from the Athens creditor – which he'd had a heck of a time paying back – and the expected tab at the store, he had never taken money from another person in his life, and he didn't intend to start owing anyone now. Especially a friend. Business and pleasure didn't mix well.

214

Mahala bit her lip and leaned forward. "Don't let your pride be your downfall."

He glanced at her in surprise.

"I know – in your shoes – Jack would be the same way. Your marriage and family are most important."

"I know that."

"Then ... remember what I said."

He knew she was right, hard as it was for him to admit it. Dylan nodded.

The buggy had stopped. Satisfied, Mahala let him help her down. In that moment, he felt insanely glad she was with him. She was a bright and determined woman – and one who now had powerful connections. Maybe between the two of them they could get through to Carolyn and get to the bottom of what was going on.

As Dylan turned to face the walkway, he froze in shock. Someone was standing at the door of the familiar townhouse, someone facing out like a guard on duty. Indeed, the man stood at attention in a blue uniform, a musket clasped at his side!

Dylan rushed up the steps, and it was only the soldier's move for his weapon that kept Dylan from grabbing him and shaking him. "What's going on here?" he demanded.

"Back off, Sir! Take a step down."

"Don't tell me what to do. This is my wife's family town house, and I believe her to be inside. What's happened? Why are you guarding the door?"

"You are Mr. Dylan Rousseau?"

Dylan felt Mahala come up behind him. "Yes! Now move out of my way!" He made a move to push past him, but the young man blocked his path with weapon raised horizontally.

"You will *not* barge inside this residence. Mrs. Rousseau is with Captain Gregory Jackson. She is being questioned under suspicion of possessing a portion of the lost Confederate gold."

"*What?*" At that moment, the man could have easily knocked him to the ground.

"*Confederate* gold?" Mahala echoed from just behind him. "But that's ridiculous! How could Mrs. Rousseau possibly have come into possession of such a treasure?"

"That's exactly what we aim to find out. Now, I'm sure the captain will be eager to speak with you, Mr. Rousseau, but he's given me strict orders to let no one else inside." The guard's pale blue eyes flicked pointedly toward Mahala.

She drew herself up. "The captain will want to speak with me as well," she said. "I am a dear friend of Mrs. Rousseau. She called on me only a few days ago and was preparing to leave town on my husband's steam boat this morning, when you detained her."

"Ah … well, that does change things." The young man looked rather surprised at Mahala's willingness – even eagerness – to be taken in for questioning. Dylan silently blessed her bravery and devotion. "For the moment both of you can enter and wait in the sitting room. After – that is – you surrender your side arm, Mr. Rousseau."

Dylan glared, but he removed his pistol and suffered the Yankee to take it and further pat him down. He wanted to give him a swift kick when the man slid a hand inside his boots to check for hidden knives. Finally satisfied, the guard led them to the front parlor and pulled the dividing door to 'til it clicked. Before exiting he said, "Be quiet, and do *not* attempt to leave this room."

Mahala turned to Dylan and asked, "What do you know about this?"

"Nothing, I promise you! You?"

Mahala shook her head.

"This must be some crazy misunderstanding. But whatever they ask us, please follow my lead. If Carolyn *has* done something regrettable, I'll do everything I can to lessen the impact on her."

"I think the most important thing is to get to the truth, don't you?"

"Of course … but she's a mother. The mother of my children. If there's a fall to take, I'll take it."

"Dylan–"

"If you can't respect that, leave now!" he snapped.

She looked taken aback, as if he had just proved something she suspected. Then her face hardened. "I'm not going anywhere. And *you* had better calm yourself. Whatever is going on, whatever these soldiers say, you would do well to remember they are in authority here. Getting their backs up will *not* help your cause."

Dylan accepted her advice. "I'm sure you're right," he mumbled.

She put a gentle hand on his arm. "In an hour everything will be settled. You'll see."

Dylan nodded, wanting to believe it was just a simple mistake – but all his instincts told him otherwise. How many secrets had Carolyn kept from him? How deep did the deception go? Was there another man? Some unsavory connection that had brought these suspicions upon her? And how could he defend her against what he didn't even know?

Mahala seemed to share his uneasiness, despite her confident words. When he glanced at her, her brow was furrowed. "Dylan … I'm remembering something Carolyn said the day she visited me. Remember when I told you I thought it was about money?"

Dylan nodded.

The next second his heart sank as the soldier from the porch opened the door. He tried to wipe all expression from his face.

"Captain Jackson will see you now," he said, his eyes shifting to Mahala. "Both of you."

They rose and followed him into a room two doors down the hall, at the back of the house. The library. Inside was the expected officer, a tall, lanky man who stood at a table pouring himself a drink. His long dark hair shot with silver touched his collar, and when he turned, Dylan saw that a patch covered one eye.

"*Captain* Rousseau," he boomed out with exaggerated emphasis. "Just the man I've been longing to see!"

"There's no need for the use of outdated military titles," Dylan stated, having stopped on the threshold. "Just tell me where my wife is."

"She is in another room ... *resting*." He smirked.

Dylan took several strides forward. "What have you done to her? God help you if you've harmed her."

The guard placed a hand around Dylan's arm, but the captain held up a long-fingered palm. The guard allowed Dylan to shake him off. "What a low opinion you take of a fellow officer and gentleman. I assure you she is fine. We merely had a conversation. Now I'm going to have one with you."

"I would like Mrs. Rousseau to be present."

"What you would like is immaterial at the moment," the older man replied, his face hardening. He splashed amber liquid into a glass. Dylan's eyes followed on the movement. It had been three days at least since he'd had a drink. His hands felt twittery, his palms sweaty. To his surprise, the Yankee officer seemed to sense his fixation and turned to look at him. "Although," he added thoughtfully, almost calculatingly, "I would not be so ungracious as to presume to drink alone."

To Dylan's surprise, the officer held up the glass, offering it to him. Without thinking, he leaned toward the drink – until he caught sight of Mahala's steely glare and froze in place. He shook his head.

"No, thank you."

Jackson gave a soft chuckle. "Sit down, then."

Dylan and Mahala moved to acquiesce.

"So, Captain Rousseau – you have left a distinguished career in the glorious 8th Georgia Regiment for the hills of North Georgia. How's the farming there?"

Dylan clenched his teeth before answering. "The Garden of Eden," he muttered.

The captain barked a laugh. "Not very profitable, eh? So I hear. Tell me, is your family here on the coast able to be of much help to you?"

"Who said we needed help?"

217

Jackson steepled his fingers. "Let's see … our friends at the courthouse tell us you're still in possession of all your land. So – if you're not raking in the money selling whatever it is you grow up in the mountains, and you didn't take a loan from anyone, perhaps you parted with some family heirloom?"

Dylan shook his head. "What? What are you talking about?"

"Just answer the question. Did you take a loan, or did you sell something valuable?"

"No!"

Jackson leaned across the desk. "Then how did you come to pay the entirety of your land taxes – in advance – in gold?" As he spoke he opened a purse that Dylan recognized as Carolyn's, shook it and dropped four gold coins on the desk between them.

Dylan was stunned, but something told him he shouldn't let this predatory man see that. He bit the inside of his mouth. The captain's one good eye, a piercing green, weighed every nuance of his reaction. What had Carolyn done? Where had she come up with that money? Suddenly, he knew he was going to have to lie to protect her.

"We had some set aside."

The captain sat back and laughed.

Mahala's eyes darted from one man to the other.

"Exactly what your wife said when I first asked her the same question. But the thing I can't figure out is – why then did you live in privation for the last year and a half?"

"What makes you think we did?"

Jackson took a swig of his drink. "Ah, the freedman," he intoned with mock disgust, "they are just so … *disloyal* these days. Just a few coins on a palm and they tell all. Your wife's nanny assured us it was commonly known in Habersham that the Rousseaus were – how shall I say it delicately – *hard pressed.*"

The captain was enjoying his cat and mouse game, but Dylan's patience had almost expired. Why should this man know anything of his business? What gave him the right? He clenched his fists again. "This is ridiculous. I told you we set some aside for the taxes. I'm going to the civil authorities. You have no right to barge into my wife's family home, harass her, hold us for questioning, and on what suspicion? What evidence? When your behavior becomes known there will be such an outcry you will be court-martialed." Dylan rose, placing a hand under Mahala's arm to indicate that she should do likewise. But Jackson's next words froze him.

"A cavalryman from Tennessee came to your home in Habersham County last July, did he not? Ah, I see you remember. Let's talk about him. I assure you I am well within my rights to continue this conversation. If I have to ask you to sit down again, Captain Rousseau, I fear I will not be so pleasant. I might actually act like a barbarous Yankee."

218

Dylan's legs weakened, and he dropped into his seat, his stomach churning. How did this Union captain know about the drifter? His mind darted, trying to discern what to hide, what to reveal. If only he knew Carolyn's part in all this, he might have some clue how to proceed.

Jackson seemed to read his mind. "Yes, your wife told me all about the Tennessee trooper, after – oh – several hours of conversation. She claimed he arrived sick with pneumonia and passed away shortly thereafter. That she found the gold in his blanket roll." His eyes narrowed. "Did you send Mrs. Rousseau down here in advance to pay your bills with stolen gold? Did you think you'd then escape any suspicion by running away together some place? Mexico? The Caribbean? Is that where you came in, Mrs. Randall?"

The officer's sudden attack on Mahala made her breathless. "What?" she cried. "No! Mrs. Rousseau indicated to me that she intended to go to her family's plantation in Liberty County, Brightwell. That could hardly be construed as the plan of a guilty woman!"

"Exactly so!" Dylan cried, seizing the opportunity. "I did tell her to pay the taxes ahead of her visit, which might extend for some time. Then, when my business allowed, I came to join her."

Mahala's blue eyes flashed to his, and he gave her a swift quelling look.

"Interesting," Captain Jackson said speculatively, playing with one of the gold coins. "She gave no indication she expected you to join her, and the clerk who took her payment said she gave *him* the impression she was acting alone – like she didn't want you to know it was she who had paid off the taxes."

Dylan swallowed. "That's stupid. What husband does not know what his wife is about?"

"Indeed. So ... you are saying you knew about the money from this cavalryman?"

At that moment sounds from upstairs, which had at first equaled the muffled movements of footsteps, crescendoed into a loud groaning like that of furniture being slid across the floor. Dylan latched onto the distraction, demanding, "What in the world is going on up there?"

Gregory Jackson was unruffled. "My men are searching the premises. Mrs. Rousseau insists she has parted with all of the cavalryman's gold, but I would hardly be doing my job if I took her at her word. And you, Captain Rousseau–"

"*Mr.* Rousseau." The Yankee's use of his former military title was nothing but an insult, and Dylan had had enough of it.

"As you wish. It intrigues me, Mr. Rousseau, how you keep answering my questions with questions. What about you, Mrs. Randall? Are you feeling helpful today? I hope you might be more understanding of the requirements of my duties and the value of my time. Did Mrs. Rousseau tell you of her plans when she visited you? That she was in town to pay her bills?"

Mahala shook her head. "I – no. She did not mention paying any taxes, but that was not unusual. She was not in the habit of discussing her financial affairs with me."

"Did you, at any time, give her money? Either by her request or yours?"

"*No.*" Mahala looked impatient – and slightly edgy.

"Did she at any time give *you* money – for safekeeping perhaps?"

"Certainly not!"

"What did pass between you, then?"

Mahala's face was red, indignant. "A friendly visit. She brought her new son to show me, and as I have already said, told me she would be for some time at Brightwell, if my husband's steamer could take her there."

Dylan relaxed just a fraction. Mahala was going to be true to his instructions and not mention whatever she had been about to tell him in the parlor.

Jackson stood up. "Then, if it is all as you say, you will not mind if a few of my men escort you home and have a quick look around?"

Mahala jumped up. "I certainly would!"

Jackson's dark eyebrow winged upward. "Do you have something to hide?"

"Yes! What's going to look to my neighbors like collusion with Yankees!"

The captain burst into uproarious laughter, taking Mahala's arm almost with affection. She bristled like a disturbed porcupine. Dylan rose as the officer steered her to the door. He felt terrible that Mahala had been involved in this – especially knowing her struggles for acceptance in Savannah society.

Jackson murmured patronizingly in her ear, "We can be discreet."

Mahala jerked her arm away and cast an agonized look at Dylan.

"I'm so sorry," he murmured.

"Oh – one more little thing," Gregory added. He turned to Mahala. "Did Mrs. Rousseau ever mention to you that she thought Mr. Rousseau might join her at Brightwell?"

Mahala looked between them again. She bit her lip. Dylan knew she would not lie so directly. "No," she said softly. "She did not."

"She did not say, or she did not think he would come?"

"She didn't think – he would come."

With a brief, sorrowful glance, Mahala allowed herself to be escorted into the hall, where further instructions were given. Dylan felt a growing despair. Things were spiraling dangerously out of control. As silly as their accusations and assumptions might be, Dylan knew who held all the cards.

The moment Jackson was back in the room Dylan cried, "Carolyn is innocent of any wrongdoing! We both are."

The dark-haired man examined him, standing only inches away. Finally he said in a level tone, "I will agree that you seem strangely uninformed of many particulars of this situation, despite your heroic attempts to convince me otherwise. Your wife's behavior, however, is highly irregular. She contradicted herself several times in the course of our conversation. In the light of what you have said, I will speak to her again before I make a decision."

Dylan's heart thudded. "A decision. On what?"

"On what to do next."

"What does that mean? I demand to see my lawyer! We are not at war. We will not be held prisoners."

"Yes, Sir, you are to be held, as is your wife, until I determine what charges to bring against you, if any."

Dylan was growing desperate. He briefly considered fighting his way out of the house – he might take the captain by surprise, and the young recruit at the door would be no problem if others did not come running in time – but that would not help Carolyn. He could not leave her here, even to go for help. Maybe they would bring her to him and he could finally begin to understand the meaning of this nightmare. "What if it's true about the gold," he asked, "and it was Confederate gold? How were *we* to know that?"

"That is part of what we'll try to determine. You attest to the truth of your wife's story about the cavalryman?"

There could be no harm in it now. "Yes – yes. There was a man. But he was delirious by the time we found him. He told us nothing, not even his name."

"And you did not notice the unusual combination of gold coins – some of them quite rare in public circulation?"

"No – of course not." He had not noticed it because he had not seen them. Was that what had made them suspicious? "A gold coin is a gold coin, right?" he added, hoping to prompt the captain into giving more information.

But "hm" was all the captain would say. He latched onto Dylan's arm. "I'll take you to a room now, one that has already been searched."

"Let me see my wife."

"Not yet."

"My children, then." Funny how once they had been threatened he thought of both boys as his. His anxiety for his brother's son was no less than for his own.

"They are safe in the hands of the freedwoman."

As the captain nudged him up the stairs, Dylan turned to him and snarled, "If they are not, you'll live to regret it."

"You are not in a position to make threats. And stupid ones at that. We are hardly in the habit of mistreating babies."

"I know all too well," Dylan spat out, all the old bitterness rising to the fore, "what your kind is in the habit of doing."

Carolyn sat alone on the bed, clasping and unclasping her hands, trying to think, trying to pray. But she realized there was a ceiling between her and heaven, not the literal one, but one of her own making. She'd taken matters into her own hands. Now she must figure out what to do next.

The captain had told her Dylan was here before he had her escorted upstairs. The unexpected arrival of her husband in no way served to alleviate her anxiety. Instead, she had stumbled up the stairs in shock and dread.

Sitting here thinking, she could only surmise that Henrietta had convinced Dylan to come after her. Why had he agreed? Out of anger? Out of duty? Pride? Even if it had been from a belated sense of shame, what did he possibly imagine he could convince her to come back to? More of his abusive neglect, his long, drunken absences? The idea made her angry, but that emotion quickly paled beside the fear. Now that he found her in this state, he would learn all that she had done, and he would turn on her with blame and recriminations.

She would rather be left to the Yankees.

She thought she heard his voice and jumped to her feet.

A door closed and locked down the hall while she waited, breath held. At last, shuffling footsteps came in her direction. Her door unlocked, and the captain stood there … alone.

"Please come to the library again, Mrs. Rousseau."

He gestured in front of him and she walked past with slow dignity. While caustic and cunning, he had been respectful thus far. Still, she was on edge, knowing he had all the power on his side – just as much power as Edward Wilde had wielded against the women of Chennault. The thought made her shudder, the lurid imaginings rising from the back of her memory.

The man behind her noticed and chuckled. "Pleased to see me?"

She ignored that. When they were in the library again, she inquired, "What did my husband say?"

"I will ask the questions, please."

Carolyn bowed her head and bit her lip.

"I have spoken with both Mr. Rousseau and your friend, Mahala Randall."

Carolyn's chin shot up. "Mrs. Randall was here?"

He gave her a quelling look, but the spark of hope remained. If Mahala knew what was going on, she would organize support.

Captain Jackson seemed to read her mind. "She will be occupied all afternoon and evening. She is graciously hosting several of my men as we speak." A self-satisfied smile played about his thin lips.

"Tomorrow the Randalls will put a stop to this fiasco," she shot back.

"Tomorrow you will not be here. I have decided that the only way to find the answers we seek is to escort your family to your home in Clarkesville, to conclude our investigation there."

"What? No! I won't go back there. I have answered your questions, and you have charged me with nothing."

This time both eyebrows raised, even the one above the menacing patch. There was a red scar running through it. "Would you prefer for me to charge you now?"

"With what?" she cried, though her voice squeaked.

He leaned forward. "You know what you did. You knowingly spent money belonging to the Federal government. Despite your husband's insistence to the contrary, I believe you did so without even his knowledge."

"He said that?" Carolyn gasped.

Jackson continued as though she hadn't spoken. "I need to be quite sure about that part, though. I also need to determine whether any more of the treasure is hid at your lovely mountain retreat. And, I'm struggling, I must admit to you, with a niggling uncertainty as to the demise of the unlucky trooper."

A blossom of dread opened inside Carolyn's middle. "What do you mean?"

"Awfully convenient, wasn't it? Delirious with pneumonia?"

Carolyn's mouth fell open in horror.

"That's why I'll be taking our regimental surgeon along for the ride."

"You plan to dig up a dead man?"

"If necessary. I believe in being prepared one hundred percent. So I'm graciously letting you know my plans, and I'm also saying that if there is anything unsavory we might find at – er – Forests of Green – it would go better for you to tell me now."

Carolyn stood up, though her legs were trembling beneath her. "All that I have told you has been true. You will find everything just as I said."

"Then you have nothing to worry about."

For a second, the spot of guilt on Carolyn's conscience throbbed so painfully she was tempted to confess all. Yes, she had suspected the money was Confederate gold. But they could never prove that for sure. They could never try her for what she might have *thought*. Carolyn looked at the uniform, the hard brass buttons, and her anger rose. It didn't really matter what the truth was. The vanquished always had something to worry about. If he chose, Captain Jackson could squash her under his booted heel like an ant.

And from the looks of his smile, he would enjoy himself.

CHAPTER FOURTEEN

wo hours later, Carolyn, the hired mammy, Devie and Jacob were herded onto the front porch. There on the street, the carriage waited, Dylan's horse tied to the back. Carolyn froze when she realized Dylan was already there, too. Dressed in a nice frock coat, trousers and fedora hat, looking more presentable than he had in months, he stood next to a Yankee sergeant. He turned, and their eyes met. She could not read his expression. And though Captain Jackson was watching with his usual observant interest, she could not make herself go to her husband.

Thankfully Devie relieved the awkward moment by flying down the steps into Dylan's arms, shouting, "Uncl'yn!"

The captain did look at Carolyn questioningly at that, but she ignored him, going down to stand by the embracing pair. She was forced to tell the invading officer enough. Her marriages – past and present – were none of his business.

Dylan searched her eyes and scanned her person. "Were you harmed?"

Carolyn shook her head, momentarily disarmed. But he turned away from her, scooting Dev into the vehicle and allowing the nurse to get settled with the baby. When he handed her in, the touch of his firm, supporting fingers surprised her with a jolt of need. If only things were as they should be between them … how she could use his encouragement, his embrace. But then, if things were as they should be, she would not be here in this predicament. And he was as angry with her as she'd feared.

She frowned as Dylan climbed into the carriage and sat opposite her. They had a split second before the captain joined them. Dylan took it to lean forward, his face intense, and hiss, "Why didn't you tell me?"

As though she could answer now! Even as he spoke the vehicle tilted, and Jackson's slick, dark head butted into the doorway.

"No Yankee!" Devie burst out in genuine alarm. He had seen enough bluecoats on their trips into town to absorb the typical reaction to their presence.

Jackson looked taken aback. Devie was scrambling as far away from him as possible, into the very corner of the carriage.

"Hush, chile," the mammy said, clawing him out to her side.

"Come sit with Mama," Carolyn urged. Her son hastened to do so. His small, solid weight created a reassuring warmth on her lap. From that vantage point he stared with wide, unblinking eyes at the officer.

Carolyn had her own object of interest. She should be preoccupied with the danger she was in, planning what to do or say should things go badly in Habersham. But Dylan's presence distracted her. First there was the mere fact that he was there at all. Then, there was his strange behavior which began on the train ride. As the miles chugged away, Dylan's brows lowered. Not in anger, but with a sort of anxiety. He rubbed his neck and forehead as though the noise and motion were giving him a headache. He stared pensively out the window, a sheen of sweat on his brow. When repeatedly the clanking rhythm of the tracks beneath them slowed on their approach to the many small depots along the route, his leg jostled with such impatience Carolyn imagined he shook the whole car.

She considered his tersely whispered question and grew angrier by the mile. Why. *Why?* She would give him *why,* and he would be sorry he'd ever asked. He'd come all that way to force his presence upon her uninvited, and now he thought he had a right to his anger? Everything she had done he had driven her to. Everything was his fault.

At first Carolyn had felt surprised gratitude that Dylan had tried to convince Captain Jackson he had sent her to make the tax payment. Now, any gentle emotion she'd harbored withered in the heat of her scorn. She ought to let him take the blame. She could run Forests of Green better than he could anyway. If anyone had to go to jail ...

Jail. The possibility that someone might end up there had seemed silly at first. Now, not so much. And that someone would most likely be her. But surely not! She was a woman, a mother of two small children who relied upon her.

With a sinking stomach, Carolyn realized this was why Dylan had lied to protect her. She glanced at him again, knowing that at one time any form of dishonesty would have eaten him up inside. Did it bother him now? Was that why he was so uneasy? Was he plotting what to do if his lie wasn't enough? Or blaming her like she was blaming him?

Being forced to return to Forests of Green when she had so nearly escaped was a sour draught for Carolyn. Watching the familiar landmarks slide by, she chafed in silence as the carriage approached the house. Once she had welcomed each one with a sense of belonging. Now, with the bitterness of lost opportunities, her love for the land – like her love for the man across from her – had turned to repulsion. One couldn't grow a crop on parched earth.

Last night they had stayed – ironically – at the Commercial Hotel, but Captain Jackson had placed Carolyn in a separate room with the children. Apparently, he wished to discourage any plotting or collusion between herself and Dylan. During the hours of darkness she had tossed and turned, but Dylan appeared rested today, and far calmer. He was quiet, lost in his thoughts. What had happened to change his frame of mind? How could he be so composed while she was picturing Henrietta's shock and distress, their humiliation before Lydia, Ham, Samson and Tania, and the literal tearing apart of their home?

Indeed, it was far worse than she had pictured. As soon as they arrived, Jackson had Carolyn show him where the cavalryman's equipment remained in the barn. His second-in-command gathered up the items. Then Jackson insisted she take him to the spot by the pond where the Confederate had been buried. After she had done so he returned her to the house – to the kitchen. There the soldiers had corralled all the workers and the family. Dylan was attempting to reassure his mother, answering her constant flow of questions in a low voice. They glanced up as Carolyn entered with the Yankee commander. Carolyn could not bring herself to look at Henrietta's blanched, suspicious face. She took a seat, her back stiff.

Samson glanced at her with concern, but Tania was smug, her lips compressed knowingly.

Jackson went to stand before the hearth, one hand on his sword hilt. "This farm has been commandeered by The United States Army under the suspicion that a cache of Confederate gold was secreted here. We believe the money arrived last summer on the person of a Tennessee cavalryman who then died in the parlor of this house. We also believe at least part of that same money was spent by Mrs. Carolyn Rousseau on property taxes in Savannah – and ... we will be speaking to authorities here in Clarkesville as well. A thorough search of the premises is now underway. We will interview each one of you one at a time. You should answer our questions fully and truthfully, holding nothing back. This is for your own benefit. Until you are called, the family will be confined to two rooms above and the freedmen to the cabin just outside the big house – just as soon as those places are cleared. Any questions?"

"Yes, Sir," Tania spoke up. Carolyn winced at the sugary sound of her drawl. When Jackson turned to acknowledge her, the young black woman asked, "Did Miz Rousseau confess to hidin' Confederate gold?"

"Yes," he responded, his eyes leveling on Carolyn. "She did."

Carolyn jumped up. "No! I did not!" Her gaze swung wide to entreat everyone gathered in the room.

"That will be enough, Mrs. Rousseau," Jackson retorted. He jerked his dark head for a guard to take charge of her.

"That's not necessary," Dylan said. His gaze on her was hard, pointed, appealing to her to spare them all some dignity.

Angrily Carolyn shook off the soldier's grasp. She gulped back a sob and turned to follow her captor into the hallway. She would not cry in front of them. But the shame crowded in on her so that the minute she was alone – locked in Dylan's bedroom, of all places – she fell across the bed and muffled her sobs in the mattress. She was completely powerless to decide her own future or even the course of the very next day. The presence of the Yankees was merely an extension, a visible symbol, of the helplessness to which she had long been captive.

When a knock on the door sounded, she stiffened. But a pitiful cry alerted her to the reason for the intrusion. She jumped up. In the hallway beside the guard stood Lydia with a mewling Jacob in her arms. Carolyn took him without a word.

"You all right, Miz Carolyn?"

Carolyn just shook her head.

"There be anythin' you need ... food, water?"

"The cradle," she said. Her eyes darted to the soldier, the same blonde, flat-faced man who had escorted her when the captain wasn't near. "It's right next door."

The Yankee nodded. Carolyn waited for him to bring the requested item in. "Can I not go to my own room?" she asked as he lugged the walnut rocking cradle across the floor. "My things are in there."

"I'm sorry, Ma'am. It's being searched now. Your mother-in-law will be staying in there tonight."

Carolyn sat and unbuttoned her bodice as soon as the door closed. The idea of sharing a room with her husband filled her with a dread she couldn't dismiss from her mind. Even nursing the baby did little to calm her. Jacob seemed to sense her agitation and flailed his arms and fussed. She had him on her shoulder when a knock came again, and the same guard let Dylan in the door. Carolyn stood and turned away, still patting her son's tiny back.

"I guess they're no longer worried about what we might cook up now that we're home," he said mildly, not moving into the room.

Surreptitiously Carolyn's fingers worked to close her bodice. "Are you happy then?"

"What?"

Carolyn turned. She couldn't keep the viciousness from her voice, and the sight of him standing there so innocently filled her with fury. "That you got your way? I'm back here, aren't I? That's what you wanted."

"This is *not* what I wanted."

"You followed me to Savannah to insist I not go to Brightwell because your stupid pride would not allow it. What would people think if I went away and didn't come back? That you were a failure? That you couldn't provide for us?"

Jacob whimpered and stiffened like a little poker.

"Carolyn, please," Dylan said. He rubbed his forehead.

"What, am I giving you a headache?"

"I do have a headache, but I was going to say that you're upsetting the baby."

"Since when do you care about the baby?" Carolyn patted furiously and then abruptly tucked the child in his cradle. "Heaven forbid I question you. Heaven forbid I embarrass you."

"Questions I expected, but we could try talking a little more quietly."

"Oh, right, your head. I guess you could use a drink about now. Didn't have access to your normal stash these past few days, hm? If you call the captain maybe he'll give you a toddy."

Dylan stepped forward and grabbed her arms. "Stop it! I haven't had a drink in five days. That's why my hands are shaking and my head is pounding. But not because of the little inconvenience of your arrest. Because I *chose* to be sober. For good."

"Oh, right. I'm supposed to just believe that. As soon as the Yankees leave you'll be just the way you were before, and all of us will be at your mercy. That is, if they don't haul one or both of us off to jail."

At her venomous response, Dylan strode away, making a sound of frustration as he raked his hand through his auburn hair. It stood in spikes while he paced. "I can't pretend I'm not upset at what you did. You kept something huge from me. And why? Because you didn't trust me. But when I look at that –" he paused, his hands out – "why would you have? When did I show you I *was* trustworthy? When was I there for you? When you left – before I even knew about the gold – I realized I had driven you away. I don't know how, but I want to make things right. That's why I went to Savannah. Because I couldn't let you go without telling you I was sorry." He turned and faced her. "So – I'm sorry. And with all that's going on now, I think that's still the most important thing."

Carolyn stared at him, uncomprehending. In his crib, Jacob whimpered. She could hear the clock ticking. "That's it?" she said. "*That's it?* After all you've done you think that's all you have to say?"

"I know I need help–"

But she didn't wait to hear his excuses. Anger like the spring flow on the rice fields poured through Carolyn's veins, and she rushed at him, pushing and pounding with her fists. He staggered back under her onslaught, taken by surprise.

"You're sorry? You think that fixes it? You idiot! It's all your fault! You scorned me and ignored me and left me, and now *you're sorry?* Oh, do let me forgive you! Let me fall at your feet!"

"Stop, Carolyn."

"No! It's not that easy! I hate you! I *hate* you!"

Carolyn sobbed. She pounded. She expected him to grab her flailing fists, her scratching nails, and force them behind her back. But she became aware that instead, he'd looped his arms loosely around her and just stood there, turning his face when necessary but taking her abuse. Shocked, she stopped hitting but sobbed harder. She could barely hear Jacob in his cradle crying, too.

There was a knock on the door.

"Not now, private!" Dylan's deep order was issued like the man in the hallway was under his command. He tightened one arm about Carolyn's waist as her knees buckled and slammed the other hand palm flat on the door, forbidding it to open.

There was silence except for Carolyn's weeping.

Dylan dragged her a few steps into the room and cupped her head. "I *am* sorry," he whispered. "God, I'm sorry for all I've done to you. I talked to Him last night – for the first time in ages – and saw clearly then what I should have seen all along. I couldn't let you in. I was so screwed up from the war, so sure I would be a failure that that was exactly what I became. And most painful of all, I was trying to be someone I wasn't. I was trying to be Dev, because I thought it was him that you wanted."

Carolyn had no words. Coming now, the words he finally spoke were too hard to comprehend. Exhausted from stress, sleeplessness and her outburst, her legs started to give way again. Dylan picked her up and laid her on his bed. She felt too raw and untrusting to tell him she'd just wanted him to be him.

Jacob was still whining, so Dylan lifted the baby from the cradle and walked around patting him, forehead furrowed with deep thought. His confession hung in the air like incense, not going away, not allowing Carolyn to ignore it. She watched him with tears sliding from both eyes and asked the question foremost in her muddled brain:

"How can I know that you mean it? And how can I know that you'll do what you say?"

Dylan shook his head. "Something my mother said before I left for Savannah has kept rattling around in my mind. A Scripture, actually. 'Til I die I will not remove mine integrity from me. My righteousness I hold fast, and will not let it go.' I've let a lot of things go. It was a slow process that started during the war. I want to get some of them back. I can't do it by myself, but with God, with you ... if you'll give me a second chance ... and I guess I'd have to ask you to take that on faith, too ..."

His voice trailed off as he lowered the now-sleeping infant into the cradle. He gave it a gentle tip and set it rocking. As he walked over to her side of the bed, Carolyn turned her face, suddenly ashamed.

Dylan misinterpreted her gesture. "You need time," he said in a dull voice. "I understand."

Yes. A lot of time. But instead of responding again in anger, Carolyn quietly confessed, "I've done wrong, too."

He was surprised, but he didn't deny what she said. "Yes," he admitted softly.

"How did we get to this point?"

"God help us."

Dylan climbed into bed and stretched out carefully, not beside her, but over her. He held himself up on his elbows and tenderly moved a strand of hair that was stuck to her cheek. She turned her head to look at him with wide eyes.

"Do you believe me? That I'm sorry?"

Her lips trembled. The pressure of his body over hers had initially panicked her, but suddenly she realized it was nice, rather like a shield that had long been absent. "I believe you feel that way right now."

"But not that I will in the future?"

"What if it's your pride – just not wanting to let me go?"

His eyes darkened with sudden vehemence. "Curse my pride. What do I have left to be proud *of*? Except you, and the boys. We may have nothing left, Carolyn, but if we have each other … if we have each other … I will take what the Lord leaves me and count myself blessed."

"And if He leaves you nothing?"

Dylan's jaw clenched. They couldn't pretend that wasn't a possibility at this point. "I doubt I'll respond as well as Job did. But I hope I can trust Him to take one day at a time, this time with honor."

Carolyn reached out tentatively and brushed his hair. "There you are," she whispered. "You've been gone a long time." And she started to cry silent tears again, but they were different now.

He drew a ragged breath, fighting some inward battle. He placed his hands alongside her face, his forehead to hers. When he spoke, each word was labored, and she knew what risk he took. "I love you."

There was a long silence in which Carolyn's breathing was shallow. She couldn't lie, but she could test him. She said it softly, almost gently, honesty a tentative gift. "I don't hate you."

To her surprise, Dylan laughed quietly, causing her to tense beneath him. At least he hadn't grown angry. It gave her enough leeway for another admission.

"You've hurt me so much."

"I know. I'm sorry. Forgive me? Please?"

Something clenched inside of her, then released, and a shudder worked its way through her body. "Yes," she whispered. She felt Dylan's ragged breath of relief, and his warm lips on her skin, and she was floating in a place where time did not exist and pain could not touch her, a blessed place of harmony and union and complete surrender unlike she'd ever known.

That night, there were no nightmares, no leaving, only healing, truth and wholeness in their joining. One good thing had come of their estrangement, Carolyn realized: no more comparisons. Confessions were whispered in the heat of lovemaking and promises in its tender afterglow.

When in the wee hours of the morning Carolyn brought Jacob to the bed for his feeding, Dylan curled tight behind her, his lips upon her bare shoulder, his warm breath on her neck. She shivered in exhausted contentment, but his next words brought her to alertness.

"I lied to the captain to protect you. I told him I made you pay the taxes with the gold. Pretty sure he knows I was lying, but that's not the point. I thought it was a man's honor to shield his wife, but I'm not sure I know what honor looks like anymore. It's been so long since I've seen it."

Carolyn stiffened, then said, "I think it's right behind me. And I think that's why your lie is sticking in your craw. There's no honor in shielding the guilty."

Dylan was very still. "You knew it was Confederate gold?"

"I suspected."

He pulled back almost imperceptibly. A glance over her shoulder told Carolyn he was digesting this news. "I told you I had done wrong," she admitted. "A year ago I would have told you, and we would have gone to the authorities together. Instead, I undermined you by keeping my own nest egg and deciding to use it when things looked impossible. I knew you would not take help, and I was determined to hang onto all we had. I thought no one would worry over where the money came from so long as the bill was paid. I justified my selfishness and dishonesty and my lack of trust in you by blaming you."

"And I made that awfully easy."

She held up a hand. "But it's *my* decision that could cause us to lose it all."

"No, Carolyn. I'm just as much at fault."

"You couldn't control the weather, the reverses."

Undaunted, he concluded, "If not by failing to provide then by failing to be there for you." He traced a pattern on her arm with his forefinger. "But we *can* control what we do now."

Carolyn knew what he meant. "You think we should talk to the captain and trust his mercy."

"No. I think we should talk to the captain and trust *God's* mercy."

She sighed deeply. In her soul, she knew it was the right thing to do. But memories of what she'd learned about Chennault, things she would not tell Dylan, froze her with trepidation.

"If we go together – if I tell him we have something to say but will only do so together – will you go with me?" Dylan probed.

He couldn't know her hesitation came not because she didn't trust him, or God ... but the captain. And why.

"Of course," Carolyn said. "But ... could we maybe pray first?"

"I think that's a wonderful idea."

They were both washed and dressed, and Dylan had just finished tying off the end of Carolyn's braid, when the guard came to the door. With him were Lydia, holding a breakfast tray, and Devie, who ran into the room screaming "Mama!" and nearly knocked her down with his leg-clasping embrace.

"Your lil' boy was missin' you," the soldier said. He cleared his throat and looked pointedly past them.

Carolyn realized he had not dared to deliver the child to them after Dylan's stern injunction. "Thank you," she returned, holding the boy in place against her. As Lydia placed the tray on the floor in the middle of the room, Carolyn fixed an eager look upon their jailor. "Can we see the captain?"

"He's busy right now."

"Please, we must see him right away."

"We have something to tell him," Dylan added.

"I'll pass that on. He'll call you when he's ready."

Carolyn nodded and sat down on the rug to eat with Devie. "Let's have a picnic," she suggested in a happy tone.

As the door closed and locked, Dylan came to join them. He smiled and tousled his stepson's hair. Responding to the new atmosphere between the adults, Devie grinned. He was more than ready to believe they were having an adventure.

They divvied up the eggs and toast while Carolyn laughed and reached for a steaming mug of coffee. "Who did you stay with last night, Devie?" she asked her son.

"G'amma!"

"Grandma, was it?" Dylan smiled.

Dev. Jr. nodded and put a piece of bread in his mouth. Then he suddenly patted the floor beneath him and around a mouthful of crumbs said, "Home."

"Oh," Carolyn murmured.

"Yes, you *are* home, and everything's going to be fine now," Dylan said, drawing the child into a partial embrace. His eyes rose to meet Carolyn's. She knew his words were intended to reassure her as much as her son, but the guilt at all the trouble she had caused was finally catching up with her, now that she had accepted her burden of the responsibility.

232

When they had finished eating, Carolyn went to stand by the window. She cradled her mug in her hands as she gazed out. The morning was bright and cold, with a late November wind that tugged wrinkled leaves from the branches. Suddenly she stiffened.

"Dylan."

"What?"

"Come see."

He rose and joined her at the window.

In a strangled voice Carolyn whispered, "Look there. They're digging him up."

From Dylan's window they could see the pond. Two soldiers with shovels were laboring under the oak tree while the captain and the doctor – recognizable by his green sash – stood waiting in their blue uniforms.

Dylan's jaw tensed. He put a hand on her waist. "This will only help us," he reminded her. "They'll find nothing."

"But it's a desecration. Poor man! And they can make up whatever they want if that Yankee doctor vouches for it."

Dylan shook his head. "No. Come away from the window." When she hesitated, morbidly fascinated, he repeated, "Come."

She turned away, took his hand, then reached her arms around his neck. Dylan embraced her, rubbing her back, murmuring comfort. She melted at his touch, having yearned for it for so long. It was so satisfying to her parched heart that there was no room for remaining bitterness. God had done that, surely.

Carolyn turned her face up for his kiss and caught sight of Devie still seated on the rug, a half piece of toast clasped in his jelly-smeared hand. The expression of wonder and confusion on his face arrested her. She realized he had never seen his parents act so.

"Dylan, look," she whispered again, this time with a tinge of laughter.

He dragged his face across hers to behold the little dark-haired boy on the floor. A chuckle rumbled in his chest. "Oh, but we have a lot to make up for, don't we?" he murmured. He held out an arm to Devie and said, "Come 'ere."

The toddler jumped up and ran over.

"Three can hug," Dylan added, bringing his stepson into the embrace.

Devie accepted the new concept with enthusiasm. He streaked grape jelly all over Carolyn's skirt.

"If everything goes bad from here," Dylan said, "if the Yankees cause us trouble – and if they do, we *will* fight it – and we'll win ... but if they do, if we lose the farm and the house in town, *this* is worth it." His arms tightened around them, and his gaze wandered to the window, his face softening with compassion. "Even if I were to die tomorrow, I won't be like that poor soldier was, left alone with nothing but memories."

Carolyn buried her face in his neck.

"From here on out … together."

"Together," she agreed.

The peace that she felt in Dylan's arms, in the room, continued like an underlying current, even though Carolyn's mind kept straying to the scene by the pond, even though she anxiously awaited the time when they would be sent for. She knew Dylan felt the same. All the while they played with dominos on the floor with Devie, stacking and restacking them so he could knock them over, Dylan's eyes kept meeting hers. It was well after lunch, and their stomachs were starting to ache from the lack of the meal, when finally that time came.

"The captain will see you now," their guard told them, gesturing them ahead of himself. "In the library."

When they entered the familiar room, the captain rose from behind the desk. Atop it Carolyn saw the haversack that had been buried with the cavalryman, filthy now and partially disintegrated. She shuddered. Averting her gaze, she sat down.

"I understand your time together has made you eager to speak with me," Jackson said, his one eye sweeping between them, looking for crumbs of information. "Perhaps I should have closeted you sooner." He seemed to find humor in the idea.

Dylan suppressed a perturbed expression and said, "We do have something to tell you. My wife and I haven't been entirely forthcoming."

Jackson laughed at that in a pleased, hearty manner. "I can't imagine! 'My wife and I' now, is it? When before you could hardly stand the sight of each other! What a rich and fascinating marital history you must have!"

"Personal observations are unnecessary – and ungentlemanly," Dylan said through tight lips.

He succeeded in interrupting the captain's guffaw, but the man only sobered slightly. "Well, as eager as I am to hear the grandiose new tale you've concocted for me, Mr. Rousseau, I will be a *gentleman* and be forthcoming. We've examined the evidence, interviewed your acquaintances as well as the property clerk in town, and searched your premises. I've come to my conclusions, and nothing you say will alter them."

Dylan's jaw twitched in that typical Rousseau manner that belied irritation or anxiety. "Out with it, then. We're ready."

"No, wait," Carolyn said softly, though she had felt the blood drain from her face at the officer's statement. "Whatever you have decided, whatever you may think of us or plan to do with us, I can't rest until the truth is all out. I was angry and defensive before, but now, I want you to know the whole story ... and I want a witness. *That* man." Carolyn turned and gestured toward the open doorway, where her young blonde guard stood.

"Very well, although I warn you, you are probably not helping yourself."

Carolyn waited, lips pressed together, until Gregory Jackson had the guard enter and stand just inside the room.

"Well?" said Jackson.

Carolyn's hands trembled in her lap. "Everything I told you was true, except I didn't tell you how bad it was, or how desperate I was. That soldier you exhumed this morning, he came just as we said, ill with pneumonia and delirious. He died of his illness in our front parlor. We didn't kill him. I tried to save him. Mr. Rousseau and I both did. We went through that haversack there ..."

Her voice went on, telling of the burial, their attempt to run the farm on their own, the bleak months with no rain, the failure of the crops, not once, but twice.

"When I found the gold rolled up in the soldier's blanket in the barn, I thought it was a God-send, sent to keep us alive if things got too bad. I didn't tell my husband because we were – estranged." Carolyn glanced down. "Later on, I had heard the story of the Confederate gold and what happened at Chennault. Yes, I thought this *could* be part of that money, but I talked myself into believing I had as much right to it as anybody. I see now I was wrong. The treasure wasn't a God send. It was a temptation straight from hell. Keeping it secret was like a poison inside me. It ate away at me until in desperation I did what I never would have done before ... used the money to try to save our family's legacy. But the price I paid ... well, it was almost everything. Maybe it *is* everything. But I see now a legacy isn't in houses and land." Carolyn paused and reached for Dylan's hand, briefly meeting his eyes and blinking tears back from her own. "It's in family, and faith. And I beg of you now, take the gold we paid back from the property clerks and give us another chance. Take everything we own if you must. But please, please, leave us each other."

Carolyn's tears were falling freely by the time she finished speaking. The captain seemed unsettled by her emotional plea. He rose and strode over to the window, looking out while she attempted to compose herself. Dylan handed her his handkerchief. His look communicated pride and love. It steadied her enough to draw a shaking breath and wait calmly.

"Captain," Dylan offered, his voice breaking. He reached again for Carolyn's hand. "If there is any price to be paid for what has happened here, I entreat you as an officer and a gentleman – let me pay it. My wife has still not told all. I may not have known about the gold, or told her to spend it, but I forced her hand just as surely as if I did. The war ... trying to be a farmer

...." His words trailed away as he struggled for control. "I used to be a minister, you know. Well, I got far from that. Let's leave it at that."

"I used to be a banker," Jackson said from the window, not turning around. "I'm far from that, too."

Dylan glanced at Carolyn, seeming to gain hope. "Mrs. Rousseau is a mother with two small children. They need her. We all need her."

Jackson turned then and gazed at them. "I know what she is, Mr. Rousseau. And neither that nor the most touching resurrection of your love changes my decision one iota."

Carolyn's heart thudded heavily in her chest.

"Please," Dylan said. "I know you have the power to overlook this. Just take the money and leave us in peace."

Carolyn winced and closed her eyes. She knew what it cost Dylan to beg from this man.

There was a long silence.

"Peace," Jackson murmured. "Now there's an elusive commodity. I don't think many have it these days, vanquished *or* victors. Congress is taking control from the president, saying he isn't punishing you Southrons harshly enough for your rebellion, saying Southern senators can't sit because we're still in a state of war. We are still at war, aren't we, but it's not out there," he gestured to the window and the land beyond, "on battlegrounds. It's in *here*." The captain hit the breast of his immaculate uniform. Carolyn watched transfixed, searching for a sign of sympathy, or softening, realizing her fate hung on his next words. He sighed deeply before he went on. "Thankfully for you, I don't agree with Congress. The suffering needs to end. Peace can never be reached until it does. You may think I've been diabolical in my search for the truth, but that's what it has been – a search for truth. Not an attempt to trump up unfounded charges. We've seen no signs that you've hidden more of the gold. Your people back up your story. Your reputation in town is sound. And the poor son of a gun we unearthed this morning showed no discernible signs of foul play. So it comes down to the question of motivations. You used government funds as your own. Yes. But can I prove you did so knowingly? Do I want to spend time trying to? No."

"But we told you –" Carolyn began. He cut her off with a sharp gesture. She let out her breath in a gasp. "You're not going to press charges?"

"These are desperate times. What would I have done in the same circumstances?" Jackson shrugged and walked over, towering above them. But his posture was no longer threatening. "Bringing back six hundred in Confederate gold may not put another star on my collar like hauling in a bigger cache plus an arrest might have, but what do I care? I'm a banker, right? What I care about is the bottom line, so I'll do as you ask – take the money and leave you in peace."

Carolyn sagged against Dylan in relief so profound that for a minute she was without words. Dylan found some. Drawing her up beside him, he stood and extended his hand to the man in the blue uniform. "Thank you, Sir," he said quietly.

Jackson surveyed him a moment, then grasped Dylan's hand and shook it. He looked him in the eye. "You have a lot going for you. Don't forget it again."

"Thank you. I won't."

"Oh – one more thing." Jackson reached under the desk and thumped a heavy object down beside the haversack. "Here's your side arm. Try to resist the urge to shoot me as I leave." He gave a roguish grin. "Well, I'll be out of your hair."

"Wait," Dylan urged. "Won't you and your men stay for dinner ... as our guests?"

Surprise flashed across the older man's hardened features. Then he smiled, genuinely now. "I appreciate the gesture, Mr. Rousseau, but I know you'd all be more comfortable with us gone. A lot less mouths to feed, too, though I must say that Lydia is a good cook. None too happy about cooking for *us*. And that Tania – a firebrand. Gave me quite the tongue-lashing for implying you might have brought the cavalryman to an early end."

"*Tania?*" Carolyn couldn't believe her ears.

"Yes, Ma'am. She thinks well of you. They all do. Like I said, you've got a lot going for you. I wish you better luck in the future."

"Thank you, Captain," Carolyn whispered. Tears of gratitude filled her eyes. "But I think it has little to do with luck."

The next morning, Carolyn did not want to get out of bed. The emotional turmoil had taken its toll. The day before, once the last of the troopers galloped down the drive, she had eaten a mid-afternoon meal, laid down, and not risen since. Now, with the pale late autumn light inching its way across the floor, she snuggled in Dylan's arms, happy and content.

"We still owe all those taxes, you know," he murmured, kissing her ear.

"Shhh." Carolyn rolled over and kissed his eyes, his nose, his mouth.

"And we still don't have money to pay them."

She sighed. "Who cares? I don't care if we're poor as church mice. I'll live in a barn with you."

"We're not poor." His lips skimmed over hers. He rolled her under him and kissed a path down her neck and chest. He raised his head, his dark eyes suddenly fierce. "We are blessed beyond measure, and I'm going to find some way to make this work. I won't lose you again."

Carolyn wrapped her arms around him and studied his face. There was hope there, and joy, but also now – a tinge of fear. "You won't lose me."

"I never stopped loving you, you know. Not for one second."

She had just surrendered to his passionate embrace when there was a knock on the door. Henrietta's tentative voice came. "Hello? Did you know it's ten o'clock?"

Dylan rolled his eyes.

Then a tiny fist pounded on the door. "*Let me in*," Devie demanded.

"Now we know the real culprit. He's probably driving her crazy," Carolyn murmured.

"Again, our fault. We got the honeymoon all in the wrong place." Dylan laughed and handed her her wrapper. "It's open!" he called.

Devie charged across the floor, his short legs pumping. He attacked the bed steps like a general going to battle. "Me hug, too!" he cried, throwing himself on them.

Carolyn laughed and snagged him to her. "Quiet – you'll wake the baby," she said, nodding toward the cradle where Jacob slumbered, one fist beside his cheek.

Dev made a face to show how much he thought of *that*.

Henrietta's eye peeked around the door frame. "Lydia and I have lit a fire in the parlor. Why don't you come have tea and toast there? I think a quiet day would be nice. We can talk, plan."

"That sounds wonderful, Mother," Dylan agreed much more patiently.

Pleased, she nodded and withdrew.

"Would you like me to help you get the children ready?" Dylan asked.

Surprised, Carolyn hesitated, then agreed. She told him where he would find clothes for both boys. As she dressed herself, she kept peeking at his progress. The sight of Dylan bent over his son, putting knit booties on Jacob's tiny feet, did strange things to her heart. She had an odd feeling, like if she let him out of her sight, he might disappear – or worse, that the old Dylan might return.

Within less than an hour, the family assembled in the parlor. Everyone seemed to *not* want to bring up their financial troubles. But as Lydia poked the fire, Henrietta knitted, and Dylan rolled about with Devie on the floor, Carolyn realized that addressing their problems would not destroy them. Together, they were strong enough together to face the future, whatever it held.

"I think we should see if the Moores want to buy the town house," she announced, cradling her tea. "If we sell it, there will be more than enough for the taxes on the plantations. And hopefully The Marshes will find another buyer soon, too."

Dylan flipped onto his side to answer her, but Devie jumped on his head. Carolyn tensed, waiting for Dylan's impatience – a flash of his temper at the boy, his defensiveness at her suggestion. But he only swung the child's legs out of the way, told him "easy" and patted his bottom. "They don't have the cash for that. Hiram makes barely enough to pay the rent."

"That's too bad," Henrietta said.

Carolyn glanced at her in surprise. Henrietta, too? Carolyn had expected her mother-in-law to resume her protests over the idea of parting with the city property.

Henrietta looked back at her. "What? Can't an old woman change? We've all got to work together on this. I won't oppose any necessary sales, but we can hardly toss the Moores into the street now, can we?"

Carolyn smiled.

"Maybe one day they'll be able to buy," Dylan added, "if Hiram gets a promotion. If we need a place to stay in town after we let the house go, we can always use Carolyn's family's home."

Henrietta brightened. "True."

Dylan continued, "I've also been thinking about what we can do. Thinking about Van Buren again."

Carolyn threw him an incredulous look.

"No, not the vineyard," he said quickly, teasingly. "His orchards. Apples have always done well here. Maybe we can add to our own orchard."

"It's a good idea – should bring in a little more income each fall," Henrietta said, nodding, "but it won't pay the taxes in January."

"My parents would help if they could," Carolyn said, "but I don't think they have near enough set aside. According to Mother's last letter, they are just barely making ends meet."

"Like everyone," Dylan said. His forehead creased. "Hmm. I assume we need a miracle, then."

At that very moment there was a rattle of carriage wheels.

"Someone's here. Maybe it's our miracle." With a smirk Carolyn set down her tea and went to the door. She stopped there in astonishment. "I don't believe it," she said aloud.

Henrietta pressed in next to her. "What? Who is it?"

A handsome carriage stopped before the house. The door opened and Jack Randall emerged, handing Mahala down. She was up the porch steps before a third person, a prosperous-looking man Carolyn had never seen, could even get out.

Mahala embraced Carolyn, crying out, "Carolyn! Are you all right? We came as soon as we could – as soon as we got rid of those dreadful Yankees and could collect Mr. Nyles. But – where are they?"

Mahala was edging past her, looking around, trying to get a view into the rooms of the house. Her gaze fell in a bewildered manner on Dylan, who was coming out of the parlor with a cordial look on his face, ready to greet her.

Carolyn stared at her old friend. She was dazed by her sudden arrival. "Where is who?"

"The Yankees, of course! Are – are they *gone*?"

"Yes. They left yesterday."

"They did?"

"They did."

"Then …" Mahala's beautiful face tightened in concentration. "You are … absolved?"

Carolyn laughed, a little hysterically, as she grasped the meaning of Mahala's visit. Mahala had ridden to the rescue. "Yes," she said. "Yes, I am!"

"Oh! Then … everything's all right? And you don't need Jack's lawyer … Mr. Nyles, of course." Mahala gestured to the portly stranger in the checkered silk vest and black top hat. He tipped his hat at her.

"I guess not." Carolyn giggled again.

Mahala looked at her as if she had lost her mind. For a long moment everyone stood there staring at each other, trying to process the truth. Then Mahala laughed, too – a joyful, melodious sound full of relief. She grasped Carolyn in an embrace and shook her back and forth in a dance of happy delight that made Carolyn laugh all the harder. Around them, the men were shaking Dylan's hand and kissing Henrietta's.

"I'm so glad you're here," Carolyn said, pulling back at last and looking at Mahala. "So much has changed."

"I can *see*. You must tell me everything!" Mahala demanded, and Carolyn knew she meant all the details, just like old times, after they had shared their story in company and could be alone together.

"I will," Carolyn promised. She felt Mahala measuring her, noting the changes. "But come in. You must stay a while, since you've come all this way. We can tell you what happened over lunch."

"*Lunch*?" Mahala asked. "But do you not know what today is?"

"Thursday?"

"*Thanksgiving.*"

"It *is*?" Carolyn held her hands to her flushing cheeks. Beside her, Dylan and Henrietta laughed in equal amazement. In the stress of their circumstances, they had completely forgotten the holiday. "Oh, dear," she added. "I'm not prepared for *that*."

Mahala smirked. "Don't worry. I am. I brought a ham."

"You brought a ham?" Carolyn repeated.

"Well, I thought you might need help feeding a bunch of Yankee soldiers. I try to come prepared."

Dylan stepped up beside Carolyn and put an arm around her, a gesture which Mahala quickly noted. He beamed. "In that case, my wife and I would be pleased if you would join us for Thanksgiving dinner."

Minutes later, Carolyn was still in a daze as Mahala joined her, Henrietta and Lydia in the kitchen. She did note that Jack and Dylan slipped out the door, talking in low voices. She suppressed a slight swell of panic. It was not likely if Dylan was with Jack that he would come back raving or drunk – or that he would disappear altogether, she told herself.

Lydia had already put sweet potatoes on to simmer. Now they took down their precious store of brown sugar, molasses and walnuts to create a soufflé. Mahala sliced pickled peaches while Carolyn added dried leather britches to a pot of salted, boiling water, adding a ham bone from the meat which had been brought in.

"Can you stay a while?" Carolyn asked Mahala hopefully. She passed close to her and confided, "I'm sorry for the way I was in Savannah. I was – not myself. I want to make it up to you."

Mahala smiled. "You don't have to make anything up to me. I understand. It's enough to know things are better now. They are, aren't they?"

"Yes. So much better. He followed me to Savannah to apologize, you know. Now that we're together – and this business with the gold is settled – we can learn to be a family ... regardless of what else may happen."

"You mean ... financially."

Carolyn hesitated. "Yes. But it doesn't seem to matter so much now."

Mahala smiled secretively. "Oh, Jack has some ideas about *that*."

When dinner was almost ready and everyone came in to tidy up for the meal, Dylan caught Carolyn and pulled her under protest into the butler's pantry. His eyes were shining.

"I think we may have our miracle."

"What did Jack say to you?" Carolyn asked with suspicion.

"He offered me a loan – with interest, to save my pride, but at a reasonable rate. And a five-year pay-back period. And the option to invest next year after we have a little cash in his shipping company and railroad stocks that he's sure will pay great dividends. Carolyn, I'm going to do it!"

"You're o.k. with a loan?" she asked warily, watching him.

"It's a loan, not a handout. I can learn a lot from Jack. For the first time in years, I'm able to actually *hope*."

Carolyn smiled. "It's a heady thing."

"But you still don't quite believe it, do you?" Dylan sobered, passing his thumb over her cheek.

She hesitated, then shook her head. She squeezed her eyes shut. "This all feels like a dream. Everything is happening so fast. I keep thinking I'm going to wake up and it's all going to be back like it was a month ago ...

that if I let you out of my sight, or say the wrong thing, you'll ... be like you were."

She was half afraid he would grow angry even at her admission.

She felt, rather than saw, Dylan grimace. Or maybe she just heard it in his voice. "God forbid."

Carolyn opened her eyes. There was pain and guilt on his face.

"I've beaten you down, haven't I?" he whispered. They had touched on these things during the night, open wounds they had tried to begin to close with words and urgent love-making, but now, in the light of day, it was glaringly apparent that the holes they had left in each other would take time to heal. Dylan cupped her face and drew her head under his chin. "I'm sorry. I'm so sorry. I swear I'll make you trust me again."

Carolyn snorted gently. "Not like I don't have to work on the same thing. I haven't exactly been forthcoming since we got married."

Dylan released her body, but not her face. He looked intently into her eyes. "Let's be honest with each other, starting now. Brutally honest, if we have to. This is going to be hard. There will probably be a dozen times in the next month that I'll see that look in your eyes and know you're not sure of me. And I'll probably still wonder at times if you believe in me, if you're ... *comparing* ..." His voice trailed off, but when she tried to protest, he silenced her. "I know. But it will still take time. And we're still going to have to go without. It may be years before we can clear our debts, and even then ... I don't think life will ever be like it was before the war. I don't think – even if I manage to exorcise my demons –" he grinned crookedly – "*I'll* be like I was, before. But I vow to you now never to quit on life – on *us* – like I did. Will you promise me the same thing?"

Carolyn's eyes swam with tears. All the things he was saying, they were real. It was the broad light of day, with the odd jars and containers of the butler's pantry about them, the murmur of voices and the clinking of dishes being set in the very next room. She wasn't dreaming. She nodded.

"Say it," he whispered.

"I promise. But what I really need to say most is, Dylan, I love you."

He groaned and rubbed his cheek along hers, catching the salty tears that dropped from her eyes. She felt like her heart would tear right through her chest, it throbbed so intensely. Dylan wound one hand in her hair and crushed her lips to his, sealing their promise.

A moment later she gasped and put a shaking hand on his immovable chest. "Our guests are waiting!"

"So glad it's finally not *me*." He moved to claim her mouth again.

"You must *stop*!"

"You think *you* can't let me out of your sight? Imagine how I must feel!"

She wiggled away from him. "But it's *Thanksgiving*." Her hand fluttered at the back of her head, trying to tuck in a stray lock of hair that his fingers had loosed.

Dylan grinned. "So it is. Here, let me help you with that."

Minutes later, they all gathered around the big dining room table. She could hardly take her eyes off Dylan, with his very obvious impudent grin, but eventually she did. She looked around at all the bright, beloved faces. While they passed the food and told their tales and the wind whistled outside, Carolyn said her own silent Thanksgiving prayer.

The visit with Jack and Mahala was wonderful. The news from the outside world was encouraging, too. New lien laws had been passed that would give farmers better access to credit and more time to pay their debts. This news brought a new purpose in their work that lingered after the Randalls departed. Dylan spent hours chopping firewood and making the outbuildings snug for the livestock while Carolyn canned the last of the fall produce. In the evenings, she and the other women, including Tania, with whom a tentative peace had been achieved, shucked corn and snuck time to sew on their secret Christmas projects. There was a camaraderie among them all, black and white, old and young. But the nights were the best. Those were the times she could lie in Dylan's arms and listen to the beat of his heart, listen to him tell her and show her that he loved her and would never leave her. For two weeks, peace held sway. But when the nightmares returned, Carolyn was angry. What had she left undone? How had she failed?

When one night he didn't want to talk about his dream, putting her off just as he used to, she recognized the sickening emotion churning inside her chest. Betrayal.

"I thought we were going to tell the truth – the brutal truth, if need be," she insisted, resisting his efforts to hold her.

"Where the truth will *help*. In this case it won't."

"It's so much a part of who you are. So much of who you are now was formed those years you were away – and you won't talk about it. I want to know why. It's like there's this whole part of you that you hide from me."

He sighed. "No," he said softly. "I hide it from myself."

"That's not good."

"I don't want to be reminded … of all the ways I failed."

"You were at war. You did what you had to, right?"

"Sometimes I did more."

Carolyn sat up, looking at him. His words chilled her, but she had him talking – she wasn't about to let him quit. "What do you mean?"

But his face hardened. He shook his head.

Tears eased from the corners of her eyes as she turned away, pulling the covers over her.

Dylan tugged at her shoulder. "Why are you crying?"

But it was Carolyn's turn to shake him off. If he wouldn't let her in, she wouldn't tell him how it hurt.

The next morning an early ice storm held North Georgia in its grip. Fires crackled in all the hearths. Sleet and snow splattered against the windowpane behind Dylan as he sat at the desk in his office. He looked up from the accounts as Carolyn entered and placed a book with glaringly empty pages in front of him.

"A journal?"

"I thought if you couldn't speak the words maybe you could write them down."

"Carolyn–"

"Just try. Think about it. See what happens."

"You'll be sadly disappointed."

"I don't think so. Take your time. Let me know when you have something."

"So we can burn it?" he asked with feigned hopefulness.

Carolyn shook her head. "It wouldn't count then. You need a witness."

His face twisted with pain. "Not you."

"Who else?"

The nightmares did not stop. They increased until they came almost every night again, as if Dylan's resolution to change had opened a tiny wound through which an impossible amount of trouble determined to flow. Even when the good news came that the Savannah lawyer had located another buyer for The Marshes property – giving them a first installment to pay back the Randalls and a bit of breathing room – the tension inside Dylan did not ease. Carolyn was afraid as she saw the shadows return beneath his eyes, the anxious movements of his hands, the way the slightest loud noise or unexpected encounter made him jump. When he took to riding out at night when the insomnia was at its worst, she feared she would lose him again. And she couldn't bear that.

Carolyn knew that something deeper was going on than mere nightmares, however horrifying they might be. Dylan was fighting the internal war of which the Yankee captain had spoken, fighting for the essence of who he was and for control over his own future. It was the aftermath of that period when survival had been foremost. There had been no chance to process it all then. It was all coming out now. Or trying to. Only he wouldn't let it.

Christmas Eve night came, and Carolyn awoke to find the bed next to her empty. She hadn't heard him leave this time. She slid on her slippers and shuffled down the stairs, running her hand along the banister. There was almost no light, and she realized the moon had set. It must be near dawn. Noticing that lamplight eased out underneath the study door, she breathed a sigh of relief. Carolyn pushed on the door and saw Dylan sitting there behind the desk. Just sitting. His expression was flat, unsurprised at her appearance.

He stood up. "Merry Christmas," he said calmly, and walked around past her.

"Where are you going?" Carolyn asked with a trace of panic in her voice.

Dylan stopped and turned to her. In his haggard expression she saw a tenderness that eased her fears. He took her face in his hands and kissed her. "I'll be back soon."

She watched him with her mouth agape. Only when she turned back to the desk did she notice the ink stand and the brown leather volume lying closed in the center. She hurried over and opened the cover. She fanned through the pages. They were filled with Dylan's neat script! Her stomach twisted. He must have been writing the nights he left their room. And he must mean now ... that he was done.

Carolyn grabbed up the book and the lamp and hurried upstairs to the bedroom. She wrapped herself in a quilt before sitting down in the rocking chair, the lamp placed on the table beside her. When she opened the journal to the front page, her hands shook.

She didn't know what to expect – haphazard accounts of Dylan's various dreams or perhaps a diary of his emotional struggles – but what she saw was a careful chronological account of his time in the service, from the first day he'd joined up in 1862. His first skirmish was recorded in words that made it sound like it had happened yesterday.

May 1862. Meadow Bridges, VA. Pursued the Federals with Companies A, B and K deployed as skirmishers. I couldn't bring myself to fire at them. Those were real men in that field, with real families waiting at home. I aimed for the tree line, but my hands shook so bad I probably killed someone by mistake. The possibility stole what little sleep I would have gotten as we finally reached Richmond's defensive positions. It was a swampy area, and everyone got lice. Everyone except Dev, it would seem. Seeing him again brought back all the old resentments, and I had to hash through them again with my own inward battle for peace. I could tell he didn't understand why I avoided him. It was easier that way. I didn't want to hate him. Not anymore. So I hated the lice, the rain, the heat, the war.

June 1862. Garnett's Farm, VA. A shell exploded right next to Devereaux, killing the man under it. His head just pulverized into a trillion minuscule specs of flesh, blood and bone. I pictured it being Dev, and I knew that even though I couldn't discuss <u>her</u> with him like he'd wanted to just before the battle – he was my brother, and I had to save him. I drug him all the way across the field under raining lead. The ground crawled with our wounded like flies on a carcass. But no harm touched me. I believe God wanted peace in our family, peace between brothers.

August 1862. Thoroughfare Gap, VA. The Manassas Gap Railroad ran through the gap, and we had to follow it to Manassas Junction to reach General Jackson before the Yankees could fall on his sundered army. The 9th GA ascertained for us that the gap was held strongly by Union artillery. The job of companies A and B (under 30 of us then, as I recall) was to scramble up the thicket to find out how far on either side the bluecoats held the turnpike. Up we went, until a voice from above asked, "Who's down there?" I think we all realized at the same time that we had met the enemy. I saw him, then. A sandy-haired boy younger than me rising in the thicket almost close enough to touch. He looked as startled as I did. His rifle was at the ready; mine wasn't. He picked a bead on my left breast. At that range it would have undoubtedly been the end. But as I threw myself backwards I saw him do what I had done at Meadow Bridges. His shot shattered the tree limb above me.

I never told anyone just how close I came to death that day. I couldn't even breathe by the time we made it back down. If only the story ended there. God, if only it did! For I know now this day was my personal turning point.

We were ordered back up, to take that gap. What are the chances I would encounter that same sandy-haired boy in that tangled brush? Most of the regiment passed under the range of the Yankee guns, but I got off to myself, so when I ran across him again it was just me and him. We both leveled our muskets at each other, and I could read the surprise along with the hazel glints in his eyes. I was faster. I'll never know if he would have shot me this time because I shot him first. I watched the light fade from those eyes and his body topple down the hill. I'd made a soldier's decision, but every fiber of me screamed murder. And didn't stop screaming for weeks afterwards.

Carolyn paused and lowered the journal, her heart squeezing for Dylan. She knew the tender and idealistic boy he'd been – a minister, dedicated to saving lives, not taking them. This, then, was the first face that haunted his dreams.

She read on, hearing a further hardening in Dylan's description of the battles at Second Manassas and Antietam Creek, where minutes after watching a glorious Confederate advance under waving battle flags he'd seen his comrades hamstrung by rolling cannonballs and blown to bits by shells. He described the incidents in details that made her wince. Even by the Battle of Gettysburg the following summer, where Dylan had found honor and recognition in defending the retreating wagon train of wounded, he and Dev had been unable to talk about what had happened between them over her. He had accepted that she was his sister, but the wounds had remained unhealed – until that conversation at Dev's deathbed.

After Gettysburg, Dylan's faith had shriveled. Lee had issued a proclamation calling for the troops to confess their sins so that God would cease to punish them. Many of the soldiers, Dylan included, had begun to believe the Lord was withdrawing His favor because of their unrighteousness. Dylan became convinced that he'd been right all along; God frowned on the scourge of slavery and would wipe it out through the war. But his path had been set. Honor dictated that he could never go back. So he'd closed his heart and plowed on with relentless determination. Anger, bitterness and violence became a way of life. Bits of battles from late in the war, just before and after Dev's death, jumped off the pages at Carolyn, setting her heart racing and her fingers clutching the book she couldn't put down.

> *November 1863. Outside Knoxville, TN. Chased the Yankees to the city and put the fear of God into them. I ran out of ammo when we cornered them in an apple orchard, saw a fat merchant-looking little man blubbering over a hand wound, and swung the butt of my rifle at his head. I heard his skull crack and took his full cartridge and haversack.*

> *May 1864. Wilderness, VA. Came across a Yank in a small clearing in that tangled hell, and we both yelled at each other to surrender. I ducked his misfire and wrestled him to the ground. Was not successful until putting a finger through his eye. It was easy after that. We could all hear the screams and moans of the wounded left*

to the flames our fight had started in those ghastly woods, dying awful, slow deaths that night.

June 1864. Cold Harbor, VA. In one day we mowed down 7,000 men from behind our strong entrenchments – like wheat before a scythe. Some of the other men were appalled, but I was amazed and relieved that I felt nothing.

Horrified, Carolyn looked up. The faint winter sun was shining through the drapes, making the lamp unnecessary. The words kept echoing in her mind. *Amazed and relieved that I felt nothing.* What must that have looked, and sounded, and smelled like? How could one become so desensitized that the brutal death of 7,000 men had no effect on the psyche? No. Not no effect. A suppressed effect.

A motion near the door caught her eye. Through her tear-clouded vision she saw Dylan, head lowered. At that moment he looked more like the boy of ten years ago than she had seen him look since. Her heart softened, but the horror still held her in its grip. Dylan must have noticed, for he did not approach her. His words seemed to hang between them, filling the air with shame and doubt. Carolyn put her hand out. He crossed the room quickly then, took her hand, knelt beside her. Bowed his face to their joined knuckles ... and keened the most unearthly sound she had ever heard. It went down her spine like lightning, and she bent over him in an attempt to shield his pain. She cradled his head against her as wave after wave of repressed anguish rolled out of him. Each cry tore her heart. It seemed she sat there forever, holding her husband, and still she knew the catharsis was only beginning.

EPILOGUE

Christmas 1868
Habersham County, Georgia

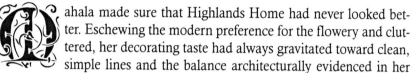ahala made sure that Highlands Home had never looked better. Eschewing the modern preference for the flowery and cluttered, her decorating taste had always gravitated toward clean, simple lines and the balance architecturally evidenced in her Federal-period residence. Now, with every surface waxed and polished, and greenery gracing the mantels and windowsills, the spirit of the holiday filled every room.

Seated around the dining room table with Mahala and Jack were Martha, Henrietta, Carolyn and Dylan Rousseau. Mahala's step-brother Jacob and his new bride were enjoying a cozy holiday on the farm he'd recently purchased from Mahala. Tomorrow they would come into Clarkesville with Ben and Nancy Emmitt. It was a shame their Savannah family could not be here, though, thought Mahala. Sunny, Sylvie and Andrew, Ella Beth and Daniel, and Grace Ellis would all be gathered tonight at the Ellis family mansion. But the decision to be here had been right. Mahala could hardly wait for Jack to get around to the news they had to share. But she had to be patient.

"That David Dickson and his new blood and bone compound has started another guano craze," Dylan was saying, as he tucked into his roast goose with sage and onion dressing with appreciation. "Last fall I broke ground ten inches deep. This spring, we put out the fertilizer two hundred pounds per acre, turned it and subsoiled. I can't believe the results we've seen."

"They say he's single-handedly extended the cotton belt fifty miles north," Jack agreed.

"It's so good to finally be able to sit around a table and have positive things to discuss," Henrietta put in, looking up from ensuring her sauce tartare did not touch her potatoes and peas. "It's been such a hard few years."

Indeed, she spoke the truth. Recently, Reconstruction Acts had been pushed through by a Congress intent on punishing the South, restoring military rule over civil government in Georgia as though the war had just ended. Under General Pope, Atlanta had been made state headquarters. When Pope was replaced by General Meade, people had hoped for a lighter hand – which they had not received. Robert Toombs had returned from exile to organize the Democratic Party, which had rallied to protest the election of a Republican governor. But Jack had often been discouraged with the Democratic Party, for the same prejudice of pre-war days often slipped through in its rhetoric. It had been hard for Jack and Mahala to know where to place their allegiances.

"Don't take us wrong, though," Carolyn put in. "We know better than to put all our eggs into one basket. All we need is a boom or bust cycle to ruin us again where cotton is concerned. We did quite well this fall with our expanded apple orchard. The progress is in pennies and dimes, but it's progress." She smiled, placing a hand over her rounded abdomen. She was rosy with pregnancy, set to deliver Dylan's second child in March. Of course, they hoped for a girl.

For three years now, Mahala had hoped for a child of either sex. The past two years, she'd cried out from her heart to God, asking why He did not bless her union with Jack. There had been rocky periods in their marriage because of that ongoing heartache. But she and Jack had never gone back on their love for each other. She knew he'd watched her tonight, surprised at how well she was handling Carolyn's obvious impending maternity, and her interactions with handsome little Dev Jr., who was having his dinner in the kitchen, rather than using Mahala's crystal goblets and new Thompson's Old Liverpool china plates, with their gold trim and six-pointed star of dark pink flowers. She was inordinately proud of those plates.

Jack was resplendent tonight in a hunter green waistcoat and his best black frock coat. His eyes sparkled as he teased the Rousseaus, "Just maybe you'll see progress on a bigger scale sooner than you think."

"What do you mean?" asked Dylan.

"I'm so glad you asked!" Jack grinned and sat back from the table. "To answer that, I'll have to go back to what I told you about Northern industrialists like Thomas Scott and Moncure Robinson. Remember when we discussed how they wanted to extend rail lines south, and eventually west, using the remains of the old Southern lines?"

Dylan nodded. "Yes. But Southern Democrats have feared – probably with good reason – that would bring unbalanced power and corruption."

"I shared that same concern. When Scott first got his Air Line going, I was excited about the potential of it, but even I knew the Southern directors he appointed were just front men answerable to his own cronies. As you know, we've spent a good bit of time in Atlanta this year, lobbying and attending meetings. I've been trying to use what contacts I have in this new government to open the Air Line to investment from native Georgians."

"And did you succeed?" Carolyn asked, leaning forward.

"He did!" Mahala squeaked, unable to hold it in a moment longer.

The reaction was immediate – clapping hands, expressions of joy, exclamations and questions, all around the table. They all knew what a railroad through North Georgia would mean. Had known for a long time. A rail line would allow local crops and goods to ship to wider markets, and allow tourists ease of access to the natural attractions they'd long endured hard journeys by wagon to enjoy.

"We're going to reopen the hotels!" Martha announced.

Jack waved a hand at all of them, trying to shush the clamor. "We're getting ahead of ourselves. I haven't told the whole story yet!"

Everyone settled down and gave him their attention, though the excitement in the room could not now be repressed. "*I* didn't accomplish this. It was really Algernon Buford, president of the Richmond and Danville Railroad. There was a meeting in Atlanta we just came from this month. He addressed the group and asked why we should let strangers control the Air Line. He's pledged $100,000 of his own money towards the $500,000 needed to build the first twenty miles north of Atlanta. Then he got the city council to renew a $300,000 pledge in municipal bonds. Next, we're going after the Georgia legislature and private citizens."

Carolyn laughed. "I have no doubt *you* will be the first investor."

Mahala reached out to clasp Jack's hand. "That's what we were so excited to tell you. Not just us, but you. Jack was so eager to come back to Habersham, not just to plan for reopening our hotels here, first The Palace and later The Franklin – but to enlist your support. Even a little money invested in this will pay dividends, Dylan. We're talking about a new era for the South."

"A new era we've fought hard for," Jack added.

Mahala saw Dylan brush a tear from his eye, and she looked away. Carolyn had shared with her how difficult Dylan's journey since the war, even since they had been cleared regarding the Confederate gold, had been. At last he'd been able to vanquish the silent army of ghosts that had plagued him. No one knew better than Dylan how hard-fought the new era would have been.

"And you men can talk about all those investments when we adjourn to the parlor for eggnog and lighting the tree," Mahala announced in a cheery voice that broke the sudden mood of contemplation in the room. "Right now, it's time for Maddie's Christmas pudding!"

"No doubt, there will be some grievous fault with it," Martha muttered behind her napkin, causing everyone to laugh again.

Later that night, when they had waved off the Rousseaus, and Martha had stretched and announced she was heading up to bed, Jack and Mahala returned to the parlor. A maid scuttled off with a tray of empty eggnog glasses, leaving them alone with the big orange cat who had claimed Highlands Home long before they had. They'd named him Amber. He was curled up in front of the hearth, sleeping. The candles at the windows and upon the limbs of the pungently-scented fir tree gave a cozy glow. Mahala paused to admire the scene. Jack came up behind her, putting his arms around her middle.

"I think that went well," he commented. "My compliments to the hostess."

Mahala smiled. "Thank you, although it was your news that stole the evening."

"I am excited to be able to help the Rousseaus in a bigger way than we could before."

"They seem to be doing well. They seemed so happy tonight. Did you hear Carolyn say Dylan had even volunteered to help fill in for the new Presbyterian minister when he needs it?"

"No, that's wonderful." Jack nibbled her neck. "I was especially proud of *you* tonight."

"How could I not be happy for Carolyn?" Mahala whispered. "She's my dearest friend. And we have been so blessed."

"Yes, we have. I must say I don't think I could be happier, either."

Mahala turned in his arms. "Are you sure?" she asked. "Are you very, very sure?"

He frowned at her, suspicious.

"That there's not even one teeny crack in your heart to hold one more ounce of happiness?"

Jack pretended to think about that, rolling his eyes up to the ceiling. "Um … nope. I don't think so."

Mahala put on a martyred expression, shaking her head and giving a little sigh. "Well then," she said, turning back around to look at the fire as if disappointed, "I guess you'll have to wait for your final Christmas present."

Interest sparked in his voice. "You got me something else?"

"I might have," Mahala replied evasively.

"Well, give it to me."

She smirked. "I will." She placed his hand, palm flat, below the waistband of her dress. "In eight more months."

"Oh. *Oh.*" Jack sounded like he might collapse, but Mahala didn't turn around. She smiled, looking into the flames. She could just see him now, the green-eyed, brown-haired son she'd dreamed of that night long ago at Forests of Green. That joy she'd once longed for. It had caught up with her many times over. The future now was truly bright as gold.

The End

ABOUT THE AUTHOR

Denise Weimer

ative Georgia resident Denise Weimer earned her journalism degree with a minor in history from Asbury University. Her magazine articles about Northeast Georgia have appeared in numerous regional publications. She is a wife and mother, a life-long historian, and for many years directed a mid-1800s dance group, The 1860s Civilian Society of Georgia. Her first two books in The Georgia Gold Series, *Sautee Shadows* and *The Gray Divide*, were released in 2013. Book Three, *The Crimson Bloom*, debuted in spring of 2014.

Other Books in the Georgia Gold Series:

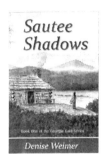

Sautee Shadows:
Book One of the Georgia Gold Series
By Denise Weimer
ISBN: 978-1-933251-66-0
April 2013
$15.95

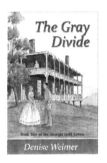

The Gray Divide:
Book Two of the Georgia Gold Series
By Denise Weimer
ISBN: 978-0-9881897-2-0
September 2013
$15.95

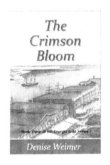

The Crimson Bloom:
Book Three of the Georgia Gold Series
By Denise Weimer
ISBN: 978-0-9881897-4-4
May 2014
$15.95

Books are available nationally through bookstores and online booksellers. For more information about the Georgia Gold Series and Denise Weimer visit: www.canterburyhousepublishing.com

CPSIA information can be obtained at www.ICGtesting.com
Printed in the USA
LVOW11s0622020914

401832LV00005B/10/P

9 780988 189799